Flashback and Purple

Sue Hampton

Contents

Dedication

@Greenpeace
with deep gratitude and respect.

PART ONE

A week in October

Chapter One

Annie Capaldi had read somewhere that when we wake, our unique consciousness is only made possible by the particular physical body that houses it. Which was annoying, because it had taken her decades to cut loose emotionally from that body and develop an interest in the possibility that she might have a soul.

These days Annie needed rather more time each morning to sharpen the blurred edges of that conscious self. So for a while, from bedroom to shower to kitchen, all she processed was another wet October Monday. She could, if required to prove that she wasn't completely out of touch with the wider world, have named the Prime Minister and identified the year as the one that followed 2012, when she had been an ambassador at the Olympic Park. But for a while the new day came with no date tag. No frisson or fanfare. In fact, as she dropped the rinsed-out marmalade jar into the recycling bin, she felt a familiar kind of vague security in the knowledge that, thanks to the Word files on her laptop, the week ahead of her already had a recorded outline and tabulated schedule – all backed up somewhere in the memory she trusted to shake itself awake in its own good time.

But it was the BBC Breakfast presenters who announced the number. The key to open the door. With the remote control in one hand and a coffee mug in the other, she was left staring for a moment at the blank screen, the date a left-over she had no time to digest, like the toast crust on her plate. And as she continued, through the clatter of mug and plate in the sink, teeth cleaning, lip balm and the clink of car keys, the number followed, in foreground and bold, centred.

Twenty-five years in the job, to the day. With marriages and reigns, didn't twenty-five mean silver – half as good as gold?

Stepping outside into rain she hadn't even guessed, Annie found a car she'd almost forgotten, probably because twenty-five years earlier Arthur had taken the VW, leaving her to the train. As she turned out of her drive, it struck her that she was a leftover herself, the single survivor of every change. But wasn't she entitled to feel some kind of satisfaction, or sense of achievement? Who stayed in a job for twenty-five years these days, apart from the Queen?

She was hardly expecting to be greeted on arrival at the hospital with a silver watch, surprise party or even a round of applause. It was such a private anniversary, barely worth a mention. But she hadn't seen it coming. She'd been too busy, busier than ever, leaving the hospital at eleven the night before. Too focused. Too exhausted for sharing and much too alone.

She could text Leigh at the first junction, with one number, a few words and a jolly exclamation mark, conveying nothing but the fact. But that could trigger Leigh's own memories, a version of events she dreaded to imagine. Annie was fairly sure that Leigh held on, through her own career, to old grievances. Did she still resent the mother who'd put work first, abandoning her as a toddler for patients who needed her more?

"Do you think it's been easy?!"

"I didn't ask you to make it so hard!"

Annie hoped her daughter might understand one day. That step into the job twenty-five years ago was not only the hardest but very probably the first she'd ever taken with her eyes open and her heart full – a conviction as well as a commitment.

Turning to Radio Three, she found some Copeland and turned it up louder than usual. No time for nostalgia. Numbers had no meaning. Life was a continuum and only people counted.

Two new patients expected today, a lunchtime meeting about the new building and *As You Like It* to be presented in bite-size chunks, nearly forty years after she last read it, to a girl in a wheelchair who wouldn't speak.

Ethan A. Garrett. Ethan saw the child opposite slowly mouthing his name in syllables. Or perhaps it was said, but softly, the way little kids read everything aloud as if they couldn't hold onto the words unless they heard them out there in the world. But the District Line tube had started to move off at the same moment, so for Ethan it was a silent movie scene, without much colour. Most of the male commuters in his carriage wore black, grey, white or cream, as if there was a kind of uniform or pact. Like football supporters they signalled their membership of the crowd. Even the few tourists all shared brands, fabrics, styles. He was the odd one out.

The little girl must have noticed him, from his long hair to his sandals, before she read the name on his ring binder. Kids older than her had thought him a girl – or called him one anyway. Even at her age, she probably noticed the notebook and pen. Not a Kindle in a leather case, or the kind of tablet you didn't swallow.

"Yeah," he might have mouthed back if the kid had been old enough to understand, *"hippie out of time."* But then she'd probably got that already.

"What's that boy writing?" the girl asked, loudly enough this time for everyone to hear.

"Shh," said her mother and looked the other way.

At twenty-three Ethan didn't mind being a boy. *Man* could sound scary these days. This mother was nothing like his, but she was closed off too. He'd like to find out what her eyes held.

The girl stared back at him, unguarded, almost as if she thought he couldn't see her looking, like a witness at a police station with a screen between them to protect her identity. Ethan had no objection. He was thinking metaphors, his pen beating time in the air – closer to a tic than conducting. But she was right in his eye line, swinging her brown legs and her black plaits but still looking hard. What was she thinking? Maybe he was the first beaded poet in her short, urban life.

He winked at the girl – the little one, because in spite of the make-up and curves her mother couldn't be much older than him, could she? Looking more alarmed than surprised, the child pulled at her mum's shiny sleeve. Eyes back on his lined page, Ethan reminded himself it wasn't really 1968. *Stranger danger* was the message, from buggy to grave. Well, the mother would think he was strange enough. Better pull down the blinds.

He reread the words that waited on his page for the next connection. But now the mother and daughter in their chain-store clothes and plastics had become the poem. Their relationship as he glimpsed it was part of his day. And so was their story, though he had no idea where they were going and what or who they'd left behind. He wasn't going to provoke Mum into pulling the alarm cord by attempting actual inter-human communication, but this was life, not art – real, mysterious and other – and he had to capture them somehow, outside and in.

If he didn't, it'd be like taking a gift to the charity shop unopened.

The train stopped at South Ken. and most of the tourists filed off. No dinosaurs or space rockets for his subjects, then. Feeling like an artist with models he had to paint blindfold, Ethan risked an upward glance and found the girl's eyes meeting his – head-on, as if she'd been waiting. In the moment of contact she puckered her forehead, lifting her chin. With concentration she attempted to close one eye. As she squeezed the lid shut, she opened her mouth as if there was a hinge.

Her first wink? With the open eye as narrow as a stitch, she needed practice. But Ethan couldn't help a small smile and a discreet thumbs-up.

"What's his name?" asked the girl in a high-volume whisper.

Ethan half-expected the mother to stiffen at once and drag the child to another carriage. But when she said, "That's his business," he heard no padlock clicking.

The woman looked at her fingernails, decorated in some kind of tiny pattern. Which could be fine art achieved with a steady hand, or a set that came in a pack with glue. And either way, why? Poets needed the kind of empathy that got inside details like that and made sense of them.

On the next page of his ring binder he drew one nail life-size, replacing the shapes he couldn't see properly with oak leaves and spiders' webs. If he looked up at the mother instead of the child, would she think he was targeting her money or her body? He began listing adjectives for the scent surrounding her.

"I'm Coralie," he heard. "It's my birthday. Do you live in a tree?"

Ethan's mouth fell wide open. His shoulders shook and a kind of chuckle came out quietly through his nose. He saw the mother's eyes brighten. Her grin was embarrassed. The girl's head turned up to weigh her mother's reaction and then back towards him, smiling. She'd made her audience happy. A small, throaty giggle escaped and her legs started to pedal.

"Happy birthday, Coralie!" he said. "I'm Ethan, and no, not yet. But I'd love to be a bird, wouldn't you?"

"I can fly."

"Really? Wish you could teach me. I've been trying all my life."

"Let the man write, Coralie." But the mother wasn't pulling the plug, because the look felt soft. Thoughtful.

"I was born in the wrong millennium," he told her directly, omitting Coralie. "I'm not sure I'd find anything to miss in a tree house." She didn't comment. People were looking and listening but Ethan felt the momentum gather. "Boris could plant a city of high-rise trees. I'd call that an improvement."

"Couldn't be any worse," she agreed. Ethan heard the change. No smile and no brightness now. "Come on," she told Coralie, warmth draining away, "this is our station."

She took her daughter by the hand and, slipping her handbag over her shoulder, led her stumbling a little towards the door as the train drew to a stop.

"Bye," Ethan called to their backs and the opening door.

As they walked down the platform Coralie looked back and waved. Ethan flapped a pair of denim wings and caught the start of her smile as she turned away.

Maybe the poem wasn't in the people but the space they emptied, and the tiny, atomic changes they made to any composition before they left it behind.

He didn't think Coralie felt the sadness, not yet, and that was sad in itself. But of all the thousands of passengers he'd travelled with, she was the first to engage him in philosophical and creative conversation. Now she'd disappeared and taken with her a secret mother he'd never even name. Their world might have intersected with his and then, like balloons, they could all have swelled and lifted off. Instead their circumferences had only rubbed for a moment, sparked and spun apart like repelling poles.

Not much chance of ever seeing them again. But would it count for anything, re-mix or reorder anything at all, if he found the words to hold memory together?

And would Coralie remember him – for a week, a day, an hour?

"Who was that man, Ethan A. Garrett?"

"Just a tree hugger, Coralie. Probably hiding a nest in all that hair."

Ethan's ticket wouldn't take him much further along the line. He'd better find somewhere to breathe for the rest of the day, or let it find him.

11

Annie found herself calculating her chances at the wheel. In the cold and wet, the standstills always felt so bleak and angry. She needed music, not an old man's soggy phone-in story about the first time he heard Elgar as a spotty youth. After all the talk, the concerto was cut short by the same headlines that had already depressed her half an hour earlier. A pity, thought Annie. The piano chords suited the weather but rose above it too.

Was she harder now, less patient? In her defence, she was sure twenty-five years of budgets, curriculum changes and negotiation with consultants would have the same effect on anyone. Maybe kids with spinal injuries made the rest of humanity look like petty, pedantic dramatists who'd abandoned all perspective. Best not to wonder what the kids in their wheelchairs would think of her now, if they knew how feeble, outside work, her resolve could be – and the size of her problems.

Which were?

"Come on, then," she said aloud. "What *are* these 'problems', Annie? Apart from talking to yourself in traffic jams?"

Lack of sleep, she ventured, but then nobody made her work till midnight. A slow, seeping surrender to obesity? Only if she allowed herself a rom-com overstatement just as loose as the blouses she'd started wearing to veil midriff bulge. She might have gone up two dress sizes in twenty-five years but who said solid was bad?

For most of those years, she would have put Leigh near the top of any list. But surely her daughter was old enough at last to take on her own problems, instead of *being* one.

Which left Arthur. Arthur, who had left her a significant twenty-six years ago, and was therefore entitled to take some credit, not just for the hidden meaning of a so-what date, but for a whole career. Without his infidelity she might never have ventured back into the workplace at all. She'd be reading novels and weeding borders until it was time to cook like Nigella. And then he'd kiss her in the hallway, with "Mm, what's cooking?"

Arthur still? Always Arthur? Would she never have enough of loving him, and just stop? Wasn't there an expiry date on mourning a living man?

Annie saw the memories like dominoes tipping. Arthur: no longer hers on that first day at work, but calling, bright and caring, to wish her luck the night before. Not as an ex who'd ended the marriage, but as an old friend, full of faith in her. "Big of him," her friend Gillie had said, but it would have been worse, wouldn't it, if he hadn't called? If he'd let the day go unheralded, when it was the most important of her adult life – after meeting him, marrying him and giving birth to his baby? The long, wide-awake night before the day had been guaranteed with or without his good wishes. But she'd certainly blamed him for the time spent sitting on the side of Leigh's little bed, watching her sleep and silently begging her to survive the separation she wouldn't forgive.

Twenty-five years ago, that October day had been drier with a stinging wind. She hadn't worn enough, assuming the wards would be warmer, but all that glossy hair she used to wrap round curlers should have offered some kind of insulation. In the mirror Annie checked the present-day model as if for the first time all morning. Now her style was more Peter Pan than Dynasty, but grey-white. Like the house, it took care of itself.

Ah, movement. Annie was driving again, sloshing noisily and terrorising pedestrians with her wash of black water. But not for long; the pace slowed again and she was edging ahead only to stop like Grandmother's Footsteps...

She needed no photograph to place herself in the scene. Her first day at hospital school; walking across the car park in new shoes that weren't quite sensible enough because she didn't want to look matronly at thirty-one. An episode of action sequences from a TV world before they ran around with hand-held cameras on the set. Thank God there'd been no mobile phones, or she'd have called the child minder to check she'd got everything she needed, but really to be sure Leigh's howling had stopped.

The now-familiar walk across concrete had seemed so long that day, as she'd tried to secure her hairstyle but also to seem, in case anyone was watching from a window, more confident than she felt. It had been weeks before anyone told her that the head of school she was 'temporarily' replacing had cracked up a few years short of retirement.

Ah, free flow... until she stopped at another junction. Annie blew her nose. It had run on that day too, as the wind scoured and her eyes watered. But she'd hoped she wouldn't cry at any point, because she'd been making a brand new habit of that for some time, and she didn't want any child paralysed from the waist down to think it was pity – or

13

any new colleague to dismiss it as sentiment, inappropriate, self-indulgent and a very bad beginning.

It was hard to be sure but she believed she'd got through without tears, even for Arthur – except possibly in the Ladies at her first coffee break, and that was a scene she wasn't going to replay. It was a good beginning, wasn't it? She fooled them all and believed in her own performance. Wasn't that the secret of all success?

Just as she'd begun to feel encouraged by Vivaldi and violins, the Blue Tooth system muscled in with its high-octane ring tone. Leigh had a habit of persuading her she needed gadgets she'd lived without all her life and she really must fight back. Calls that filled the car made her feel hunted.

Arthur. At eight thirty-five? "Yes?"

"Annie!" he cried. "You got cats and dogs down there?"

Since Arthur couldn't give a simple thing like rain its proper name, Annie found herself picturing a long-forgotten Persian Blue carried around like a teddy in Leigh's arms, until it was squashed by a car. She was tempted to remind him of that small carnage, in a tone that insinuated his inability to remember consequences.

The rain drove faster. And now the clutch control made way for progress, but the conversation was backed-up.

"We may have snow here tomorrow," he said at last.

"I get the weather on Radio Three, Arthur," she said, "too much of it. Are you all right?"

This time the pause was his. She knew she'd been prickly. But then she'd just been back in a time when she'd felt buried under the debris of the marriage he'd wrecked. It was hard to adjust to the present, with its *amicable* online friendship and café catch-ups, with gardens or galleries thrown in.

"Ah, that's the thing, you see. It's all over with Carole, really over this time. I know you two get on…"

"Ah." It was amazing, thought Annie, how disposable relationships could be. "So Carole's actually gone?"

"Apparently she had to be out of the house before her fiftieth birthday. I've never understood numbers."

"They mark time, I guess."

"Thanks for that."

Was he cross? She couldn't let it stop her. "And time is just a way of

14

bigging up that little thing called life…"

"Bigging up? Does that come from the same phrase book as *bitch* and *ho*?"

"Elevating its status, Art. But there's someone else, I suppose." Couldn't he call Samaritans or a chat show? "That seems to be the pattern. We're good at moving on these days. And now, I am, finally!"

Of course he couldn't know that she was being literal now, wheels turning, relief surging. She started to explain, "The traffic's a pig…" but he cut in.

"I'm so sorry I hurt you, Annie."

"Yes, I know," she said, knowing he'd hear the outbreath. "You've told me before."

First, after explaining that he loved Lorelei Tacq and was moving out. But Annie couldn't watch that particular episode, not now.

Once again in a disarmingly affectionate letter about money a couple of weeks later.

And then not for quite a while, at the end of which he was presumably too busy being sorry he'd hurt Lorelei in the process of falling for Carole – who quoted him, a couple of years later, on the same subject: *"Artie's so sorry he hurt you, Annie. Lorelei was such a tragic mistake."*

This, she thought, was a mistake now: the Blue Tooth that brought him in, the traffic, the rain, the time slipping away. But he was talking, more pauses than usual, wistful and sorry for himself, drifting, apparently with no idea that the words he said were not just here in her car at 8:37 but in other moments, houses, coffee shops. Even at her desk. And she had less control over where they took her than of this car of hers on the loud, dark road.

On the most recent Edinburgh visit, when Leigh hadn't gone with her and Carole had sent apologies that she couldn't join them this time, he'd said it again, with lingering eye contact that almost compelled her to throw tea in his face.

"Well," he said now, "you didn't deserve it. Carole's highlighted that herself. She likes you rather more than me, it turns out."

"Well, yes, of course… and naturally our daughter likes Carole more than me."

"She does? Why 'of course'?"

"I just meant… we all have ways… even Lorelei."

15

"Lorelei? Do we have to bring her into this?"

But, Annie thought, she was there, wasn't she, even in her absence? Lorelei had been tragic all on her own, fragile, insecure and completely incapable of playing stand-in mummy to a sullen child. She couldn't have received her infant visitor with more disgust and fear if it had been a cockroach in her designer lounge.

"No, this is about you and Carole," she told him, not sure she could continue at the next roundabout.

The name prompted a rush of narrative, just as musical in its lilts and theatrical in its feeling as any radio station. Required to make no response, Annie tracked the road like a learner. Carole 'through new eyes', a Carole he called 'a stranger', a Carole he 'had to say' he could 'never understand'...

Carole: all warmth and intimacy. The third Mrs Capaldi embraced everyone – except Lorelei – both physically and emotionally. But Annie was glad she'd stopped short of complete trust, the kind she didn't do anymore. She had no plans to share Arthur's shortcomings with his third ex over a bottle of wine.

"Leigh will be sad," she interjected, at what she hoped was the end of a lengthy Carole-themed paragraph. It was true. Carole was a hi-spec step-mum, every box ticked.

"Does Leigh do sad? I don't see much of her."

"You moved to Scotland. I couldn't whack her off by Royal Mail."

"In fact, Annie, do we have to talk about every female in my life except you?"

Annie was approaching the roundabout. And some slick male was determined to cut in, as if a bigger car and younger hair gave him the right...

"Listen, Art, I need to negotiate this traffic. Email if you'd like to. I could call you tonight."

Not content with muscling in, the other driver showed her the finger. Arthur would be so livid – if of course he had the slightest idea that she was trying, while he talked, to live...

"I just wanted you to know," said Arthur. "It's all been such a huge mistake."

Another one? But which was the biggest, since he'd had sixteen years of marriage with Carole, seven with Lorelei and five with her?

"O.K."

"O.K.?"

Which part of O.K. could he not interpret?

"Speak later. Bye now."

Did he ever consider the damage words could do?

Chapter Two

The bench in the churchyard garden was dark with rain but Ethan couldn't wait for the sudden sun to dry it. Looking up at the clock tower, he saw that the chat with his tutor had been far from quick. He was hungry. Counting out two pounds eighty-seven from his back pocket reminded him of a theory he'd shared with Sam; that chocolate was not only the cheapest lunch in London but also the most satisfying.

"That's because you're such a little boy," he heard her reply. How long ago? A month, two? While she was still on his side of the world.

At the time he thought she liked the little boy in him, who refused to make way for a suit and a mortgage, but it was hard to tell with Buddhists. Had she liked him at all, or just the fit they made – paths intersecting, bodies joining – and the wordless place not far from Nirvana where sex took them?

Unless on that journey he'd been travelling alone?

"Come with me if you like, or not," she'd told him. "Up to you."

"Do you want me to?"

"Ethan…"

He knew what that meant: he never learned. The subjugation of feelings to the spiritual. The end of desire. The surrender of the ego. He wasn't meant to need her, or need her to need him. He just had to be, like the grass and sky.

It had made him feel like those parakeets in Richmond and Kew. But at least they could fly. Sam had flown too, overlooking the impact on her carbon footprint.

He'd chosen integrity even if she called it conformism.

"How would I explain to Dad," he'd asked her, "after the money he's 'lent' me? *Sorry, Dad, but I'm not finishing the thesis because I'd rather just breathe, preferably in Tibet?*"

"Follow your own path. That's all I'm saying. Not mine, not his, not your tutor's path. You're the one who has to walk it, just you."

He could picture the dust on her sandals. He could feel the heat on the reddening skin at the back of her neck, where the hair trailed from its scoop.

Given his tutor's recently-expressed concerns about progress and the need for more research, Ethan smiled grimly at the appeal of flight just now. But it wasn't really about escape. The kind of studying that mattered most was really an awakening. He must find a new awareness: of all life's textures, sounds, shapes and patterns, the breath-taking intricacies. As clouds scattered he looked at the dark stone of the old church and the spire reaching up to a pool of blue. His stomach rumbled, just a blink ahead of the hour's chime.

Around him the pigeons seemed oblivious but a crow on a high branch answered back. Bully, he thought, eyeing it. Gangster. Psychopath. The intelligence of corvids was an idea more terrifying than anyone in this straggly little urban garden dreamed. With a brain-to-body mass ratio similar to apes, their mental capacity would make a great subject for a PhD but Ethan's stomach wasn't strong enough.

He put down his notebook on the bench and searched his backpack. The chocolate bar in the pocket had softened out of shape, its coating cracked open but the toffee underneath sticking firm as he tried to separate it from the wrapper. Old, but still sweet.

A man was walking in through the side entrance, his raincoat loose enough to be an artist's smock and stained, too. Definitely not his celebrity father, who only wore brands these days. Ethan looked down at his own red, brown and yellow trousers, settled in folds, and the left-over black varnish chipped on his toes. How different was he really from the raincoat guy, heading towards the thick church door – to pray for a job, a bath, a wife?

People were a greedy species. Peace: that was all and enough, if Ethan could only track it down inside him.

"O.K. if I sit here?"

The voice made him turn. It was a middle-aged woman in a dark grey professional suit.

"Go ahead."

"No one promised sun," said the woman, producing a bottle of water.

"That's the kind of surprise I like."

"Right. Me too." He glanced at the plastic as her squeezed bottle crackled.

"We'll all be buried under these things one day," she said, "won't we? I keep meaning to break the habit."

"Like her," said Ethan, squinting at a girl, cross-legged on damp grass smoking weed.

For a moment the woman looked blank, probably less familiar than Ethan with the smell of cannabis.

"Ah," she said. "Ouch. All right, I'll do it. Last bottle of water."

He didn't suppose she meant it and was about to tell her that along with habits and mind sets, laws would need to change.

"It's not much of a garden but I like it," she said. "I came here on my first day at work twenty-five years ago today and it feels just the same."

"You work at the hospital?" he guessed.

"Yes, I'm head of the hospital school." She smiled. "I'm Annie."

Ethan hadn't been ready for the handshake as he gave his own name. His might be sticky with the chocolate but as smells went, it was a good one to leave behind. Her grip was business-like.

"I study," he added. "Theoretically for a thesis, but mostly trees and crows, and light on stone." He smiled too. "It's a full-time job."

He'd never seen her before. No poem in those sensible shoes. An off-the-peg woman, a statistical example, always meaning to... The bread in her home-made sandwiches was chunky and irregular, fresh enough to break up.

"That's my father," said Ethan, looking beyond her and raising a hand shoulder-high.

His dad always had the same purposeful stride, as if he had one of his tombs to examine inch by inch and artefact by artefact, and there was no time or budget to waste. Even at fifty-something he still looked as if he could run, climb and drop by helicopter as required.

The woman stood, screwing the lid on her bottle.

"No, you're all right," Ethan said. "Stay. You got there first. Eat your lunch."

"It's fine, really. I'll find somewhere else."

A nice woman. It was pointless, couldn't she see, the sacrifice just as stupid as any competition? Ethan shrugged. He'd spent enough energy.

She must have dropped the water bottle just as his father spoke his name. It rolled towards a plastic bag smeared with mud and stuck to the path. Ethan's dad swooped down on it faster than a pigeon on a chip and wiped it on grass.

"Thank you. That's very kind."

"I told Annie she was entitled to sit," said Ethan.

He watched her face for recognition but if she knew who his father was, she was a long way from star-struck. He suspected his dad was moving into charm mode.

"Do finish your sandwiches, please."

"I will," she agreed. "Eleven minute lunch hour." She looked up at the church clock.

"Annie, I'm Mark. You've obviously met Ethan."

"Mark Garrett," she said, with a small smile of recognition. Ethan admired her refusal to sound impressed.

His father nodded. "Don't be fooled by his youth," he continued. "He lives in the past. I guess that's why the possibilities of mobile phones pass him by. Like the advantages of turning them on."

"I understand, Ethan," she said, and smiled. "I sometimes want to beat the bits out of mine."

A chunk of cucumber fell out of the bread, followed by a slice of tomato which sprayed her shoe.

"I meant the bits in my phone," she added. "Not the sandwich. Contrary to appearances."

Ethan's dad offered her a tissue and she thanked him and used it. A pigeon swooped down on the salad ingredients, only to scorn them. Lifting its head, it made a noise that could have been a complaint.

"Ethan's like the pigeon," said his dad. "He'd rather have junk food."

A ring tone butted in. A hospital school lost without its head? She stood to answer it, apologising, walking away and lowering her voice. Ethan looked at his father in a way that meant, *Well? Do you need me to play Cupid?* But then Annie was walking back.

"I have to go. Nice meeting you both. Good luck with the thesis – and the next tomb."

"Nice meeting you too, Annie," said his dad.

She walked purposefully away, still listening to her phone but telling whoever had called her how hard it was to hear.

"You could have got her number," said Ethan, guessing at queues of adoring women at his father's book signings.

"Stressed. Thinly veiled by good manners. Good heart too, but much too stressed. Google it, Ethan, I know it's an unknown concept. S t r..."

"Ha."

"How's the dissertation?" his father asked. "You can tell me over lunch."

"I met a mother and child on the tube," Ethan told him. "I know they're a poem. I just haven't written it yet."

Annie was used to being called back to work during her lunch hour but it was a long time since she'd had to cut short a conversation with one attractive man to talk to another.

"No, Arthur, I can't," she told him. "And I can't talk against the traffic!"

Crossing the road as all sound was lost to London, she pictured him slouched in an armchair. Arthur wasn't really attractive anymore, not by objective standards, but then neither was she. Although Mark Garrett had behaved as if he thought so, at first, but then he was probably the kind of man who expected women to flutter at his intellect and fame.

"Art, hold on a minute!" she shouted.

What kind of man was Arthur, really? Did she even know? Because the student boyfriend with come-to-bed eyes had morphed, after leaving her, into two more husbands that weren't hers, each one a different version of the original. And now the one-liners, teases and unabashed compliments travelled across the gap their lives had made and he didn't even seem to notice.

Currently, however, they made way for questions – which she could hear as she arrived back on site and headed through the smokers towards the hospital entrance. He wanted to know why she couldn't meet him if he came down to London next weekend.

"You're busy?" he pushed. "Not with paperwork? Life's for living, Annie. When do you play?"

"I'm not seven, Arthur. I'm busy, really..."

"Is Leigh around, this weekend I mean?"

"You'll have to ask her."

"Are you all right?"

Was that a criticism? "I'm tired," she told him. It struck her that for twenty-five years she'd been exhausted by love of him.

"Why are you being so frosty, Annie? How many hours per week are you working these days?"

"I've no idea." Finally finishing with an ex-husband was not the kind of thing people did in the middle of revolving doors. "I can't do it anymore, Art."

"The job?"

"No, Arthur, you!"

Annie cut him off. *Arthur,* she tapped. *Please don't try to call me again. I don't want to speak to you. I don't want to listen.*

She pressed Send and wondered what would have happened if she'd tapped in a different kind of truth, along the lines of: *Arthur, I love you and would happily overlook the last twenty-five years if you could make me believe you really love me too.*

Of course part of her wished she had. That was the problem, the one she always came back to. But for now she would tread the corridors slowly, finishing lunch as she walked in a way that would affront her mother who thought eating on the move was simply uncouth. She'd rather be working than taking calls or texts from Arthur and trying to find out whether it was possible to stop loving someone because of an intention, or the date.

As she swallowed a large bite of sandwich her ring tone sounded again. Impatiently, she read not *Arthur* but *Leigh.*

"Darling, are you all right?" she asked at once, because Leigh had made it clear that she was far too busy to eat lunch or call her mother.

It was hard to make out the answer, but the tone was brusque. Possibly aggrieved. She identified the word 'Dad' and the adjective 'unsympathetic', which she only guessed was being applied to her. Annie waited – partly because she thought there might be more to come and partly because she was trying to make a best guess of what she'd heard.

"Mum? Are you there?" was louder and clearer than the rest and possibly even more accusing.

Annie considered and, at the fullest volume she could manage, answered. "No, I'm not," she shouted, with a big, bright-eyed smile. "Not to your father, Leigh, not anymore. Not after today."

She turned off her phone and made a point of not glancing in any direction but ahead. If anyone had heard her, she couldn't care less. Turning a corner, she loosened her shoulders and breathed out slowly. Emmy Fern-Battiston and Sanamir wouldn't find her unsympathetic.

She had a job to do.

In the empty schoolroom Annie remembered the chalk dust that used to cloud in sunlight. Twenty-five years ago there had been no technology to wipe obsessively with antibacterial cloths. The place used to smell of Dettol but no one had heard of MRSA. Alice Triviani, who still wanted to be a barrister in spite of the car crash that put her in a wheelchair, used to read one crime thriller after another, donated by a smoke-soaked mother who never wore rubber gloves. Patients didn't die – not of infections caused by wall-charts or textbooks, anyway. Since, the paperwork had multiplied, the curriculum had changed more regularly than Rod Stewart's wives and the kids had... *like*... a brand new vocabulary.

Gloves on, she tapped *As You Like It* into the search engine, thinking Emmy would connect more easily with Hamlet or Lear. After all, her life seemed to have become a tragedy. What drove a fifteen-year-old to jump off a railway bridge? God knew how she felt about having failed.

At half-past one, Annie went to fetch her from the ward.

"Hey, Mrs Capaldi!" called Sanamir, her black hair in her hands as she tied it in a loose pony tail, probably the twentieth of the day.

"How was the curry?" Annie asked her.

"Lame," said Sanamir from her wheelchair. "Like seriously lame."

Sanamir glanced at Emmy. Including her was a kindness but Annie didn't suppose she expected a response. They might be in the same school year following similar syllabuses, but she wondered how much real-life experience they'd shared until now. And whether Emmy would share anything with anyone. It had only been a week so far but the girl's silence was packed so hard, it was difficult not to feel crushed. A whole long week of failure to connect.

Annie remembered from the one full week of her whole career that she'd spent off sick with flu – long before the days of texts bleeping cheerily at the bedside – just how different time became, how heavy in its emptiness. The function of work: to spare people that. To set aside the question of happiness, making sure that life-evaluation fell off the end of a to-do list that never shrank.

Sanamir was talking about her Science teacher at school and his habit of knocking equipment around the lab with his big gestures. Annie smiled as the girl simulated his flinging arms and wide eyes, but when they both looked to Emmy she was wax-work still. Not just the legs that

24

wouldn't walk again, but the clear, young skin on her blank face. There was a clock on the wall ahead and her green eyes – extraordinary eyes framed by fair lashes, with scatterings of freckles on high cheekbones and deep forehead – seemed focused on it. As if she was watching the red second hand clicking around it. Years ago Annie had taken it down on the grounds of cruelty. But next morning, while she was in a meeting, it had reappeared, still issuing its moment-by-moment reminders like a malicious hiss in the ear.

Standing beside Emmy, Annie thought better of a hand on her arm. Too soon. It seemed to be a day for over-thinking when instinct usually served her well enough.

"I've been catching up on Rosalind and Orlando," she told her. "It would help if I knew how much you've done already." She glanced at Emmy, who showed no sign of having heard. "Well, you can always stop me if I start on something you already know."

With a hostile stare, perhaps? Annie would welcome one of those. Or a scream? Was that what Emmy needed to let loose?

"I know nothing," said Sanamir cheerfully. "Is there a movie?"

Annie said she'd check and started to push Sanamir's chair into the schoolroom next-door, telling Emmy she'd come back for her. Teaching was almost always one-to-one, but she'd hoped the company of a lively girl with some interest in 'doing Shakespeare' might encourage her. Now she saw that it only gave her the space to be silent, to absent herself more easily and absolutely. But if she split the lessons they'd each get half as much time, which wouldn't improve Sanamir's chances of making it to the courtroom of her parents' dreams in wig and gown.

Leaving Sanamir looking at the cast list, Annie returned to fetch Emmy, chatting about Hollywood and who could fill the key roles. Johnny Depp? Nothing. Not a flicker. Annie realised she didn't know any actors under fifty. Leigh said she should be watching Hollyoaks and X-Factor and reading vampire novels if she wanted to relate to teenage patients. But there must be a way of making a connection that was deeper than that, one that was human and timeless. There always had been, in the end, before Emmy.

"Is there something you'd like to do instead? Will you think about it?"

She'd already tried nail varnish, hair curlers, cake baking, board games, cards, origami, paints... Emmy loved horses, her mother said, or

25

used to before the 'boyfriend business'. A business that seemed to have made a hell of a loss.

As she wheeled her into the schoolroom, Annie noticed Emmy close the green eyes. She must still be in pain and sometimes when her breathing quickened she let it show, her mouth unable to hold its line. But this signified resistance. It was the best she could do to make herself untouchable.

No sooner had they joined Sanamir than Emmy pulled out her I-pod from under her cardigan and plugged music into her ears. Sanamir gave her a questioning frown and sighed at Annie, who addressed herself to the cast list and plot summary, making sure she distributed encouraging glances equally to both her pupils.

It was only a matter of time.

Chapter Three

At the tube station Ethan watched his father disappear down the steps. His hair was thinner these days and he carried a few more pounds but when he turned, the wave he gave Ethan was the same.

It took Ethan back. Not to boarding school goodbyes because they were ten a penny and just a matter of a boy setting off for the station in lace-ups, with a suitcase and a backpack. This wave transported him to a beach but it had no name. Pebbles or sand? Seaweed anyway, clinging to the rocks and feeling creepy under his toes as he tried to swim out and his feet floundered for the surface below. Had his father abandoned them mid-holiday once, for a dig that went deeper than the moats round Ethan's sandcastles? And did it matter?

Maybe people who'd smoked less weed could caption these backward glimpses and give them a date and a location. All Ethan knew was the feeling. Sad. Isolated. Lost. Because then, when his mum and sister Daph shared a mysterious secret bond and laughed with the same laugh when he wasn't being funny, his dad was the one he loved most. But it didn't matter now, except when it came back like the waves. He'd thought his dad would understand about the thesis and the future he couldn't imagine. But he didn't. He wanted Ethan to conform and consume like everyone else. And the wave brought back the disappointment.

I can't forget that you didn't get it.
What kind of dad gives his son no credit?

Ethan used to write a lot of lyrics but other people's music never fitted and in any case he had no voice to sing them. The old lines sounded like rap now in his head, and there were more to follow as he walked away from the station steps.

When I'm in my hut like a shepherd with no sheep
I don't want your hand waving through my sleep.

"Be a performance poet," Daph had said, last time he saw her, before she went skiing for Christmas. "They're cool. You know, fashionable." The laugh was just the same even though she'd be twenty-six soon.

It was hard to love her now that she was living in the U.S. with a hedge fund manager – and got hysterical that time he spilt coffee on her shoes – but he must kept trying. He must take more time to open up and understand. No condemnation. There had to be a place where they overlapped.

"I love you, Dad," Ethan imagined himself saying as he headed for the river. He pictured the wave coming to a standstill and the smile clearing away. Now his dad was a widower who spent more time writing papers or fronting TV programmes than actually digging around in barrows. He should understand that everything and everyone had the capacity to change.

Dad? Ethan used to stress the word like a question, as if it was a favour he needed to ask. He used to want to go with him and be an archaeologist too. Now he just wanted to live in a different time, when it wasn't too late.

There was rain in the air, nicking the surface of the Thames. But he was back at the funeral, where he hadn't been able to say the words, not 'love' and not 'Dad' either, because his father was so whole and smart, with his brand new shirt looking bright white round his neck and his social skills peaking to meet and greet.

The past was endless, overwhelming. Ethan willed himself alive and alert in the present. There were people everywhere but he didn't see them. He hated being absent and cold, as if life wasn't human and only in his head. Swarms of strangers moved in silence around him. Maybe he should try to connect with just one, like he had with Coralie and her mother.

How would he choose? Ethan saw a guy who had to be homeless watching from a wall. He was bearded and Biblical, like a prophet but with jogging trousers and a body warmer. One foot kicked the wall where he sat, his head just registering the rhythm in a small, steady nod. Against it rested a grubby board, breaking up at the corners; it read EVE OF DESTRUCTION in red capitals and underneath, smaller, RUNNING OUT OF TIME.

Ethan nodded too. "You're right there," he said.

The prophet didn't seem to see or hear. One of his trainers had a sole that had unpeeled and been fixed – with gum? Ethan smelt the roll-up held in gloves with no fingertips. The guy narrowed his eyes as he inhaled, looking through Ethan to the burger stall. Counting the coins in his pocket, Ethan looked at the price list.

A large bald guy and his equally large wife were choosing, losing patience, less than happy that the stall holder's English wasn't compatible with their Geordie accents. The smell made Ethan queasy. By the time they'd loaded up their Styrofoam tubs, squeezed on ketchup and sprinkled salt, Ethan was wondering how any stomach could survive this stuff. But he ordered, grinned and gestured about the rain, thanked the guy and waved away the change. Carton in hand, he looked back to find the prophet gone, along with the sign. No trace. Like a Jesus from the tomb.

Looking around for someone who might accept a burger from a hippie, he glimpsed the board between bodies, not high but at stomach level. A shout. A clash of board and flesh. And a couple of skinny white boys had the board, holding it high, passing it above the prophet's head like a ball in a scrum, dodging, running. The prophet didn't move but only watched as his warning was hurled over the wall into the river.

The lads swaggered off without glancing back. The prophet stood in the space made by passers-by who turned away and moved on. Ethan didn't move either. The apocalyptic message was face down on the surface of the river, making a landing spot for a fat, noisy gull. Then it thudded against the wall, tipped and sank. But the prophet wasn't looking at the water. He was still standing, eyes narrowed on something Ethan couldn't guess. Thinking? Or making sure he didn't think at all?

"You all right?" Ethan asked, and offered the burger. "Hungry?"

No answers. But the man took the food and walked away. Then without turning, he held up a hand – another kind of wave, a thank you, a reply. In any case, enough. Ethan smiled. But what was the life expectancy of a guy on the streets like that – forty? Maybe his message about time running out wasn't so much an ideological warning for the masses as a kind of identity card?

Ethan felt sorry. He could have tried. Lads like that needed someone to show them the truth. Intervention didn't have to be led by the fist.

Not much anyone could have done to help his mother. That was what the hospital said. What was the running time on shock when an active forty-five-year-old woman dropped dead one day of a brain haemorrhage?

It's not the love that hurts but the space that gapes
wide, wide as the ocean
where the love ought to be
the story at bedtime
love with an eye on the watch
I heard the TV speak your language
when it called your name
mother
you were a tile-flat pillow case with paper-cut corners
you needed more sockets to keep your world spinning
and here I am
in the shadows
where the moon is enough
just trying to be still.

Some poems hung on after he'd cut them smaller than a banker's old credit card. And the bad ones had the tightest grip because his brain was just a spectator.

"It's more like therapy," he'd told Sam in the silence after he read it aloud. "Than a poem, I mean."

"Yes," she said, wrapped in the duvet on the sofa, holding the folded paper in both hands. "Maybe you should get some."

Maybe she'd meant, *Don't expect that from me.* As if he asked for anything.

Ethan walked on, close to the river, watching its surface as if the prophet's board might bob up like a corpse in a movie. He might never get better at poetry but he needed to improve with people. It wasn't always easy to tune in – even with Sam, who took his breath away but said that it was tacky when he told her so.

Tacky things clung and she didn't want him stuck to her. There must be a way of knowing people where their spirits cried out to be known, without attaching yourself to them like a parasite that needed to be picked off. Eaten, even. He had no idea what his mother's spirit would tell him if he found it, out there, inside him, in photos or stories passed on. He'd thought Sam was all spirit, a faerie in jeans, but she wanted things that weren't him. It was a discipline and he'd only just begun to

30

understand about needs, how few they were and how easy it was to bury them under waste. Life under landfill.

The poems were there, hidden like the prophet's words, but breaking out like shoots. Someone said the Brazilians had the vocabulary for each element of the love phenomenon: for the look, the tightness of anticipation in the chest, the separation, renewal, dread. But no one could ever capture it with labels or strategies. Love: he wondered how it could be all we need when it was such a yawning gap, an absence.

Ethan told himself he no longer chose the love people sang about. Love was about being, about breathing each moment as a microbe in a biosphere, part of the universe, sustaining not consuming. Or stardust waiting to return to base… Maybe no one had ever told the prophet that.

Slow had its downside. Sometimes he forgot to act.

"You're a Buddhist now?" his dad had checked, as they headed out of the graveyard garden.

"I think I just am," he'd answered, which made his father smile.

"I'll take that as a yes," he said.

Ethan wondered whether Annie from the hospital had felt the disconnection. But she seemed too focused on her own priorities and they were good ones after all.

Ethan would hate to dismiss people the way his father did, reading and then discounting her with that careless certainty of his. He'd rather be like Coralie, taking a good look and trying to understand. He hoped education wouldn't close her eyes. Her mother's had started off suspicious but they'd grown younger as she'd let that go.

He should have got her name.

It was six-eleven. Still at her desk, Annie turned on her phone but saved the three voice messages from Leigh for later. Clearly her daughter was not as busy as she liked to make out. Seeing a text from Arthur, she deleted it unread. How small her world was, really. In five hours of constant posting, blogging, tweeting and virtual following all around her, only two people in the global network had tried to communicate. And only, in both cases, to disturb the equilibrium she needed to restore.

Professionally her day had yielded zero communication with Emmy, not even glances, shrugs or scowls. Nothing to fill blank boxes. An optimist would say *ongoing* or *TBC*. One day, any day now, Emmy would give it up. How dark the pain must be, how tightly it must wrap her, to make her choose isolation.

Annie had already begun to wonder how alone she would feel when she cut all the arteries of work. Today it struck her, shutting down the computer, that in her life she was a long way down the path. Which had taken her, via dolls, cartoons and dress-up parties, to a kitchen with a TV she could snipe at, correct and very occasionally applaud in her dressing gown.

"Still here, Annie?"

Zelda, the paediatric staff nurse, was leaning around her door. She looked so smooth and breezy in her dark blue uniform and shiny bob that she might just have arrived early for the night shift. It made Annie feel old and discoloured – like a photograph her mother had presented recently, after a clear-out, of a prize-winning speech she'd made as a girl about the rights of animals.

"Just off now," said Annie, aiming at brightness.

A brief exchange established that neither of them had any plans for the evening, the difference being that Zelda had a husband to do nothing with, except on Thursdays when they learned to tango. Which Annie thought was quite touchingly *something*.

The photograph reminded her. It really was time she visited her mum and low emotional energy shouldn't cut it as an excuse. "What happened?" her mother had asked, thrusting the limp old cutting at her, as if she expected an answer more detailed than, *"I was eleven, Mum."*

Of course, by the time she reached her, it would be what her mother called 'far too late' but when was that any different? Annie packed up her bag and said her goodnights on her way out.

There had been no anti-bacterial hand cleansing dispenser twenty-five years ago when she ended her first day. Then she'd left imagining Leigh throwing her arms round her knees. But when she made it home she'd found her asleep, a trace of resentment in the thrust of her lips. Annie wished she could remember more clearly what it felt like to pick her up, kiss her forehead and stroke back her delicate, fair hair.

Walking towards her car, Annie realised she had finished earlier that first night, but she'd thought of the same people with the same feelings: stabbing, bruising longing for Arthur and two shades of guilt towards her daughter and mother.

So much for progress.

Twenty-five years ago Annie's mother had been half of a marriage, and there had been no red cords to pull in emergencies. No need for visitors to press the doorbell and bang repeatedly before the front door opened.

Annie waited on the doormat, shivering without the coat that lay across the back seat of her cosy car. She checked her watch as she heard the ring in the hallway and wondered about using her phone. Not many minutes after seven. Maybe she should have called, but experience showed that if she estimated an arrival time and the traffic was thick, she'd be held to account – for her mother's conviction that she was upside down in a mangled car on the motorway.

Hilda Mills opened the door but stepped back at once and told her to come in and keep the cold out. She was in her loose plaid pyjamas, which Leigh said were definitely Men's – a result of haphazard internet shopping that she considered a mischievous as well as triumphant delight. Hilda liked to confess each purchase with a sheepish smile: "I couldn't resist it! Such a clever idea!" Looked at from above, her hair, now thin enough to streak scalp through, suddenly reminded Annie of guitar strings. Specifically Arthur's, the ones he used to strum when she fell in love with him. Imagination could be such a destructive thing.

"How was your day, dear?"

"Fine." Not much point in trying to share an anniversary with a mother who for most of those twenty-five years had considered her job an inconvenience. "What about yours?"

For a moment, as Annie watched her mother moving to the kitchen to put the kettle on, she tried to picture her as she used to be, twenty-five years earlier – at the same age she'd reached now. A particularly indigestible equation. But this Hilda Mills had eradicated all the previous versions, even though the smaller, lighter and slower model seemed only loosely connected to the young mother who became the town councillor and then the widow.

"I emailed Babs in Brisbane," she said, "but I couldn't work out whether she'd be up. She can't see the screen very well so I used font 48, Arial, bold."

In Annie's memory Babs was loud, made-up and amiably saucy. Suddenly it seemed odd that her mother had sustained an improbable friendship from school into her eighties and across to another hemisphere. What, apart from repeat stories of hockey injuries and unjust detentions, did they write about? Probably her: the divorcee who

33

worked too hard and let herself go.

"You're so lucky, Mum," she said. "You're not exactly a burden on the NHS."

"I should hope not," said Hilda, as if she'd be ashamed to be ill. "Any news of Leigh? Is she dating again yet? They leave it so late these days. Bodies peak." She giggled, heralding some naughtiness to follow. "She'll be past her sell-by date."

"I wouldn't mention that idea," said Annie, smiling. "No men in her life as far as I know. At least, no one special."

She wondered, as her mother handed her a mug of tea, trailing a drip down the handle, what that meant, exactly. Lovers, one-night stands, collisions, but no actual love? Not celibacy, surely. That was her own style, not her daughter's.

Carrying a tea tray through to the lounge, Annie realised that having asked after Greg, she was paying no attention to the news. There was always so much of it: of Greg himself, his wife and kids, grandchildren and dog, car and holidays. In absentia he was for Hilda the good son with the firm marriage and even firmer faith, a success story to share. But in person he always seemed to be less of a favourite. Annie supposed Christmas at his place would be overcrowded again this year, thanks to 'The Lord' who was always an extra guest at mealtimes – presumably the only one who didn't mind the chipped mugs, smeared cutlery and hairy cushions. While Hilda, muttering asides, would mind most actively of all.

Christmas. How, Annie wondered, had she survived twenty-five of them since Arthur left?

"Oh," said her mother, pouring from the pot, "Arthur sent an email."

"Arthur! What about?"

"He called it a catch-up. It was one of those PCC ones, you know, meant for 72 people at once. Is that what you do these days if your wife leaves you? Maybe it's so they can all adjust their Christmas card lists."

"BCC," said Annie. She shook her head. "He's a piece of work."

Her mother's look could have been called askance. She was always complaining about new words and phrases she claimed she couldn't interpret, and then taking pleasure in using them.

"I don't understand. Can't a piece of work be good or bad? C minus or A plus?"

"Ah," said Annie. "Yes, it can. Very much so. But not at the same time."

Deciding Arthur would be overmarked on C minus at the moment, she sipped her tea. Her mother began to talk about a headline on BBC Breakfast about nursing homes. Annie could understand her concern but the news of neglect had become a preoccupation. She couldn't imagine allowing herself to be so irrational. Except...

"Arthur wants me back, apparently," she told her, and lifted her eyes and brows with something that must have looked like amusement.

"Ah," said Hilda. "That'll pass."

Annie smiled into her tea as she stirred it. Now the wisdom. Nail on the head. The clarity of experience.

"He's trying to convince me that I'm the one feeling that doesn't pass."

"He can't work out what to do with his shirts."

Yes, Mother, thought Annie. *Indeed.* "I'm not the best person to help him with that."

"No, because you never wanted to learn. It's the same with Arthur, dear. You don't want to learn." Hilda added a teaspoon of sugar to her half-empty cup. "I wish you would."

"Me too."

It was a murmur and her mother didn't hear it. Or didn't let it stop her. It was a while into the story that Annie realised this was one she'd never heard before. Not naughty school girl antics but a revelation.

"That's the trouble with the Internet. People can crawl out of the woodwork. He expected me to believe I was always the one – always kept a candle burning, he said, all through forty years of marriage, children and grandchildren. Would I like to meet for dinner, when really he wanted me to move in and keep his house tidy and his bed warm!"

Annie knew she must look astonished. "When was this? Who?"

"A couple of years ago. Keith Marshall. Pay attention, Annie. Not everything's about you." Hilda chewed her lips and pushed the biscuit tin towards Annie, who ignored it. "He'd been a widower for a few months. I gave him short shrift. The slightest encouragement and he'd have been on the doorstep with flowers."

"But... did you ever love him, all those years ago?"

"I can hardly remember!"

Annie wasn't sure whether to believe that. But surely, if companionship could have spared them loneliness...? Did this sad old

35

man really deserve such scorn?

Hilda wiped her nose. Astonished, Annie recognised the hankie she'd struggled to embroider when she was about nine. It wasn't as white as it used to be, but like this octogenarian ex it had re-emerged from another time to shock her.

"I can't believe you've still got that!"

"I had a clear-out and there it was, between sheets. The stitches are bumpy, but it's good cotton. Things were made to last..."

Like marriage used to be? Or the feelings of an old man? Like her love for Arthur, anyway. Even if *his* was a delusion, triggered by domestic ineptitude – and the abrupt cutting off of his sex supply. Her cheeks heating, Annie wondered how high her mother was keeping her thermostat these days.

Hilda was mid-story, complaining about some shoes she'd bought recently. Now she went to fetch them to prove her case. Annie looked around the room, skimming the photographs. The bungalow was tidy and dusted daily. Hilda managed everything still and that was good, an achievement. But it had never before made Annie feel ridiculous, transparent, a child again. If her mother was wonderful, then she was a mess, a joke.

Hilda returned with a flapping sole on a cheap, girlish pump of a shoe and finished her story, apparently satisfied with Annie's automatic responses: siding with her against the shoe shop, a company 'that should know better' and the level of craftsmanship in the UK today.

Hilda placed the shoes unexpectedly on the tablecloth and adjusted their angle to make them parallel.

"You won't let him work his charm on you, will you, dear?"

"No," said Annie, remembering. "Perish the thought!"

It was one of her mother's favourite phrases. Hilda nodded but she looked dubious, probably because Annie was unconvinced herself, rather wishing her mother had given the old widower a chance. The idea seemed both comic and touching.

Hilda brought her up to date with the loneliness and poor health of other widows. "Being alone doesn't have to be miserable," she ended, as Annie stood with her handbag on her shoulder, regretting the second biscuit even more than the third refill of tea.

"Well," said Annie, "it must be great if you choose it."

She had a feeling more people should make the choice, people destroyed by their toxic partners. But that wasn't Art. Arthur made his women happy, until he met the next and, even then, he hoped his cast-offs would enjoy their new friendships with their substitutes. And with him, too, because in his words, "It seems crazy to me, Annie, to be so close to someone and then part and never see her again." Which she used to consider a kind of innocence, or unforgivably stupid.

"Leigh's a modern woman," said her mother, admiringly. "But modern isn't always best. Do you remember those marvellous shoes I always wore for Sunday strolls – over thirty years they served me, five miles at a time – unless it was really wet underfoot?"

Annie assured her she did and kissed her cheek, promising to call the following evening. Her mother's skin was cool and baby-soft. The feel of it, which must be familiar, surprised her all the same. Love was so contradictory. Now that their conversations at the bungalow had continuity gaps, reversals and the kinds of spark that come from faulty wiring, she made herself excuses to stay away. And then found herself unable to sleep for dread of the time when there would be no one there to visit, the flimsy old lady lost along with the fresh-air rambler and bedtime storyteller.

Annie started the engine. Such an odd visit, full of plot twists! Arthur seemed to have embarked on a kind of mad campaign, and apparently Hilda wasn't the only one who'd lost touch with the rules.

Finding an annoying celebrity confessing ignorance about classical music on Radio Three, she changed to Two. *"Maybe she's in need of a kiss."*

Oh God in heaven. Not that, not now.

Annie cut off Paul Rodgers, but in the basement of a convent that became her hall of residence (twenty years before they demolished it) Arthur was dancing already and singing along with the lyrics. Not well, but confidently, because she was in need of his kiss – any time, but best of all now, and he was sure of her, since *Miss Prim*, as he'd called her, had already allowed him into her single bed.

There were plastic bottles of cider rolling about in corners and fag ends trodden underfoot. Her friend Gillie was working her arms like a witch at a cauldron. The heat glued Annie's blouse to her back; her hair, moving independently, brushed damp against her cheek. She reached out and linked fingers briefly with his, then spun away and focused on the floor and walls, the shapes she made, the curves and sway that were for him. Pretending to dance with Gillie as if he didn't exist, when all she could think of was the body and hair and smell that were Arthur Capaldi.

The guitar cut loose and all the soul girls with their shoulder pads and cheek glitter cut loose with it, most of them drunk, because this was a late track to fill the floor before the smooching started. As Annie danced for him, she heard him shouting the chorus. She knew he was watching her. Before she could turn back, he pulled her by the arm so she stumbled into his boy-chest and kissed her. Why wait for a slow-dance? His hand curved over her breast. The other was on her backside, lighter. His tongue was as confident as his dance moves, more. Her eyes were closed and her arms loose around his neck. She could smell the gel in his layered, New Romantic hair but this was the music he loved. As the song ended they were still kissing.

Rain began to spatter Annie's windscreen in the darkness but she'd be home soon. Maybe she'd surprise Gillie with a phone call, if she still had the same number she'd last used about a decade ago. She'd have to face Leigh's texts but really, there was no obligation to reply. Leigh often chose silence herself.

Chapter Four

Coralie didn't seem sleepy yet but it must be after eight o'clock. Crystel closed the book very quietly and murmured, "Goodnight, little one." Even though in the day she might call her *sweetpea* or *honeypie*, *dreamboat* or *sugar*, at bedtime she was always *little one*. It was a kind of signal. Crystel stood slowly and leaned over to kiss her cheek.

"I'm not little now. I'm five."

"You can be a big girl," said Crystel, "and still be my little one."

"Even when I'm in the top class?"

"Even when you're top of the top class!"

Coralie kept on smiling but Crystel wished she hadn't said that because she hated the world being competitive, even in primary school. Mums should watch their mouths. She knew that from the playground. A fat white woman had sworn at a teacher the other day, in front of everyone, fag and fingers jabbing close.

Coralie wanted another kiss, a pucker-up one.

"Did you have a nice birthday?" Crystel asked, smiling when Coralie nodded hard. "Night now, little one."

She closed the door quietly behind her, and realised she was tired even if Coralie wasn't. She must write the teacher a note. Tummy bugs were good because schools didn't want mess to mop up or germs to spread. Crystel knew her mother would wag a finger but what harm could it do losing one day's learning? Schools were above themselves these days. Like Madam, who wouldn't be best pleased if she found out how long she'd been at her flat that morning. Well, she'd left the place smelling of lavender and tidy too. If she'd skimped – with Coralie sitting in front of the big TV colouring in and asking with every ad break, "Have you finished, Mummy?" – she could make it up next time.

Madam was the only one she couldn't just come right out and ask by email, *"I was wondering, might I have Monday off on account of my little girl's birthday, no pay of course?"* The others didn't mind. They knew she was a hard worker and a good mother too. Mrs Harris said she'd be great value at twice the price, not that she was offering a pay rise. Crystel could see the money was nothing to Madam. Otherwise how could she be living in a flashy apartment like that when she wasn't thirty yet?

Crystel checked out Facebook. Lots of happy birthday wishes for Coralie, from her aunties in Detroit and Manchester and her gran in Tortola. Her old schoolfriend Aimee was out drinking on a Monday night, but she was always wild. Lucie posted about having a fab day with her goddaughter – *Birthday Blessings, Coralie* - before she went off singing in a gospel choir. Lucie was a churchgoer and said charity was just love. When they were girls their mums had been best friends and Crystel's had called her a good influence because she studied hard and said sex was only for marriage. Now Lucie looked bright and shiny with her bump. Crystel could have done with paid maternity leave herself five years ago, but then some people would say Lucie had earned it, with exams and a husband too.

Thanks for today Lucie. Coralie was still colouring in fairies up to bedtime. X

Crystel was just going to message her cousin Lynnette, to find out whether she was still dating the customer in the expensive suit who'd left her a fifty pound tip and asked for her number, when she remembered large print on a notepad. Ethan A. Garrett. She'd never have remembered David Smith or John Green but an off-the-peg name like that wouldn't sit well on a long-haired guy in patchwork trousers. He was a weird boy with a weird, old American name and the cutest smile she'd seen on anyone over ten. Crystel had thought he might smell, but the scent of him was only herbal or earthy, not quite dope, and his white-boy, sandy dreadlocks were still damp from the shower.

There he was on screen: Ethan A. Garrett, outdoors, with long, loose hair blown back from his face, maybe eighteen years old. A whole sixty-three friends and nothing posted for nearly four years! Crystel paused with the cursor on the Message box. What was she thinking? He wanted to live in a tree. But he wrote poetry and his face was kind.

She clicked to be his friend. Why not? He wouldn't see it anyway.

No computers in tree houses. Maybe he was the only guy in London without a phone. His head was full of serious things like the meaning of life, not *omg bad hair day* or *where's the fucking bus?* Crystel still longed to study philosophy and understand the big ideas. Her R.E. teacher said she was heading for an A before she fell pregnant with Coralie. Her mother said it wasn't too late, she didn't have to be a cleaner all her life and she should study part-time at evening school. But with the rent just gone up and the electricity bill bound to be higher than ever with no summer to speak of, Crystel couldn't see how.

Ethan A. Garrett had been to private school. So he'd walked away from money and that did him credit. And it made her angry too in a way, all the same, because she could use some, without having to ask Madam for extra hours and finding a message saying, *Impossible, I'm afraid, Crystel. Would you take extra care around the taps in the sink, something of a blind spot?*

Crystel put down her phone. Her own little kitchenette needed clearing. As well as the sink full of pans and plates there were chunky colouring pencils on the worktop where Coralie had been sitting while she made late supper. Crystel collected up the crayons and dropped them into the pencil case, noticing that the yellow was worn down because every fairy so far had a big head of hair that was long and blonde. She sighed, wondering who'd decided that the only shiny fairy fit for the cover had to be golden-haired, with skin a shade paler than her pink dress. In fact, who'd decided that fairies looked like Princess Diana? Why couldn't they be cheeky-faced with chubby brown legs and black curls? Someone needed to make some rules about presents for girls. Boys too, probably. She hoped Ethan Garrett had never made a gun out of sticks or fingers.

She wondered where he was going with his bare feet in floppy old sandals and his old-style notebook, and whether he shared his squat or whatever with some posh drop-out girl who never shaved her armpits, but painted his nails for him. That was sexy, in a way.

An email came through, from Madam. Title: *Disappointed.* Shit, thought Crystel, guessing, reading fast...

Dear Crystel,

I wish you had explained your intention of bringing your daughter to work with you today. I could tell that you had not been here for much more than half an hour even before a neighbour mentioned it. I need to be able to trust anyone with the keys to my home and feel that by trying to pull the wool over my eyes you have been disrespectful as well as deceitful. Therefore I am terminating our arrangement. Please drop the keys through the letterbox by tomorrow evening.

"Shit!" muttered Crystel. "Oh shit, no."

No best wishes or good luck, just her name with a whole load of business stuff underneath that must come up automatically. Crystel stared back at the last two sentences.

Fiercely she deleted the whole message, gone. No way was she going to answer that. How exactly did Madam reckon she could tell a quick lick from a deep clean when she couldn't be bothered to do her own vacuuming or stick a brush down her toilet, even though she had no one to take care of but herself?

Who overreacted like that anyway? What exactly was her problem?

It wouldn't do people any harm to try to understand what other people's lives were like before they wagged their fingers in her face. And why couldn't this neighbour of hers mind her own business? That money would leave a hole she'd have trouble filling and Madam had better not bad-mouth her at dinner parties.

All right, O.K. Someone had to understand what *fair* meant. She found the message in Trash and typed: *When I bring the keys I will do the extra hours I owe you. My Coralie is five today and I wanted to take her out.* That was no good. Madam would report her to the authorities for missing school. She deleted the second sentence and added: *Apologies, Crystel.* After she'd sent it she realised she hadn't used Madam's name or *dear* or *yours sincerely.*

Crystel washed up the dishes but no reply came. If she asked Lucie to pick Coralie up from school she could fit in another couple of hours at Madam's apartment, which was only right but more than she deserved. Apart from the notes that said *You missed a bit* in different, roundabout, corporate-type words, this was the first time Leigh Capaldi, manager of some kind, ever bothered to communicate. She was the kind of person who wrote *Thank you* when it meant she wasn't grateful at all, ever.

Picking up her silent phone, Crystel went back to Facebook and Ethan A. Garrett. Scrolling down his wall she saw a poem there, a short one:

Free is a falling
Sky, time to be
Clouds, a breath
Sun, your morning come again
Like sea's arrival and return
No traces left
But the echo of a murmur
Scattered like sand

Crystel didn't know much about poetry that didn't rhyme – even what made it poetry except the missing bits you were meant to guess. But this poem of his was dreamy, and romantic without the love story. She pictured him scrubbing words out the way he'd done on the tube, but this whole thing might just have rushed in like the waves he was writing about. Or been strung together, bead by bead, reaching for the words by instinct, the way she liked to make bracelets. She must start some for Christmas or she'd be panicking again, last minute.

Crystel didn't suppose it was great poetry, yet it took her places she didn't usually go. It made her look out of the window and really see. But the poem was full of a shy kind of brightness and the street was only black, with gold broken up by rain as if the edges were soft as paint, not hard. She knew once street lamps used to be lit with a real flame, but that wasn't cosy like it sounded, because Jack the Ripper stalked the streets in a black cloak and that made her shudder.

Hi Ethan from Coralie's mum on the tube. I like the poem.

It was true; she did. There! She'd left it on his wall now, not that he'd ever look to find it.

Her ring tone sounded and she grabbed the phone quickly, chipping one nail. When her sister asked what she was up to she didn't mention Ethan A. Garrett because Lou would call him *weird*, but she told her all about Madam, making sure she didn't raise her voice even when the anger came through. And leaving out the plan to give her ex-employer every second of the cleaning she'd paid for, because Lou would only say, *"Are you crazy?"* or tell her to piss in the kettle.

"Oh, there are plenty of bits lying around in the fridge," Annie had assured her mother. But visualising a mangled tube of tomato puree, an ounce or two of cheddar and four-day-old rocket that had probably spent the day biodegrading, she turned the car away from home. After all, she should be celebrating the date some way or other before it passed.

Americans said people passed, as if death was a variation on a driving test. As if it gave you wings instead of wheels, a better kind of freedom. Annie supposed she was closer to death than a birth that happened to be hers but sometimes felt as long ago as the big Nativity. That was the difference twenty-five years made. Suddenly it was ridiculous that when she'd begun her job she'd been so young but had hardly known it, hadn't felt it through the weight of responsibility. Now she could make impulsive decisions to eat out alone and it made no difference to anyone.

The town centre car park was shiny with black puddles but the rain was easing. She'd been meaning to try the place for a while because of the décor and the flowers in window boxes on the pavement outside. But she'd missed the chance to sit under a purple tasselled sunshade during the three or four days of summer that had tempted her. Now as she opened the door there was no assault of hot air. The smell was incense of some kind, more souk than church. There were sofas in a corner, draped with the kind of throws Leigh called messy. On one side, old painted shelves stocked health products and food for people with allergies or convictions. Glancing around, she saw teapots, second-hand books, slipper-ish harem shoes in a basket, a lamp with camels supporting the light fitting and a bright pink shade bumpy with mirrors and beads. Moving in towards the tables, she could smell food cooking: spices, herbs, oil.

An elderly couple who might be retired anthropologists glanced up from their wooden platters and greeted her. The only other customers were five women in their late thirties or early forties, heads together and open paperbacks in their hands or on their placemats. One of them smiled in Annie's direction. Another turned, the novel in one hand, and raised the other in a still kind of wave. It was that sort of place.

What she could see of the kitchen reminded Annie of her first as a wife, in the nineteen thirties semi where Arthur complained that if she came in, he had to do a Sylvia Plath and lose his top half in the oven. From this narrow space a woman appeared, in wide multi-print trousers and trainers, with a long, worn apron over her tunic and hair hidden in something Annie couldn't name. Her face was open and her skin clearer than Annie's felt, although she might have been close to her in age. She smiled, so warmly that Annie wondered whether she was mistaking her

44

for someone she knew.

"Welcome," she said. "Nice to see you."

"A table for one, please," said Annie. She'd said that so many times. Maybe it was the date that made it hurt again, just a little.

"Take your pick," said the woman. "There's an upstairs too if you prefer. It's got a whole different feel but it's quiet. This is only the third time I've opened on a Monday evening – for the book group, really."

She smiled at the table of women with their paperbacks. One of them cried, "Thank you!" and another said "You're a sweetheart, Amira", extending a thin black arm ringed with bracelets.

The town where Annie had lived most of her life was feeling the frisson of a multicultural tinge to its whiteness. When Leigh called it snobby and two-faced she didn't bother to defend it just because it was quiet with manners. But this café was different. She liked it already.

Amira told them how welcome they were as Annie climbed the steep staircase and turned into a long room soft with fabrics and shiny with coloured glass. Nothing matched. No sets or pairs. Every light fitting, tablecloth, chair and cushion had nothing in common with the rest except its individuality. Drawn to the window seat, Annie remembered Jane Eyre and thought Amira would be glad to see her occupy it, feet up, like a child daydreaming. But she sat at a small round table.

Below, the traffic was sparse. She could hear the water gush around the wheels but there were few people on the pavements to be splashed. On Monday nights in middle-class suburbia, with rain falling in the darkness, only commitment or loneliness drew the residents from their sofas and TVs. Apart from the need to escape.

Looking at the menu, Annie found some words she didn't know and practised pronunciation alternatives in her head. Laughter rose from the book group below. She hadn't recognised the cover but she didn't suppose the title was *Crime and Punishment*. What was that sex book Leigh had read, taking offence at the implication that she was a victim of hype? "At least I'm not a victim of worse things, Mum," she'd said, and when asked to explain, only told her, "Think about it."

"If you mean age," Annie almost retorted, *"just wait."* But it was a conversation she didn't choose to begin.

Now, turning at the sound of a rustling skirt, Annie saw a freckled girl appear with a pen and order book. An Art student, perhaps, with no make-up. Her coppery hair was caught up in a wooden slide, Japanese

45

style.

"Hi," she said, softly. "I'm just checking you're all right. Take your time if you need to."

"Thanks," said Annie, "but I don't. What do you suggest?" She stopped, checking the prices which were downright cheap.

The girl looked thrown. "You'd like me to choose for you?" she checked, and when Annie said, "That would be lovely!" she said she'd ask Amira and turned towards the stairs.

"Oh, and a large glass of red wine, please," added Annie.

The girl turned. "Oh, I'm sorry – we don't serve alcohol. But there are juices and smoothies, and twenty-seven yogi teas…"

"Surprise me with something you guess I've never had."

As the girl disappeared with a slightly anxious smile, Annie breathed deeply and re-ran her order. Something she'd never had. Like any kind of illegal drug or a first cigarette. A paranormal experience. Surgery, colonic irrigation, a mud wrap or hypnotherapy. A five-star, white-sand holiday, or cocktails by a pool. Any cheese that wasn't some shade of plain yellow, and anything on her plate that could have climbed off again if it hadn't just been submerged in boiling water until its skin colour screamed. Thank God. An affair with a married man, or a woman of any status at all. Flowers from any man on any day when they weren't virtually obligatory. A blind date. Sex anywhere but a bedroom, in spite, early on, of suggestions Arthur called 'imaginative' and she called 'mad'. A toy boy, a sugar daddy or a ketchup sandwich with or without the crisps. "You don't know what you're missing," Arthur had told her, grinning, wiping the red smear from his short-lived moustache with a forefinger.

Annie supposed she should look at Leigh's texts. She'd read *Why aren't you looking at your phone today?* followed by *Dad seems to be having some kind of midlife crisis and I'm trying to work here* and *Call me* when Amira creaked up the stairs with a small tray and a tall glass full of something thick and green.

"Nature's pick-you-up," she said. "Mondays can be tough, especially when the sun's been hiding all day."

"Yes," said Annie. "I gave up looking for it." She looked down into the liquid that now sat close to her nose. Fresh mint? Broccoli? She hoped she didn't look unsure. Unadventurous. Dull.

"You're not waiting for anyone? Niamh forgot to check."

46

"No, not today."

"The food will be with you in five minutes. Nothing you're allergic to?"

"I can't think of anything."

"Nothing you just can't stand?"

"Nothing you could serve on a plate."

Annie smiled, a little embarrassed, but Amira laughed, her head back. Annie wondered what she was picturing as the head of Art Capaldi took shape, with Caravaggio darkness.

She glanced around her and started to tell the woman how 'nice' the place was, in words other customers must have improved on already, but Amira thanked her, smiling.

"Make yourself at home," she said. Oddly, because Annie was just thinking that for all its space and thick, distinctive character, and in spite of her limited travel which didn't extend beyond Europe, that was just how the restaurant made her feel.

Alone again, Annie realised that though she always took something to read, she'd come out without her Kindle. And there was no way she was going to set up her laptop on the embroidered tablecloth among the poppies, or work on her phone like Leigh. She wandered around the room, looking at the shelves, but everything was ornamental, and must have caught Amira's eye on a market stall, if not in Marrakesh then in Camden.

She turned at the sound of feet. Amira was holding a paperback, but not the book group read. She put it down on Annie's table with a smile, murmuring that it was from the collection downstairs and she must feel free to come down and search for something she preferred if she hadn't grabbed the right thing.

Annie thanked her and picked up SOUL THERAPY. Although she'd never met anyone called Kinzi she thought the writer must be female.

"Sorry about the condition," said Amira. "I think it's what they call pre-loved."

Annie smiled, even though she hated these new, touchy-feely phrases coined for profit, but it occurred to her that so was she. Except that, built into the marketing term was the idea that a buyer was ready, while embracing an object's history, to lavish on it a brand new love of his own.

"I'm definitely post-loved myself," she said, imagining how

47

mortified Leigh would be if she were opposite this confessional mother. "My daughter calls me an over-sharer if I use the L-word in a public place."

"Share away," said Amira. "Life experience is too valuable to keep to yourself. That's why Kinzi wrote the book."

Annie wanted to ask why Amira had chosen it for her but in fact she only said, "I couldn't hold you up, really. I'm fine. I'll have a look."

She opened the book at the first page and pretended to start reading. But as Amira rustled away she imagined the answers if a hundred people were given the title and asked for the first word it triggered by reflex. Soul Therapy could be chocolate. The sea, or flowers. An early morning forest. Beethoven.

A restaurant owner who knew nothing about her could see what she needed. Like her mother. Like Gillie, who had told her during that phone call she never returned. Like Carole, who had implied as much with a light hand on her shoulder as Art queued for drinks after Leigh's graduation.

It wasn't Arthur she needed, but the strength to put an end to love. Her soul therapy of choice!

After one delicious course, she paid the freckled student while Amira was busy and left the restaurant none the wiser about what she'd eaten. Back home, she indulged in conditioner when she washed her hair, then lay in bed. When the phone rang she allowed the recorded message to speak for her.

"Mum, are you there? You can't avoid us forever. I'm worried now and I could do without this on top of all the crap I'm dealing with at work. Call me – please. Tomorrow?"

Annie began focusing on breathing, but the next call followed less than ten minutes later, just as her eyelids had begun to set and her body had found a shape it could hold.

"Annie..." Arthur paused. "I just wanted to let you know I'm coming down to stay with Leigh and catch up with both of you. It'll be good to talk, if you don't mind listening. You know you're my dearest friend. I'll call you tomorrow."

Too late to move. Annie took a deeper breath. Did Leigh know anything about this?

So, she thought, eyes decidedly closed, she'd have to listen. She was good at that. As long as there was no chance to talk, express any thoughts or feelings she might have, about the past, present or future.

But then she felt tempted to call him back: *"Listen, Art, maybe in the circumstances you need time alone before you jump on a train – time to consider who I am to you, since it doesn't seem entirely clear."*

Not now. No soul therapy in that. She needed sleep to give her distance – as much as possible with Arthur heading southwards any day.

No picturing him, searching for words he couldn't find. No imagining his face across from hers, or the double bed where he'd be alone soon. There was nothing more exhausting than a marriage brought to a sudden stop, and nothing less conducive to sleep.

"The wisdom of Annie!" she muttered. "I should start a blog."

Chapter Five

Ethan woke late, aware that he'd dreamed one of those epic muddles that left him in mental disarray, all energy sapped. In there somewhere was a chaotic narrative he'd love to hold on to, so he could reshape it and find a theme. His poems all had one, even though as they formed he didn't know what it might be. Labels didn't always do the job. Now the dream left him with the same feeling that words couldn't quite pin down. His mother had been dying again, repeating her biggest role. But she'd been absent too, not just dead but out of reach, the other side of a wall he couldn't climb even if it was there. He had no memory of feeling the bricks or scraping his knees like he did that time as a Sixth Former when he broke back into school at two in the morning. It was a memory that might have been a dream too, even as he stumbled through darkness, mud and blood on his hands, and thought he heard her say his name.

Maybe that was what haunting meant. She was dead but alive again at night when nothing was real.

If Sam had been there to listen, he would have told her, "And then she morphed into you, the way dreams go." He'd tried to explain that same change before, after a similar dream, and he could tell she hadn't liked it much.

"How am I like your mother?" she'd asked. "That's a question for you, because you need to know, but I don't."

Then she suggested meditation and the dream soon drifted away into the clouds that wrapped London around.

It was Tuesday now and a whole week since he and Sam became a pair of exes. Ethan looked at a new sky, edgy and on the move. Wind and rain, not a lot of brightness promised. But he didn't want to lose the dream even if it troubled him, because in it, Sam had made way for Coralie's mother and, if he could word what she did, he might understand why she was there in his dream and what there was to learn. Without understanding, being was just a selfish act. Sam had gone solo to tune in to the wisdom, like the teenage Sioux alone in the wilderness with the Great Mystery, but he was looking out on London. And he wanted to understand the other lives people picked up after their own dreams. That must be why Coralie's mother was haunting him too.

"If you want to sleep with her, go ahead," he imagined Sam saying. "Feel free. It's not a problem."

Sam felt free. She called Western ideas about monogamy and romance oppressive and deluded respectively.

"I love you," he'd said, not long before she packed.

"That's a formula, Ethan," she told him. She thought he was conventional. "It has no meaning."

Ethan supposed some part of him wanted to sleep with Coralie's mum and Sam would say, dead straight, "I know what part." No blame.

But in the dream he didn't touch her. He only observed her, not just in the carriage but walking at the foot of trees. Where were they? Somewhere he'd been, like a park, or somewhere her parents or grandparents might have grown up? Hadn't it been lush and hot?

No cheating, Ethan, he told himself. Tell it like it was. Coralie had been there too, drawing monsters in his notebook.

"I want to have children one day," he'd told Sam once in Hyde Park, because two little girls were running across grass to a little bridge over sunlit water.

"No one should have children just because they want to," she said, "especially not now." Sam scorned the things people wanted.

"It seems to me, Ethan," his dad had remarked over yesterday's lunch, "you don't know what you want."

"I want nothing," he'd declared, but his father only laughed. Apparently his archaeologist father had discovered over his longer life that human beings were inescapably greedy and full of dissatisfied longing.

Ethan had forgotten to greet the morning with gratitude and there would be no peace without stillness.

He breathed deeply and closed his eyes.

Crystel felt like a burglar as she turned the key with the familiar jiggle and tug she'd had to learn without tips or warning on her first day. She fronted the mirror in the hall, trying to firm up. Not guilt but bravado. She wasn't just returning the keys; she was tilting the see-saw. And if Madam ever thought twice about her own behaviour, the rethink might do her good.

With the TV on in the kitchen just for company, Crystel listened to the names of food ingredients she'd never bought and wouldn't know how to spell: shitake, fenugreek, hing, tempeh, galangal. As she scrubbed the sink, then sprayed and wiped the worktops, she repeated some of the words and felt like a witch reciting a spell round a cauldron. Crystel could still remember some of the lines from Macbeth.

"Out, damned spot!" she muttered, shifting a tiny tea stain – and laughed, imagining what her sister Lou would say about her reciting Shakespeare in rubber gloves. Ethan A. Garrett would know whole speeches because they were real poetry, better than his.

Stepping back, Crystel could imagine little stars twinkling off the shiny surfaces the way they did in the ads. The floor was still wet under her damp little trainer socks, but spotless. She turned off the TV and tiptoed out. The carpets were vacuumed and the surfaces dusted, so with only the bathroom and en-suite to do, she should be out in half an hour.

Rapping the best ingredient names – "Galangal, crazy girl, dancing girl, you sway and swirl" – she was running the tap to rinse off the cream cleaner in the washbasin when she heard a noise. A door. Crystel turned off the tap and stood, looking through the gap into the hallway. Her starry pumps were splayed on the doormat and her handbag bulged next to them.

Madam. Crystel knew what she looked like. Not from the interview because Leigh Capaldi was too busy to come and meet her in person, so had sent her mother on a day off – a nice-mannered, white-haired woman who'd given her the wrong idea about the daughter. Since, Crystel had studied the photographs. But life was always something else.

The real thing was too skinny and her hair needed a good conditioner but her clothes were boss-style, classic. Crystel had always wanted a trouser suit, with a jacket that curved over a plunging silky blouse. She made sure she looked at her straight.

"What are you doing here?"

"I'm cleaning."

The tone ended up smartass and Madam didn't like it. Her mouth opened but Crystel got in first.

"I owe you for what I skipped on Coralie's birthday."

"Don't try the sympathy card, Crystel. You were dishonest with me and now you're being dishonest again."

"With rubber gloves? How's that?"

"I don't want to argue. I haven't time. Please hand over the keys and leave."

How could she have no time, all on her own with no one to spend it on but herself? Crystel didn't move. "The keys are in the kitchen."

Crystel began to tug at the yellow gloves. Arms folded, her ex-employer just watched her struggling with them until a hole split one palm open. Crystel dropped them on the tiled floor and walked into the hallway, where she found a two pound coin in her bag and shifted her feet into the pumps. Behind her she heard Leigh Capaldi emerge from the kitchen. Crystel turned to offer her the coin for the gloves, but found her wearing a different face.

"The kitchen's sparkling," she said. "I came home early to sort the place out because my father's landing on me with no warning – but you've done an amazing job. You didn't need... I'm sorry."

Crystel stared and waited.

"Look, Crystel, I was hasty. It seemed like a big deal but not anymore. Shall we just forget it?"

"I've made other arrangements."

"Really? You couldn't carry on?" Leigh Capaldi put her hand to her forehead, dragging her hair back.

Not a daddy's girl, then, thought Crystel. Stressed, not happy, no love in her life.

"Look, will you think about it, please?"

In her head Crystel could hear Lou telling her Madam didn't fancy cleaning her own toilets or trying to find someone else to do it. But something else was going on.

"I don't know. I'll have to see," she said, as Madam stretched out a hand that meant 'stay', as if she was a dog, called to heel and jerked around. Then she disappeared.

"I need to go," called Crystel. "For Coralie."

Madam was back, with a plastic bag containing something thin and flat which she held upwards like a tray. She pulled out a rainbow arc of coloured glass pieces, fitted mosaic-style on a painted wooden curve with no proper shape.

"Take this for Caroline's birthday."

"Coralie."

"It's a clock. Maybe she can't tell the time yet…"

"No, she's only five."

"But she might like the colours. It was a present from my mother when I bought this place but it doesn't fit." She looked around. "Well, you know – I'm into minimalism."

Crystel thought rich people could afford to be.

"Maybe I'm still a teenager in her eyes," Madam continued. "Anyway, I was going to take it to the charity shop but I never have a minute."

Was that a joke? Crystel looked at the hands, which were shaped like strings of big fat raindrops. There were no numbers. Not very helpful for Coralie.

"There's no need."

"Please."

"All right. Thanks."

"I'll be in touch, when my father's gone. I've no idea how long he plans to stay."

Crystel wanted to tell her not to bother. She wished people wouldn't spin from heads to tails. But she needed the job and Madam had a face now; she had two.

Seconds later she was leaving with the clock, avoiding eye contact because it was hard to know how to look at Leigh Capaldi, or what she saw when she did.

It was in the Internet café that Ethan decided. He wasn't going to finish his dissertation; it only stopped him living. His dad talked CV as some kind of justification but Ethan didn't want that kind of job. Life was a gift. The natural world, children, love and creativity were all free and precious. And he wasn't going to lose touch with life's gifts because he was too busy competing in a corrupt Capitalist economy that only valued wealth and prestige when real success was being the best he could be.

His cousin was a doctor and that was great, but Ethan couldn't heal the sick, or even teach them like the woman in the churchyard. The best

54

thing he could do in the world was no harm. Tread lightly. Rise above greed and ego. Live as simply as he could, without squandering the earth's resources, find the poetry of being and strive to understand.

He'd been in limbo so long, isolating himself and calling it discipline. There was more than one way to study and Ethan intended to keep doing it all his life, with every step.

In the email to his father he tried to explain.

Once you told me about turning up, barefoot, at the Spanish Steps or The Bois de Boulogne, any square in Amsterdam or Rome, and finding someone else with long hair and a tie-dyed cheesecloth shirt who'd take you back to his hostel or squat.

And give or sell you drugs, but his father skimmed over that bit because it was the community that counted. Acceptance. Soul-mates connecting.

At Ferningstone it will be the same: like minds meeting and working together, sustainably. No drugs except fresh air and sunlight. They won't turn me away. Maybe I'll do an apprenticeship. We all have to learn a new way of living.

There are places I'm going on the way so I don't know how long it'll be before I get there. I'll write when I've settled in. People should write letters. We'll save a dying art.

It was what Ethan had told Sam before she left.

"Don't wait on the post, Ethan," she said.

Now he looked back at the email. Once he'd sent it, he'd log off before his dad could reply.

Ethan

Ready to sign out, Ethan thought of Facebook, surprising himself. He entered his home page and knew why when he found Crystel's face. Whoa. A connection, a crazy one. She liked his poem – but that was just schoolboy crap. He should have deleted it long ago but it was a record of who he was and he couldn't lose touch with that. The journey only continued, no need to clear away the footsteps behind.

But he'd made a decision now. He sent a message:

Leaving London but will check Facebook on Tuesdays.

Why Tuesdays he had no idea, but it seemed like a plan. Manageable. *Off to excavate the past*, he added, but deleted it. So that was what he was doing. But it was his past, not hers, and she didn't need it. Ethan closed, exited and paid up. The place was quiet. It couldn't

55

survive much longer now everyone took walking, talking Internet with them to the park, the shops and the loo. Everyone but the poor who gathered, separate in silence, paying for a line of communication on the Worldwide Web.

Outside, he wrapped his scarf round twice over his sweater. Thin drizzle peppered his face and clung to his hair.

It was time.

Crystel sat on the bus, talking on the phone to Lou. She was trying to tell her about Madam but the story was hard to tell the way it had happened.

"Bitch!" cried Lou. "Probably a cokehead."

She was late night shopping. Crystel guessed she was fingering through a rack of tight little dresses.

Looking down on the carrier bag she was keeping upright between her legs, Crystel started to tell her sister about the clock. It was hard to describe.

"What – a present! Guilty or what!"

"It's not suitable for kids. She just doesn't want it. The whole thing got really weird and I don't know what to do with it."

"Sell it on Ebay."

Crystel agreed to that vaguely but she knew she wasn't going to sell it at all. It was wild and a peace offering in a way. And in time, Coralie might love it. No one else in her class would have anything like it. If she looked at it, time would seem bright and exciting, special.

Suddenly she didn't want to talk anymore because Madam had tried to be nice, even though it didn't suit her and she needed a lot more practice. And she was obviously upset about something. Like some other power-dressed graduate woman getting promotion over her or M and S raising the price of sushi. Claiming bad reception, Crystel told Lou she'd speak later and looked out on the high street. Were those people rushing up and down it as tense as they looked, or was that just her? She hoped Coralie had good news: gold stars or smileys, ticks for adding up or a painting on the wall.

A fat woman in a beautiful sari moved down the bus and sat next to her. Crystel moved the bag before the colours got splintered, and rested it carefully against the edge of the seat by the window. She checked Facebook and saw a picture she didn't recognise at first. *Ethan Garrett has confirmed you as a Friend on Facebook*. Crystel smiled, catching sight of her mouth lifting up and rounding her cheeks in the glass. *Ethan Garrett posted on your wall.* She clicked and there it was: *Hope Coralie had a great birthday. I haven't looked at Facebook for months but I'm in an Internet café. I'm glad you got in touch. Namaste.*

Her mum would say Fate was working overtime. *Namaste.* Crystel mouthed it, heard him say it. The Indian woman smiled as if she heard too, or read the smile. "Good to see the sunshine after all that rain," she told Crystel.

"Yeah," she said, "hope it lasts."

Not much point in starting a dialogue if it would be months before Ethan A. Garrett looked at his wall again. Maybe it was enough that she met a poet who wanted to live in a tree. But there was another message. The poet was leaving London. Tuesdays? This was turning into a weird day.

Time to ask the fat woman to move if she was going to make it out at the next stop.

Repeating, "Excuse me," as she squeezed along, Crystel made her way off the bus, picking up a call from a cousin with boyfriend trouble as she stepped down to the pavement.

"Can I call you back, Mina? Gotta run to pick up Coralie now."

Thinking that people without kids could never understand the panic, she heard a shout. Turning, she saw the plastic bag held high. The woman wobbled breathlessly. The driver looked impatient.

"It looks fabulous," said the woman as she handed it down to her. "I nearly kept quiet and took it home."

A corner was shining out. Crystel tucked it back in and folded over the edge of the bag.

"Thanks," she said, tempted to hand it back with a "*You like it, you keep it,*" but walking on.

She would have been sorry to lose it.

Chapter Six

Six-fifteen. Where was he? Leigh checked her phone. Nothing. What was she doing, rushing around after two men, fitting clean sheets for both of them at their convenience? She poured herself some red wine. There was no guarantee that either one of them would show. Her dad seemed to be wading around in a mid-life crisis of total confusion. And the way he kept contradicting himself, veering around like a teenager, she wouldn't be surprised if he rang her at midnight to say he'd charmed Carole back over supper in a fancy restaurant and cancelled the whole trip.

Maybe Kyle's wife had cancelled her own plans. Was that why he'd gone off the radar?

Leigh had an important meeting tomorrow and she wasn't going to let either of them screw it up. She sat at her laptop, but five minutes in she turned off her phone. She was pouring a second glass almost an hour later when the doorbell rang.

Leigh checked the mirror in the hall, pursing her lips to blend the red wine stain into her crimson lipstick and fingering through her hair. She swore at herself, or him, and opened the door.

Kyle was holding a bottle she hoped was expensive. Rain dribbled down its cold curves. His hair gleamed damp under the outside light.

"You turned off your phone."

"I was working."

"I'm impressed."

He touched her breast with his free hand and kissed her. Longer than the first, in his office, the blind spot behind the door. Wetter than the second, in the car park at five thirty-eight one evening, in a brand new, sleek black car she was meant to desire.

"I've been impressed," he said, "for a very long time."

Not as impressed as I've been, thought Leigh, but his ego was big enough already. She took the sparkling wine, told him to take off his shoes and let him follow her into the kitchen.

"Nice place," he said. "We must be paying you way too much."

"Fuck off, boss."

She held the bottle in his direction as she released the cork, and laughed as he ducked. His hand went to his hair.

"That's rain," she told him, and licked a droplet from the top of his head. "Eugh," she grimaced, then smiled. "Sweat and conditioner."

He shoved her away, grinning. "You're mad!"

"My dad helped me out with a deposit, FYI. There's no way I could afford a flat in London on my wages." She sipped the wine, too sweet for her taste.

"My heart bleeds. Daddy's little rich girl, eh?"

"I didn't say that. He's coming to stay tomorrow so this is a one-off, Kyle."

"Francoise gets back tomorrow too. So better not waste time."

Leigh hadn't done this before but it was amazing how much a sex-starved woman could learn from bad TV. She reached behind and unzipped her dress, let it fall and stepped out of it, smiling as if she had no anxieties whatsoever about whether her breasts were as he'd imagined when she stood by his desk, or her stomach less than smooth. As if inside her, nothing was flung into disorder and she had all the experience he was counting on, because he had to know it didn't matter. The earth might move and she hoped she could blag her way through to some kind of quake but lives wouldn't change. One night only, she told herself as he unthreaded his belt.

At bedtime Coralie held onto Crystel's hand and said, "I had a bad day."

She'd been bouncing when Crystel collected her, chatty through supper, laughing at her DVD. What was it about the pillow that brought bad things back, in spite of the fairies around her head? Darkness, or being alone?

"Did you get your maths wrong, little one?"

"No!" So indignant, as if she'd never made a mistake! "I got all ticks."

"Go, girl!"

Crystel made a fist for her to meet with a smaller one but Coralie didn't smile back.

"Norah said my dad's a badass."

"She didn't!" Crystel shook her head in disbelief. "Don't you say that. You don't repeat those words, all right?" She stroked Coralie's arm in case she sounded angry. "Norah doesn't know what she's talking about. You just hold your head high like you're not listening when people say mean things. Then they'll stop, you'll see."

"Where's my daddy gone?"

"You know he passed away, honey-sweet."

"You mean he died?"

Crystel nodded, and pulled up the duvet closer to Coralie's chin.

"That's why he doesn't send birthday cards like Norah's daddy?"

"That's why." She smiled. "No post boxes in heaven. But he still loves you as much as any daddy, even that Norah's."

That did it. "I love him too," said Coralie. She paused. "I think I do."

"So sleep well with those fairies, little one."

"I will."

Coralie pressed a kiss on her lips. Crystel could smell the tomato from the pasta but she wasn't going to fuss over teeth cleaning now. She pulled the door so there was a gap the way Coralie liked it.

She'd like to ask Ethan Garrett about pretending that was really lies. Talking fairies and heaven, a loving daddy smiling down from the clouds, when the truth was she never told Finn what he wouldn't want to know, so that Coralie wouldn't grow up with a drop-in daddy who didn't give a shit.

Well Norah may be a little cow, Coralie, but truth is she's right on target. Your daddy's no good for you or me or anyone but himself.

Maybe truths like that got told one day when the time felt right – once Coralie had grown up strong and clean, without him there to teach her things no kid should know. It wasn't her fault her mother wore her heels too soon and learned her pride too late.

She looked at her phone and there was a different kind of guy, just when she'd been thinking of him. A guy who was leaving.

Crystel didn't know why she felt disappointed. Ethan A. Garrett had said, right off, that he wanted to live in a tree. So now he'd gone to find more nature than London could rustle up. She'd known him for all of four stops on the tube and even with the messages he'd probably exchanged more words with Coralie.

Sounds exciting. Be happy.

What else could she say? Not *I'll miss you.* She waited, but there was no reply. No *Ethan is typing...* because Ethan had better things to do. And so did she, like living in the real world: the one with no fairies, heaven or poets, but stuffed with ironing.

Leigh couldn't sleep. Eleven twenty-seven, she read on the small flat screen beside the bed. Kyle must have seen its flash of pale violet light.

"Turn it off," he said, sleepily.

With his back to her – smooth and long, a faint new smell – she'd been lying still, trying not to think beyond him and the warm trace of him between her legs that left everything stirred, even deeper than he'd been. Was that normal? She could barely remember. Now he turned towards her.

At work his hair stayed behind his ears. Now it fringed his forehead and cheeks. A wife would stroke it away, and maybe his did. A lover might kiss where it had been. Leigh didn't kid herself that because the opportunity presented itself, she'd earned the right to tenderness on top of sex – on top of time beneath him, next to him, and waking in six hours' time to find him there.

As Kyle's mouth closed light and wet on hers, his hand curved round her breast. Maybe, she thought, he felt conned by her uplift bras. His other hand reached down, long fingers making her draw breath. He wanted the same again. Because it had been so good for him too, or because it was a chance for her to improve on performance?

"You're not one of the twenty per cent," he murmured at the sound of a text arriving, and kissed her again, "who use their smartphones during sex?"

"I'm not American," she said, "or under twenty-five. And it's your fucking phone."

Not casual or active enough but those weren't the admissions he wanted to hear. He'd be shocked if he knew, perhaps panic-stricken. Not the time to tell him she hadn't had sex for nearly a year. Not the time to ask him if he ever came twice a night with his wife.

Slower, gentler now, he was making her forget, her eyes shut and hands spread as her arms lifted up and out.

"Condom," she whispered as his head lowered closer to her shoulder.

61

"Quick."

He jerked away, fumbling on the side of the bed. The tissue box fell to the carpet. He swore, and rolled away.

"I'll put the light on," she said, reaching for the switch on the lamp.

"Don't bother," he said, reproachfully as the brightness narrowed his eyes. "The moment's passed."

Something in his voice prevented her offering to bring that moment back and snatched the confidence that she could. His face looked a lot less attractive as he twisted it from the light. The pack he'd been feeling for lay waiting on the bedside unit all the time, hidden underneath the used sheath wrapped in tissue.

Had he bought them for her or were they from a secret supply, for use when his wife was away? Maybe he didn't need them at home because they were trying for a baby. God! Three times a bitch. With her mother, with Crystel (in spite of the clock that made no difference and that she didn't want) and now with someone's husband. She turned off the light.

Kyle had his back to her now but he wasn't asleep, or pretending to be.

"What do you want from me, Kyle, apart from a second orgasm?"

His shoulders did what might be called sinking, of a horizontal kind. He rolled back towards her.

"That about covers it," he said. The darkness was too thick to tell whether he smiled but she couldn't hear it in his voice. "That's what you want too," he murmured. "You've been wanting it for months so don't start pretending you're some kind of victim just because I can't marry you."

He was right. They were in it together – for now, at least. But would it have hurt him to go easy on her, to play the game instead of shoving the pieces off the board? It made her hate him. It made her remember how he'd put her down when she started the job, because the computer had some program she didn't know and there was so much to learn so quickly.

"How many times have you cheated on your wife, just out of interest?"

"Never? Is that what you want to hear? Just for you." He held her head in his hands and kissed her mouth softly. "I'm here, Leigh, with you. We both chose this." The kiss was more forceful now. "And this."

He was big again, nudging. He reached across and fitted the condom. What difference did it make? It was only sex. No pretence. Tomorrow he'd still be there, in the same office, business-like and on-task. And she'd still be alone in her tastefully-decorated flat, wondering how to manage her father. And hoping her mother might resume that job, if she could overlook two wives as easily as Kyle could overlook one.

Men could have heart attacks doing this as Kyle did it. Leigh cried out, addressing the God she'd loved as a teenager. As he thrust, her hand left his shoulder and went to the top of her head, down the back of her neck. Her mouth shaped *"No"* but made no sound. There was good and hard, and there was more: point-making, lesson-teaching, silencing. He climaxed at last, kissed her forehead and fell away as if she'd pushed.

Leaving him to peel off and wrap the condom, Leigh went to the bathroom, legs vaguely unsteady, still breathing fast. She felt sore. Why was she thinking of her father? He'd never won an argument this way – had he? She looked in the mirror, mouth full and red with a little lipstick spreading from lip-line to skin. Her eyes were too bright. Or was that just the light that drenched her? She was far from sober, but not drunk enough.

"Leigh," she heard from the bedroom. "I'm missing you."

Fuck you, she thought, and laughed at herself. And the English language her mother thought she curated. She pulled the cord and lost her face in blackness.

Chapter Seven

Annie's coffee break came late next morning. Emmy had an infection and steps had to be retraced, backs covered, paperwork in place. A twelve-year-old boy called Declan Garroway, injured without a helmet on his big brother's motorbike, was due for his first lesson as soon as he'd finished physio. His file was dense reading. But sometimes she thought she should skip the psychological profiles and let them start their new worlds like babies, with no syndromes, disorders or anger management strategies round their necks. Declan might be a kitten.

Annie turned on her phone to find no messages from Leigh but three from Arthur.

Moody weather but what a landscape.

Railway magic. I'm flying. What time do you finish work? I could meet you at the hospital.

Call me when you get a break. I'm reading one of your favourite novels.

Annie sighed. Apparently he had no recall of what a working day was like. Didn't he read distant male stuff that felt like an intellectual exercise rather than a story? Even if he'd really remembered what her favourites were, she had no time to talk about Carol Shields or Anne Tyler and no idea how late she might get away that evening. She was thinking out a reply when he called.

"How are you? You sounded off-colour yesterday."

Did that mean grey? "I'm fine. I just found your messages but I can't say when I'll finish and Leigh will be expecting you for supper."

"And you. I suggested a take-away. You know what she's like in the kitchen."

"I hope you didn't. She watches enough cookery on TV. I'll see you there, at her flat. I've got to go now, Art."

"What are you wearing?"

"What! You sound like a dirty raincoat perv!"

Zelda's mouth opened. Annie rolled her eyes theatrically.

"Tell him suspenders and a black lace basque!" whispered Zelda.

"I look extremely dull, Arthur," said Annie, smoothing her navy blue skirt across her thighs. How had that ladder sprung in her tights?

"I just can't wait to see you," he said. "I thought you could give me a preview, like a movie trailer."

"There are no best bits," she told him. "See you later. At the flat, not here."

She looked at Zelda. "My ex-husband seems to think he's in love with me," she said. "The timing's handy because his current wife's just left him."

In twenty-five years she'd never vouchsafed anything so personal, but then there hadn't been a lot to make anyone gawp delightedly the way Zelda gawped now. Annie had no idea her soft round jaw could hang so slack.

"You should have let him come here," said Zelda unexpectedly. "I'd sit him down and tell him not to mess with you."

"Thanks," said Annie. "I appreciate the thought."

She could tell him so herself, of course, but she'd rather avoid one-to-one time for now.

Dad called, she texted Leigh. *Will try to be at yours for takeaway by seven. Don't let him choose the chippie. How are you today? X*

The answer was instant: *Having a shitty day. Headache from hell. Meeting going from bad to worse. Dad's timing was always lousy. Wish he'd just make up with Carole and stop being weird. X*

Annie turned off. Her daughter sounded in need of soul therapy herself.

Stepping out at the station he used to know so well, Ethan had to look down at his billowing legs to be sure he wasn't in school uniform. No lace-up shoes from Enid Blyton days. He wiggled tough old toes spreading in his sandals like symbols of freedom.

The corner shop was a nail bar and the café where he used to sit with his notebook and drink herbal tea had shut down. No sign of Joe's Print Place, where Joe used to give him a special deal when he submitted poems to magazines. Crazy, he thought. So much change in so little time. But not as crazy as sending an eight-year-old boy away to a place that pretended the world never did any changing at all.

The school on the narrow road was the largest place in town, its front lawns bigger than the petrol station forecourt opposite and just as smooth. Ethan could smell the grass being trimmed, but the figure on the ride-on lawnmower was as unfamiliar as the sound.

"Let me have a go," he'd asked Hissop. No one had a Christian name, in spite of all the praying.

"More than my job's worth," Hissop had said. He had the thickest, blackest beard Ethan had ever seen, with specks of grass in it. He rubbed it a lot, probably to squeeze out the grass along with anything else that might be hiding there. Hissop could have been his first poem if he'd only known in those days how rare those gifts would be.

For the first few years he'd gone home for weekends once a month or so but that was before the call to the principal's office. If his mother had known, she wouldn't have sent him away however much time his dad spent in the ancient world.

"My dad's like Indiana Jones," he told the other boys.

"What, with a gun?"

"No! What for? There are no Nazis anymore."

"What about Willoughby?"

Once Mr Willoughby spotted Ethan refusing to sing the words of *Onward Christian Soldiers* in the chapel and beckoned him over on his way out.

"It's against my conscience, sir."

"How old do you think those words are that you refused to sing?"

"Old, sir."

"So generations of pupils here have been singing those words along with people all over the world but you're above them, is that it? You're taking the moral high ground over archbishops and prime ministers?"

"I'm not taking anything, sir."

"You're taking liberties, Garrett. My office at lunchtime."

He'd reported at twelve-thirty, to be given a headset.

"Something to listen to as you run five times round the rugby pitch."

Mr Willoughby had found a recording of the hymn sung by choirboys and put it on a loop so that as he ran, the mud hitting the backs of his calves, the rhythm of it outpaced him. For a bully from

66

another era, Mr Willoughby was a techno-whizz.

Why hadn't he told his father?

Because he didn't tell him much. He was a boy of few words that weren't written. Somewhere in his father's loft was a box full of jotters with dates but for now he was travelling light. He was going back because he had to move on.

He'd arrived with his slightly-twisted ears all too visible under a brand new haircut and left with them pierced, but hidden under a thatch that ended stiffly on his shoulders. The nickname Dumbo had made way for Woodstock on account of his musical taste. Or Weed, on account of his habit, overlooked by an older, gentler housemaster – because he had an idea that he might have met his dad in Marrakesh, and a vinyl collection Ethan dreamed of possessing.

Lesson time. The place must be packed with boys but not one was on the loose. This wasn't a place Ethan liked to admit to, then or now; wasn't it bad enough to have a dad on TV? Not that anyone in his year had been impressed by that. Someone who'd been a prefect when Ethan began was an adviser to Cameron now. Someone else wrote for The Financial Times. The principal used to talk about them being captains of industry and Daph said one of his classmates, who'd visited one summer and flirted with her, was massive in Google.

For a moment he remembered his dad parking the car on one of the few occasions he'd driven him there.

"*Let's Do The Time Warp Again*," he'd said.

When Ethan started, there was still one teacher in the place who'd taught his father Latin. Mr Stevington hadn't concealed his disappointment. "Speak up, Garrett. I never had to prompt your father."

Why was he here, when he'd sworn he'd never go back? Why not begin at the maternity ward, or the playgroup?

Because this place was in his dreams. It had stolen his childhood and made him a misfit; first lost and abandoned, then dark with resentment, but always intense in his isolation. He was still an outsider of course, but by choice now, and choosing to come back. He'd take a good, slow look and, with the air deep in his lungs, feel no fear. No nausea. No alienation. He'd embrace what it had been and leave it behind.

Out of the chapel door stepped a squat figure in black, with spidery hair straggling thin from his scalp. Mole! More rounded, but not squinting through round lenses anymore. Ethan smiled, unsure whether to call a *"Hey!"* when he couldn't remember the Chaplain's real name. But Mole glanced across the road and saw him, lifting a hand. Ethan was touched that he hadn't forgotten. But he supposed motherless boys were a smaller minority than the druggies and loners.

"Ethan?"

Ethan stood and grinned. Mole advanced, belly first, more of a poem than ever. He held out a hand several short steps away as Ethan crossed towards him.

"What a wonderful surprise! What brings you here? I'm on a free period before Mysticism – have you time for coffee?"

"Yeah," said Ethan, "coffee would be good. Thanks."

"I've got double chocolate cookies and Mary will have real coffee brewing so your timing's perfect!"

"Improved, you mean?" Ethan looked at his wrist. "Still no watch."

On cue the clock on the tower chimed, dragging down hands the length of Ethan's arms. Mole's smile became a hissing-balloon laugh. He was the easiest impression of all.

"If I whisk you round this way," he said, "we might be able to get away without signing in and badges. We're very corporate these days. If admin knew you were here I'd have to come up with targets and a risk assessment. I trust you don't have any cannabis on your person?"

"Gave up."

"Ah, good. Clarity helps, doesn't it? You introduced me to *O.K. Computer*, of course – do you remember – and it's quite a revelation but I need to sandwich it in between Tavener and Bach or I feel myself drowning, you know, and not bothering to wave."

Ethan remembered the sense, with that poem, that the last line was targeting him. "Dodie Smith," he said. "Yeah."

Mole led him between spiky bushes to the Chaplain's house. It dated back to the nineteenth century, which made it a recent extension.

"Never thought I'd welcome you back to the Folly," said Mole, jangling keys and trying several before he slammed the knocker instead.

"Yes, I guess I was a regular," said Ethan, "for a heathen."

Mole's gassy laugh alerted his wife who took a mere second to connect the visitor with his schoolboy self and clapped her hands as she cried, "Ethan Garrett! What a blast from the past!"

She was the one who could have walked onto the set of *Sons and Lovers* with her short cardigan and plaid skirt, and hair that crinkled around her head like a bonnet. Mole pointed out that Ethan must be all of twenty-three.

"You won't ever change," she said, smiling, "and become a merchant banker, will you, Ethan?"

"No immediate plans," grinned Ethan.

Mole laughed. "That," he said, "would be the day I retire."

Ushered in, he kicked off his sandals even though Mary told him not to worry. Then it struck him that his feet were more visibly dirty than the tougher soles he'd left behind. Entering the living room, he saw the angle-poise lamp that still reminded him of a pterodactyl on the swoop and the enormous bookcase he used to search for unlikely titles. But he looked straight up at the *Light of the World*. He hadn't seen Jesus knocking – golden rather than Palestinian, but kind in a muscular, woodcutting way – since he last walked out of this small, flatly-carpeted room. And he hadn't known how well he remembered it.

"Holman Hunt, right?" he said, because he could hear Mole telling him once when he asked. An action replay on a ten year time lapse.

"Yes, such a warm painting," said Mary, handing him coffee in a cup with a saucer. As it rattled he realised how cold he'd been. He took a biscuit too and thanked her. Mole turned on a gas fire.

It was amazing how much time could be wasted with details that were only facts. They were so interested; their politeness was breathtaking as they skipped over his father's series, books and awards to focus on him and what he'd done, read and studied since he left. They even remembered that he had a sister. It was more warming than the Jesus painting, and comfortably odd.

But for Ethan it was all a preamble. Now that he was here he didn't want to delay any longer. He declined another Fair Trade cookie even though it would be good to take a couple away when he left.

"You know after my mother died?" he began.

"Yes," said Mole, "you kept looking up at that face up there instead of mine. I wish I'd known what to say to you. I hoped the painting might communicate something I couldn't."

"I didn't say much either, did I?"

"You were in shock," said Mary. "What were you, twelve, thirteen?"

"Yes," said Ethan. "Can I tell you now, what I didn't tell you then?"

Mary sat down at the other end of the sofa, one hand on the saucer and one on the handle of her cup. "Of course."

Mole took the armchair facing Ethan, a flushed cheek full of chewed cookie. He swallowed. "Please," he said.

Crystel was on Facebook, on the bus between jobs. It wasn't Tuesday but Ethan might have the chance to look sooner. *Coralie remembers you. She drew a picture of you in a tree. I wonder where you are.* It was strangely exciting. She Googled Ethan A. Garrett but there was no Wikipedia article so he hadn't won any poetry prizes or done anything to make him famous, like throwing eggs at the Prime Minister. There was a page on Mark Garrett, though, an archaeologist who was such an expert that the BBC used to call him in as an adviser and then let him front his own show on The Incas. In the photo he had the same look in his eyes whether he was smart for an awards ceremony or digging in the desert. It made Crystel smile because it was Ethan's look. The section called Personal Life mentioned a wife who died ten years ago – and two children, Ethan and Daphne. So Ethan had a celebrity dad, and he'd lost his mum when he was just a boy, which was so sad and must have made him sensitive. Crystel felt glad because she'd been right about him all along.

There was an email from Madam, hoping Coralie liked the clock. Crystel knew what that meant. Madam needed her servant back. *I'm keeping it for when she's a bit older. I can carry on cleaning if you wish.* The reply came straight back: *That's great because my father is staying. Thank you. If it takes longer to clear up because of him and his mess I'll pay you extra.*

She thought that sounded disrespectful, as if Madam's father was a naughty boy. On Facebook, her cousin Lynette's status announced that her well-dressed customer had proposed, with a ring. *Amazing, Lynette. Be happy.* Crystel hoped he was good enough for her but in the picture he looked old, maybe forty. Her mum and her auntie wouldn't know whether to be suspicious or start looking for hats. But Coralie would love to be a bridesmaid.

Now someone was messaging: Bailey Greaves. *Who rattled his cage,* her dad would say, Bailey being her parents' neighbour and supposedly sweet on her even though he was never single for five minutes.

hey crystel you want to meet up later for bowling or a movie
No babysitter Bailey.
i could come round

70

In your dreams.

She clicked off the conversation box and stood to make her way off the bus. Did nobody romance anyone nice and steady anymore?

Ethan realised as he looked around the room to avoid the faces that he still hadn't retrieved Mole's actual name.

"People thought I was crying all the time, or choking back tears like boys are meant to do, to be brave. But I wasn't. I don't. So I thought there was something wrong with me."

"Oh, no…" said Mary, with a shake of the head that didn't stir her frame of hair.

"Like the tin man, no heart. I couldn't tell anyone I wasn't heartbroken because I thought I ought to be."

"Leaving home can feel like loss," suggested Mole. "Perhaps you'd already adjusted to a form of bereavement…"

"By putting a distance there," finished Mary, "emotionally, between you and home?"

He smiled at their connection before he nodded. But how could he be sure?

"I already felt like a freak. I'd been crying at night for years, under the sheets. Now I couldn't do it – even with practice! I was the boy who didn't like his mum enough to cry, or resented her for not liking *me*, for sending me away."

"Ah, parents have ideas about boarding school, Ethan. It's not personal," said Mole.

"You mean I was a soft boy who needed toughening up."

"It's a theory. A bizarre one. But it seems to suit some children…"

"Who rise above it and thrive," put in Mary, "but sometimes it's just plain cruel, for the sake of some advantage they believe it gives their child."

"I don't," Ethan said. "At least, I do, but that's why I hate it." He looked at the pterodactyl about to strike. "Sorry – it's your job, your choice." Mole waved his hand. "They told me it was practical because of dad's travelling and her business…" He nearly said no one asked his mother to set up a company and enjoy it more than him. But he knew she couldn't help who she was and what she needed. "Can a mother and son be mismatched? How does that work genetically?"

"We're all much more complex than D and A," cried Mole. "Thank

71

God!"

Ethan smiled. Mary offered more coffee and he accepted. Mole looked at his watch, which was probably older than Ethan felt, rose and apologised. Hands in pockets, he looked awkward. Ethan hoped his classes didn't give him a hard time for being uncool.

"Yeah, you have to go. No problem," he told him.

"Do stay if you'd like to, Ethan," said Mary. "You're more than welcome."

Ethan stood. "Thanks, but I'll make a move. It's the start of the journey, really." What was he talking about? He had no idea where he was going next, but that was the point. He was open and ready.

Mole clasped his hands and told him how wonderful it was to see him. Then he rushed off. Out of the window Ethan saw him scuttling, tightening his belt on the move.

"Maybe the past is still another country," Mary suggested, "even when it's so recent?"

"Yeah," said Ethan. "Or I'm another person."

"You've got so much life ahead, Ethan." She smiled. He supposed people their age must be envious of that but, with the planet self-destructing, it felt like a scary gift. It just seemed rude to point that out after they'd been so kind. They were so full of hope, for him and the world.

"Thanks for the coffee," he said. "And the listening."

"Not at all. You've made our day. We always wonder and no one ever comes back, unless they have something to sell."

She took him to the gate and waved him off with a wide smile.

"Maybe we'll see you on the next demonstration," she called.

"I'll be there," he said.

His step was light.

Chapter Eight

Outside Leigh's flat Annie breathed as slowly as possible before she rang.

"You're late," was Leigh's greeting. "Dad's pissed already."

Annie felt the apple juice tugged from her hand. Leigh wore a frilly Fifties-style apron that would barely protect a mini skirt, over a long black dress that clung to every contour and matched her bare toenails. Annie's skin felt old all over.

"Really?" she whispered.

"I am not!" called Arthur.

Leigh seemed in a hurry, leaving Annie removing her boots as she rushed back to the kitchen.

As Annie struggled on the doormat Arthur appeared. Without waiting for her to overcome the boots, he leaned in for a kiss, two. She wobbled and had to reach out for support. He held her arm.

"It's your mother who can't stand up!" he announced.

"Are you cooking, Leigh?" she called, and then, lowering her voice again, asked Arthur, "I thought we were having a takeaway?"

"Me too," he muttered, "but she's following a recipe from a TV show and I'm not sure she's been having much fun. You didn't bring any chips?"

Annie raised her eyebrows. "Do you need help in there?" she called past him.

"No," came from the open doorway. "Just sit down and talk to each other, will you? But not about me."

Arthur stood aside, grinning with one arm outstretched, allowing her to step in first. Even at nineteen he'd had old-fashioned manners, when he chose to apply them. They'd made her giggle.

Leigh's lounge wasn't homely. For Annie it always felt like the oversized reception space in a company trying to look cultured as well as successful. Arthur craved colour; Leigh muted it. A few neatly abstract paintings of matching size lined up with precision but Annie thought them as dull as they were chic.

"You look great, Annie."

He followed her in and sat opposite her, leaning forwards on the edge of the cream leather sofa.

"At the end of the day I've had, I doubt it," she told him. "We've got a new boy. Motorbike victim. More than averagely foul-mouthed."

"Little fucker!"

So Leigh was right: the booze had loosened him. Annie could see the naughty-boy amusement through the deadpan pose. She knew him too well. Deciding to ignore him, she helped herself to a couple of dry-roasted nuts.

"Sorry," he said. "You're fun when you disapprove."

"You're *not* fun when you show off."

"I know," he said, "it's not big and it's not clever. Poor kid. I'm afraid Leigh's been plying me with alcohol."

"Liar," said Leigh, back again and tightening the belt on her little pinny.

"Nice apron, darling – very pretty," Annie told her.

"It's retro."

"I should have kept the one your gran made when I was little," said Arthur. "She only wore it on Christmas Day for sipping sherry."

"Don't try to pin me down for Christmas, either of you," warned Leigh. "I'm not planning on celebrating it. I might go away somewhere hot." She pulled a tense smile. "Dinner's ready. Kind of. It doesn't look like it did on screen."

Annie assured her it was bound to taste good.

"It'd better. It took me hours to find all the speciality ingredients in Waitrose. It would have been cheaper to fly out and pick them myself."

"Madness," Annie said. Leigh frowned at her. "I meant the carbon footprint on food." Leigh couldn't have looked more disgruntled if she'd told her she'd gone vegan. "Not your fault!"

Art laughed loudly and winked. "We appreciate it, sweetheart. We really do. It's very kind of you to put me up for a few days, and even though you see me as a hopeless reprobate who should enrol for AA, I shall endeavour not to leave behind any unshiftable stains."

Annie smiled, then realised she probably resembled the proud mum of a clever boy.

"He's been reading *Pride and Prejudice* on the train," explained Leigh, with deadpan amusement that was a kind of mock despair.

"Ah," said Annie.

Arthur was always entertaining in Wickham mode, but shouldn't he be working towards Mr Bennet by now? She tried to take the plates through but was told to leave them and sit down at the table. Which she did. Leigh's good humour was apparently only for her dad.

"Don't worry," whispered Arthur, once she'd hurried off, "she'll be eighteen soon!"

"Shh," Annie told him as he began to pour her wine. She stopped him, not only with, "I'm driving!" but also a hand over the glass. The result was a red spill – through and off her fingers onto the marbled table top, and in a drip onto the pale beige carpet.

"Holy shit!" gasped Art. He hadn't changed his favourite way to swear in thirty-four years. "Napkins?"

There were none. He pulled off a sock and dabbed the table with it, which seemed to hurry the wine spill on its way. Tugging the other, he tried to absorb the liquid from the small pool on the carpet. Trying not to feel like a teenager herself, Annie ventured into the kitchen to soak Arthur's socks in salt water and ask the cook for a cloth.

"Oh, for God's sake, Mum!" complained Leigh.

In spite of her father's encouragement to leave it or her plateful would get cold, Leigh persisted in kneeling down and scrubbing with foam by the side of Annie's chair. The smell from the stain remover made the dish even less tempting. Arthur wiggled his bare toes like a boy on the beach and poured himself some wine, sitting up straight and holding both glass and bottle with exaggerated firmness.

"Go ahead!" Leigh insisted as Annie waited to begin. "We'll eat in the kitchen from now on. I was trying to do everything nicely."

"You have," they said together. The unison was unnerving but pleased Arthur visibly. "Please leave it and sit down," added Annie.

Leigh's phone to the side of her plate made a quiet heartbeat. Arthur glanced at it.

"It's Kyle," he read from the screen.

Leigh stretched upright, cloth in hand, and reached for the phone –

taking it into her bedroom.

"Arthur..." began Annie.

"I don't know her, Annie! She's so uptight. This Kyle guy must be SAS. Anyone else would be terrified to go near her."

Had Arthur been frightened of Lorelei and what she might do? "She's not always like this, really."

"Not in Edinburgh, she's not! I suppose she's always in holiday mode then."

"And she loves Carole."

"Everyone loves Carole!" He lowered his voice to add, "I've already been told off for screwing up – as she pointed out, *yet again, Dad.*" He ate a mouthful, with silent-movie suspicion as his jaw worked. "It's good of her to put up with me but I hope you realise I'm here to see you too."

"You can't stay with me, Arthur."

"All right. But we need to talk, just the two of us."

"Go ahead." Annie looked at the half-closed bedroom door. Arthur put down his glass. Annie tried to think, work mode, tactically. "But I think... before you say anything, with or without red wine in your bloodstream, you need to recognise a few things."

He nodded encouragingly. "Tell me."

"That you're in a kind of shock. It's such a short time since Carole ended the marriage, and she might want to reconsider anyway..."

"She might. I won't."

"O.K. But acting – reacting – in the heat of the crisis isn't... well, advisable. Right now you're emotional so you're looking for a sticking plaster."

Arthur held up a thumb with just such a plaster attached. "Single man and can lid! No training!"

He started to tell a story about meatballs in the Edinburgh kitchen and how they'd been worth the bloodletting, with oven chips to soak up the sauce. Annie felt impatient. This was important.

"But maybe we all need to reflect, before we make some kind of... And it may seem easy to fall back... into old patterns."

"You're not an old pattern, Annie. You're the one thread that's never cut because you're the lifeline." He grinned. "I didn't rehearse that. But it's true."

"Only because we have our daughter."

She looked down at her food and, even though she wasn't enjoying it much, attempted another mouthful. She could feel him staring. But was that true? Did she believe that without Leigh she would have severed all contact after he left, in spite – or because – of loving him?

The daughter in question reappeared.

"You're not eating!"

She took the plates to reheat in the oven. In her absence Arthur pulled a mock grimace, like a schoolboy who might be in line for the cane, while Annie smacked her own hand. Then Leigh returned with a smile that seemed, to Annie, found or applied.

"Sorry to abandon you like that," she breezed, all airy grace. "Is it all right – the food?"

Arthur used the word 'surprising' while Annie resorted to 'interesting'. Leigh shook her head.

"I tried," she said. "It's not my forte, homemaker stuff. I'm out at work all day with no kids or dogs to mess the place up but it seems I need a cleaner. Crystel. I'm thinking of promoting her to Life Coach."

"Good idea," said Arthur, less than tactfully. "Trial her and then send her northward. I'll double what you pay her!"

Leigh didn't seem amused. "And you know the joke? She's on her own, with a child and God knows how many jobs, and no prospects of ever owning a place like this. And she's younger than I am."

Annie reached out a hand to their daughter. Leigh allowed it to rest a moment before she removed hers from underneath.

"So no one said life was fair. Anyway, don't flirt with her, Dad, all right? I nearly lost her. Keep a low profile when she comes. I'll get your plates. Bloody TV chefs. I bet Crystel can cook too."

Left alone with Art again, Annie glanced at him. In his case, a low profile might take some work. He drank his wine and smiled seriously – a rare species of a smile, but she'd seen it before. It was his wedding day smile as she approached in white.

"You're a wise woman, Annie. It's part of your attraction. Before we steel ourselves for this genuinely bizarre dish, I want to tell you I love you. I believed I did, in Edinburgh, imagining you across a table from me, but now that you're real, I know I do. It's clear."

"Arthur…" She sighed and looked around the room, seeing nothing.

"I want to make it up to you, all of it, years of stupidity and mad delusion – when I should have been with you, raising a family, a son, another daughter..." He turned as Leigh approached with the plates, held in oven gloves that might never have been used before. "So take the time you need, to do everything you advised so wisely." He looked up at Leigh. "Thank you, darling. I'm really hungry now."

"What?" asked Leigh, sitting down between them along the egg-shaped table and looking from one to the other.

Arthur winked at her. "We'll tell you when you tell us all about Kyle."

"Funny!"

Annie looked from one to the other. Father and daughter could keep things loose, most of the time, with banter. She couldn't wink and she wasn't sure she had the timing or tone to be genuinely funny off-page.

But they were 'we' again, a family of a kind. Would he be making these proposals, regardless of being dumped by a wife everyone loved, if that wife had been able to give him the son he slipped tellingly into the picture? Or a daughter likely to be sunnier as well as curlier?

"How's Carole doing?" asked Leigh. "Have you cheated on her again, Dad?"

"Again? No!" He held up both hands, an innocent suspect. "I think the boot may be on the other foot," he announced, as Annie felt his bare toes brush her leg, probably not accidentally. She removed temptation.

"You're kidding," cried Leigh.

Annie noticed no disapproval in the way Leigh received this news. It looked more like excitement.

"I could see her with a toy boy," she added. "Sorry, Dad. But you have to work on a marriage if you want to keep someone like Carole. Three attempts and I don't think you have much idea."

"Thank you, darling. If you're running Marriage Guidance sessions I'll sign up for a course and benefit from your decades of experience."

"Half a century doesn't seem to have taught you much."

"Excuse me, darling! I was not romancing anyone at seven. I was nearly nine when I sent Jennifer Emery a Valentine." He smiled at Annie but it must have been obvious from the stiffness of her face that she hadn't quite managed to enjoy the jokes so far.

"But you'll be seeing Carole," persisted Leigh, "to talk about the house and the bank account?"

"She knows where I am."

"How long are you planning to stay, exactly?"

"That depends," said Arthur.

Even though Annie was looking, discouraged, at how much food remained on her plate, she heard the smile that shaped the words.

Leigh asked about her step-sisters and Annie backed her up with an "Oh yes? What are they up to? Any nice young men on the scene?"

She felt Leigh's scorn as her plucked eyebrows illustrated it, vividly. But Arthur had taken his cue.

Answering as Mrs Bennett, he talked eligible bachelors, refinement and Edinburgh's pitiable lack of both. And the consequences for her poor nerves. Annie found it funnier than she wanted to show, since he needed no encouragement. Through it, Leigh's smile flickered on and off as she interrupted, telling him to stop being stupid – "I just want to know about their careers and cars!" and "Dad, hairstyles? Weight?" But Annie remembered how instantly she'd adored the big step-sisters that came as extras with cuddly Carole.

The impressionist released a big laugh the moment the impression finished.

Annie felt herself grin down at her plate, but as she ate she felt Arthur's eyes on her and knew that was exactly the feeling he intended.

At Ethan's B and B, he had more hair than the labourers with their hard hats and overalls, but brought in less dirt and left no fag ends behind radiators. The floor in his room was sticky, as he discovered when he sat to meditate. It smelt like the butcher's near his school, on Thursdays when the lorry came to collect the unsold meat before maggots moved in. He thrust open a window and sent a few flakes of paint scattering like dandruff, but the street air carried in petrol, metal and McDonalds.

Anyone more than underweight might get trapped in the en-suite bathroom between the door and the shower unit. But the water was hot enough to wash away the pubic hairs left behind by a previous guest and send one rather blue beetle running for cover behind the toilet. Which didn't flush, but oozed at the bottom.

He guessed his father planned itineraries and had a secretary to eliminate possibilities like this. Here even Sam would forget to embrace suffering and demand her money back.

Ethan greeted the day with palms joined and raised to the grey sky through the window onto bins. He was open. It would lead him.

At breakfast, in an odd colonial verandah of an extension facing the road, the plastic tablecloth smelt like warm old milk and the man-made lilies appeared to be rusting. But it was only when his baked beans arrived tepid in a bowl, with two triangles of cold white toast on the side, that he felt sick.

"Thank you," he told the woman with smoky candyfloss hair.

Paying in cash, Ethan thought of the prophet by the Thames and hoped he'd found a roof overnight. Everyone was a poem, he told himself. And a fraud. And a version of what they might have been.

He was going to the seaside.

Crystel woke to a text from Madam. *Sorry Crystel and no worries if you can't but is there any way you could give me a couple of hours today while my dad's out, time and a half?*

Thursdays were the only days she met Coralie from school. Crystel tensed.

Sorry no have to see the teacher.

What about this evening? You could bring her if there's no one to mind her.

We are having our hair cut by a friend. Sorry.

She waited but that seemed to silence her. Coralie appeared looking sleepy. She slid into Crystel's bed and pulled the duvet up to her chin.

I want to give you a pay rise. 40 per cent. Let me know if you have any flexibility.

"What is it?" asked Coralie.

"Nothing, babe. Madam trying to buy me."

"Is it Thursday? You're coming to pick me up from school?"

"Yeah, course I am. You finished your reading book?"

"Nearly."

"You can finish it on the bus."

"Out loud?"

"You betcha! Then everyone can enjoy your voices."

Crystel picked up her phone. *I could give you two hours tomorrow lunchtime.*

"Have you told Madam she can't buy you?"

"Yeah. Not for sale. Slavery ended."

"What's slavery?"

"Tell you after breakfast. We need to roll."

"Roll me!"

Crystel got out of bed. Coralie emerged from under the duvet and lay width-ways on top at one end.

"I'm the sausage and this is the pastry!" she cried.

Another text. *Great. I'll get my father to go out.*

"Mum! You need to roll me!"

No need I can work round him. "O.K! I'm ready to roll!"

She wrapped Coralie down to the end of the bed, each push slower as the package got fatter – and gigglier.

You don't know my father. Thanks Crystel.

"Why do you call her Madam?" asked Coralie, and began the struggle to escape.

"Because she's full of herself."

"The duvet's full of me!"

"I know, and if you can't get out you'll get no breakfast."

"I can! I am! I'm out!"

Stumbling over the last part of her quilted cocoon, Coralie followed her into the kitchen.

Chapter Nine

At the passenger ferry Ethan saw a woman who could, from behind, have been his mother – at least, his memory of her, with a casual but expensive jacket and well-groomed hair held in place against the wind. He pictured her looking out to sea while the ship throbbed. When holidays began badly she was nil by mouth – coffee, crisps or words. Because his father was never ready until ten minutes after the time she'd insisted was the absolute latest they should leave the house.

They must have been to the island five times, maybe six, and mostly in sunshine. Today the water looked grim under unbroken cloud.

"Why can't we just take it easy?" Daph asked most summers, when their father presented the expedition for the day. Shanklin Chine, a castle or two, Osborne House, the Needles. "We went there last year!"

"You went to school last month," their dad pointed out, "and you'll be back there next month too!"

"Holidays aren't school," said Daph.

"Well, in a way they are," Ethan told her.

Daph didn't like Ethan being on the learning side, the trekking, wildflowers and binoculars side which meant picnics in woods and afternoons in museums, when she could be shopping or eating cake in a tea shop. But after their mum died she wanted to go again all the same.

"No," said their dad, "not there without her. It was always for her."

Well, now he was back. Walking off the ferry he realised that his dad liked to live in the past even on holiday. He used to call this Enid Blyton Land. But hadn't his mother called it home?

The wind off the sea bit hard. Ethan remembered the horizon being jammed up with yachts, and trying to count them when they looked no bigger than flies joining their wings in a swarm. Last time at Alum Bay,

Daph spent a lot less time looking at the pinks, browns, lemon and silver of the cliff edge than the whole range of plastic souvenirs filled by the shedding rock.

"Consumer," he'd called her.

"Nerd," she'd retorted.

Well, the labels still fitted. But he should have come back with Daph now. They could have retraced steps together and tried to understand what it all meant: their separateness that would never knit, their parents' awkward loving that sometimes fluffed up cosy and sometimes wore threadbare. It seemed to him that when she wasn't sparking off with his dad or still in bed with him at half-past eight on Sunday mornings, his mother had no love left over for a boy she thought found fault with her. And he did, for falling short of an idea of motherhood he'd gathered from books and films and dormitory talk about cake.

It was all right for Daph. The two females were thick as thieves. He told her so once and she said, "Better than being thick as a short plank."

"Two," he corrected her.

"Two?!" she cried. "Why? There's only one of you! No one will ever want to marry you!"

"Who says I want to get married?" he asked.

Because he never understood how it worked. Parents were supposed to be steady and affectionate with each other – not scrapping one moment and embarrassingly intimate the next.

Anyhow, there was one passenger this time and one guest to book in tonight. Daph wouldn't understand why he wanted to go back to an island that didn't do nightlife. The one thing they shared was horror at all the restaurants offering crab and chips.

Not many outsiders in October. Ethan tried not to feel disappointment: in any of it, in his memory or his impulses. He'd see what he could find.

Annie was on the way to work. She'd have to warn her mother by phone that Arthur was planning to turn up later for coffee. In Annie's experience it was always harder to be cross with Art Capaldi in the flesh. Most of her mother's visitors were elderly and female as well as rare, and he'd do his best to entertain. Annie could imagine the pair of them pronouncing with authority on her feelings, problems and needs, and even if they characterised her in rather different ways, there was no way either of them would shift their point of view. She expected Hilda to quiz Arthur about his intentions, and Arthur to be as direct as he'd been with a wine glass to hand. Unless he'd thought up some tactics...

As the traffic stalled she made the call.

Her mother was delighted, and checked whether he still liked Battenberg cake. Annie said she really couldn't say since she hadn't been his wife for a quarter of a century.

"There won't be any need for the two of you to talk about me, Mum," she added. "I can speak for myself."

"What else do we have in common?" asked Hilda. "He's anti-monarchy and he can't stand Bing Crosby!"

"Ask him about Leigh's boyfriend," suggested Annie. "He might have gathered some evidence by then."

Now that was a tactic.

Arriving at work, Annie told Zelda the story of dinner with Leigh, who wouldn't appreciate the way she described the food. "The gnocci balls ended up fusing into mush, with lumps. But the sauce broke up, you know? Like an oil spill in a harbour." It was mean, really, so she added how beautifully their hostess had set up the table. But she couldn't tell the story of the wine/carpet disaster because that would involve mention of Arthur.

Not that anyone knew, because she'd never said, "In fact I'm still in love with my ex, silly me!" She'd only ever talked about how likeable Carole was and enthused over Edinburgh. She couldn't feel quite that ridiculous in the workplace and carry off the role she had to play with any conviction. She picked up her bag and locked her office door. Business mode only.

Which was hard enough with Declan, and no easier when she remembered Arthur's 'little fucker' at the sight of him. The boy was a pale streak with a turned-up nose and a brace on his teeth. But as soon as she tried to divert him from motorbikes, F1 and Arsenal to subjects more likely in theory to earn him a GCSE, he looked as if he'd like to mow her down with his wheelchair.

"I need a fag," he told her in the school room, ignoring the table where she was setting up the laptop with its lesson on long division.

"How are your tables?" she asked. "Nine times? Sevens?"

"I get moody if I go too long without a smoke," he said. "Like withdrawal. You've been warned."

She explained with a smile that she expected respect. He pulled a face and repeated the demand.

"You're telling me you're addicted," she said. "We can get you help with that. In the meantime, let's see what you can do with these numbers…"

"I don't want fucking counselling. I want a cigarette."

"Declan, come on. Language."

As she looked at the program, hoping the graphics and sound might divert him, he wheeled his way towards the door. Annie dashed to bar his way, calmly reminding him of the way he needed to speak to her. At which point he spat on the floor as he left. Lesson over.

Even the good-humoured Sanamir was anxious when she came back from physio, because her father was visiting that afternoon to talk about exams. Annie said she'd do her best to talk to him first but Sanamir was hard to reassure.

"I can't handle pressure," she said weakly, her eyes filling. "I can't."

"I know," said Annie. "I hate it too. There's no pressure here, not anywhere in the building. It's banned. If the cameras pick it up anywhere on site, Security descends on it, escorts it out and ejects it. And sets the dogs on it."

Sanamir's full, deep laugh was a surprise and Annie smiled to hear it for the first time. She was talking like Arthur already – sharpening up the skills she'd need to outsmart him? But also reliving the smell of him as he kissed her goodnight: red wine and garlic, butter and sweetness, aftershave, fabric softener and warm flesh.

This was work and he was messing her up already, butting in where she was safe. Next to Sana, but absent as always, Emmy was flicking through a magazine. Annie watched her turning pages like a shopper with a rack of mixed sizes. Then she stopped. What was she reading? Something she cared about?

"Anything interesting?" Annie asked her, without confidence. With Emmy, best and long shots seemed to be the same.

No reply or reaction of any kind.

"Can't be more interesting than Shakespeare, though, Emmy?" she asked, enlisting Sanamir's support.

"Not unless it's shoes," said Sanamir.

She was wearing the most exquisite jewel-look sandals that networked up her ankles and shone red, blue, green, gold…

"You'd better lock those up when you're in the shower," Annie told her, "or I might take them for a very long walk."

Emmy didn't seem remotely aware of the sandals that every female member of staff coveted openly. Her own feet were in old trainers.

"Emmy's hair looks nice washed," Sanamir told her. "Vanilla's my favourite smell."

It was a worthy attempt but Emmy kept on reading. Annie murmured agreement but suggested starting Act Two. Maybe, without appearing to listen, Emmy was absorbing the characters, plot, themes and killer lines.

Luckily Sanamir was happy these days to take a part or two and they had some fun with Touchstone and Jacques. Emmy didn't smile but she didn't frown either and only yawned silent objections. Annie had a theory that when it came to the exams she might astonish everyone with A stars, but Zelda thought she was just as likely to write nothing but her name.

"Though to have her and death were both one thing," Annie quoted. "What do you think that means?"

"He's dying for love of her?" suggested Sana.

"But he's talking about possessing her – having her – as death."

"I don't get that."

"Maybe it's the longing that's exquisite and the possession that ends the obsession."

"Oh, like a reality check?"

"Yes, exactly. No one can live up to the ideal the lover imagines," Annie paused before adding as nonchalantly as possible, "in that state of unfulfilled desire."

Sanamir grimaced. "I don't believe that. Love must grow with understanding. There's no point otherwise."

She was clasping her small, beautiful hands. Annie felt touched by her innocence. She didn't like to ask about arranged marriage in case she made any ignorant assumptions.

"But Shakespeare was a romantic, wasn't he?" she asked Annie. "He wrote all those love poems."

"He did, yes, for more than one lover. Maybe it's possible to celebrate the ideal and the ecstasy and at the same time recognize that love may have a sell-by date."

Sanamir shook her head. "The character was wrong, right? I mean, it's a happy ending?"

"We'll see," said Annie, smiling.

She glanced across at Emmy, as she often did, in case there was anything on her face that she could read and verbalise. But what she saw she couldn't name. Emmy was crying without a sound.

"It's only a play, Emmy," Sana told her quietly.

"Can I get you anything, Emmy?"

Emmy wheeled herself away.

Ethan hadn't planned it, but Dimbola must be next.

"It sounds so boring," Daph had said, when their mum told them it was the home of a Victorian photographer called Julia Margaret Cameron, who captured every cultural celeb of the time.

His dad said the list included Tennyson and recited from *The Charge of the Light Brigade*. Ethan couldn't see that recklessness made people into 'heroes' just because they died – when up to that point they were carrying sabres to lunge into human organs and sacrificing horses in the process.

"Rhythm doesn't make it right," he said.

"What about rhyme?" Daph asked. "Does that make it right? As in 'You're a geek, each day of each week'."

But at Dimbola, he had been left behind in every room, lingering over the black and white portraits. The wide-eyed females all looked dreamily forlorn and the wide-browed men were ancient and severe. Especially Tennyson, who deleted his audience completely, as if he was sitting on Mount Olympus rather than one of Margaret's chairs.

"What's so interesting?" Daph wanted to know. "They're all dead," she'd added, as if that was the worst crime they could commit.

Now Ethan realised he'd rather go to the museum than anywhere else he remembered. The B and B proprietors were very helpful about buses to Freshwater and by lunchtime he was paying his entrance fee to a white-haired Miss Marple-type woman on the desk. It wasn't the kind of place where you had to queue and in fact the three other visitors were in the café, but that was a small part of why he chose it. Most people didn't know or care. "Never *heard* of her!" had been Daph's protest, cueing one of their mother's acerbic set pieces about women being 'subjugated' to men in those days. "Not anymore!" Daph had cried. "In your dreams, Dad!"

The woman on the till had blue eyes that rounded when he answered her question about having visited before. With respect? With delight at meeting an unlikely soulmate?

"When I was a kid," he said. "Blew me away."

"Oh, me too! I'm an addict!"

She gave him a leaflet and asked who he admired among contemporary photographers.

"I prefer this," he said, waving the leaflet. "It's authentic. You see the world as they saw it. You know – a different place."

"Absolutely! That camera of hers captured spirits."

She was still scrabbling for change. Counting it into his hand she asked whether he'd ever been to the island's pop festival.

"I suppose Hendrix and Janis Joplin are history now too," she said, regretfully.

Ethan struggled to imagine her with wild hair flailing, beads swinging. She winked as if she read his mind, and told him, "Enjoy!"

Even though two houses had been joined as one, the place was hardly a mansion. No erotic statues or exotic shows. At the end of the family history exhibition there was Annie, *my first success*. Eleven years later Ethan still thought her a kind of angel.

He remembered his excitement at discovering the mess, mechanics and danger of Victorian photography: poison, fire risk and eggs for gloss. It made Julia Margaret seem what his dad called 'intrepid', and Daph said, "Like me!" once he'd explained what that meant. "Not Ethan," she added. "Ethan's a wuss. Julia would have loved his girly hair."

The house felt quiet now, but alive all the same. His mother had approved the whole package: opinionated JMC bossing her famous sitters around, her good taste and pioneering of the science within the art. Until his dad said, "Ah, but she worshipped these guys. Effectively, she was washing their feet."

Remembering, Ethan wished he'd respected his mother more, as a woman with a Science degree and a career…

The next room was full of Victorian faces, mainly young and ethereal. Or sexless, anyway. Ethan loved Ellen Terry, even then. Now she was intimidating, untouchably perfect as she leant against a papered wall, fingering a simple necklace. A goddess. Though her eyes were lowered she wasn't demure or sad either, just unknowable. Could Julia Margaret have found that in Sam? In Crystel? Daph had ridiculed the photographer's trademark instruction of 'Big eyes!' by obeying it, looking like a Dr Who alien in the control of a Dark Force.

Reminded that these Victorian trendsetters thought you could pick out a murderer in a crowd, he decided that Virginia Woolf's mum looked more likely to dissect human organs than cuddle her little girl.

When his mother wandered these rooms, absorbed by the images, what did other visitors see? A woman pretending to be in control and almost convincing herself? An achiever afraid of everything she didn't know how to do? A mother gazing at the black and white children as if she'd forgotten the full colour ones who came with sound?

Being alone made a difference, sharpened things. This was what a poem should do, expanding a moment to open up time.

For his dad it had all been 'a bit arty farty'. He preferred pyramids and hieroglyphics, temples hewn from rock that staged more primitive rites. Ethan didn't mind how far back the past took him. Every glimpse was a revelation and he tried to let go of the present and feel a way in. He didn't blame Victorians for being Victorians, the rich for being rich, or Tennyson for the big head his admirers gave him. But in the twenty-first century there was no time left to mess about, experimenting and missing the point. It was time to get it right.

One room had been taken over by rock memorabilia, with quotes both from locals and the front men of bands who'd played the festival since the late Sixties. In it he found a man in a parka, silently following the exhibition around, oblivious to Ethan. With a cap hiding most of his hair and a cowboy scarf high under his chin, he was hard to age.

A crowd stretched along a wall. The Summer of Love. The man moved in and examined it. Then he turned with a faint smile behind his glasses.

"That's me," he said. "Near the GIRLS WANTED sign."

"Yeah?"

"I didn't write it. Didn't get a girl either – as far as I remember."

Ethan grinned. "Who did you hear?"

"Slept through a lot of it. Off my head. I'd do it differently now – I mean, that was music. You recognize what you've lost when it's gone – as Joni Mitchell would say. Life's like that. With the big failures you don't get to re-sit and up your grade."

"No." Not when Earth had taken too much punishment and people paid the price, thought Ethan, but evangelism stuck in the throat. He chickened out unless people like this met him half-way. Still a wuss.

"They don't tell you how many of us had mental health issues. Still have. Life is one bad trip, you know?"

"Ah."

"You look like you want to go there but don't be fooled."

"I won't. I don't."

"We won't get fooled again!" sang the man, with one arm swinging to air guitar.

"Right."

"That photographer woman in there never saw the real world, the dirt, the disease. It's all the same kind of lie."

Almost inadvertently Ethan murmured, "I guess we'll never learn how to live unless we find out how to read the past."

"Ha!" cried the guy, eyes suddenly big enough for Julia Margaret. "You're not wrong there!"

Ethan did what his sister would do and moved away, making for the stairs. Of course it was what he was doing, at twenty-three – trying to find out how to read the past. As if the personal mattered, when the future was at stake and living had to be for the future, for kids like Coralie. That was a child Julia Margaret would have been gagging to capture with light.

He didn't stop for coffee, but as he left he asked the white-haired volunteer whether she happened to know of any Internet cafés in the area.

"I'm not sure the Island's on the Internet yet, dear!" Then she winked, because for a moment he'd believed her.

"Ventnor!" called the man in the parka, thudding down the stairs.

"Ah," said Ethan. "Thanks."

All the way around the coast! They'd never managed to walk that far with Daph in tow but he'd do it now, sea below and sky above. No need to measure distance or hours. He'd get there. He waved as he left.

Eating lunch in her office, Annie found three texts from Arthur. *Hungover but no less clear about you, Annie.* Then: *Daytime TV is even emptier on a giant screen. How are you doing?* Finally, as if it had occurred to him that she was working: *Busy I guess. Don't let the little fucker jerk you around. XXX*

Maybe he was hoping for a call but she had no intention of repeating her words of wisdom. Until he had sorted out his feelings, she couldn't see the point in discussing the Turner Prize or the cost of rail travel, whether Federer was finished, the Aussies would ever learn to lose or if the Labour Party could recover its soul. Reading his messages again, she wondered why he had to use the vocabulary of an American when that soft Scottish accent he'd brought with him to university had been so musical. Was he louder now – or was that just the booze?

Yes a busy morning. Lunch break will be short. Speak later. That was certainly non-committal but cold too. *Don't leave coffee grains on the worktop!* She hoped the exclamation mark made it jokily conspiratorial, as opposed to the kind of nagging he would already be getting from Leigh. With his daughter and ex-wife both at work, how had he imagined he'd spend his days? Couldn't he take a stroll along the South Bank and check out what was filling the Turbine Hall at the Tate Modern? She offered the suggestion and turned off her phone.

"I've loved you so hopelessly for so long, Arthur," she rehearsed in her head, *"that I can't handle the hope you're giving me in case you reconsider and snatch it away. You have no idea how I've lived with this love that you think you've rediscovered, as if it was in a drawer all along and you never looked for it. Mine wasn't hidden or forgotten. Mine was with me every day and every night you shared a bed with another wife. Year after year."*

How could she tell him anything of the kind while he was on the rebound, re-evaluating in a way that most women would dismiss as a mid-life crisis and probably on the verge of buying a motorbike or an electric guitar?

"You all right, Annie?" asked the young primary teacher who came in twice a week.

"Fine!" she breezed, but five minutes later disappeared to the Ladies to check.

In the mirror she saw an image lonely men would scroll past on a dating site. What made her lovable anyway? Only airbrushed memories and regret, a desire to make amends or recapture the youth he found hard to let go.

Annie combed her hair and noticed, as she applied her coral lip gloss, the little tucks above her mouth that weren't there last week – were they?

Coralie said her teacher looked a bit like Miss Honey in the Matilda movie. Crystel thought that was a stretch. Miss Howell was just one of those blonde white women who didn't need make-up or heels to look fresh. She spoke like she'd been to a girls' school and been taught by nuns, but Crystel supposed she went out on the lash on a Friday like everyone else with no kid at home. Maybe the school was a shock to Miss Howell but she had a coping mask that almost smiled. Coralie said she wasn't as nice as Miss Honey but then who was?

Crystel was late in the end. Only a few minutes, because of the bus, but she didn't want anyone thinking she was an irresponsible single mother like some of them, smoking over their buggies and cursing at their kids. Coralie wasn't bothered about a few minutes. Crystel could see that the moment she looked up from the desk where she was reading. But she read the accusation in the doll face the teacher lifted from the computer screen.

"Hello!" she cried, almost sing-song. "You wanted to see me?"

Miss Howell invited Crystel to sit down. Coralie squeezed onto Crystel's lap in the space under the table, reached for her book and kept her eyes on it.

"I hope Coralie's happy? She's doing very well."

Was the teacher expecting trouble? Crystel hoped she didn't come across that way.

"That's great. Good girl, Coralie." Coralie gave her a smile and a thumbs-up before she returned to her book, mouthing silently. "She likes school but someone called Norah's been bothering her…"

"Not today," said Coralie. "We were partners today. She's my friend now."

What? Crystel looked down at her curly head. "Yeah? That's good then. But you remember yesterday…"

"I thought it might help to put them together," said Miss Howell.

So she'd noticed – but that was good. She'd have to trust her.

"Thank you," said Crystel. "But maybe you can keep an eye?"

"Certainly." Miss Howell sat up straight as if she wanted to stand. "Most fall-outs last less than a day. Girls especially – they can be in tears at playtime and holding hands in the lunch queue. Was there anything else?"

She sounded like a cashier at the bank. This was *her* girl. Crystel almost rose herself but then she said, "I don't understand the targets. I mean, the way they keep on coming."

"Sorry?"

"As soon as she gets one ticked off there's another. Like the pressure never lets up. When I was her age it was just fun, sand and clay, you know? We must have done our letters and numbers but I didn't feel … like…" Crystel paused. "Evaluated all the time."

Miss Howell's cheeks looked pinker now. "I hope no child ever feels under the pressure teachers feel, day in and day out."

"It must be a tough job," said Crystel. This was a girl really. She probably stayed in at nights, planning and marking when her friends were out partying. "I don't know how you do it," she told her encouragingly. "I guess if I want to get rid of targets and testing I'll have to write to the Government."

"If you start a petition," said Miss Howell, "I'll sign it."

Crystel smiled. This was just a human being and her life wasn't so easy. "I'll let you get on with your work," she said. "You should set a deadline. Walk out of here and have your own fun."

"That's what my fiancé says." She sounded sad. "It never happens."

"Make it happen tonight. Surprise him."

"Thank you. Maybe I will."

Miss Howell looked at the clock on the classroom wall, just the same old round white face with a black rim that Crystel used to try to read to find out whether it was Story Time yet. Taking Coralie's hand, Crystel remembered the wacky rainbow clock and it made her think of Ethan, who would love it if he hadn't given all that up. Possessions like watches and phones. Meeting deadlines and targets. She wondered, as she led Coralie down the corridor, where he was and what he was doing.

Chapter Ten

In the mirror, Leigh could see what her mother meant. She looked tired. Not that her mother would guess why, never having conducted a furtive and heady relationship founded on opportunistic sex.

Resourceful, he'd said, in her review. *An imaginative approach.*

Well, now she was imagining Francoise, the wife she'd meet before long at the Christmas party. It was time to end it before he did.

Another text came through as she showered: a list of things he wanted to do to her. It was a game he played on the way to work. The next round would be at the office, where he'd be cool and crisp, avoiding eye contact, even if they found themselves by the water dispenser at the same moment and his hand could skim some part of her body unseen. He wanted her to be more reckless, called her 'chicken'. But he had no idea how far beyond her old limits she'd moved.

He was a boy playing spies or undercover cop. She was his playmate but sometimes she felt sick. Real, shaky nausea.

Her sexual vocabulary exhausted, she sent no reply. The clock on her phone screen suggested she must be thinking too much and moving too slowly. She pulled on a grey sweater dress Kyle had called a second skin, tied her hair in a high ponytail, outlined her eyes with kohl and let scarlet lips do the rest.

Along the coastal path, the wind off the sea kept seizing Ethan's hair and trying to beat him with it. For a while it made him feel alive. It was real and raw and he chose it – nothing protecting or numbing him, nothing separating him from the elemental. It would clear the fug. With no sign of any other walkers, he ignored the nagging seagulls trying to spoil his meditation and started to feel like a monk in one of those abbeys set apart from the world. But ruined refectories were evidence that monks were occasionally allowed to eat. Ethan had mistakenly swallowed his two squares of chocolate much too early.

Below, the sea's mood wasn't improving and it was hard to name its colours but they didn't include blue. Industrial? Was that fair? There was beauty in bleakness, joy in weariness. His heart felt full. But it was hard to tell, as the sky darkened, whether he was in for a soaking or just stepping into the last hour of daylight.

At the next pub he asked how far and was told he had another twelve miles to walk.

"At least!" called a guy with a shaved head and a plate full of chips.

Ethan was offered a room by a woman with plum-coloured hair and gold hoop earrings who called him 'lovey'.

"That's winter rate," she said, voice lowered. "Breakfast included and - drum roll please - free Wi-Fi. If you see my husband, see if you can explain what that is." Giving him the key, she told him, "I'm Marian, lovey. I've got a hairdryer you can borrow. Give me a shout if you need any help." He realised his hair was steaming. She winked. "I like a man with dreadlocks."

He thanked her and insisted on finding his room without an escort. It was tiny, with corners shaved by eaves. A bad painting of yachts in a flat blue sea made the real thing out of his little leadlight window look wild and bleak. The only moving ship he could see was a tanker on the horizon, its colours rusty. The peace and action of summer felt carefree in his memory, but it was just another dream, or lie.

After a hot shower he towel-dried his hair and fell asleep on the neat single bed, waking surprised by dreams of warm, wet kisses with eyes firmly closed.

But disturbingly, no face.

"People make a big deal of sex, Ethan," his dad told him once, after they'd watched *The English Patient* just before another new term began, mainly because of the cave paintings of the swimmers. "It's love that matters and there's much less of it about."

"I know," Ethan said, eyes ahead. That was his way of drawing the line.

"Right," said his dad, and smiled. "You're a quicker learner than I was, then!"

By that time his mother was dead and he didn't want to know how much sex was 'about' for his father. Of course he'd never been able to imagine it between his parents. And schoolboy Ethan avoided the schoolboy shagger-braggers, shrugging off stories of scaling walls and buying condoms from public toilets for the benefit of the Convent girls across the field.

"You're kidding!" Daph had said, when he told her Sam was his first. "Ethan, that's so sad."

He wasn't sure which meaning she intended for the adjective. Maybe Daph had been given the same fatherly advice, but what would their mother have said? He knew nothing about her, really, that wasn't domestic. As if she had no previous or inner life at all.

Ethan sat up on the pub bed and realised he couldn't relive his own life without uncovering the human being that was his mother.

But he needed food. Returning to the bar, he couldn't help noticing the landlady's startling lipstick, a shade darker than her hair. Ethan chose tomato soup and locally-baked bread for supper and, during the process of ordering, being served and eating hungrily, absorbed a series of winks, some of them long-distance. Novels were full of women her age, predatory or generous but always unfulfilled. But he'd never bought into the storyline, not for a minute, until Marian touched his shoulder as she cleared his bowl and plate and he smelt the perfume behind her ears as well as the onions on her fingers.

"I do a lovely apple pie," said Marian. "Can I tempt you?"

"Apple pie sounds great," he said.

"Cream, ice cream or custard – or the lot?"

"Just the pie, thanks."

Boarding school boys knew about apple pie beds but Ethan had thought enough about sheets. Waiting, he looked around for a poem. The place felt empty spite of the Italian League football on a widescreen TV, but around the open fire it was warm. This could be the most traditional pub in Britain: nooks, horseshoes and a toby jug, a laminated menu that pre-dated the Tandoori and the Chinese take-away. A game of darts between fat men in football-style nylon shirts and the smell of hot fat right through.

Wind threw rain at the windows, as if the sea was crashing in. He wrote some words in his notebook, starting with nouns that brought back the coastal path, but there were no adjectives in tow that were fit for any page. And the verbs had all been used, and cranked up until they lost the power they were reaching for – the power of the earth, sky and water.

The pie arrived, but this must be Marian's husband, his thumbs large and red but nicotine-tipped.

"Anything special brought you to the island, then?"

"Retracing steps," he said. "I used to come for family holidays as a kid."

"Dead in winter."

That seemed to Ethan to be another example of line-drawing. He thanked the man for the pie, which was solid, dry and cool in the middle. His mother was dead in December, at the same sort of age as this man's wife, and her idea of dessert was cheesecake from the freezer.

"Excuse me," he said, "the free Wi-Fi?"

"On your device."

"I haven't got any devices."

"Really? Off the radar, are you?"

"Kind of, yeah."

"As long as we won't be reading about you in the papers? Headless corpses and all that?"

Ethan wasn't planning a reply to that anyway but Marian signalled her husband over. As Ethan arrived at the landing that led to his room, she appeared behind him with a key and pointed to a door marked PRIVATE.

"I'm guessing you want to message some girl," she said. "Or some lad, it's all the same to me. You can use our PC for five minutes, O.K?"

The computer was old but live. Ethan thanked her. He emailed his father: *Where did Mum's aunt and uncle live on IOW?* And added that he was fine. Then he went into Facebook and messaged Crystel: *I've been to my old school which was weird. Now I'm on the Isle of Wight where I used to come as a kid. It was never this cold and wet. Google Julia Margaret Cameron and Dimbola and tell me what you think. There must be poems here but they're hiding like the sun.*

Maybe she was putting Coralie to bed because no answer came. No tick to mean she'd seen it. But his father's email was there in the Inbox, all alone: *Ventnor, I think. The street began with S but I can't get it just now and anyway he died. What's up, Ethan?*

Nothing. Thanks. They didn't do kisses, upper or lower case. Ethan exited and emerged to find Marian dusting the banisters and window sills with cerise feathers on the end of a stick.

"You're all right if you want a bit longer, lovey," she said.

"No, that's fine, thanks," he said.

What would Crystel think? That he was mad? His dad was probably coming to the same conclusion.

He shuffled along to his room as if he had all the time in the world – which, in a way, he did.

At her desk Annie knew she should be pleased to be finished early on a Friday. Not five-thirty yet. So why the delay? She turned on her phone and imagined six texts from Arthur. But while she was tidying, shredding, and watering a gerbera that showed no signs of rebirth, a call came through from Leigh.

"I've been trying to get you for ages!"

"I've been working."

"Women are meant to be able to multi-task! Anyway, I've got to get home and pack. Something's come up and I'll be away overnight, back late tomorrow evening. Some meeting in Chester. I don't want to leave Dad alone in the flat, and I know he's hoping the two of you can go out to dinner."

"He's an able-bodied adult, Leigh."

"What?"

"I mean, he could manage on his own."

"Is that a no? You don't want dinner with him?"

"He can call me himself. You get yourself off to Chester. He's not a seventeen-year-old who's going to trash the place while you're gone."

"Can I have that in writing?" Leigh sighed. "Can't he stay at your place?"

Annie was conscious of her breathing but which words were best? She couldn't find them and Leigh couldn't wait.

"You have a spare room, Mum."

"I'll talk with your father. Have fun in Chester."

"I told you, it's work!"

Annie told her she hoped she might enjoy the trip anyway, without meaning to. It struck her that as a mother she had the cover of almost-jolly resilience pretty much mastered. She'd had no idea twenty-five years ago how undaunted she could pretend to be.

There were only three texts from Arthur, the last of which told her he was being abandoned, and asked her out to dinner anywhere she could recommend.

She could take him to Amira's. He'd be face to face, with no alcohol, and she'd remember soul therapy. It would be clearer there: the difference between what she wanted and needed. But he'd have to get the train back to London – or stay overnight.

There was no solution. If she ate with him in London she'd be driving back late and be washed up in the morning.

It was an opportunity, with no Leigh around. But Annie felt an alarm she couldn't have explained to him or to anyone. Was it the thought of sharing a bed with her ex-husband for the first time in twenty-six years? Or the fear of telling him there was no way that would happen, no way she could allow it, because at her age she needed sleep and if they had sex she wouldn't sleep again, not that night or the next or even once he was back in Edinburgh? That peace she'd been working towards through all these years alone would be over.

Easier to be ill. She began to claim a headache by text but erased it. She wanted to understand how he felt, and if she stayed at home with the TV he'd be calling every half hour to ask how she was.

The phone rang as she stood in the office doorway unwilling to leave.

"Annie! Has it been a bastard of a day? Let me look after you. Come over to the flat and I'll order us a curry. And massage your neck. Your favourite movie's on Channel Four – the Graham Greene one where he hates God…"

"That's not my favourite movie, Art. It's depressing. You get Barber's Adagio over the grave."

"Ah. But you also get Ralph Fiennes's bottom. Leigh said you're partial to that."

Annie flushed with embarrassment that felt ridiculous. Was she fourteen? Her own bottom certainly wasn't and Arthur's wouldn't be improving with age. That film was for evenings alone in pyjamas. "I'm going to head home. I'm really tired. Maybe we can all do something when Leigh gets back. Friday night theatre? A Saturday matinee maybe? Why don't you go online and choose?"

"You're avoiding me, Annie. Please don't."

"Speak later!" she cried brightly, walking down the corridor. She ended the call.

On the toilet, phone in hand, Crystel caught herself smiling in the bathroom mirror. Then she realised Ethan had sent the message some time ago and might not see a reply if she sent one. No one else messaged her that way, with proper sentences like a book, about poems hiding like the sun.

I haven't been out of London much. Have a good trip. Wrap up warm. She pictured his bare feet in sandals. He didn't look like he ate enough – maybe because he was too busy with higher things. She wished she could remember a joke to tell him because he took life dead seriously. Unlike the other guys she knew. They didn't even take *her* seriously. *I told Coralie's teacher I don't approve of targets.* She thought he'd approve of that. *She is well and bouncing.* She sent it off and wondered how long it would be before she heard from him again.

This time five years ago, when he was at his posh school, she was struggling. No flat and no clue about babies or how to be a mother to one that never stopped crying. Now Coralie was part of her. If she didn't mention her in a text or message, making out she was young and free like most of her friends, it felt wrong, like a married man alone in a bar without a wedding ring. As if she wished Coralie away, when she didn't, no way! Not now. It was different when it was new.

"There's no such thing as post-natal depression," her mother had said, so sure that Crystel felt a surge of anger. "It's just panic. You get over it when you get on top of the routine. You've got to accept that's what your life is."

Her mum still didn't understand how to help. Even after she moved into her own place with Coralie, she was always demonstrating, explaining and taking over, "so you can rest." Crystel didn't want rest. She wanted peace and that was something else. Sometimes now she thought she'd found it, with Coralie. Like when the two of them were sharing the same sunshine in a park or the same story at bedtime. When there was nothing between them to make the connection feel loose, or spark off and hurt. Ordinary moments, good ones.

"You're a good mother," Lou told her, but what would Lou know? She was what their mum called 'off the rails'. They laughed about that a lot; it was a running joke.

"I don't want to be stuck on a track," Lou had said in Top Shop the other week. "I wanna de-vi-ate!"

She'd grinned and held up a black lace top, smoothing it over her breasts till Crystel had to slap her hand, but she didn't buy it. It wouldn't have stretched that far. Lou stretched a lot of other things, including the image she liked to broadcast, of a bad girl who'd give guys a good time, but really she was a fun auntie with a big laugh. Not hard like she pretended, in her leather jacket with big gold zips and buckles. But that loud, deep voice carried across a market and turned nervous white women into meerkats. Lou just had no plans to end up on her own with a baby and no clubbing.

"I'm not stuck on any track," Crystel told her, while Coralie looked at the jewellery, but Lou didn't seem convinced.

And standing there in a shop where she couldn't afford new clothes, Crystel could map her life out like a train line. But that was then, before Ethan Garrett.

How would he picture her now? Not on the loo! Crystel washed her hands, watching another smile grow on her face. Craziness. She had to remember what was real. No sound from the small bedroom. Padding across the landing, Crystel peeked in and there she was, asleep in that flat-out way of hers, both arms reaching towards the door.

"Limbs akimbo," she told her a while back. Then she had to explain both words, which merged to become Coralie's favourite. It went on for weeks, months – on the sofa when she jumped, in the street, it was chanted and sung. Now it was stuck in Crystel's head like a rhythm on a dance track.

"If I had a rabbit," Coralie had said, just days ago, "I'd call it Limsakimbo."

Crystel pointed out that you couldn't keep rabbits in a flat. "Anyway, rabbits are all tucked-in and neat."

"But their *ears* are akimbo!" cried Coralie and stuck hands above her head.

A day or two later they were watching a wildlife programme about Africa and Crystel said, "Look! Limbsakimbo!" because a young giraffe was having trouble with all four splaying, knobbly legs at different angles.

And Coralie said, "We can't keep a giraffe in the flat!"

"Maybe not," said Crystel. "Its head might burst up through Number 4's bathroom floor when Mr Grumpy's in the bath."

He lived upstairs and didn't like the sound of babies crying, but he wasn't grumpy anymore because he'd died in September. Crystel didn't even know until she came across his daughters in the lift with an old, dark brown wardrobe. Then she recognised his grubby checked hat sitting on the top of a bin liner full of clothes. She didn't tell Coralie Mr Grumpy was dead because it wouldn't be right to call him that now, but she didn't know any other name.

No one could live as if death never butted in and turned things upside down, even five-year-olds. Coralie seemed to cope quite happily with a daddy in heaven. But then he'd never been real like Mr Grumpy, who smelt of cigarettes and sweat, and always wore the same old mac with a torn hem that dangled behind like a tail.

Crystel thought of Granddad George, whose time had come too early when his heart just stopped. Like Coralie's jumping lamb that frisked one minute and froze the next. Power cut off. A whole different way of sleeping. Crystel hadn't got used to being without him yet but she had the feeling sometimes that he was still on her side. She'd feel his belief in her when she needed it.

She slipped away with a last smile for Coralie, leaving the door ajar and thinking that for his own reasons, Ethan Garrett believed in her too.

Annie did the maths as she looked at the clock in her car, to find out whether the journey home had really been quicker than usual. No, just an illusion, probably caused by the traffic jam of nose-to-tail thoughts, all agitated but none of them leading anywhere in her head. To Annie's surprise and relief, Bluetooth hadn't served up Arthur, more impatient than any driver and possibly just as frustrated. Only silence.

Maybe he was calling Carole instead, or sitting in the pub opposite Leigh's flat, befriending the males and making the women feel interesting. It was quite a service to womankind, really – not ogling, chatting up or smarming as a response to breasts, hair, legs or lips but looking full-on and focused. Taking playful and genuine pleasure in every woman's company and showing respect even when he had to fake it.

"What the hell do you see in me?" she asked him in his absence, with a last look in the rear mirror before she locked the car.

The carpet that greeted her looked in needed of a vacuum and, hurrying upstairs, she found the contents of the washing basket nudging the underside of the wash basin, but Annie felt tired as well as hungry. She checked the fridge. Maybe macaroni cheese: Leigh's favourite for years before she fell in love with Jamie Oliver and required fresh herbs and garlic mushed with a pestle and mortar.

Maybe she'd shower and then treat herself at Amira's. The house felt cold.

Just after half past seven she was in her winter-weight robe, drying her hair and losing interest in anything more energetic than TV and bed. As she turned off the hairdryer she heard something unexpected. The doorbell?

Maybe Lilian next-door had taken in a parcel. Like Hilda, Annie had taken to ordering all kinds of bits and pieces online, but without the triumphalism. It was a habit she meant to break before shops went the way of Banda machines. Surely that wok couldn't be here already?

Not a neighbour in fact. Or a Jehovah's Witness, or a canvasser for the local elections which she suspected were approaching. Arthur was at her door, looking rosy-cheeked and a little breathless. He had something like a sports bag over his shoulder but when he unzipped it, he reached in for a bottle of champagne.

"Still cold," he said, handing it across the doorstep to her. "It's bitter out here."

Annie stepped back to let him in, but without words. Was this what trances felt like?

"Unlike you, Annie Capaldi. You were never bitter, were you? That's a wonderful trait."

He kissed her, both cheeks. She smelt spirits.

"I have almost no food in the house," she told him.

"I haven't come for food," he said. "Though I admit eating would be an acceptable kind of add-on. Have you got eggs?"

She thought she had.

"I'll make omelette," he announced, kicking off his shoes.

Annie had an unwelcome Bridget Jones flashback but he was no Colin Firth. "I can make omelette, Art." She was blocking him and he noticed.

"What's up? Have you got a man in the bedroom?"

Not jealousy. Just a joke. About as likely as a unicorn in the garden.

"Only Ralph and his bottom," she said. "He can recover while we go out for dinner, poor baby. I know a fantastic place, probably unique." She looked at her watch. "There's a fast train back to Euston at 9:36." She might be making the numbers up. "And 10:06. Every half hour."

"Great, but slow down. This is good champagne. A hint of peach, your favourite."

She thanked him and in the kitchen he popped it open with no need for a mop. She dug out champagne glasses that might not have been used since she bought the place, hoping his eyesight was as fuzzy as hers because they were probably less than crystal-clear.

"Cheers," she said, trying to pre-empt any more lavishly worded toast he might offer – of the sort that might alarm her as the bubbles fizzed up her nose. They chinked glasses.

"To you, Annie Capaldi," he said, so tenderly that she could have slapped herself for never changing that name. For Leigh's sake or hers? His eyes looked moist. Oh God. She couldn't meet them.

Then he asked about her day and she was glad to tell for a change. He'd soon emptied his glass and poured more, topping up hers by less than the centimetre she'd cleared. Was alcohol a problem now, really a problem? No more than average, surely. She supposed he might as well enjoy a couple of glasses now, since Amira's place was dry. And that would certainly be a way of finding out.

"I'm lagging behind," she said, "and it's going to my head anyway. Empty stomach." She patted it, wishing it backed her up. "Contrary to appearances."

"Stop!" he told her. "Don't put yourself down. You never used to do that."

"I had no reason. God, young people are clueless."

Their smiles meant Leigh, who must puzzle him too. Annie took her glass upstairs, where it sat forgotten amongst age-defying creams that came with a price tag similar to champagne. Just her best jeans and the turquoise shirt with embroidery. Not the time to lose confidence in every item in her wardrobe, the skin under her eyes and the colour of her teeth. She reminded herself she'd left all this behind.

Annie sprayed on some Body Shop perfume from some grateful parents, fresh and bright, but not sexy.

Why not? Only because. And because. And because. Annie averted her eyes from the mirror and slung a shiny little bag over her shoulder, the one made of old crisp packets, which Leigh said was bizarre. Did everyone grow odder with age? Maybe young people were only afraid of their own latent eccentricity, clamping down on it with the standard vocabulary, taste and habits. With no idea that by fifty they'd have forgotten the lid and it'd be bubbling out all over the place.

At the bottom of the stairs, Annie glimpsed her ex-husband and current date from behind, touring her lounge. His jacket was too young for him, a little zip-up job meant for twenty somethings. In the gap between its hem and his trouser belt, a creased shirt spilt out. But from the back, with his tummy off-camera, he looked less chubby than chunky, and the hair still trying to ripple down his neck was ridiculously strokeable. Even now she knew how her fingers would feel, just there, when he couldn't sleep.

Both intent and typically at ease, he was pausing to read the spines of her paperbacks and examine the photographs – mainly Leigh at various ages up to graduation, each smile stiffer than the last. But also a studio portrait of her parents not so long before her dad died, with Hilda's resistance to the extravagance equally tight across her face. Arthur looked and smiled. She wondered what he could be thinking.

She watched him move on and around, picking up a group shot at a school reunion. She'd been dusting it for so long but now she saw it again, felt it. Here was a day that had left her stunned – that sadness should be so commonplace and, in spite of the laughter, so dreary. That time could work so much damage and bring such disappointment and pain.

Turning, he smiled. She had to stop him.

"Don't tell me I look years younger than anybody else in that picture or I'll never believe another word you say."

"You have style, Annie. Effortless."

"You mean I let myself go, cheerfully."

"Compliments aren't meant to be confrontations." He replaced the picture on the shelf. "I remember some of those women."

"Yes. They were all at our wedding."

"Of course," he said, smiling as if he didn't feel the sting in that at all. "How's Gillie these days?"

"Oh, same as ever." How stupid, she thought. As if even Gillie could escape time unscathed! "I must call her."

As they left the house she seized the opportunity to tell him the stories. Beginning with Carrie and her severely autistic son who had to be cared for away from home because of the violence of his temper, she moved on to Meg's double mastectomy and Greta, who'd lost her husband to Motor Neurone's after years of nursing him. Not forgetting

Helen, abandoned after twenty years of what she thought was a good marriage and now computer dating with some hilarious stories to show for dates that weren't amusing at the time.

Arthur laughed, sympathised and asked questions. They'd all be touched and impressed by his memory for female details.

Then he asked how much further they had to walk.

"You need to exercise more, you know."

"I will. I've started now! You're dragging me miles!"

His arm brushed hers. It felt warm and fleshy. Their hands hung so close that she wondered what she'd do if he took hers in his. Lift up her head and kiss him? Maybe she should. Rather than waiting to see, wouldn't it be better to take control, and judge in the light of available evidence and good sense?

"It'll do you good," she said, eyes ahead.

"You do me good. Always did, always have."

Annie smiled, but not at him. Only at the fence and the squirrel running along it, illuminated by a street light ahead. He knew her smile; she knew his smooth talk. They walked in step.

The bed in the purple hotel room was wide and white under the covers, the pillows so blissful that Leigh told Kyle she defied any princess to detect a whole frozen pack of peas. Not for the first time, he had no idea what she was talking about. In any case he clearly had no desire to talk at all.

They were progressing through foreplay when his phone rang and he swore. Extracting himself from underneath her, he reached for it. Leigh glared at it, then him. His eyes fixed her as he put one finger towards her mouth.

Leigh blanked him. Some women would run a shower with the door open and sing, or caress and tease him until he couldn't shape the words. Or take the phone and say, *"He's very busy just now."* She turned away and, standing naked near the door, brushed the hair he'd tangled.

"What! Which hospital?" he cried. "Is he all right? What happened?"

Leigh looked back at him. His father must have had an accident. Leigh knew nothing about him, or where he might live – probably because married lovers had no families.

Focused, he was listening now. All Leigh could hear was a female voice, no obvious distress.

"Are you sure? Call me later. Give him a cuddle from me."

A cuddle? This wasn't the Kyle she knew – not until he ended the call: "Yeah, sure, he'll be fine. He's a soldier."

Fastening her bra, she guessed. The adjective that would slot in before the final noun wasn't *old*. Kyle shook his head, both hands briefly to his mouth, as if he'd forgotten her. He closed his phone. Then he loosened again and turned to her, not a lover anymore but not a boss either. He was a father.

"Dan was at a sleepover and tipped back on some ride-on trike or car or something. Cut his head. He's having stitches." He ran his hands through his hair. "I didn't mention Dan, did I?"

"No," she said, stepping into her knickers. "Funny, that."

"He's three." He grinned. "He's all over the place."

"But currently at A and E." Leigh zipped her skirt. She could do this. "Is he all right?"

"Yeah. Quite a lot of blood apparently, but he's being brave."

"You're not going?"

"No point. He'd be stitched up and home by the time I got up the motorway. Don't worry." He reached out a hand. "Come here, you. Unfinished business."

Leigh looked away. So the Dad role was a walk-on part and he'd walked off again. Leigh picked up her blouse from the back of the chair, smoothed and slipped into it, keeping her eyes on the fabric and buttons, on her own fingers moving quickly.

"What are you doing? This is because I have a kid? I'm not cheating on him!"

"Not with me, no, not anymore."

"What! Come on! You think I'm some sort of scum because I'm not treating a little accident like a big drama and rushing back, just to find him fast asleep in his own bed?"

"I'm going back to my room to prepare for tomorrow. One of us needs to know what we're doing."

"Answer the question, Leigh. I asked if that's what you think." There was an edge to his voice that she'd heard on the phone to suppliers. She just needed her shoes now, if she could find her bag.

"You're not my superior now."

"Technically, since this is a work trip, on expenses, I am. And this is a meeting right here. So sit down and get your laptop out, Miss

Capaldi."

"Fuck off, Mr Hart." She chuckled through her nose. His name had never seemed darkly funny before.

Now he was smiling too, as if he'd decided this was a game. She closed his door and was heading back to her own room when she decided to find a restaurant instead, in case he came knocking. How could she be so hungry? Because she was as heartless as him, but a lot less consistent.

Stepping into the car park, she remembered he'd driven. The hotel was off the A road, near a roundabout that must lead back to the town centre, and she had no coat. Her shoes showed off her legs but they weren't meant for walking.

A gust of wind made her clasp her elbows and press her arms to her stomach. Behind her she heard the door that led into reception swing open, but paid no attention, wishing she hadn't given up smoking: a reason to stand out there on an October evening, alone. She clicked on her mother's name on her Contacts List without thinking why or what she might say.

At the touch of a hand on her backside she spun round.

"Come back and let me warm you up," he murmured. "Work up an appetite," he whispered in her ear, "and have a really good dinner. And go back to bed."

Kyle kissed the back of her neck, took her hand and led her inside.

Arthur liked everything about Amira's until he found that, however many times he flipped the menu, there was no mention of alcohol. Amira herself appeared just at that moment and Annie introduced him by name only, with the unsettling feeling that Amira knew everything, perhaps more than she knew herself.

"What, no booze, Amira!" he cried. Annie felt embarrassed. As if there were no Muslims in Edinburgh. "What's that about then?"

"It's about health, in fact," said Amira with a smile. "It's better for your body, you know, Arthur, to give it a miss now and then."

"But there's an off-licence almost opposite," he said, cheerfully, "so it might be *then* but it won't be *now*." Annie saw he'd amused himself, but what she felt was embarrassment. "I take it you've no objection?"

"I have," said Annie quickly. "Let's order from this wonderful menu. It all looks so good."

Once they'd chosen, he smiled. "Did she used to be an infant teacher?"

"No," said Annie. "A rehab counsellor, I believe."

He raised his eyebrows and grimaced. Then he nodded, grinning. "You got me! You've got much better at that! All right, sweetheart, you win. No booze." He sipped his lemon and mint water, blowing the steam. "Just the intoxication of being out on a date with you."

"Please don't talk like that."

"Like what? As if I'm romancing you? That's what I want to do, my dear Annie. I might not be as slim or athletic as I was the first time round, but I want the same as I did then – you, and to make you happy. And I know I didn't make a very good job of that before..."

"You did, for a while. I was very happy. Stupidly happy."

He laid his hand on hers, running his fingers along hers and in between. It felt so erotic that she snatched her hand away, as if she'd touched a hob that hadn't cooled.

"So was I, you know I was. I don't know what I was thinking. Lorelei's a witch! But I do believe we could be happy again." His best smile was back again; it still made him glow. "I'm happy now."

Amira appeared with starters, naming each component. For a while they ate, only exchanging appreciative remarks about the food. Annie heard herself, with some astonishment, telling him about the dish she'd had last time, a dance class she might join and revisiting Dickens. As she talked between mouthfuls he smiled, nodding encouragingly. When she stopped, he reached one hand across the middle of the table, cupping it like a beggar.

Annie looked at it. "I can't give you an answer yet," she told him. But what exactly was the question?

"Just give me your hand, Annie. Let me hold it."

To have and to hold, she thought. *Until Lorelei do us part.* When it didn't seem remotely possible, he'd left her. In spite of their simultaneous orgasms twice a week, three times or even four, he'd been in love with someone else. But was this possible now, after everything? She lifted her hand from her thigh, reached across the square wooden platter and rested it in his. No stroking this time. He just held on and looked her in the eyes, as if he knew he'd used enough words. It was meant to be a promise.

She wanted to believe it.

Suddenly she rose and he released her hand. She told him she was going to the loo and, seeing Amira in the kitchen at the foot of the stairs, avoided a smile that might be sympathetic, a warning or just supportive, because it was too late now for anything but loving. Annie's legs weren't shaky and her balance was perfect. Her head was clear. Emerging from the toilet, she looked at her face in the mirror above the towel and found it oddly unchanged. Mature and professional – but flesh and blood, with just a suggestion on her cheeks of some kind of graph peaking inside, somewhere that might not be her soul but was hers all the same.

She'd have to hope that unnamed part of her would lead, because if she tried to remember she'd be lost. He wouldn't get the train.

She held on to the banister all the way downstairs, slowly, carefully, like a partygoer in heels. There was no one at their table but Amira was behind her.

"I think Arthur might be ignoring my health advice," she said, looking at the door where he was grinning and holding a bottle of red wine by the neck.

Chapter Eleven

Ethan woke early to sky that was vivid blue.

"Thank you," he said, at the window.

"I am me," he told the waves at Chale Bay, once known as the Bay of Death because sixty ships were lost there in almost the same number of years.

"I am free," he announced at St Catherine's Lighthouse, the whitest point on his route.

"We have today," he realised at Packaster Cove, where there were still phone boxes with directories, and his great-aunt's address ready and waiting for him.

Coralie woke excited because she counted just five days before the advent calendar started, and this year hers hid chocolate.

Leigh woke alone to work on the morning's presentation, glad she'd slipped out while Kyle was sleeping. He was as harmful as cigarettes and harder to quit, but she'd get through Christmas before she started looking for jobs.

Annie's alarm clock rang the traditional way, with a judder. Silencing it, she remembered the man beside her. Arthur swore loudly and rose briefly from the sheet.

"Sleep on if you like," she said. "I'm dropping into work to pick up some stuff I forgot. I'll leave you some spare keys to lock up."

She couldn't touch him now, though his back was uncovered and almost unblemished. The youngest part of him? She pulled the duvet over his shoulders.

"Thank you darling," he said sleepily, and rolled away.

Annie ran a bath. She smelt of him and wine and spices. It had been so long she had almost forgotten the other smell lingering between her legs. Who had likened it to marzipan? As the water steamed she listened for sounds of him stirring, and realised there was nothing he could say that she wanted to hear.

He wouldn't wake, but when he did, he'd have some hangover. He wouldn't rerun it like she could, on a third of the alcohol, a quarter. She doubted whether he even knew he'd come too soon, like a teenager, and left her crying. Annie locked the door before she stepped into the bath.

No time now. Stupid of her to leave those documents behind but it wasn't the first time she'd had to drop by on a Saturday and she couldn't see any alternative. It would save her trying to judge, if she stayed to greet him, exactly how to be.

The man she'd loved all her adult life was in love with her again, in her bed, and everything had changed. He wanted to make her happy. But when he'd been on top of her in the darkness, all dialogue ended, no longer linking fingers or holding each other eye to eye, she couldn't be sure he knew where he was and why. Or with which wife.

"Arthur," she'd whispered, as if he might have forgotten his own name too.

But he only grunted, and kept on, oblivious. *"I love you, Annie"* was all she needed him to say, the way he used to at moments like this, when he'd place his hand lightly on the side of her face. It would have been enough and more. That he left her behind didn't matter beyond the moment; after so many years, any sex was good, or satisfactory. And it wasn't the first time he'd been too drunk to bother with romance, but that was then, before the loss of him, of hope and self-esteem and the future she'd counted on.

Annie stepped into the steaming bathwater and watched her legs redden as she sat. She'd run it too hot, to be really clean. It felt sore now where he'd been; uncharted territory, more or less. Her skin pricked. A spot burned on her forehead. As the water drained, she rubbed herself dry as quickly as possible, before finding something to wear in the spare room wardrobe, to avoid disturbing him but also the need for words.

For a wordsmith of sorts he'd had so few in her bed not long ago.

"What do you love about me?" she'd asked – breathily, because he was shaking her body awake and every part of her felt wide open, even though her eyes were shut and she hoped his were too. And because this was heady now, reckless, extreme. She felt flooded, carried on a tide, and very possibly at sea.

"Everything," he gasped, and then there was no more to say.

Then, as he lay sleeping only seconds later, she'd turned towards him, curled and still, listing silently everything she'd loved, long ago. *Being on the same sofa. Hearing you whistle. Looking at the same painting in a gallery and guessing what you thought of it and what it triggered in you, because you were inside my mind. You were behind my eyes when we faced the world together. I loved the show-off with his air guitar.*

She loved the past, she told herself, not the present. But then she found it: the dip where his throat met his chest, just as it used to be. Soft, and senselessly vulnerable.

"Still here," she said, touching.

Why couldn't he have bought himself some chips at Leigh's, doused them in ketchup and watched movies on her enormous satellite TV? Or courted her with a walk by the canal, an exhibition at a gallery, or candlelight?

Six forty-nine a.m: a time he'd never welcomed. In the kitchen, she tiptoed, and found a cereal bar to eat in the car, even though she really didn't need to set off so early. Not that it was possible to beat the traffic, already starting to stack up at the first roundabout when their daughter's name appeared, in red letters on her dashboard.

"Oh, darling," she imagined. *"I'm so glad you called. I wanted to tell you I had sex with your father last night. Though he might not remember himself."* Why had she been talked into this kind of all-seeing surveillance that snatched away the convenient excuse, the necessary lie?

"Leigh?"

"Mum? You all right?"

It was one of those quick check questions that assumed the answer so Annie said, "Yes, O.K."

"Dad didn't answer the house phone last night, or his mobile. Did you see him?"

"Yes, he's fine. Good luck with the meeting. Is it important?"

"Yeah, of course it is!"

Annie heard her sigh in the pause. Irritation with her mother or something else? "Leigh? Is everything all right? I'm sure you'll be brilliant." No one would argue with her, surely, or dare to criticise.

"I'm in a bad situation, Mum. It's pathetic. I'd like to murder my boss but I think I must be in love with him. It's not much of an excuse. And he's a total shit."

"Oh, Leigh!"

It was shock she felt. Not at the story, but the telling. She felt the start of a tear and rubbed it away.

"Mum? You're supposed to offer motherly advice, you know? Words of wisdom? It'll all end in tears – that kind of thing."

"I'm sorry. It's just the timing." She was talking about bad traffic and ice on the roads, warning Leigh to take care when she interrupted.

"Look, forget it. I've got to go anyway. I suppose Dad's the one I should be asking about infidelity. I hope he's all right. I hope the flat's all right!!"

And am I all right, wondered Annie? It hadn't occurred to her daughter that she might not be. But how could Leigh, who hated Lorelei with such passion, possibly have become 'the other woman' compromising someone else's marriage?

"Call me later," she invited her. For more reasons than one, she decided she must concentrate on the traffic.

Ethan's hair was alive with wind by the time he reached the address he'd copied from the phone box. The surname made the search a lot easier. Any schoolkid called Yettimen must learn patience, day after day, but he remembered they'd been childless, these two. Maybe that was the point?

Ethan's skin felt tight and overheated in spite of the temperature lifting off the sea. He must look like a wild man who might have slept on the beach.

But the house he was looking at was newly-painted and bright white, with a dark blue door that would be arced by roses in summer. Not showy but boxy, it was a house for one. The tiny garden, which spiked with wild grass and lay still with pebbles, looked almost Japanese. But perhaps that was just the stripped-back emptiness of winter. He had no clear memory of the old house big enough for the family the Yettimens never had, even though they'd welcomed his own more than once when he was small. Like his mother before him.

Ethan hadn't thought beyond introductions. All morning he'd been talking and thinking words for sea and sky, birds and wind, paths and plants and insect life. And Crystel. He'd been feeling alone and exposed and stirred up to some silent form of full volume, as if everything inside him was as intense as it was unknown. He was and he would be. Understanding was all.

Just as he thought his great aunt might be out, or in a nursing home, the front door opened. The woman standing there was almost six foot and all angles. Her cheekbones were firm above sagging skin. Knucklebones lumped as her misshapen fingers held the door, and her legs had a blue-white seam down the middle of bare flesh. She looked like the survivor of another era. He couldn't imagine how long her basket of hair might be if she un-wove it.

"I'm Ethan A. Garrett," he said, "A for Alastair. Your great nephew." She didn't react. "If you're ..." He'd forgotten her name! The phone directory had said *Mr. T. Yettimen*.

"I am," she said. "You were five the last time you visited but your core's just the same."

"Right," he said. Her eyes were grey and went so deep he felt psychoanalysed. "Sorry to land on you without warning. I'm trying to find out more about my childhood, and you knew my mother before I came along. She stayed with you for whole summers."

"She did."

She swept him in with a long, vigorous arm, encouraged him to sit in a cane chair that seemed to be unravelling in places, and poured him something she called rhubarb wine. Ethan sipped. He had the feeling it might interfere with his balance. Producing his notebook, he sat forward on the edge of the chair, avoiding spikes.

"You're not a journalist?" she checked.

"No! I'm a poet. A searcher, really."

She sang a snatch of a song about needles and pins and laughed. "A pop group before your time. Before your mother's too but I taught her the words to go with the embroidery. It wasn't her greatest gift but I could only show her what I knew. What do you know, Ethan? What do you want to know?"

"Everything? Anything, whatever..." He drank. "This is good stuff!"

She nodded, turning her glass. "We walked a lot. She collected shells and arranged them in patterns. But mostly she was in the sea, living up to her name."

Ethan was puzzled. Catherine?

"Tom was the one for nicknames and rhymes. He called her Aquamarina, or the Water's Daughter. Even Sealia, spelt S E A L ..."

Smiling, she flapped some flippers and made a nasal sound that Ethan thought would scare a whole colony off whatever ice was left.

He chuckled, but remembered Daph's acute teenage embarrassment at anything he approved as wacky. Like this great aunt whose name he just couldn't recover. It struck Ethan that time wasn't just a thief and a cheat but a murderer too...

"Why didn't you come to the funeral?" he asked. "That's just a question, not an accusation."

"Tom was dying. I didn't invite you to his, my dear. Much too soon after hers. It wouldn't have been fair."

Ah, thought Ethan, Uncle Tom and Auntie Evelyn! Evelyn Yettimen had sidestepped his question but she looked him in the eyes.

"I thought you wanted to know about your mother as a child," she said, "not a corpse."

It didn't sound shocking the way she said it, with the last word slow and almost lilting.

"Yes."

"Not that she's a corpse anymore. She's an angel, fully fledged. Tom said so when she took flight." She lifted up her arms like wings, curving her hands at the tips. "That's our destiny, all of us, as long as we don't block out the light. Your mother lost sight of it for a while but it came back at the end, and now she's nothing but! Pure light!"

"Ah," he said.

The old skin was far from rosy and what he saw when she smiled was not a full complement of teeth, but she didn't look her age, which must be well into her eighties. Ethan thought she was entitled to let the dreams in. But he guessed his hard-headed mother outgrew shells and decided her Auntie Evelyn was bonkers.

"Your mother was a gift. She was a joy when she was small. She was!"

It sounded almost insistent, as if she read his doubt. Ethan nodded encouragingly as she continued.

"She made up sea songs and we all had to learn the choruses. She wrote secret messages in the sand for the birds to read from above, in bird language with brand new letters. Childhood is magical if you just leave it alone."

So his mother once had imagination. But he wasn't sure whether that was thrilling or very sad. He said he supposed the island was less interesting when his mum was a teenager. Evelyn nodded.

"Of course. Young people want what they want. Old people can't wait to get rid of it. Oh, the relief!" Her wide grin showed the gaps where the teeth should be. Daph would call her a batty old crone. "After your grandparents divorced," she continued, her tone slower and deeper, "your mum spent more time with us than she would have chosen and I think the island's charm wore thin for her. Not enough hip young men and nowhere hip to meet them. She went her own way."

"She cut off all contact?"

"Not quite." She paused and stood to look out of the window, as if the past rolled out with the sea. "She had no time for letters and we were no use on the phone. I like faces. You have a bright one."

"Thanks."

Suddenly she lifted a finger with an "Ah!" before disappearing. Ethan rose and crossed to the window, watching the wind drag clouds ragged across the glass. The water rocked as it roared slowly in. A dog chased a stick while its owner followed stiffly.

His great aunt returned with a cake tin, explaining that she'd made the flapjacks a while ago and they were quite hard for old teeth but Ethan might take his chances on one. Which he did, cheerfully.

"You didn't come over to the mainland? I don't remember you visiting." Ethan was sure he would. The wine was like medicine; he was getting used to it.

"We never had a car because Tom could see what they did to the earth long before people thought twice about carbon. Tom's health failed and across the water was too far. We had what we needed here."

"But she brought us to visit you when I was small."

"Twice." She quoted the months and years. "She loved it here. Love doesn't die unless you kill it and she never did that."

Seeing her tears, Ethan felt awkward. He pictured the Head's office and speccy Mole, a cartoon figure then, solid in black and warm with compassion. The Head beginning the speech, a very short one... He never seemed to like boys, as if they were a bitter aftertaste. "I'm afraid your mother has passed away." It made her sound light as a cloud, untouchable and impossible to hold back. But which euphemism was most cowardly, the biggest lie?

Ten years later Evelyn sat silently, her narrow shoulders firm, unshaken by her crying. Her cheeks were damp and a tear hung on the edge of her chin but when it fell he must have missed it. Watching wasn't easy and it was his mother she was mourning. If that was what she was doing.

"Forgive me," she said and blew her nose. "You'll love her too, when you get to know her. That can take time. But in the end there's more than enough of that, without the distractions."

He presumed she meant eternity. But even if that lay ahead, in some form nobody could even guess, why did he have to wait to die just to know his own mother? Ethan was starting to feel the kind of anger he'd been managing his whole life, but why? Because this old woman loved his mum more than he did, or because she'd understood some prototype of her he'd never seen? As if that would be her fault any more than it was his!

"You're howling at the moon, Ethan," she said. "I can hear you. It's all right. The moon can take it. I'm glad you came. You're going to play your part in the healing, I can see that."

"Healing," he echoed, as if he had no words of his own. He stared at the flapjack on the Art Deco plate.

"Past and future. I think they're safe in your hands."

She looked at hers and turned her wedding ring; then she clicked her finger straight. Ethan heard the bone snap back.

"You haven't... you haven't really told me what she was like."

She looked up at him, surprised. "I thought I had. Can't you picture her, out there, with the wind in her hair? If you listen you can hear her calling. *Evening! I saw your mermaid!* That's what she called me, Evening. It suits me better now." She smiled. "She had her storms, but plenty of blue skies. Plenty of theories, too, and not just about mermaids either. I wish I'd written them down in a notebook like yours." She looked at it. "I don't suppose you'd show me?"

"I don't..." he said, feeling precious. Or inadequate. "It's work in progress. I may be wasting my time."

She shook her head. "Impossible," she said. "That's you on those lines, and between them. Send me one when you're ready, if you are. I'm just being nosy. I'd like to get to know you too."

So Ethan talked, about his dad and Daph, school and going back to find it again, Sam and his unfinished thesis no longer in progress, and meeting a young mum on a train and not being able to forget her. And non-violent direct action to save the life of the earth and its children, like

Coralie. Evelyn listened without comment, nodding often, and assenting with a kind of hum that must make her creased lips tingle, like playing the comb and paper.

Maybe the sensations lingered longer than the constructs. So much was lost already and he didn't know how to find it again. He'd been there an hour and a half and his cheeks were warm now. She said he could stay as long as he liked but he needed time alone. Promising to keep in touch, he rose to be held in a long, loose hug and though she was his size and his build, she told him he was thin.

"You must feed your brain and soul."

Then she waved from the doorstep as he reached the small red gate. Ethan looked out to sea. Then he waved back.

"Hey, Evening!" he called. "I saw the mermaid!"

She smiled and nodded as he walked back towards the cliff path.

Chapter Twelve

Sitting on the bus, Crystel posted a photo on Facebook that she thought Ethan Garrett would like. In it she wore no make-up and her feet were bare. Lou had taken it when she found her in pyjamas at 19:34, and posted it round her own friends because she'd thought it was funny.

Then Crystel hoped Ethan wouldn't find it because you could see the shape of her loose breasts through the spotty fabric – even though there was *no way* the pyjamas were sexy, which was the whole reason Lou laughed and reached for her phone. Looking at the picture again, Crystel thought it was better of Coralie. Being 'twins' was her idea. She said, "You're nicer to cuddle with no buttons."

Crystel couldn't imagine what it would feel like to hug Ethan, but she had the feeling his mother should have done it more often. She glanced up and out of the window. Not far from Madam's stop now. *Madam Allright* was what Coralie had called her that morning, before Crystel had dropped her at Grandma's. If it was all a lesson not to judge too fast, Madam learned it first. Like how to get ahead in the world.

Crystel let herself in. The door opened on a mess of bags, clothes and shoes all over the hallway. In the spare bedroom the curtains were drawn, the bed hadn't been straightened or smoothed and the cover was at an angle. So Madam's dad was an old man with bad eyesight and worse habits. Two separated and in-turned socks left her sniffing her fingers. Worse than her little brother Denny after football.

She checked, calling, "Hello?" but the whole place was empty. In the kitchen she found a couple of brown-stained mugs and a milky bowl with cereal bits stuck to the sides. It was dark outside now, too dark for tourism. There were three wine bottles in the recycling bin, un-rinsed, with a bitter tang to breathe as she touched them. Madam's father was most likely a merchant banker who ate four-course lunches with different booze to wash down each one.

The envelope Madam had left for her was half-hidden under a newspaper, the heavy kind. There were toast crumbs all over it, scattering when she lifted the pages. *Crystel, sorry, I owe you ten pounds. Circs beyond my control as they say. Will pay next week. All a bit hectic at the mo with guests and last-minute trips for work. Don't take any cheek from Dad. He's a bit of a lothario* (crossed out) *a charmer (in his own eyes). L x*

Leopards and spots, thought Crystel. Madam was L with a kiss now but she obviously didn't expect the black cleaner to understand long words. Now Crystel had to remember to nag her for the extra money, and she hated that. It was demeaning. And she could spell that too.

She was bringing up a shine on the draining board, with an American talent show on Madam's flat little kitchen TV for company, when she turned to find a man with a wet umbrella. Twinkly eyes to prove Madam right, but too much belly and hair crying out for the chop.

"You must be Crystel," he said, reaching out a business-like hand. The rest of him looked more like an artist or an old pop star who didn't know how to stop.

"Mr..." Crystel paused as their hands met. Not Mr Madam or Mr Allright.

"Arthur Capaldi," he said, smiling. "I won't get in your way."

Crystel turned off the TV, told him not to worry and kept on scrubbing with cream cleaner while he boiled the kettle. He was sure she'd like a cuppa and she said that'd be nice if he was making one. Crystel liked his soft Scottish accent. Without really looking, she'd registered clothes that cost plenty but weren't cared for. Typical man, more interested in how she looked than what his own reflection might warn him. With no attempt to leave her to get on, he sat down and began chatting, just assuming she was paying attention. Which she was, up to a point. His subject was living in London with Madam's mum before Leigh was born, and how things had changed. Then he stopped.

"I'm being rude. Tell me about yourself, Crystel."

She didn't stop. For one thing, where to start? What did he really want to know?

"You're busy. Ignore me," he said instead.

"Sorry – it's just time," she muttered without looking up from the

121

draining board she was shining.

Sitting with the paper open, he flicked the pages over but the stories he found only triggered his own. He was the kind of man who thought everything linked back to him like a cue. Crystel kept working. No way he was going to give Madam the impression that she'd cut corners to be friendly. He wasn't as easy to screen out as TV but she didn't bother to pay much attention until she heard something that made her look up and say, "Huh?" when she meant, *"Pardon?"*

"Yes, I know, a bit of a shocker! Confessions of a foolish man! I've been in love with Leigh's mum through two more marriages. And last night I *think* I managed to make her believe me."

Crystel guessed that meant he'd got her into bed. She couldn't have looked convinced even though she turned her eyes back to the sink, because he said, "You don't believe me yourself?"

"I've got no opinion," said Crystel. "I don't know much about love."

"Ah," he said, "you're young, but you will,"

She thought he'd forgotten the tea so she turned it on to boil again. He took the hint but, stopping just as he was about to pour water onto the first teabag, added in a different voice, "Since we're talking love, shall we have a glass of wine instead?"

"Not for me," said Crystel, "thanks. Tea's fine. My love's mainly for my little girl. Safer that way."

"Wait till she's a teenager!" he grinned.

The next thing she knew he was placing a mug of tea beside her, spilling some but wiping it with a thumb. She could tell without watching him that he wanted the wine, even before she caught him looking at a bottle in the fridge when he returned the milk.

"I have to tell Leigh when she gets home," said Arthur Capaldi.

That he hadn't left her many bottles in her wine rack, thought Crystel.

"I hope she'll be pleased," he continued. "All kids want their parents to get back together, don't they?"

"I hope not," said Crystel.

He was blocking the worktop she needed to clean, first one end and then the other: looking for sugar, scattering brown grains where she'd just wiped and announcing that he didn't think he'd eaten 'all those very expensive cookies'. He picked up his mug, leaving a milky brown ring where it had been.

"Are we talking about the father of your little girl?"

"Not if I can help it, no." She cleared away his mess. "I don't mean to be rude, about you and Mrs Capaldi." She realised there were three of those. "The first," she said.

He laughed out loud. "I'll call her that! Mrs Capaldi the first! It makes her sound American and fat, with a cumulus cloud of sprayed hair! And those soft slacks with sharp creases!"

Crystel didn't laugh. It wasn't her job to decide whether it was funny, or tell him there were no slacks in the twenty-first century.

"I just didn't realise until the last few days," he said, all smiles. "I mean, I suspected. There was a voice now and then – but not the kind you share with your shrink. I suppose the love was dormant, and now..." He grinned and lifted both hands, including the one with tea wobbling around in it. "Ka-boom!"

Crystel wondered what he'd be like if he'd gone for the wine. Why was he telling her this anyway? Was it a rehearsal?

"You're sceptical," he said.

'About men?' she thought. Yeah. Including him. Returning to the fridge he poured himself a large glass of white wine.

"What about Leigh?" he asked, and drank. "She's seeing someone. What can you tell me?" He looked almost gleeful. She half-expected him to rub his hands.

"Nothing," she said. "She wouldn't be happy. And I don't know about her private life. Sorry."

"Worth a try," he said. "I'm the one who should be sorry. You've got a little girl to get home to and I'm holding you up."

She didn't deny it, although she was working extra-fast. His phone rang and he pulled it out of the back pocket of his jeans, muttering before he answered, "Mrs Capaldi the third."

Crystel began to move, to give him privacy, but he held out a hand and shook his head. She heard him say, on his way to the kitchen door, "Carole! How *are* you?" as if she'd just had an operation. Then it went very quiet as he wandered across to the lounge. If Wife 3 didn't know yet about Wife 1 being the one he loved all along, he didn't seem to be breaking the news. This Carole must be doing all the talking and there was something about the silence at his end that told Crystel it wasn't easy listening. Maybe it was money talk. Rich people fought a lot about money in celebrity divorces.

The oven needed a lot more work than usual. The Capaldi family might make a good story to tell Lou but she wouldn't like it if their dad was messing about like Madam's. He must be well into his fifties. If the lifts in a tower block were down he wouldn't make it far up the stairs before he needed the paramedics.

She heard him swear and realised he was heading back into the kitchen. But he wasn't angry or shouting. He had a sympathetic voice although his face didn't quite match it.

"All right, I'll get a train as soon as I can fling my stuff into a bag... Early as you like tomorrow, yeah... Bye." Still holding the phone, silenced now, he sighed. "She took the dog with her," he said, "ignoring the legal consensus on pets in custody battles and the importance of giving them a choice. But now she's off on a cruise and Janey's got an ear infection. Which means the kennels won't take her. Janey, that is – a Golden Labrador, dopey old girl." He paused. "And she wants a divorce so no problem there. But to cut to the chase I have to go back to Edinburgh so she can go to the Caribbean. And they talk about 50/50 splits."

Did he really expect her to comment? Crystel managed a kind of smile, but that was for the Caribbean, even though she missed Granddad George more.

"Sorry, Crystel," he said. "You're a good listener. And the soul of discretion, I suspect?" His smile faded and he sighed. Then he turned his back to her as he strolled towards the hallway again and tried to call someone else. No luck. Another try. A phone ringing faintly, and an answerphone he cut off. He was back. "I need to leave a note. You wouldn't know...?"

Crystel pointed with a rubber-gloved finger to the square notepad of sticky notes in one corner. He bent over the worktop and scribbled, then stuck the note down.

"It was nice to meet you, Crystel," he said. "I need to pack."

She noticed he took the wine glass with him. Five or ten minutes later he stood in the kitchen doorway, pretending that he hadn't been looking at her butt as she scoured the oven. She turned round, still crouching.

"Take care, then – and I don't mean with the breakables! All the best. There's a decent guy out there somewhere. When you find him, don't let dogs with ear infections get in your way!"

She heard him shut the front door hard and then remember the keys, which landed with a clunk and a jangle.

The News was on TV. She looked up at the screen as the presenter switched on her serious look. "What was that all about then?" she asked her, but all the suited woman had to say was stuff Crystel wouldn't want Coralie to understand.

She brought the empty wine glass back from his room and washed it. Then she moved on to the lounge, which was all shaken up. There was nothing she couldn't fix but it all took time. And she hoped Madam would find all the things Arthur Capaldi had left lying around the place after she'd only guessed at a place to shove them out of the way. Filling gaps on the glassy shelving, making sure there were no angles, she thought about Ethan, who wouldn't keep fat hardbacks by TV chefs and comedians. He'd read poetry and philosophy. The only book Madam kept with *History* in the title was about fashion, from wartime to Vivienne Westwood and Princess Kate's High Street look. Not a black woman to be seen until the last chapter.

Crystel vacuumed, polished and dusted until the lounge was its normal self, a space where no one would feel at home. She was wondering how much longer she'd have to stay when she was interrupted by noise in the hallway, a whole load of it: the sound of heels, jewellery tinkling and a few swear words. Best keep busy, Crystel thought. She dragged the vacuum cleaner into the hall, looking up to see Madam padding towards her in feet people still called *stockinged*. Her sealed lips were blood-red but her face looked whiter than usual. She slid a laptop case from her shoulder and let it rest against the wall.

"I thought you'd be finished," she said and looked at her watch. Before Crystel could object she put a hand to her forehead. Sure sign of stress. "Ignore me, Crystel, of course you're not. I'm home early." She looked into the lounge. "Have you seen my father?"

"He left a note," said Crystel. "He's left. I'll just do the hall carpet, yeah?"

"A note! I don't believe him! I was going to cook."

Crystel turned on the vacuum cleaner, but a moment later she swung round a corner to find Madam standing there, and pressed it off again.

"Do you want a cup of tea or something?" It sounded a bit like an accusation. Crystel hesitated. "Coffee? A glass of wine if my father hasn't cleared me out?"

"It's all right thanks. I want to get on, get home."

"Of course you do. You're better off without a man, Crystel. If they're not slobbing around your home they're trashing your life."

"Only if they get the chance," said Crystel. It was a reflex because she was picturing someone who would have done both if she'd let him. She wasn't sure Madam liked it.

"I'll let you get on then," she said, plenty of sharp edge. As if the cleaner was getting above herself.

"I had the same conversation with your dad... Mr Capaldi," Crystel told her as she walked away. Why say that? How stupid could she be? Now she'd be quizzed.

"He talked to you, then – but not me."

"Well, you weren't here. He left a note."

"I've read it. It's like a joke with no punch line."

Crystel assured her that she didn't know anything except that the dog was sick and there was a divorce to sort out. She had a feeling she really did know more than Madam about her own parents but it might be tactless to admit to it.

"You'd think he could get it right third time round, wouldn't you? I mean, I love him to pieces but then I like hopeless philanderers. Otherwise known as shits."

Crystel decided to ignore that. Madam sounded like Lou now she'd loosened her City bitch accent.

"That's my trouble," finished Leigh Capaldi, and laughed.

"There's a real joke," said Crystel, "an ancient one from Roman times or something. The patient says, 'Doctor, my arm hurts when I do this,' and lifts his arm and ..."

"I'm not really in the mood for jokes now, Crystel, sorry."

Crystel shrugged. "It's more than a joke." But it was spoiled now and maybe Madam wouldn't laugh anyway – not being one to take advice like: 'Then don't'. She'd headed off to make a call in her bedroom and shut the door.

Leigh Capaldi made Crystel feel lucky. 'Blessed', Granddad George would say. It was his favourite word. Something made her remember the rainbow clock and wonder whether Coralie would like it after all, as an extra surprise at Christmas.

The challenge that was Declan kept Annie busy. It might be Saturday, but at least with all of that, experience counted, shining a light on ways through. Glad of the solitude and the focus, she was in no hurry to leave.

It was nearly four by the time she turned on her phone as she crossed the hospital car park. Five texts: Art, Art, Art, Leigh, Leigh, Gillie! Telling herself Arthur's digital sweet nothings and innuendo could wait, she opened her old friend's first. *Hey Annie, I'm in London for a few days and was hoping to hook up over the weekend. Call me. The disco diva. X* Smiling but not sure how to respond, Annie wondered why, after thousands of empty Saturday nights Gillie could have filled, she'd waited until there was a man in her life again – albeit same man, old life – to complicate it.

Leigh next.

I've been leaving you voice mails. Dad has buggered off and I'm in a mess. Ah yes, darling, she thought, he's been with me. But where was he now?

Mum can you call me? I'm pissed off with Dad. He comes down to stay when I'm working and then clears off because of the dog. Dog? Janey? He'd gone back to Edinburgh?

Annie felt her mouth fall out of line and shape. Her intake of breath sounded sudden and sharp inside her. She read Arthur's messages in reverse order.

Lastly: *I'm hoping I told you I loved you. XXXX*

Second: *My memory of last night is a little fuzzy but I hope you can tell me I wooed you well. You're a whole lot more than I deserve but I intend to change that, if you'll have me. XXX*

The first: *So sorry to have to rush off. I will kick the dog when I see her but must try to avoid doing the same to Carole. Seriously, Annie, it was wonderful to see you. As if none of the rest of it ever happened. I'll call later. XXXX*

Annie found her car and stood beside it, as straight as she could, her breathing conscious. She unlocked and waited for a moment before stepping inside. All right, she told herself. All right. So he'd gone, but nothing was any worse. Not for her, anyway, although what was going on with Leigh she dreaded to find out.

Her hands on the steering wheel, she was about to start the engine when she decided to call Leigh first, then Gillie. Not Arthur, not yet, not now. Leigh didn't answer, which was something of a relief, so she tried Gillie.

"Annie! Say we can meet tonight!"

Had she always been so loud? Annie could hear a million cigarettes in her voice.

"Well, I don't know, Gillie. How are you?"

"Alone in London! Where are you, Annie? Name your Italian, Indian, Mexican, and I'll be there – especially if he's got a restaurant!"

"Well…" Annie hesitated. Gillie was very possibly the only person she knew she could tell, in painful detail, everything she'd been rerunning, in her body as well as her head. Just to hear the words and what they meant out loud.

"All right. Yes, O.K." She must lose the reluctance and sound fun again. "I know a good place in the West End. Can you get to Leicester Square? I'll leave the car here and jump on the tube. I could see you at the National Gallery exit by five?"

Gillie was whooping like a fan at a concert. Annie wondered whether she still loved Rod Stewart. She felt an edge of excitement, as if meeting a very old friend for dinner was like camping at a festival or hitchhiking through Europe. Not that she'd ever done either, but Gillie had. Gillie would have new stories and they wouldn't be about a four-by-four, a new sofa or endless paperwork – or the achievements of her children, because Gillie had none.

I'm sorry too that you've had to leave so suddenly. Would that echo for him like it did for her? *I'm meeting Gillie soon! She's in town and it'll be great to see her. Let's talk tomorrow evening. XX*

By then she might know what to say.

Chapter Thirteen

A text announced that Gillie had found a restaurant and was waiting with wine. The place was already crowded but Gillie had chosen a table right at the front by the window, framed and illuminated. She was wearing numerous shades of purple – sparkling around her neck and draping her body in spirals and swirls. Annie's smile felt big and free, not least because she vividly remembered her friend saying that in her 'gallery' shops this one colour was banned. "I have to tell the artists no purple. Public won't wear it." And Annie never did.

On Gillie it was like a power surge. She'd been size 16 the last time they met but there was much, much more of her now. Not that it made her less arresting – probably more. She was startling even in London, her short, spiked hair a deep wine-red.

Standing, flesh squeezed, she stumbled back with a laugh. Annie leaned to embrace her. She'd been the only English student in their year who never wore a bra to lectures although her breasts were, in Arthur's words, 'slaves to gravity'. Now, even with support, they'd almost reached her belly.

"Love the hair," Annie told her.

"Never too old to play! You're looking trim, Annie. Are you still a workaholic?"

Annie's answer was evasive but she could see the conclusion Gillie drew. In the absence of a life, she was guilty as charged. Even before a waiter had checked on a drinks order, Annie had begun internally the same old flashbacks they shared. They were memories that left everything else so thin and faded in between that it could all be covered by words like 'nothing', 'not much', 'too tired' and 'quiet now'. But she had to try. She'd never flunked a job interview yet.

After a pause to order – wine for Gillie but iced water for Annie, whose head was tight – she found herself rejoining her own work-dominated bio as seamlessly as a DVD on hold for a bathroom break. Gillie loosed her shoulders, sighed and shook her head. Annie stopped.

"Sorry. Enough. "

"No – no, you need to talk. We all do. If men did more of it they'd be a lot more bearable."

Annie could think of an exception. "But you've heard all this."

"You're telling it differently this time. As if you've let go at last."

Annie's lips parted. Of Arthur? Was that what Gillie meant? She shook her head. "That's so... odd, really. Is that how it seems?"

"You sound like you're putting it all in place, finally, back in the past where it belongs. About bloody time, but that's his fault, not yours." Gillie lifted her eyebrows and hands. "Uhuh, no defending the indefensible. I know he can't help being Leigh's father but in my opinion he's been yanking your strings unforgivably for the last quarter of a century and it should be a hanging offence. Anyway, enough about you!" She smiled, and sipped the wine as soon as it was delivered. "You're allowed to ask about my love life but you'll need some kind of chart."

She chuckled. That sound was more papery than it used to be.

Annie's ice chinked against her glass. The lemon slice on the side nudged her nose and splashed it.

"Behave," Gillie told her.

That used to be Annie's word in college days, usually spoken with a smile but occasionally a nervous one. Now she rolled her eyes.

"I take that back," said Gillie. "You've behaved all your life. Time to stop! But way too late for me to learn, of course."

Annie felt less than ready for all the men Gillie had found wanting. But Gillie had apparently heard more than enough about the one man Annie wanted herself. She sidestepped with some dull questions about her friend's trip and hotel. The restaurant was already busy, mainly with pre-theatre diners, and it crossed Annie's mind that even though she was less likely these days to climb on a table to silence the clientele with *R-E-S-P-E-C-T,* Gillie was better value than a musical.

A waiter took their food orders. After which, unprompted, Gillie began a story about a very bad artist who'd fallen in love with her. Annie was at first an avid audience, but found her concentration wavering as the words linked back to her own bed, with Arthur in it.

"I broke a kind of duck last night," she blurted, as Gillie paused to drink her wine.

"Duck? One of those long-necked wooden ones that won't stand up and look so cute you want to wring their necks?"

"No! A duck as in cricket." Annie grinned but she felt herself flushing too. "As in not scoring. Which is all rather laddish and I don't know why I'm resorting to such terminology anyway."

"Annie Capaldi, do you mean what I think you mean?!" Gillie slapped the tablecloth with one hand. "Tell me it's a toy boy!"

"I could tell you that," said Annie, "if that's what you want to hear. But no."

"A girl, then?" cried Gillie as the food arrived. She didn't even look at the waiter, who only a few minutes earlier had been in danger of a wink. Neither did she stop talking, while Annie smiled and thanked him. "I've often thought it takes a woman to really appreciate the female."

Annie picked up her cutlery.

"No boobs involved?" pursued Gillie.

"Not one." Annie had no idea, now, how to finish this. "However horrified you might be, I'd rather you didn't repeat this for everyone to hear." She waited – for some kind of promise?

Gillie's thick eyebrows were overacting while her smile hung on, uncertain. Her hand wound an invisible clock.

"Spit it out!" she hissed. "I'll just swallow so I don't do the same. Not good with tomato and olive oil."

"It was Arthur," muttered Annie, looking at the door, "last night." She wanted to call it exquisite, ecstatic, or even claim that it left her half-dead. She felt her lower lip trying to sag and lifted it as brightly as she could.

"Tell me you mean Ashe. Miller. Scargill?"

"I think at least two of those are dead."

Gillie turned her wine glass on the table. "But the one in question obviously isn't. In spite of all my curses."

"Gillie, please. I can't do this if you won't understand."

"I would if I could, Annie. I'm trying." Was she angry? "Maybe you can help me but I wonder if you understand it yourself."

Annie felt silenced, shamed. This was such a mistake. Why Gillie, whose solution to the problem that was Arthur had once involved blood, vultures and a heart plucked while still beating?

"All right," Annie told her now, pushing back her chair, "I'm going to the loo to give you time to think of something helpful to say."

"I'm being as helpful as I can be, Annie."

"I mean it."

"So do I."

As Annie rose, Gillie laid a warm, fleshy hand on hers and pressed, telling her the food would get cold. But without a word Annie broke away and, after several dead ends, found the Ladies, one surprising step down and smelling of pine disinfectant. Above the dusty fake flowers in a woman-shaped plastic vase, she looked in the mirror at her own face.

Anyone would think from her watery, pink-rimmed eyes that she was the one who'd gone three times over any reasonable limit last night.

Was she really a fool? Was this love that just wouldn't lie down and die with everything else, some kind of justification, enough? Tightening her muscles from the shoulders up, she attempted authority, aiming to see a professional woman with enough life experience behind her to reach her own decisions.

The door opened behind her and Gillie filled it.

"They're keeping the food warm. I need a fag but this is even more urgent. One shag doesn't mean you're committed. Forget the history. In relationships, the past means nothing unless it gives you reasons to get out. And I rest my case."

"Gillie, he's all I've ever wanted."

"No, he's all you've ever had."

Annie couldn't argue with that, even though she remembered Gillie telling her at university that she'd have *had* him herself if her best friend hadn't got there first.

"Come back and eat, Annie. And talk to me, and I promise to listen…"

"With an open mind."

"As long as you promise the same."

Annie nodded and followed her back to the restaurant. Gillie exhaled deeply as they sat down, but said nothing. Instead she watched the food returning, thanking the waiter with a quick smile that instantly disappeared without trace.

Annie sipped water. She wasn't really hungry. In the silence between them everyone else in the restaurant seemed animated.

132

"I wasn't planning to tell you this," said Gillie, "because the past is so over."

Annie's face felt stiff; her chest was a match. She prodded the pasta with the fork. "You did have him, didn't you?"

No answer. Now Gillie was frowning, her forehead creased. "Oh God, Annie, we're talking light years ago when I was skinny! But I think so…"

"You think so!"

"I can't remember every man I ever slept with!"

"Not any man, Gillie. My husband."

"Oh, if we ever actually did it, that was before you married him. Come on, Annie. The point is, *he* came on to me, whenever and wherever. I thought I had a memory, that we had very drunk sex one time, but I really don't know. Did you have a stomach bug on a party night? I'm sorry, Annie, maybe I need some song to bring it back. But it's not the detail that matters, is it? It's who he is."

Gillie placed a hand in the middle of the table as if to reach for her. Annie sat straight in the chair. This was the friend who knew before anyone that she loved him, LOVED him.

"Why are you even telling me this when it might be some kind of dream or muddle?"

"Because he tried. I know that much. He was still trying after Leigh was born."

Annie could see him now, at their first housewarming, telling Gillie how sexy she looked. "He's a flirt," she said. "It doesn't mean anything."

"Maybe not. No way of knowing. In the end I warned him: if he didn't back off, I'd tell you."

"Thanks a lot."

Annie's eyes burned as they studied her food. A stomach bug. There was a sick smell on the furry old pink blanket, near the hem. It was Gillie's twentieth birthday and she'd lain there in her tiny room, trying not to imagine them dancing, telling herself between retches not to be so insecure.

He'd always wanted to bed her best friend; that wasn't news. But grope her, whisper dirty nothings, where, when? It was all the same and so was he, always the same.

"Annie, think. You're my oldest friend and I don't deserve your contempt. That feels like transference to me."

Annie chewed. What did Gillie expect her to say?

"Look, you know I've always liked Artie. Who doesn't? He's fun, he's clever and he means well, which puts him in a league above most men. But he's not good enough for you."

"You're trying to protect me?" Annie hated how feeble she sounded, in spite of her anger, but she knew it was true.

"Don't forget I've already seen you decimated. Great sex is something, sure. If you could do the male thing, and use him for that, but you wouldn't know how...!"

So, had she remembered after all, in spite of the light years, the booze and all those men she claimed? Great sex with Art Capaldi; everyone remembered that! Annie wanted to deliver some line that made her strong, or at least affected dignity and control from her moral high ground. But she must be coming across like a curled-up animal that couldn't take another beating.

"Annie?" pursued Gillie. "You need to take a good look at the whole picture. Take him back if you must, but know what you're taking."

Annie looked up. That was too much. Who did she think she was?

"I know him, Gillie. I do."

Gillie remarked that the food was getting cold again and began to eat. Annie saw she expected to be forgiven. To withhold that forgiveness would be ridiculous, psychotic, but was she meant to bow to some kind of greater wisdom and deeper understanding? Was she supposed to be grateful?

The waiter stopped to ask, "Is everything all right with your food, ladies?"

"Great!" said Gillie and took a mouthful.

"Very nice, thank you," said Annie.

Ethan anticipated what his sister would say, and it was true. He *was* the only person in the UK still using a public phone box and if he hadn't been on the Isle of Wight, he might not have found one that functioned. He heard the exclamation marks at the end of everything she said, short as the sentences were.

"Work all right?"

"In the sense that I'm *at* work, yes. But maybe not for much longer if you keep me talking."

"Ah, O.K. Busy, then? I just rang because…"

"Oh God Ethan, is it Dad?"

He reassured her, even though he had no idea where in the world his father might be at this particular moment. "You know that material world Madonna sang about, Daph?"

"I should do."

"I'm leaving it – well, as much as anyone can. For air and grass and all that."

"You back on the weed, Ethan?"

"Not that kind of grass," he told her. "I'll write you a letter if you give me your address."

"A letter?"

"With handwriting. You can write back to me at Ferningstone. There's no spell check on pens but if you make phonetically plausible choices, I'll cope."

"Very funny."

She gave him her address. He had to tear off an empty corner from the directory and write small.

"I'd better go now, but you're all right, aren't you? Not having a breakdown or something?"

"Not me." *Just so-called civilisation.*

"O.K. I'll look forward to the letter." Pause. "Seriously… I think."

She didn't sound as if she was laughing at him. "It'd be really great if you did reply," he said.

"Yeah… don't hold your breath!"

I want to love you, Ethan thought. It was the one statement he knew he'd include, probably as an opening. He used to think it as a boarder, about her, about all of them, when he felt he loved words more. Sometimes, sitting in the Prep room with the thick blue writing paper his grandmother gave him every Christmas, he thought it would be easier to write to Keats and Dylan Thomas because they were possible to know, inside out. The poems let him in.

"Daph," he said, before she could put the phone down, "describe how you look, in context, your world."

She paused. Probably pulling a face, maybe looking around.

"You've seen New York in the movies, Ethan. They build it high. This is the fourteenth floor and the sky is blue right now, O.K.? There's the hum of technology. My hair is currently Midnight Black, bob,

135

asymmetrical. Hoop earrings a Maasai would die for. Do you still spend hours flaking dandruff around you like a snow globe?"

"No. Do you still kiss Justin Timberlake goodnight?"

"That's for me to know and you to find out." She laughed. "Gotta go, Ethan. Don't get any weirder, O.K.?"

"Don't count on it."

Ethan already knew some of the questions he'd ask her in the letter but he couldn't imagine the answers. Daph might not reply this time, but one day they'd find a connection because when the rest was peeled away, that was all that was left. After all, he'd made a connection with Crystel and Coralie in minutes, with fewer words. As soon as he got the chance, he'd message her and tell her where he'd be. No reason not to.

Annie stared a moment at the keys Gillie put on the table.

"I bet you never take a holiday. You're the boss, aren't you?"

"Well, not exactly…"

"The temperature won't be Mediterranean but you might get some sun down there. I'll call the locals I affectionately call *les grenouilles* and alert them. They'll invite you for drinks, supper."

"I'm quite happy with my own company," Annie told her, "and plenty of books."

"Then you'll go? If you want peace it's perfect. Proper darkness and no mobile reception half the time unless you hop on one leg in the corner by the pool. There's enough wine for a fortnight and basic store cupboard stuff. The nearest supermarket's a half hour's drive away."

Annie admitted that she did have two days early in November booked for Christmas shopping, even though she didn't intend to go anywhere near a mall with piped carols and inflatable Santas bobbing until time had almost run out. Just in the last forty-eight hours she'd entertained thoughts of going up to Edinburgh. But she didn't enjoy dogs at the best of times and much as she liked Carole, now their roles had both changed she wasn't sure she could handle a new kind of conversation with an inevitable subject.

"It sounds perfect."

"I'll get Guillaume to put the heating on. Say yes."

In any case, if she went to Arthur's, would she be staying as his lover? Because if that was a development he hadn't quite caught up with himself, she couldn't imagine how to fill him in. And even if she did jog his memory, was the bed big enough, with Gillie lying in between them whenever she closed her eyes?

She looked at her friend, leaning eagerly, longing for an answer. Another woman, another time. Only an idiot would let imagination get in the way. It was history, like Mark Garrett's tombs.

"Thank you, Gillie," she said, because it was generous. Not an adulterer's bouquet because Gillie felt no guilt for something she wasn't sure had happened. And that was fair enough, simply common sense. "I'll accept your kind offer."

"Fantastique, mon amie. Gillie to the rescue. It'll be just what you need – space, distance, perspective and the Pyrenees. Let him sober up, sort himself out and leave you alone."

"Mm."

"No wavering."

"No wavering. I'll book the ferry."

Coralie had a temperature. Crystel hated it, feeling the heat her small body seemed to have soaked up as she lay there, damp and restless.

"I feel bad," she murmured, but Crystel wasn't sure whether she was more than half-asleep.

She whispered, "It's all right, little one, it'll pass."

She wasn't sure Coralie heard. She moaned quietly, turned over and over again, front to back and then embryo-like on her side, facing away. As lightly as she could, Crystel stroked her neck with two fingers. As if she was calm, when really some panic dial inside her had spun round towards max and her head was full of doubt – about A and E, overreacting, whether to tell her mother, how she could sleep on the floor beside Coralie's bed just to be near.

Of course she'd be fine. Kids bounced back from illness, no trace. It was a bug and Michaela in her class was back at school after two days off, posing like a brat. If Coralie ever talked to *her* like that...! "Just you wait until she's a teenager," people said, but that seemed light years away right now. She looked so easy to hurt, as if she could break or be snuffed out in a moment.

"It'll pass," Crystel murmured, more for herself than Coralie. That was what Granddad George used to say. *All things must pass.* Where had she seen that? On Ethan A. Garrett's home page, dated years back. Now he thought the earth would pass, or the time of people on it. It was scary.

137

Life was too short anyway and Coralie would grow up soon whether she liked it or not.

Crystel wanted to take that heat and those germs away and fight off the bug for Coralie. She was tough. Never even caught a cold, skipped morning sickness.

Her little girl was sleeping now, without all that tossing about. Peaceful: that's what they always said about death. But it was hard to imagine giving up on life like her granddad did, as if it was time to let go. Crystel planned to hold on tightly and if it ever came to it, Coralie had better do the same.

She'd been here before. Kids got sick and recovered but mums took longer to shake off the shock. Crystel wasn't sure she ever felt fear at all before she had a child with a hot head and no appetite.

"Love you, baby," she said.

Ferningstone was further from the station than Ethan had thought and the darkness felt more complete. But then, he'd forgotten skies like this. No neon, or shop fronts lit up like a stage. The moonlight felt soft, thin as mist and cool. The stars that London did its best to overcall were unmissably white, their patterns clear and their old names making a new sense. Like ripe fruit they seemed plump as well as bright. Words crowded in after the feelings but none of them were right. None of them were big enough for this.

How could anyone forget a canopy that roofed the earth right around, always there whatever pointless bling got boasted below? People were crazy, blinded. This was truth. This was real. This was the breath of life and he opened his lungs to let it in.

Ethan liked to think he knew time the way a shepherd knew it, but he'd been wrong. Maybe it was too late already for a welcome that meant supper, and the camp fire might be smoking ash. Maybe there was a deadline for turning up without warning. If he ever found the place at all...

"Using a phone isn't surrender to materialism, Ethan," his father said, in answer to his talk of *waste* and *disassociation*. "It can get you from A to B. Or connect you with C."

No one was right or wrong all the time but Ethan wanted to believe he could make this journey without an on-screen route. It was only relearning. People used to trust their eyes and ears, the sun and stars, a compass, an animal sense of direction. Surely Cubs still did?

A hedge swelled dark on one side of the lane as it bent. He didn't even know what made it prickly as he stumbled backwards where the edge of the track dipped away. Over the top of it he guessed at a field, stretching flat and even, its darkness closer to charcoal than black. As he looked, contours edged faint, trees rising firmer out of the emptiness. Furiously winding his torch he located the green footpath sign a few steps ahead, and a kissing gate almost hidden by the ballooning hedge.

"You can't miss it," the guy on the email had said, but that was hours ago when the outlines were still sharp.

The other boys used to think the same about the ball on the football field, but Ethan could generally miss that. Were there any poets or composers with hat tricks behind them? Ethan doubted it. Failure and difference had made him a poet. Goal scorers kept their eyes on the net.

With a backpack fatter than he was and nearly as heavy, Ethan negotiated a way through the kissing gate. He thought of Sam, but only for a moment before her mouth became Crystel's. Revving up the torch he found a notice, *Ferningstone 200m*, painted on board and wrapped onto the gate with string. Loving the earth and all her inhabitants was the only way forward. The other kind of love made things small, kept people selfish. Well, the way ahead was clear now: commitment to something bigger and deeper.

It was hard, as he followed the stony footpath, to match the photos on the website with the space ahead. He heard sheep but it was impossible to place them – left or right, high or low. He'd adjust, all his senses would. He was there to learn. Only then would transformation be possible.

No barbed wire or sentries, no security cameras or dogs. Just silence, thick with the leftover smells of an open fire, spices and herbs. The grass around his ankles was damp but he felt the air warm around him. His torch defined tents and yurts, fencing, logs. People were sleeping. Somewhere not too far away he made out the thin silvery sound of water and pictured it fast and fresh over stones.

A beam of light targeted his feet and lifted slowly.

"Hey there," said a male voice.

"Hey. I'm Ethan. I've come from London." What did he call himself – not a recruit and not a follower either? "I'm a volunteer."

"London hours, eh?" Welsh, perhaps? "The city never sleeps?"

"I didn't mean to disturb anyone."

"No problem. There might be some food I can heat up if you're hungry."

"Thanks, but I'm all right. Tired. I have a sleeping bag. Water maybe?"

"Cheap to feed, eh?"

Inside the log cabin they had reached, electric light revealed his escort; a few years older than Ethan, in jeans, sweater and a knitted hat with ear flaps that might have come from the Andes.

"I'm Rhys," he said.

"Ethan."

"Cup of tea, Ethan?"

As he zipped himself into his sleeping bag half an hour later, Ethan wished he could tell his father it really was that easy, if you wanted it to be. If you made it so.

PART TWO

The End of November

Chapter One

Half-past four already. Annie had been back at work for over three weeks but she still felt out of sync. When people asked, "How was France?" she found it hard to explain.

How it felt, waking to silence broken only by the tree stirring outside her window. That time was expansive but light too. How different she'd been, for just a while, without routines. Gillie kept one clock in the place, for its old-fashioned bell of an alarm when there was a ferry to catch. Annie shut it in a drawer and judged whether to slip out of bed in the mornings not just by the colour of the light between the curtains but by which desire felt stronger: the longing for coffee or stillness.

In that strange bed, looking across the tiled floor to the shuttered French doors, she used to lie naked. Aware, as she hadn't been for decades, of her curves, the texture of her skin, the bones that remained detectable and the spread of hair the glamorous young ripped away with bikini wax, more than once she turned to the space in the double bed and imagined Arthur: his shape, his mouth parted in sleep, the warmth of his body.

But that was France. Home was pyjamas, cold sheets and emails to postpone a little longer.

"Have you called Dad?" Leigh asked the first time they met up on her return. "He's been texting for news of you every day. Was there really no signal? I couldn't deal with that. Didn't you feel cut off?"

"Yes," said Annie, "perfectly severed, without the blood."

"Mum, try to be normal. You're back to reality now. I'm worried about Dad. He's been acting really weird since he came down."

"In what way?"

The best Leigh could come up with was 'out of it', and 'all over the

141

place'. Annie tried to distract her with holiday photographs on her phone but she soon lost interest and passed it back with, "They're all views. Haven't you got any people?"

When Annie finally called Arthur he'd sounded so pleased to hear from her that the image of him beaming at the other end of the phone shook her composure.

"Now that I can hear your voice I'm missing you more than ever," he said. "But I can see your face, just as it was at your door."

But not on my pillow, thought Annie. Alcohol had swept that away and there was no drawer where he could find and restore it. He began to talk one lunchtime about Christmas and the two of them coming up to Edinburgh.

"Stay through Hogmanay. You know how much you always enjoyed the flavour. So much more full-bodied."

Annie regretted that. *"Life's not a vineyard, Arthur,"* she thought. Leigh might have told him so. "I'll talk to Leigh but she might have plans." With a boss ensconced in the bosom of his family, she feared their daughter might be less than festive company.

She told him she was sure Hilda would be going to her brother's this year. At least there she knew what to expect: soggy sprouts, a slobbery dog, daily church and a schedule of board games.

"Has old Greg got worse?" Arthur wanted to know.

"Oh, I'm sure we all have," she told him, "in every way."

There was a pause where she expected repartee, and some kind of score. "Don't, darling. Don't say that. You're not and I don't want to be. I hope it..."

"Bye now!" she said, and pretended some kind of urgent professional response was required. "Yes, I'm coming!" A funny way, she thought as she ended the call, to avoid the subject of sex! Annie had come back from France with one certainty. If Arthur ever entered her again, he would be sober enough to call her by name and the sentence structures of his foreplay would be levelled a robust 4A according to assessment criteria. Eye to eye, they would be connected. It would be love they made and if she wept, it would be with joy.

In a dozen phone calls, a whole tail of emails and countless text messages since her return, there had been no mention of what happened after supper at Amira's and although she had rehearsed the question, "You do remember?" there had been no cue, no link, no sideways reference she could use. What was clear, from the *darlings* and the *sweethearts* and the way he'd end with *Lots of love, then,* was that he seemed now to believe in some kind of understanding between them, something restored and established.

Work was so useful. But at weekends she was expected to be free. So at the café the next Sunday afternoon she'd looked at her phone, wondering whether she dared turned it off.

"I'm stalling," Annie told Amira. "I don't know what for, exactly."

"It will all become clear," said Amira, pouring her cardamom coffee and offering dates and pistachios as nibbles. "You'll see."

Was it something in her eyes that asked for help? Amira stood a moment, then sat down opposite and listened. Annie told her that according to Leigh, Janey the dog was still keeping the vet busy and trying her dad's patience. And that the divorce papers had been served, but Annie hadn't asked on what grounds. That apparently Carole was still on holiday but whether alone or with a male or female companion, Arthur never mentioned and according to Leigh, didn't seem to care.

And then without warning, an account of the bedroom scene that would surprise Arthur began to fracture over ginger tea. Somehow, as she worded it, it shocked Annie too. Amira laid a hand on hers.

"Leigh says marriage is such shit!" Annie told her, voice politely lowered. "But we're not even married."

Amira's husband appeared from the back and raised a friendly hand. Such a kind smile for Amira, who smiled back.

"Perhaps in your heart you always have been."

Annie nodded. Amira stood. "Aren't you angry, Annie?" The adjective was almost murmured. Gillie would have shouted it but there was still a challenge in Amira's eyes. "You're allowed anger. It can be mixed in with the love and the hurt. Didn't you feel it, just an edge of it, when you looked at him lying there, drunk?"

"Oh, please, I've exaggerated. I don't know. I can't..."

"I don't want to upset you. But it's disrespectful. You deserve better." Amira picked up the tray. "I'm sorry. I don't always scare off customers with agony aunt advice."

"Presumably they don't all blurt out stories of seduction after leaving your premises!"

It was a good recovery but the word was so wrong it felt like a worse mistake. Not a seduction at all. She was his for the taking and he took her. And Gillie had known better. Gillie hadn't really forgotten.

"I have no licence but I turned a blind eye," said Amira, jug of rice milk in hand. "I shouldn't have. I didn't want to cause trouble for you."

Of course, it was her religion. Why hadn't they thought? It was mortifying. "He shouldn't have put you in that position! I'm sorry, Amira. But he would have bought wine on the way home anyway so please don't feel at all responsible for... of course not!"

Maybe she really should be angry – with herself, for allowing it, all of it.

"I'm always here," Amira told her. "Well, in opening hours! I hope you forgive my bluntness. Anger can give us strength, when it's righteous. It can be pure."

Annie nodded. An elderly couple walked in for afternoon tea. While Amira was taking their orders she slipped out, leaving a ten pound note on the tablecloth.

Two more days had passed. Now it was nearly the end of another work day and she was glad of those, even though she sometimes felt too tired to go through the motions of breakfast, driving, corridors. And time, stretching ahead.

On the bus, Crystel looked at the website again. Ferningstone. It sounded like the kind of village where the cottages had thatched roofs, but Ethan called it a community. There was a film with music behind – peaceful at first but then it gathered energy. The woman on camera wore no make-up but lots of colours in her shirt. She had presence. With her long grey hair in plaits she looked like a writer, or an artist who made pots or quilts. Her voice was light but deep. Crystel had played her speech twice already. *A community working together for healing, for the survival of the planet and its species, for a future that is sustainable and fair...* Grace was her name, as if her mother had known from the start. White as you could be, but an Indian surname. Her eyes sucked you in.

While she kept on talking, there were shots of people cutting wood and cooking, trees with sunlight shining through, children picking fruit and a man kneading speckled bread. No one looked dirty exactly but Crystel didn't see any clothes she'd allow in her wardrobe. She liked her showers and her bed with everything matching. There was a young guy with long hair, same sort of age as Ethan, same kind eyes. An Asian man, older, his hands in the air as he talked over a camp fire – Mr

144

Dosanjh, maybe. A couple of kids weaving with bright colours, looking happy the way Coralie did with her crayons and modelling dough. Crystel thought the rainbow clock might have been made by a dreamer like these.

It was all right for people like Grace to talk about the earth as if global warming might put an end to it, but mothers couldn't believe in that. Crystel didn't want to hear about now being the time to act before it was too late. She was just about to stop the film when, in the silence the music left behind it, Grace Dosanjh finished, "But we have today."

Crystel's day was almost gone. The film ended. She went back to the website with links about day visits and week's courses. But she'd never camped in her life and she didn't fancy it with the weather the way it was. She'd never heard of a yurt but the word made her think of mud, dung and straw. Would they have electricity? No mention of shepherds or their huts but it was obvious Ethan would fit right in.

Only she wouldn't. What was she thinking? She was dreaming herself! Ethan A. Garrett was a dream but she was awake now. Real life might be tough but she had to get on with it. She didn't need distractions that got underneath and threw things in the air. It was all right for Ethan with exams behind him. He'd have a daddy with a wallet of credit cards. If he got tired of sheep's butts and wet feet he could walk back to a haircut, suits and a salary.

"Never waste time lamenting what's gone wrong. Just make it right."

In the video Grace Dosanjh had said that, or something like it. Crystel wasn't sure she'd ever lamented because it made her think of olden times and women weeping with a kind of gnawing music. But it reminded her of her Granddad George. She'd been pregnant with Coralie and never cried one tear about any of it until she'd met him at the station and felt his arms right around her. Lou thought abortion would make it right – along with revenge on Finn. But Granddad George only hugged her.

She knew the top of his head as it came up the escalator. Maybe she remembered him holding her up high so she could touch his curls before they greyed.

When he saw her through the commuters and tourists, waiting between the café and the newsagents, his smile didn't lament. Or judge either. He was still using the aftershave she used to call *sunshine smell.*

They didn't pretend she had no baby belly topping her skinny legs.

145

"How are you doing, sweetheart?" he asked her, looking right at it and back to her eyes.

They linked arms and walked as she told him she was fine, not sick, not tired, just scared and sorry and running out of time to decide. That was when he said about making it right.

And what was right meant Coralie. She knew that now, because no one could look at her tucking her teddy into his shoe box bed, or laughing at a butterfly that only let her catch up before it flew on, and *lament* her. But how could she know then, when no one could tell her? Same way Ethan knew he had to leave London. Something in the air she breathed as she felt the thinness of Granddad George's arm under his soft-worn sleeve. She could picture the old, light jacket with its droopy lines fading each year on a washing line in the sun.

He hadn't come to give her advice, only love. He trusted her and that helped her trust herself.

"I suppose you think you'll go to the top of some waiting list," said her dad, once her grandfather had flown back again, "and get your own place?" But that wasn't it.

Some things were right and wrong and some you could only feel a way through. Coralie made it right. But being her mother was enough to manage, and too much some days, when she was whiny and her eyes squeezed in. Then Crystel knew in no time she'd be breaking her heart. Like Lou, smoking at twelve, smelling of it, making their mother cry. But not her. Crystel had been the good girl with the school reports that earned her fivers, even a tenner once. It made Finn harder for them to bear, with his strut and the swearing he made sure they heard when she shhhed him.

"Suppose," her father said, his teeth almost meeting and the words scraping out, "the child turns out like him?" He was standing by the doorway as if to block it.

"She won't," she told him. How had she found the certainty? She'd trusted Coralie from before she was the size of a hamster, the way Granddad George trusted them both.

And now she'd have to trust people like Grace Dosanjh to save the planet while she saved her little girl from Finn and boys like him. And judging eyes. She'd seen plenty of those. She'd imagined Madam's would always be like that, resting on *the cleaner*. But when she gave her the clock, they were full of other things.

146

Ethan Garrett had no watch and no phone to keep track of it. But even if he'd be waking tomorrow to some kind of cockadoodledoo, that didn't mean he'd escaped time.

Crystel stepped off the bus. The pile of washing waiting for her at home would take hours and some stains hung around, slow to fade. Of course Ethan never bothered with ironing, wherever he was. She would probably have met up with him if he asked, if Coralie hadn't been so sick. But in a way, she wasn't sorry because the Tuesday messaging was something to look forward to, and face to face it might be weird like Lou said. Ideas were O.K. for Facebook but with his eyes on hers there might be nothing to say.

20:07. Leigh wasn't sure why she needed to know the time, given the emptiness of the evening ahead. But looking at her sleekly minimalist kitchen clock, she thought of her father: "Nicked from the control deck of the Starship Enterprise?" She was reminded of the clock that was its polar opposite: the rainbow one that might have been made by some tree-hugger, stoned. Well, Crystel's kid might like the colours.

Now she stared at her phone, wondering whether her father might call and, if not, whether she should be the one to make the effort. He was behaving like a kid himself. It seemed a long time since his sudden visit, and she wished he could have stayed long enough for the two of them to walk arm in arm the way they used to when she visited Edinburgh as a girl. Preferably without the gales. Not that she minded those in her spotty quilted coat and fleece-lined boots, with his big hands around her mittens.

In her one and only hour of counselling – never again – she'd come up with a theory about getting to know her father as a child. "Not chapter by chapter but visit by visit." And it was exciting because there was always more to know. Surprises every time! She could picture him now, greeting his Big Issue seller by name and asking about his wife, health and kids. A little thing that wouldn't save the world, but it explained why now, twenty years later, she knew 'Sid', the Ukranian with the patch not far from her office.

Leigh had never been into politics but she knew her father was a good-hearted Leftie who could spare time and money for people and causes. Or was, before he became a flaky old boozer obsessed with his own muddle.

But could she talk to him about Kyle? She knew he wasn't the kind of father to kid himself about his daughter. He didn't exactly see her as the model of virginal innocence in a sleazy world but he admired what he called her spirit. Whereas her mother, ridiculously virginal herself, winced at her swearing and any grammar that was less than tight. Leigh was sure she disapproved of her job, flat and heels, her cooking, viewing... And her reading – or lack of it. Had she ever given her credit for anything, even all those helpful tips on how to use basic technology?

The annoying thing about her mum was that she had no idea how clueless she was outside the little hospital school that was her universe. Even when she took herself off to France like that it was just to laze around on her own, with a list of long literary novels on her Kindle and no mobile reception. Leigh was a hundred percent sure her dad would have socialised every night and made a little French go a long way.

She decided to shut down her laptop and call him, sipping a glass of wine as she waited for him to answer.

"Come on, Dad," she muttered. "Don't be down the pub, not tonight. I want you. I need you."

Surely he didn't drink quite so much before Carole left? Was that why Carole left?

"Hello?"

He sounded old. Weedy. Miserable? "Dad? What's wrong?"

"Oh, nothing, darling. Good to hear you!" Change of gear. She could hear him smiling now. "I'm just a bit off-colour. Probably caught the lurgy from the dog. It'll be fleas next. She's far more trouble than a child."

Leigh didn't say so but he wouldn't know much about that. "Is Carole still on her cruise?"

"Oh yes! Apparently it lasts rather longer than Drake took to circumnavigate the globe in The Golden Hind."

Leigh wasn't going to admit that she knew nothing about that. She'd heard him crow over the ignorance of quiz show contestants about 'proper subjects' like politics and history.

"Dad, you know I've been seeing..."

"Darling, sorry, can I call you back in a minute?"

"All right." Was he visiting the loo, or did he need to fill his glass?

When she went to bed early an hour later, he still hadn't rung back and she'd be pretty pissed off if he woke her up.

Chapter Two

The morning frost had a dull gleam. Stepping outside, Ethan saw a sky that reminded him of smudged old newsprint, dirty and running. The grass around his hut was spiked. A robin landed on the hedge, rounded and bright enough for a Christmas card. Ethan's breath clouded out over the wagon steps. The cockerel that had woken him replayed its alarm call a few fields away near the farmhouse, but everything felt so still that Ethan thought he could be the only one, with two legs or four, who took any notice. He closed the door, took a cut of wood from the pile and stoked the stove into a streak of red life. Another day and a cold one. It must have a date and Christmas couldn't be too far away. He'd have to give an answer soon. How long now since his father's visit?

"Canvas?" he'd echoed. "For the roof? How can that be tough enough?"

His father seemed to think a knife could rip his ceiling open like a train seat.

"I'm more worried about aliens with lasers," Ethan told him.

In spite of a busy schedule of interviews about the new series, his father had insisted on seeing the place before it was finished, refusing to imagine how beautiful and simple it was going to be. And any time now he'd expect him to abandon it for a London hotel, with brandy, cream and party games.

The only trace of Christmas anywhere in Ethan's world was the cactus Caitlin had given him, budding creamy pink. It made him smile. Caitlin was a twenty-first century nymph but he didn't love her and he'd had to tell her so, in case she began to remove his clothes.

"That's all right," she'd said, that cold night when she helped him make up the drop-down bed for the first time. "I understand. Friendship is a stronger kind of love. Safer too."

As he cooked himself some porridge, Ethan looked out and found her walking across the field, her long dress clinging to her legs and her thick hair splayed behind her. She was holding something not much bigger than a cigarette packet. The porridge stuck to the pan the moment he looked away to wave. Caitlin was light on the steps but he felt the temperature plummet as she opened and closed the door.

"Post," she said, smiling. Her face looked freshly splashed with icy water.

"For me?"

"It came to the farm. Rick asked me to deliver."

Ethan had given his father the address under pressure, mumbling, "I'll be on the move. I can't say how long I'll be there."

He looked at the package and saw his dad's idea of a joke: *Left field, Stone Farm...*

"I've never had mail," said Caitlin. She wiped dust from her fair eyelashes and yawned.

Ethan opened it carefully because the jiffy bag could be useful sometime. A phone. He read the note aloud.

"Whatever you decide about Christmas, or any other day or week, please accept this. It's cheap and basic, no games or Internet, just a way to keep in touch. Call me. I've put the number on your Contacts list. I've paid in more than enough for a text a week till summer."

"He misses you," said Caitlin, sitting on the end of the rumpled bed.

"Yours miss you too," Ethan told her, but it sounded lame and her look meant he didn't know what he was talking about. "They must," he argued.

He'd seen a photo of the parents she called 'The Tories', who spent Christmases in their house in Switzerland.

"Do you want to call them?" he asked. "Test it? Show me how?"

"Maybe later."

He offered her porridge but she said she'd already had breakfast at the farm with the kids. Then she smiled her faint smile and left in a hurry to walk them to school.

"Why don't you accept their offer, Rick and Layla's?" he called after her. "Their spare room? It's not getting any warmer."

"I'm snug," she said.

Ethan closed the door. He'd been in 'her' log cabin in the woods long enough to know that was wishful thinking. It would make sense for the two of them to live together and generate more body heat. Ethan thought about it most days and when Rhys had asked him one night what was stopping him he'd said, "Poetry?" He pictured Crystel, the only person he knew – if he knew her at all – who called him a poet.

"I'm trying the mental search engine on that one," said Rhys, fingers on his crown, "but nothing's coming up. You're going to have to explain."

"It'd make practical sense," said Ethan. "Poetry doesn't. It has no use."

"Good job I'm a carpenter then," said Rhys.

Now Ethan picked up the phone before he remembered. Basic model, no Internet. Well, there was a Tuesday each week. At Ferningstone no one minded him signing in and messaging, always the same slot.

"But you've never met this girl?" Rhys had asked last time, when he caught him looking at her smile on Facebook.

"Only on the tube."

"What do you talk about?"

"Her life, mine."

If he could call her now, he would. Fingering the instructions booklet, he realised he couldn't read it, not with Crystel in his head.

In her messages she reported checking the Ferningstone website for photos and spotting him in one, chopping wood. She'd ordered a book by Grace Dosanjh from her library when she returned *The Gruffalo*. When he tried to describe his home on wheels, she Googled shepherd's huts and asked, *"What does bespoke mean?"* *"It means they're playhouses for rich grown-ups,"* he answered, *"and cost ten times more than my wagon. And never get pulled from one field to another by a clapped-out old banger that runs on vegetable oil."*

Just because she painted her nails and lived in a third floor flat in Tower Hamlets didn't mean she didn't understand. But he could tell Rhys thought she was a kind of fantasy – or he was hers.

"You're a romantic, Ethan," he said.

"And this isn't?"

He meant Ferningstone: equality, community, sustainability, hope. Stars at night.

"This is grit, Ethan," Rhys told him. "Survival, not romance."

151

Was that what Grace would say? She was spiritual, a soft-voiced speaker more genteel than any aristocrat but an activist too, with muddy, splintered hands and a heavy file on MI5 records. Ethan had been thinking a lot about contradictions, and the biggest of all: how to live with a commitment to saving human civilisation alongside fear that it was already too late.

His father thought he was dreaming and would wake up to reality one day when he needed a house made of bricks, a mortgage and a salary. For him, a phone was essential to any survival kit.

Ethan read the note again. So, it was all set up, as if he was an old man who didn't know a text from an email. He picked up the phone again and found *Dad* on the Contacts list (along with his sister; a very subtle hint) and sent a text: *Thanks Dad.* Tonight he'd go online at Ferningstone and ask Crystel for her number. Was it Tuesday?

He was half-way through his porridge when a ring tone sounded, standard and shockingly loud. In any café in the nearest town, every woman over forty would be reaching into her bag. It was the sound of the world he'd walked out on. This was only going to work if he kept the thing off.

"Hi, Dad. All right?"

"I'm fine. Are you warm enough? It's bitter today."

"Yeah, I'm good. The local gangs must be lulling me into a false sense of security before they jump on my roof with butcher's knives."

"Ha. All right. Good." Pause. "Ethan, about Christmas…"

"Yeah, when is that exactly?"

"You're joking, right?"

Ethan didn't answer. He was trying to attach numbers to short-term memories.

"Everyone's coming, your Uncle Johnny, most of your cousins…"

Ethan wasn't sure he'd know all his cousins if they advanced across the frosted field like a riot squad.

"Even Great Aunt Evelyn. She said you'd visited. She was always sweet on you."

Ethan couldn't imagine her in a smart hotel with a brandy glass. Why now, wondered Ethan. What was it for?

"Are you paying for all this, Dad?"

"Yes, like I paid for your hut."

"Thanks for that, again. Really. It's great. I can't see me living anywhere else."

"Well… we'll see. Things change; we change."

"The climate changes."

"Ah! One to you!"

Ethan's porridge was cooling fast. He spooned some in, waiting.

"It's for a reason," said his father. "In memoriam, if you like. Ten years tomorrow."

"Ah." Then Christmas was close. His mother had died on her way home from lunch-time shopping. Ethan was caught out now; he hadn't suspected and it felt like a kind of smack inside. In memoriam; had part of him sensed it all along, a kind of anniversary?

Without the right words – and apparently after a decade he still had none of those – it seemed best to let the silence lie undisturbed.

"She always wanted a big family Christmas but I didn't like the idea of her spending her whole time in the kitchen and…" *Stressing,* thought Ethan. She did hers way below the surface but when it pierced through, it was sharp. "People were always doing their own thing."

Big family funerals weren't quite the same, Ethan guessed. But no one made excuses to avoid the dead the way they avoided the living.

"Ethan? You there? Have you forgotten how to use a phone? It's a two way thing."

"Ah. Yeah, right."

"I want us all to remember in a way she'd approve."

"Mm. If she would… I mean, you'd know."

Ethan couldn't argue because he had no idea, really, what his mother would want. Apart from wall-to-wall Bee Gees. She might have been a crazy little girl when Evelyn allowed her to be, but she became a straight-down-the-middle, Marks and Spencer's mother with no deviations. With him around, anyway.

"No one wants to be forgotten, Ethan. We all lay the foundations for memory. I should know. But she didn't get much chance."

Ethan didn't think he'd need to be remembered. It would be enough to believe in life after him.

Now his dad was talking about his mum wanting the best for him. Subtext: not imagining this place or this hut, the dreadlocks, the opt-out. She'd made him do Saturday morning football for nearly a year until the coach had a quiet word about his heart not being in it, and when she read his first poem in the school magazine she asked, "Where did *that* come

153

from?", as if it was some mysterious bacterium that had invaded his gut.

"Your sister's flying back."

"We have to stop that," he said. He supposed these were love miles, but Daph (or Daffi, as she was on Facebook) didn't use the L word, except for fabric or shoes.

"Yes, all right, Ethan, but you only have to pour some vegetable oil in your car. Or get the train. I'll pay for a ticket. I want you there. It's not much to ask, after everything."

"Everything," he repeated. Did that mean death, or money wasted on his education?

Forgiveness is a violet breathing scent on the heel that crushed it. Was that it? Mark Twain anyway. God/Mother Earth was better at that than the people with their feet. He mustn't judge the living or the dead. The poetry was in the pity. Wilfred Owen knew it in the trenches and Grace Dosanjh lived it. The search was for understanding, no exceptions. There was no love without it.

"Christmas is a convention. It's about excess and waste." He almost said it. His father knew anyway; everyone did.

"Ethan? We can come together, can't we, for family's sake?"

There was a bigger family but his dad knew that too – with members in Egypt, Iran, Zimbabwe, Somalia. Members unborn and at risk.

"Thanks for calling, Dad. Thanks for the phone and everything. I'll see. You know, I'll think."

"I guess you have plenty of time for thinking."

"Yeah, that's a part of it."

"Daph sends her love."

"Yeah?" Ethan grinned. He wanted to send love back but he still didn't know his sister like he knew Rhys and Caitlin. Like he knew Crystel and Coralie! But was that really possible, or were they less of a poem and more of a fantasy?

"She's done the Christmas window for the flagship store. It's great. Lots of positive comments."

Didn't Americans know how to shop, with or without displays? It might be harder to get a few positive comments on reducing their carbon footprints. "O.K. I'll call you, Dad."

"All right." Pause. "Peace, brother."

Ethan could almost hear the smile. He was always the same joke.

"Namaste, Dad."

Grace Dosanjh could bear witness to the global community, with such gentle power that only governments and big business could resist. Yet he couldn't make his own father see. Perhaps he should read a poem over Christmas dinner, the kind that would stick in their heads like a festive number one from the Seventies. He remembered something Grace had said at Ferningstone the other night about hotels in the Maldives and the fake snow and plum pudding they'd be laying on for rich Westerners for as many Christmases as they had left. The lyrics attached themselves to a familiar tune in his head.

Are you wasting earth's resources having fun?
Are you jetting off for Christmas in the sun?
There's a Santa pulled by dolphins
To an island doomed to die
So the wealthy can eat turkey, booze and cry.
So here it is, Merry Christmas, shame the party's got to end.
There'll be no future while we frack, grab and pretend.

He sang the lyrics while he crouched by the stove with more wood, editing, forgetting and finally wishing he hadn't bothered.

"Scrooge," Daph would say. *"Lighten up and don't be a party-pooper."*

Too much disturbance already. Sometimes he wondered why more people didn't just live in bed, wrapped around with eyes shut. Ethan breathed slowly, arms lifted and then falling, imagining the sun's rays: energy from the core, life-giving.

"Peace, Ethan," he murmured. "Peace, Dad. Peace Daph. Peace Crystel."

His mother was all right. She'd got out in time.

Leigh noticed that Sid's place with the Big Issue had been taken by a younger guy who could have been a footballer. His smile as she handed over the coins made her feel attractive enough to be a WAG herself and as she walked away, she enjoyed an idea that he was watching her.

For God's sake, she muttered as she headed towards the office.

Leigh had already spent far too much time trying to find a venue for the Christmas party, at what was close to the last minute. Work was no fun anymore but although she'd composed a CV she hadn't been in this job long enough to make a move credible. She'd look difficult or over-ambitious. And the truth – that her boss dismissed and deleted her, except when he was dishing out cold, sarcastic one-liners at her expense – was not exactly tellable. The message he broadcast was that he wouldn't touch her for any money. But the hidden one, for her alone, was that she'd better not count on the kind of reference she'd need.

Arriving to all the usual greetings, she became aware that somehow she was seven minutes late. No time for meaningless chat. Since she had no intention of confiding in any of her colleagues, Leigh pretended her skin was inches thick and kept her eyes on the screen. But she wished she'd kept her mother in total darkness. It was humiliating. She looked cheap and stupid. And how could her mother, who'd lived like a nun since divorce, have any clue what it was like to obsess, bodily, over a man?

Kyle emerged from his office with the work experience girl.

"My son's so excited about Christmas," she heard him tell her. The girl looked up at him as if he was Bradley Cooper. "He's losing sleep already. He reckons Santa must start loading up the sleighs any time now."

Apparently they were buying little Dan a motorised ride-in car with lights and a horn. Assuming that history wouldn't repeat itself with A & E.

"I don't believe in spoiling kids at Christmas," Leigh muttered to Henry at the next desk.

"I don't believe in Christmas," said Henry, who was gay and had recently been left by his partner of two years. As well as looking greyer and more hung over every day, Henry had given up pastries for lunch, which Leigh thought was odd. Personally, since the sex had stopped she'd been fighting a craving for doughnuts and chips.

Kyle was showing the girl a cute toddler photo Leigh had never seen. How old was she – sixteen?

"Aw, so cute!" she cooed.

Leigh shuddered and wondered whether it showed. Henry lifted his eyebrows quickly and discreetly.

"Shall we run away together, Henry – to some corner of the earth where there's no tinsel and no Slade?"

"Good idea. Unless you mean North Korea. Our options may be limited."

Leigh had an idea that Henry's options might be double hers. "You're not bi, by any chance, Henry?"

156

"Sadly, no, sweet thing. You wouldn't be safe, I promise you."

"That's comforting." Why wasn't she the kind of woman who could pat a guy's hand even when he was gay? "Thanks."

Henry glanced at Kyle and back again. God, had they all worked it out in spite of Kyle's spin? Did the smokers mutter about it outside? Looking back at Henry, she realised he thought the Christmas escape was just a joke. Of course he'd be bound to have family to laze around with, but she didn't feel like Edinburgh without Carole, who was an amazing cook and always booked theatre tickets for Boxing Day.

And her mother was behaving as if someone had died but she didn't want to talk about it. Whenever Leigh asked what was wrong she shook herself into a deeply unconvincing smile, so Leigh had pointed out recently that she wasn't a two-year-old who could be fobbed off with bad acting. The response was a brisk, "I'm fine, really." Which made Leigh huff down the phone. That was when Annie countered with, "I know you're not fine either, darling, but sometimes we have to hold on to our secrets."

Leigh couldn't say that mothers and daughters weren't supposed to have those because she couldn't bear the alternative, whether it was a no-holes-barred emotional splurge or just too much information to be questioned on, advised about or even remembered too long.

"Any time, anything I can do," Kyle was telling the work experience girl.

"He's oozing," she murmured to Henry, thinking sex appeal.

But what was that exactly, and did she have it? Had her mother ever even wanted it? Her dad presumably had it at the time of the three weddings in his life but it was hard to see any trace in the podgy version. Especially now he'd become so boozy and annoying, like a teenager who thought a winning smile and a bunch of flowers compensated for everything else.

She was thinking about Kyle far too much, and sex, and the office party too. His wife would be there and if Francoise Hart was nice to her, she might actually be sick.

"Let's go out tonight and get rat-arsed," she whispered to Henry.

Kyle was heading their way. Eyes down, Henry already looked diligent. He never stopped, even when he was on Facebook. Leigh's hands spread above the keyboard as if she was thinking carefully about what key to hit next.

"Everything sorted for the party?" Kyle asked, accusingly. "Time's getting short. What's the hold-up?"

"No hold-ups whatsoever," she said, thinking of the black lacy pair she'd worn the first night, which squeezed her thighs but didn't need to stay in place for long.

"Good. Then you can let me have it all in writing by the end of the day."

She couldn't bring herself to answer.

"Sorry? I didn't hear you?"

"Silence is assent, in fact," she said.

"Not here," he said. "Five o'clock latest. Thank you, Leigh."

"No problem."

If Annie's month was being swallowed up by paperwork, this new Tuesday morning had been eaten alive. Arthur used to have a theory about Tuesdays: the most productive day of the week, or possibly, in his case, the only productive day, Monday being post-weekend and Thursday and Friday winding down for the next one. Apparently on Wednesdays he was too exhausted by Tuesday's efforts to repeat them. Such a macho pose, while women could and must admit to working hard if they wanted a fraction of the respect that men like Arthur simply accepted as their due. She should really have told him so, instead of smiling indulgently.

Annie's columns were filling with data. Was there a noun for what boxes achieved once every one was ticked?

After lunch at a computer screen she collected Sanamir, who told Annie in a discreet murmur that Emmy had moaned through the night.

"She must have been asleep," she added. "She keeps her mouth tight shut when she's awake."

Annie didn't see how any dream could be worse than Emmy's reality. Maybe if they could access them, they'd shed light on what happened, not just before the suicide attempt but since. Emmy was at physio now. Outside, the sun had broken out in a splash of blue sky and through the glass, Annie felt a surprise of warmth on one side of her face.

"Fresh air, Sana?" she asked.

"Yes please!" said Sanamir, rolling her wheels at once. Then she braked. "Shall we wait for Emmy?"

"She can join us when she's finished," said Annie. "If it isn't raining by then. You could do with a hood on that, buggy-style!"

"What about The Act of Supremacy?"

"A ruse to get a different woman in his bed!" cried Annie, turning the wheelchair.

"Is that all I need to know?" smiled Sanamir, looking enjoyably shocked.

"As a woman, yes – but for the examiners, maybe not. We'll discuss outside."

She picked up Sana's jacket and offered her a scarf from her own bag. Sana managed to wrap it around her own neck, the pain visible a moment before she smiled and declared herself ready. Annie glanced at the windows as they turned into the corridor, hoping they reached the exit before the sun made its own departure.

"Can I have a latte?" asked Sanamir as they approached the coffee shop.

"Afterwards," said Annie, "to warm us through."

She realised she wasn't wearing a coat herself. Arthur used to tell her off about that kind of recklessness, but it was a joke, because in every other way she was the careful one. With an eye on the sky, she didn't notice the newest receptionist at the far end of what staff called the Turbine Hall because of the alternative art works that lined its walls. Not until Sana pointed out that the exquisitely dressed young woman was trying to attract her attention and wobbling on her heels as she waved.

"Annie Capaldi?" she asked. "I just tried the schoolroom. Phone call for you. There's a number to call back urgently."

Annie looked at the piece of paper. An Edinburgh number.

"It's the Royal Infirmary," said the girl.

The girl swivelled off but Annie realised, with her hands on the wheelchair, that she wasn't moving any more than Sanamir.

"I'm sorry, Sana…" she began.

"I hope it's not bad news."

Annie pushed her back to the ward, fumbling for her phone at the same time. But when the screen appeared there was nothing. Then Zelda appeared to take Sanamir. Annie found her fingers unable to connect with the keys – to match the digits on the paper she didn't have enough hands to hold.

Too many rings. Then a voice, a real one. She identified herself and waited, until she was put through, finally, to someone who could tell her what she needed to know: "Mr Arthur Capaldi suffered a heart attack last night."

There were other words, like *critical* but also *stable*. And questions.

"No, his ex-wife. The first…"

She told them to check his mobile for Carole and Lorelei and said she'd tell his daughter, their daughter.

Then she went back to the ward to explain before she left. As she collected her coat and laptop she saw Sanamir wheelchair to wheelchair with Emmy, the darker face so anxiously sympathetic she wondered what her own was betraying. She told them both, apologetically, that she might be gone for a few days. The white face was blank as always.

"I hope he's all right," she heard from behind a moment later – a brand new voice, so husky it was almost thick. Yet some of the syllables were barely in place.

Annie turned, her mouth twitching into a smile that could crack into tears.

"Thank you, Emmy."

Chapter Three

Crystel had half an hour to start wrapping presents before she picked up Coralie, who was playing with her parents. She began with the rainbow clock because that was the hardest. Once she'd laid it on the paper she took a photo of it and uploaded it onto Facebook for Ethan to see, asking all her friends whether they'd ever come across anything like it. When she'd finished the taping, the shape that bulged awkwardly under the paper looked weirder than ever. There was no way Coralie could guess what was inside. But once she found out, would she only give her a puzzled, disappointed look that meant *why* as well as *what?*

It was Tuesday. Ethan Garrett would be checking for messages. The thing about only communicating once a week was that it almost felt *too* special. She wanted her news to be funny and interesting as well as properly spelt and punctuated. It was mostly about Coralie and the questions she asked, like, "Why do boys have a different smell?", "Does God love ants as much as ice cream?" and, "If I swallow a bead how long will it take to come out?" Even though she still remembered his voice, she had no idea how his laugh would sound.

Putting down the scissors, she looked at the Ferningstone website but found nothing new. Snow was forecast soon and that might not be romantic in a shepherd's hut.

Annie knew Arthur would be the first to sound off about the train fare but supersaver tickets booked weeks in advance were not applicable with heart attacks. Annie was just glad to be on her way, watching out of the window and wondering how long it would be before the light faded. Usually she read until York or Darlington and then kept watch for more spectacular views. Today she felt unable to focus as her own face, pale as a moon, merged with back gardens, sheds and greenhouses. An abandoned factory and a river edged with rocks made way for stumpy waste where trees had been. Trackside under grey sky, much of England looked sad, Larkinesque and drab, rusting or peeling between weeds and litter. But there were highlights to come. She just wasn't sure they'd feel the same this time.

Checking her phone, Annie told herself the hospital had her number. *Comfortable,* they said. That was the way Arthur liked things. Of course he wasn't going to die. Not his style at all.

She hated eavesdropping on calls in railway carriages but this time she'd be the annoying voice displaying her life to a captive audience. Where was that bit of paper with the guest house number? Even once she'd emptied the contents of her bag on the table, all she found was a Waitrose receipt. Sighing, she bundled everything back except the phone, and glanced apologetically at the smart, rather Blairite passenger opposite, feeling like the driver who jumps lanes with a raised hand.

"Leigh," she said, voice low. "I'm calling from the train. Your father's in hospital. He's had a bit of a heart attack, but they've assured me he's all right."

"What? A bit?! How can he be all right?"

"I've heard no news," said Annie, voice raised, looking apologetically around the carriage, "since they called me so there can't be any change."

"When? How long? Why didn't you call *me?*"

"You were working and I couldn't leave you a text. I didn't know a number to ring. But in any case I didn't want to panic you. I'll be there by seven thirty or eight."

"Visiting hours will be over!"

"Not in Intensive Care."

"I thought it wasn't serious! Now you're telling me he might die before I get there!"

"No, I'm not. Darling, please don't be hysterical. In any case, he's asleep. It makes no difference. Please don't worry. Really, they've assured me..."

"I'll book an early flight. God, Mum. I can't believe you didn't try harder. He's my dad!"

Annie sighed. The silence felt as if it must be audible to the young man opposite, who was turning to the back pages. In it Annie heard

162

something she'd always suspected. Their daughter loved her father more. There was nothing she could do with her daily communication, however concerned, supportive or informed, to change that fact. He had the charm she lacked. It was independent of his actions and it couldn't be learned or rationalised.

Slowly and quietly she repeated everything she knew, little as there was of it, about Arthur's medical condition, word for word. She felt Leigh's indignation subside. She seemed to have convinced her. Melodrama on hold.

"I can't understand why you're not flying," said Leigh, critical again.

Annie didn't think *"It's environmentally irresponsible"* would be well received given Leigh's carbon footprint. Besides, she must shrink her own more systematically before she pointed the finger. Best intentions, diet-style, weren't good enough.

"I like the train," she said, looking out. "Those are cart horses! They've got those ankle sock things." Now there were sheep amongst shaving-brush tussocks. Gorse, and red earth poking through grass like a scalp through hair. "I wouldn't want to miss Durham Cathedral."

"I'll let you enjoy it."

Was that barbed again? Sometimes it was hard to tell. "Leigh, this isn't anyone's fault," Annie told her, laying the calm as thickly as she could, to reassure. And to armour herself. "Call me when you arrive." She ended the call with a foolish, "Sleep well, love," and remembered hearing the way Leigh talked to Arthur: all smiles, banter, lightness. Art-like, in fact. Charming, even when rude.

Their daughter had wanted, once the teenage years began around ten, to live with her father. And the big step-sisters she adored, of course, even though they seemed to like her rather less once she could verbalise her demands with expletives and wreck their bedrooms. It was a campaign so relentless that in the end she'd had to tell Arthur, who claimed she'd be welcome.

"If she's serious, of course! Yes, why not? Only fair I guess. You know how good the girls are with her – they've got their mother's patience. But isn't it just a protest, a way of saying she *hates* you? She'd soon hate me a whole lot more. She'd be packing her bags inside a week."

Annie had never taken the h word as lightly as Arthur, even when living daily with the symptoms he rarely saw. By the time Leigh handed

163

the phone back to Annie a different deal had been done, involving longer summers, and she never explained how or why.

Arthur never did what didn't suit Arthur, but when she'd hinted as much to Leigh some years later, she'd been told *she* was the selfish one.

"Well maybe that's the human condition, Leigh," she'd said.

"Well maybe that's a useful excuse," was the reply. Leigh had been sixteen or so, vaguely Goth, her black hair smelling of smoke. She'd just refused to eat potatoes even though Annie listed some of the vitamins they contained, because she didn't want 'two fat females in one house'.

Out of the train window, wiry trees rose out of waterlogged ground where wind tugged at dark water. *Desolation,* thought Annie, and wondered at something similar on her face.

Ethan felt a nervous tightness in his chest and throat. Crystel had his number and he was walking back across the field to take the call alone, in his new home, on his new phone. How had this happened and why did it suddenly feel so big?

Leigh reported to Henry that her flight was booked. As he laid a hand on her shoulder, she felt the shakiness again. Daddy.

"Leave now. Just go. I'll clear it. Even bastards can't argue with heart attacks."

She shook her head. It wasn't serious. It really wasn't serious. So that, she told him, would be an overreaction. Besides, there was a project she needed to work on tonight. She'd set the alarm for an early start and would be in Edinburgh before coffee time.

"Go anyway," he said. "He won't know when your flight is."

"Good idea," she said, and kissed Henry's cheek as she rose from her desk, hurrying past her boss's suited back and pretending she hadn't heard her name as she headed for the lift.

The cathedral, when it came and went, was grey under a threatening pre-Christmas sky. Annie preferred the version her memory had stored. She found herself making eye contact over the top of a newspaper opposite, and remarking that they'd left the sun behind in London. The man, who was half her age, put minimal effort into his "Mm" and quarter-smile. Annie wondered how differently he'd respond to Leigh, and whether she'd delete him with unflinching cool.

New trees in tubes gathered along a bank. Didn't saplings manage for millennia without plastic? As a species, she thought, humans kidded themselves they could give Nature a protective hand when they were the weaklings, the ones with trouble standing tall, keeping healthy and maturing. Would Arthur be tubed too?

As lawns rolled out from conservatories, so repressed they might as well be fake, she heard the train as if for the first time. Not *whoo-hoo* or *shushti-coo* at all, but a rumble that changed chords as repetitively as Status Quo. Now they passed abandoned warehouses with security cameras trained on weeded car parks – so ghostly they reminded her of Spinalonga without the sun, or Arthur's hand in hers. But she must stay alert, because the climax couldn't be too far away now, and she wanted to enjoy it from every angle, for as many seconds as possible...

"Ah!"

She heard herself in the silence of the carriage but she didn't check whether anyone glanced upward or out. It was their loss, as they worked or played on their laptops, if they missed it. Even in light close to dusk, industrial without sun, the Angel of the North stirred her to a quivery smile.

"What's it like," she'd asked Leigh, after Art had taken her up close, "to be there under that wingspan?"

"All right," she'd said, aged twelve or thirteen.

When Annie said she was envious, Leigh had wanted to know why. "It's just a statue."

"Yes, but it's so full of meaning," she'd said, and wished the claim back when Leigh wanted to know, "Like what?"

Then her mumblings about history and hope were cut short with, "I don't believe in angels anyway."

Annie thought that faced with such twenty-first century lack of imagination, Pre-Raphaelite hair and soft feathers wouldn't cut it. Angels today needed deep roots, a wide reach and cast-iron strength. Aware that she never used to have these thoughts, she wondered what the man opposite would think of her if she voiced them.

Did Art believe in angels?

"I'm about to find out," he'd say. If he could speak. If his eyes were open.

Tower blocks heralded Newcastle. No one else seemed to find the bridge over the Tyne awe-inspiring, or strain to count the bridges old and new. No one looked at the seagulls swerving without formation, or the rubble and rubbish around the sign that promised MAJOR MIXED USE DEVELOPMENT. Prime office space gaped un-let. But the smart hotel angling out over twentieth century ruins was the kind Leigh would choose for her business trips.

Annie realised she must check with the guest house. She never had found that paper – and just for a moment, as she began to search again, she lost the name too. What was the use of the street view in her head, complete with crossing and bus stop, without words? The smiling faces of the Chinese couple who ran the place didn't help any more than the smell of coffee and croissants in the breakfast room.

Annie felt her eyes brim. She didn't used to be like this, her head so full of memories and meanderings that present-day facts fell out. Arthur might die in spite of all the assurances and she'd lied to him, without the words, because deciding not to love him was pointless, a joke. She might not have the kind of faith she could present in a Powerpoint but The Angel of the North meant close to everything all the same, like a hospital school, like love.

Maybe it was true. The alcohol was a side-issue. Everyone had bad habits to bring to a relationship by this point in their lives. He loved her too and all their long time apart was coming to an end.

At the end of the gravel path she could picture, the one they'd crunched hand in hand on their first holiday together, she recollected the name above the door at last. Repeating it internally, she sent Leigh a text asking her to find the number online.

Have booked you a single room, came back less than five minutes later, with the postcode and a name that wasn't right. *This place is a little three star too but it's an eight and a half minute walk from the hospital as opposed to an hour. Had you even looked at a map?*

Thank you. X No denial of helplessness, talk of overruling or jokes about some kind of premature Power of Attorney.

Of course Leigh was right about a more sensible option with no associations. Was it really possible, after all, that more than two decades later she remembered the dips in the mattress of that first double bed, along with the lilac sprig print and the extra satin pillows he'd used for a play fight that led to lovemaking?

Annie wasn't sure how but all through her life without it she had remembered sex somehow: a kind of composite, a highlights-only blend, touch but no smell. Just a dream-state feel with no rubber or mess, idealised like Hollywood – but from deep inside closed eyes and minus the music. All those years she had kept it, up to the meal at Amira's and something so... other. Now she had a new memory she wished she could set aside because it counted for less, in the end. It was nothing.

Love and sex: two words a single mother never used with an adult daughter. Hers, anyway. The train moved out of Newcastle. Not long now.

To Ethan, Crystel sounded different from inside his phone. Younger, friendlier. He'd been a stranger before and now, what was he?

"Hey, Crystel. It's Ethan."

"How are you doing out there in the woods? I mean, your field. Are you warm enough?"

He knew he couldn't ask what he'd asked his sister, but he imagined her just as she was on the tube: small and curvy, everything smooth and neat. He heard something jingle, perhaps around her wrist.

"Yeah, I'm cool. I mean, I'm warm. Cosy," he told her. "Snug as a bug in a rug. How's Coralie? No more viruses?"

"She's good, thanks. She remembers you."

"Once seen never forgotten." Ethan hated conversation that just filled space and went nowhere just because the other kind felt too urgent, too fast. He'd waited weeks to speak to her and now he might as well tell the truth.

"Come and visit," he said. "I can sort something out – somewhere for you both to sleep."

"When?"

"Whenever. It's special."

There was a pause. Was she working out what he meant by the pronoun? Not just Ferningstone, or his hut, or even the completeness of his silence or the darkness that had fallen around him now, broken by one candle on his table. She was special. Maybe this was special too, for all its hesitations. Did she feel it too? Was that why she waited, breath only?

"I believe you," she said. "I'd like to see it."

"You will?" He told himself not to push.

"Let me think."

"Sure. Great. Tell me about your day."

167

She told him, making him smile. There was a story of an employer she called Madam who used to be snotty but had flipped, apologised and kept trying to be her friend. She described a clock so clearly he could have drawn it; he told her he wished he'd made it.

"I think someone did. I mean, not in a factory. It's not... slick. GCSE maybe? But someone got a buzz out of it, like *I did that!* You can feel it when you touch it."

"I love that feeling."

"You get it when you've written something? A poem?"

"I've only got one theme left." Did she understand? Did he sound ridiculously tragic? But how could he or anyone with eyes to face the truth get past it? "That's not true. You know about Keats and beauty? It's all around me and I feel the joy of it, I do, a lot. It's out there now, but... " Ethan felt something gape or sink and he heard her anxiety. It wasn't fair. She had a child. "It's an earth worth healing. Not crying for. I'm not good on the phone." He sighed, and knew she'd hear. "I'm sorry."

"It's all right," she said. "I believe you. I just wish I didn't."

"I don't want to bring you down, Crystel, honest to God."

Suddenly Crystel thought of Granddad George. What reminded her? A kind of tone, a gentleness. Granddad George loved birds and watched them from his bed when he was sick, catching them with his long lens and getting her gran to stick the images up around the bedroom.

"You don't," she said, because she knew what she felt was a kind of happiness. It was light with surprise, like the voice on the phone. Love and sadness. Maybe you couldn't have one without the other. If you loved something, like Ethan loved the earth, you couldn't watch it die. She hadn't even been there to hold George's hand.

"Good. I'd hate that."

"Coralie loves living things." Crystel remembered her running after a butterfly that landed on corrugated iron the other day, but thought better of it and made for a bush she couldn't even name. She wished she had a perfect story she could give him, to put the picture into words. "I don't know. I'll have to see – about visiting."

"You could bring someone else," he said. "Your mum?"

Crystel laughed. "I couldn't," she said. "She likes her comfort. It's not that... I mean, it's not... "

"Too weird?"

"Only a bit. I'll call you next time. Soon."

The last word she said to him was, "Later", even though that annoyed her in American movies. Every second was later. And what had she meant to say? That she'd come, because there was nothing she'd like more.

Edinburgh was hard to recognise through darkness and rain. Perched on its crag, the castle Annie once found tame looked grimly Gothic, without its coloured chain of tourists. Passing cars splashed her legs as she pulled her small case behind her and tried to get her bearings.

A lifetime ago the two of them had set off on foot, with a lot more luggage but always connected. She'd managed the map too, somehow, because Arthur was proud of what he called his *dysmapsia*. Walks a mile and a half long were nothing to lovers on an adventure and a limited budget, but tonight she needed a taxi. Guest house first, to dump the case and get a key for later. Then the Infirmary.

Just because they'd liked the city as young marrieds, did he have to go and live there?

In the taxi she called Leigh. "I thought I'd let you know I'm here. It's raining…"

"I thought you'd have news of Dad."

"I will do soon. Try not to worry."

"I'll let you do that – be the one not to worry, I mean. He's had a heart attack, Mum!"

Annie considered claiming the kind of worry she concealed in the interests of functioning, or a greater familiarity with crises that enabled her to breathe more easily through the latest. But Leigh never took kindly to time's wisdom shared.

"Yes," she said, wondering why she felt this composure that evidently riled. Was it just a work skill transferred? Or because he was still too boyish, too full of colour and energy, for her to believe the threat? "I'll call you once I know what to say."

Annie looked up at the back of the taxi driver's head. He was Art's age, but balding. Arthur's hair was suddenly so real she could almost smell it, close on her pillow. She supposed a daughter's love was inevitably less complex than that of an ex-wife who should really have outgrown hers.

The risk seemed suddenly more plausible as the taxi splashed through the city. Would he be on machines, with cannulas, numbers, graphs? Would he know she was there?

At the guest house she checked in, used the en-suite bathroom and left her case unopened. Then she walked, struggling against a wind that made her umbrella useless, angling it to read the signs that directed her towards the infirmary. Under streetlights and headlights the rain was industrial black, as if the city was running with oil. Yet in the air it grew steadily finer, not so much soaking as anointing her hair and cheeks. She was alive. He felt no wind and no rain.

Once through the doors she stood a moment trying to process words in big print. Intensive Care: a euphemistic title for *In Danger* or *On the Edge*. How fit was he these days? Did he walk anywhere or had it always been Carole on the end of the dog lead while he watched the History Channel?

"Not for me," she'd said, last time she saw them both, when he'd poured himself a third or fourth glass of wine.

Carole covered her glass too and they both watched him fill his almost to the top.

"You know I like my pleasures," he said and Annie looked at Carole, not sure which wife he was addressing, or whether the 'you' was plural.

By the time she reached Intensive Care she'd had significant exercise herself. Was it her imagination, or did something in the anti-bacterial air feel different – less routine, more urgent? The silence lay thick, more sombre than tense, as if a seismologist would pinpoint tears breaking in all kinds of locations. Cracks in life's crust.

Perhaps she'd had it easy, because she'd never done this before, her dad having died in his sleep at eighty-one. She smiled, recalling Hilda's story that just a couple of hours beforehand he'd asked for a fourth crumpet at suppertime, with a topping of peanut butter and honey sprinkled with drinking chocolate. But now the deaths-in-waiting around her didn't feel quiet or comforting. Here, some of the relatives she passed were young and visibly stunned. A mother and daughter clung together, heads hung and mouths gaping, in a public embrace that was utterly private all the same.

Annie reran the words of the nurse on the phone, with their subtext in the tone that there'd be no need for sobbing. The Capaldis were the lucky ones here. Maybe a shock like this was what Arthur needed if the boy was going to grow up – the medical equivalent of his DDE in mock exams at eighteen. His mother called his AAB a few months later miraculous, but in Art's account it was simple: "Time to stop messing and get serious." She might have to tell him that time had come again.

There was a board behind the reception desk, smeared with pen rubbed away. No Capaldi, not even misspelt. The nurse checked her records, then asked an older woman who told her, barely turning, that he was on another ward.

"So that's good?" she asked, as the nurse, non-committal, began to give her directions she had no hope of recalling.

Thanking her, she felt a shaky smile forming as she walked. He must be making good progress. The care he needed was no longer intensive. He would be fine. She almost called Leigh but stopped. See him first, she told herself. Be sure.

In the lift a man with a stick leaned on a girl half his weight. A woman with thick black eye liner and lips that almost matched broke the silence with a cough full of mucus. The accents around Annie were different now but this felt more familiar. She might be off to work. It was only as she stepped into the ward that she realised people were leaving.

"Visiting's over now, I'm afraid," a nurse told her.

"I've come from London! Please, five minutes? I'm here to see Arthur Capaldi."

"I'm sorry. We can't make exceptions."

Annie only stood a moment, her chest rising and tightening, before she power-walked past, glancing in at the beds, ignoring the "Excuse me!" from behind. Arthur had his eyes closed and his hair swept back from his forehead. Screens blinked information she'd never had to understand.

"Arthur," she said, and he opened his eyes. Very nearly a wedding day smile.

"Give us five minutes," he told the nurse at her shoulder. "This is the love of my life."

Turning, Annie saw the nurse shake her head as she walked stiffly away.

"She doesn't believe you either," she said.

Arthur patted the bed for her to sit down. Briefly she touched the hand, avoiding the tape that held the needle in place. It felt cool, for someone who liked to call himself a hot-blooded male.

"Leigh's flying up in the morning," she told him.

"Sorry to scare you both."

"How do you feel?"

"Tired. I'm very tired. And under the influence of legal drugs. I may talk rubbish."

"You already have." She smiled. "Did I just miss Carole?"

"On a yacht with a toyboy."

More rubbish, she wondered? Although Carole would suit blue sea and beach parties. "But she knows?"

"She left me. She's no need to know."

"But you'll need... You won't skip out of here and pick up as if nothing happened, Art."

"Don't count on it. Gym here I come." That was both deliberate and off-kilter. "Broccoli and yogurt for breakfast."

His eyes looked old but they were smiling.

"About time," she said.

"You're staying in our hotel?"

So, some things he did remember. "No, it's miles away!"

"But you're here. That's all that matters." He brought his other hand across his chest to touch hers. Should it feel so cold? She pulled the cover up to his chin even though he said he was fine.

"Leigh booked me into a place just up the road. I'll be back tomorrow." She smiled, knowing it felt faint, tense. "Try to talk sense by then."

"You'd never have left me, would you, Annie?"

In a restaurant across wine glasses she might have said they'd never know. In any case, she was leaving now because the nurse was back and looking implacable. Annie tried to withdraw her hand as she rose but Arthur held onto it. She felt reassured by his grip.

"See you in the morning," she told him.

"I love you," he said, and let go.

"I love you too." She almost said it but he must, or should, have known all along. It occurred to her that for him her love been a constant like *The Archers,* endlessly and reassuringly available... if he'd bothered to tune in.

Waving, with a zipped-up kind of smile, she walked purposefully out of the ward, holding in her head the image she'd have to word for Leigh. It wouldn't satisfy. Tomorrow they would ask to see the consultant for some phrases as clues, medical labels Leigh could tap straight into her phone and research online before they reached the exit. But he must be all right. He was being himself, albeit circa 1980. And she was the only wife who knew or cared enough to be there. She was the love of his life!

The rain was light now. Annie shook her umbrella outside the hospital, her wet hand cold. There were dark spots on her tights and the skin on her face felt grey. Why wait all this time, until it was too late for relearning? How could two lives that had diverged be reconnected at will, without all the space between them getting in the way?

Crossing towards the guest house, she told herself she was three steps ahead, ten. He had one particular lyric on the brain, lodged and on repeat, but who said it wouldn't shift to make way for another line? What if Carole jumped ship or Lorelei flew over from California? What if he loosed his tenderest smile on a young nurse with no bullshit detector?

Maybe he needed a mother most of all, and she wasn't the best candidate for that position. She wouldn't ask Leigh for a reference.

The guesthouse room was too warm, or she was. So much waste built in to life these days. The perfect white towels, fluffy as new, were too good to use. Lying on the bed, she called Leigh, fielding questions she couldn't answer adequately.

"But he's not that overweight!" Leigh protested, somewhat inconsistently. "Just solid ..."

"You know he doesn't take care of himself."

"He quit smoking."

"Yes, after thirty years."

"You're saying he brought this heart attack on himself?"

"I'm not saying anything much at all, except that I've seen him and he was cheerful, and I'll find out more tomorrow."

They confirmed times. Leigh's room would be next-door to hers.

"Night, love," said Annie.

"Mum, Janey!"

"Janey?" Annie couldn't place anyone with that name.

"The dog! She'll be alone and pining!"

"I would have thought... the neighbours will have taken her in, Leigh, when the ambulance arrived."

"Well that thought might be good enough for you but I'm going to find out. Poor Janey..."

It was too much: an abandoned dog whining as she searched for

173

Daddy. Annie had to make Janey, doubtless thoroughly spoiled next-door, wait her turn. When she closed her eyes she was too tired to think back or ahead. Annie chose the distant past, or it chose her. Arthur dancing. Like a favourite DVD ready to be slotted in again.

Arthur with baby Leigh, whirled around in his arms as if the maternity ward was a ballroom, laughing out loud at her 'gormless' face and her squashed straggle of hair.

Arthur decorating their first flat, strumming an imaginary guitar with a paintbrush that dripped on the kitchen floor.

Arthur inside her. Not the remake but the original, looking dated now...

Then he was in the hospital bed, his skin dull and his eyes liquid, like Omar Sharif seeing Julie Christie from the bus. Lips crisped, skin cracking at one corner, breath less than sweet. Not so much a brand new memory as a dramatization, surely? Unlike Zhivago, he was not about to die.

Let me sleep, Art. She pictured her own hand smoothing back his hair. The dog would be all right, wouldn't she?

Chapter Four

Waking, Annie realised that her dreams had been unusually bizarre. Not that she had anyone who'd listen if she tried to convey the content. In Arthur's opinion, her dreams were a kind of break-out lunacy to compensate for impossibly good behaviour by day – a refusal to believe in her flaws and failures being one of his more endearing quirks. She knew he'd been there, in this latest one, at the centre as he generally was, and in a bed on wheels. But the rest was vaguely disturbing and certainly surreal. Hadn't she been watching him from the ceiling, as if the body she was 'out of' was his?

She was the first guest in the dining room for breakfast and kept her book and phone to hand, avoiding any eye contact beyond a smile and a "Good morning" as others appeared. Nothing from Leigh yet but she'd be in the air by now.

The coffee was so dark and strong Annie exceeded her daily allowance, thinking how jealous Arthur would be as she broke another warm roll in half. Then her dream butted back: Gillie and Arthur in bed, screwing, with nurses all around, about their business. But not a dream at all, just an imagining, one that had been waiting to catch her unawares. A big so-what, a nothing – but a ghost all the same, just as present now as memory.

Her ring tone sounded: the least intrusive option she could find but still embarrassing somehow. Why couldn't Leigh just text? The breakfast room was filling and it seemed unnecessary to broadcast their business to guests who'd just woken. But it wasn't Leigh. A number. At 8:48. No? She told herself to get a grip as she said, "Annie Capaldi?" so quietly the hotel dining room might have been a library. Or a crematorium.

There were complications. She might like to come to the Infirmary as soon as possible.

"What kind of complications?" she asked. As if she'd understand if they told her, as if it mattered anyway. Once the nurse began to explain that she couldn't go into detail she heard herself interrupting to agree: "Of course, I'm sorry. I'm on my way."

Crossing the room, weaving a path between tables, she had to focus on the door but she felt sympathy animate the guests who'd been sitting so muted and undefined. It was as if the toys had come to life at midnight.

"It's a wonderful hospital, love. They'll take good care of him there."

Of course the woman meant to be kind but the murmur of compassion smothered as thickly as a blanket. Only tragedy could create out of nothing such a community of care. These strangers thought Arthur was going to die.

As she walked she called Leigh, but no reply. She hesitated, a little breathless, at the bleep that invited her to begin a message. What was the point, anyway? She'd get there when she got there. Planes couldn't step up a gear, could they?

Thank God, she thought, (God are you there?) that she was staying so close by. God. God, again and again, with each step. Already she could see the building rising up ahead. She repeated the nurse's words in her head but they yielded nothing new. Any minute now she'd ask, listen and try to understand.

Once on the pavement she began to run, or trot, until she lacked the breath for anything but stopping and recomposing as she lost the time she'd gained. And now she felt as if everything needed smoothing back into place, not least her face, her voice... How blithe had she been!

Intensive Care seemed tightly quiet. Everyone else seemed to be in uniform with I.D. hanging around their necks. A young nurse was on the phone, making demands. No rush, yet all the walking had purpose. Many of the patients were hidden behind curtains, but she passed a few whose closest relatives might not have recognised them, so thickly were they wrapped, so invasive were their tubes. She could smell blood. Whatever it was mixed with, however chemical the sanitising scents, Annie could detect it. Of course. It was everywhere, drying, leaking, staunched and possibly plumbed in too.

176

"Yes?" asked a male nurse.

"Arthur Capaldi? You called me. I'm Annie Capaldi."

"This way please."

At the end of the bed she stopped, unsure. But it was him. His eyes were shut. Never had she seen his skin so discoloured, so ghoulish, as if he'd been made up with a kit from a fancy dress shop for Hallowe'en. But his mouth wasn't red. Dry, it looked bruised. Not that he was breathing for himself. One of the tubes did that. She wouldn't know where to touch, even if she had the chance as nurses attended, measured, checked. So many numbers, each heavy with meaning, spoken and noted.

A young bearded man put a clipboard back in its slot at the end of the bed and looked her in the eye.

"I'm Doctor Livesey," he said. "Your husband's heart ruptured around midnight. It's a relatively common complication after a heart attack – one in ten cases maybe – but unusual when a patient has been making such good progress."

"He was making jokes!" she cried, her voice shrill, wavering.

"Is that right?" His accent was pure Edinburgh. His hair and beard were the red she'd longed for as a girl.

"He's not in pain?"

"No, we're managing that now. I'll ask the surgeon to talk to you in more detail."

"Surgeon?" repeated Annie. "He's had heart surgery? A by-pass?"

"Yes, open-heart surgery. More complex in his case than a standard by-pass. He's only just back from theatre. Let's find you a chair."

A chair? Annie stared. It seemed ridiculous that amidst all the life-and-death activity, she should sit – useless, a mere spectator. Just a concession really, but in the way. What if the other two Mrs Capaldis turned up? They'd need a bench. Or a pew, because this must be when the praying started.

"No harm in talking to him," said a nurse while she stood awkwardly, waiting.

Annie edged alongside the bed, guessing where his arm lay covered. She rested one hand lightly above his elbow. His skin was liable to tan at the first blue sky. His hands were accompaniments, spreading, opening and closing, there to express something even without the guitar. This body, though no longer lithe, always had a kind of spring. It was life.

He'd always been full of it.

Without all the external support, would he be dead now? It was only her generation that had extra time on top of the match. But he was only just into the second half...

"Arthur," she said, quivering at once. "It's Annie."

Annie, the love of your life. But what had that been: a final moment of clarity or a first sign that he'd lost it?

"They're taking care of you, Art," she told him. "You rest."

At last, advice he'd take! She looked at her watch. Not long now before Leigh arrived. She was frittering away her chance to be alone with him, but what to say?

"I've always loved you, my darling."

She could almost hear him joking, looking around the ward: *"Who said that?"* Not her style. Not her vocabulary, not out loud. But his face held its steady, empty peace. Nothing moved that wasn't inanimate, attached to him, throbbing, feeding his veins.

If he was aware at all, in any way, of where he was and how, she must calm him.

"It's wonderful what they can do now," she said, brightly. "The consultant's going to talk to me soon."

Heart rupture. But a different kind from hers when he said, "There's no easy way to break this, Annie, and you know how much I care for you, but I've fallen in love. And I've fought it, but I can't anymore."

Apparently Lorelei hated him now. She'd proved rather good at fighting too, for money. But what about Carole, who hated no one – Lorelei excepted? Surely the most exotic locations had Internet connections now?

Annie told herself she was thinking too much when she should be talking. They always had so much to say over coffee, about plays and films, the latest insanities of the Minister for Education, National Trust gardens, social injustice, young people and their phones... Their mothers too, until his had died of a heart attack – very suddenly, after decades of vigorous walks with large dogs she had no hope of controlling. "She never felt a thing, the doctors said," he'd told Annie. "Like a bullet through the brain. Over. Best way to go."

"Don't go, darling." It was unaskable. He had no intention of leaving. But suppose he had felt the kind of pain that carried only one meaning? Suppose, as he lay there, some part of him – that soul that was

178

only his and must stay intact, whatever damage time inflicted on his body or mind – knew and understood? It was unimaginable. No wonder people tried to believe the soul lived on somehow, beyond this earth. *Eternal:* the most powerful word in the language.

One summer not long ago, when they'd done the city's National Gallery again, Arthur had called the Rodin kiss 'sexy as hell' but she'd found it outsize and simply too misleading. So when she'd mumbled something about the spirit as well as the flesh he'd asked, "You've got religion, Annie?"

She'd been rather teenaged, if she remembered rightly: shrugging, evasive. She didn't know what she'd *got* but it didn't let go. A mystery to be celebrated rather than denied. A sense of something bigger than the material world as well as herself. Otherness? Was that what people meant by God?

"Not enough sex?" he'd teased, because he really could do that, now and then. Lose the plot. Lose all grip on their narrative, or live the chapter as if he'd forgotten the book.

Sex and religion, heads and tails? She couldn't possibly comment, not out loud, not to anyone, least of all him and not in a public place. But she'd moved away from the sculpture without looking back. Holding her bag to her midriff, she'd pretended to look at paintings she didn't care about, while his words replayed on a loop. He liked to tease her. It used to make her laugh when they were married and he'd mimic a speech he thought fussy, or snobby, or just too serious.

Time was a trickster now. It felt as if the screen was held on pause.

"You'll be laughing soon," she told him.

What could be funny she had no idea, but she meant they'd bring him back to himself. Like paramedics, his humour could be dark; she used to think there was nothing, for him, too serious or sacred. Apparently ambulance crews used it for therapy, or a survival strategy, but she'd never understood *his* excuse. Annie didn't laugh enough – he'd said so and Leigh joined in the refrain, the pair of them defining her and leaving her helpless to disagree.

"Leigh's on her way," she said, wondering whether their daughter would be better at this. Because her love was less, or just simpler? "Even setting aside climate change – and God knows most people do – I don't know why anyone would fly. The train journey's such an education. It's like a degree in geography and economics, with some

179

social history thrown in, and that's without the plant life. And just being in a carriage with other people is like an anthropological study. London to Edinburgh: it could be a whole TV series."

By now he'd be excited, trying to cut in. She touched his hair; it felt sweaty. Settling herself, she took him through the journey frame by frame: random shots of topiary and trampolines; the relentless rattle of a lap top on a table. One enormous crow alone in a huge waste of field; extra-large bin liners making smooth black tubes of hay. A jagged half-and-half tree that looked, as the train approached it, dark and twisted enough for an art installation called *Entropy,* but then as she stared back sprouted improbable green. *"Annie, you're waxing lyrical,"* he'd say, and she wouldn't be sure whether he was making fun.

All right, what else? She'd never told him about meeting Mark Garrett, 'that archaeology Prof' from a real TV series he must have watched. Not that there was much of a story, even with the gauche son in need of a mother.

Then Leigh arrived, heels striking at a distance...

For a moment Annie thought she looked like a page in an upmarket clothing catalogue. But in spite of the flattering new coat – a beautiful cream garment nipped in at the waist and flaring as she strode in – she looked worn. Could she really have aged overnight? Her lipstick matched the burgundy velvet collar and cuffs, but she wouldn't want to be told that some of it was on her teeth.

"What happened?" she cried.

Annie stepped away from the bed and lowered her voice. "His heart ruptured so they rushed him into theatre. Don't panic, Leigh. We'll be able to see the surgeon soon."

"Christ! He's had open-heart surgery? Rupture? God!"

"The surgery was to save his life, Leigh. He's alive." She put a finger to her lips. "Try to stay calm."

Leigh breathed out and nodded. She accepted the delayed embrace Annie moved in for, but it was too brief for kisses on both cheeks, even one. She stood beside her father, a grimace on her face, eyes wide.

"Where's Carole?"

"On a cruise, apparently, remember, or perhaps a yacht, according to …"

"But they're calling her? She has to know. Why didn't you text me when they called you?"

"About Carole? I don't know anything..."

"About Dad! I thought he was going to be fine!"

"I didn't know until this morning, at breakfast..."

"You turned your phone off overnight?"

"Well, yes, I always do. My generation... I had no reason to expect..." This was too hard. Annie was imagining it now: the calls unanswered, the phone quiet and blank by her bed, the operating table, a blood-stained glove inside Arthur's chest. "Sweetheart, we have to stay positive, in case he can hear us."

Leigh looked disbelieving. Nonetheless she sat and took her father's hand, clasping it with her own, intent on his face. Then, straightening, she switched to breezy mode, authoritative. Annie watched as she became an adult practised in managing both people and situations.

"I'm here, Daddy. You're going to be out of here soon. Heart surgery's amazing these days – I saw a documentary the other week. I'll find the consultant now."

She stood again. "Excuse me!" she called, almost imperious even though she was addressing no one and everyone. She focused on a head that turned with a clipboard, reducing the distance between the two of them with a couple of purposeful steps. "I'm this patient's daughter. We need some information here."

"Please," added Annie.

"And you need to call his wife," said Leigh, "the current one. I can do it but I think it would be better coming from you. The right words make a big difference and currently we don't know what they are."

A female doctor approached, apologising, promising it wouldn't be long now.

"I hope not," Leigh said as Annie thanked her.

Leigh felt herself cringe at her mother's grateful half-smile. She supposed the worst was over now that they'd operated but that didn't make it easy seeing him like this. She began to stroke her father's hair back from his forehead, saying, "It's all right, Daddy," three times before she registered the words she'd spoken. All right? How? What did she know? Her father was lying there, out of it, and she was telling him something she only wanted to be true. So it could be a lie.

In Kyle's case those couldn't be avoided. She hadn't been open with her mother about anything that mattered for more than a decade but with her father it was different. He didn't judge.

"I'm in a mess, Dad," she could tell him, and he'd smile and say, *"Aren't we all?"* Except that he wasn't smiling. Looking round quickly, Leigh produced her breath freshener spray and did what she could when his lips parted.

"Leigh, you can't go spraying him!"

"It's only like toothpaste. He'd hate to know his breath was bad."

"His heart ruptured!"

"You keep saying that but what does it mean? You have no idea!"

"You're right," her mother told her quietly. Leigh stared back at her a moment because that was a first.

Her father looked like some kind of chrysalis of himself. It was unbearable imagining him dancing Gangnam Style at Christmas almost a year ago. But people came back from flat-lining all the time. Carole would know what to do and say. Carole was the kind of woman who made people feel better with a hug.

"My mother sucks the energy out of me," Leigh remembered telling Kyle after sex, because one of her texts had come through close to the climax.

"Must be a powerful woman," he said, kissing under her ear.

"But I'm constantly recharging," she boasted, and he took the hint.

A hundred times Leigh had seen the way, on TV hospital shows, they jolted patients back with high-voltage shots right through. She'd tell the consultant his job if he didn't know it.

"Good morning," said an Asian woman with piled-up black curls, enormous brown eyes and the thickest real lashes Leigh had ever seen. She held out a small hand. "Mrs Capaldi? Miss Capaldi? You wanted to see me. I'm Mr Capaldi's surgeon, Doctor Jaspal."

"The patient would certainly want to see *you*," blurted her mother, holding the doctor's hand too long. Appalled, Leigh could tell there was more to come. "Has anyone tried whispering in his ear that there's a beautiful woman on the ward and all he has to do is open his eyes?"

Leigh gave her mother a glare. "Mum!"

"I mean the way they get footballers and pop stars to visit kids," her mother continued. "He likes women, that's all. I apologise. I think we're in shock."

"Shall we go to the relatives' room where we can be more comfortable," said the doctor, "and talk more freely?"

In her mother's case Leigh thought that would hardly be possible.

She extended the glare as they followed the surgeon through Intensive Care. Remembering what the neighbours had told her about poor Janey, she felt a sudden need to cry.

PART THREE

December

Chapter One

Ethan watched as Coralie piled stones beside the stream, patterning them with twigs to make what she called a picture. Her red gloves had darkened with moisture and browned with dirt. In wellington boots and a quilted coat, with a flap-eared hat tied under her chin, she looked almost solid, untouched by the wind that skimmed across the water. Ethan hoped Crystel wasn't cold.

"Now for the jewels," announced Coralie, and crouching on her haunches, began to pick berries from the ground, some of which squashed at once into her woolly fingers.

Apparently the crow they'd heard earlier was the wicked Count Cawcaw and the robin was Princess Scarlett, who mustn't prick her fingers on any thorns. Ethan and Crystel exchanged smiles as she started her narrative, with a finger to her mouth to make sure the trees listened carefully.

Crystel side-stepped away and, following as if they were joined, Ethan took her hand. She smiled.

"She won't want to go home," she told him.

"Stay," he said.

"We've got today," said Crystel, "and most of tomorrow. That's a lot of minutes and each one feels like…" She didn't know how to finish, but looked up through the trees to the sky.

"A cloud?" he suggested, and grinned. "No, a rainbow?"

Crystel rolled her eyes. "If you want," she said, and smiled. "If your imagination's big enough."

"It is," he said, wishing. A rainbow would mean sin and forgiveness, sun and rain, beauty and happiness so brief it teased, disappeared in moments and promised to be back. They'd be back – if not at Christmas, soon. The trees and the water had drawn them in and claimed them too.

Remembering her face through firelight, splintered by sparks from the logs she'd helped to chop and stack, Ethan kissed her again. Her skin was cooler now but he could still smell the wood smoke in her hair.

"I'm in love with you," he whispered as Coralie started to sing a tune that sounded improvised.

"I know," she said, smiling.

Reaching up, she tucked his hair behind one ear and kissed his cheek. She knew that her answer sounded sad as well as happy, and that he'd hear it.

Coralie stopped, straightened up and ran at his legs crying, "Cherry picker!"

That was a request Ethan couldn't deny. He lifted her onto his shoulders, holding her by the ankles that hung down like a scarf.

"You might wish you never started that one," said Crystel. She looked up at her daughter. "Careful you don't knock the tops off the trees."

"I'm going to find the stars," said Coralie. "They're hiding and they're fast asleep."

Crystel had told him the two of them slept like logs in his bed. But Ethan hadn't. He'd lain awake, stirred by her closeness a few hundred metres across the darkness and the picture in his mind of her full lips apart.

"I've been different since we met you," she said. "I see things I passed by." She smiled. "I was asleep like those stars."

"Wake up, stars, it's nearly Christmas!" cried Coralie. "You have to show Santa the way."

Crystel had already explained that she couldn't abandon her family at Christmas and she thought he understood, but it was different for him. Now that he'd found his peace here, away from the tinsel and the jingle of the tills, it would be hard to leave it behind. Especially for four-course meals in a five star hotel. But another year would follow and one way or another they'd begin it together. If they could.

They walked back towards the hut. Crystel had no idea how she'd explain it to anyone back home, even with photos.

"The sky is white as your face, Ethan A!" announced Coralie.

Maybe if it snowed, thought Ethan, they'd have to stay.

Leigh stopped on her way to the restaurant because Sid the Ukrainian was back, working his old patch. He looked shivery as he stood outside the pharmacy.

"Hey, Sid. Horrible day," she said, fumbling in her purse with fingers that felt stiff. Not enough. "Haven't seen you for ages."

"Sick," he said, and he looked it too. "You well, Miss?"

"Fine," she said, and took out a twenty pound note. And another. "How many magazines would this buy? Then you can get home, out of this wind."

Sid pushed his bag towards her and she took a pile. Not quite all of them. She could put them in the Secret Santa sack, one each. For now, she bent and stuffed them in her handbag, hurrying off with his thanks following her. It was Christmas after all. She hoped they were ready at the Taj Mahal.

Leigh was well aware of the grumbles about the day and the venue. But it had been quite effective fun telling the whole team that with her father bedridden in Edinburgh, she didn't *give a monkey's fart* about any Christmas party.

Even so, she wasn't going to let anyone else mess up the decorations, or take the credit either. And she'd rather be out of the office struggling with plastic holly and tasteless plastic Santas than at her desk with her mind on the loose. The room above the Indian restaurant was already overseen by Ganesh and Krishna, the walls were a flocky robin-red and a small silver tree stood heavily stacked with baubles to one side of the coat stand. Leigh had just bought a bagful of tacky bits and festive bobs and managed to find some mistletoe against her better judgement.

When she'd finished she would have done her bit so no one could blame her for skulking off early, before the space at the far end was used for dancing and things got as *messy* as people seemed to hope. Henry, who'd compiled the music, swore there was nothing smoochy to license groping. He'd promised to drop by after work in case Kyle did the same, like a site foreman checking up on the workers.

Hearing a text arrive, Leigh raised her eyebrows at the name Carole Capaldi. So she was finally back: *Hope you are O.K. Sorry to be out of touch. I hear your dad is making progress. Speak soon. XX*

"No thanks to you," muttered Leigh.

She could call her own mother but it was hard to know what to say.

186

Her dad might be sleeping or dopey, or worse still, a bit wild. As things stood, the Bali room was still booked for her and Henry, 23rd to 30th, at an overblown price with orang-utans built in and no refund. Now there was even more reason to escape, with an ocean separating her from her own family and Kyle's. She would visit her father for New Year, when it was no longer compulsory to eat mince pies at any hour of the day. That'd be fun, with him off the booze, especially as Carole would no longer see it as her job to book a show. On Facebook the fortyish toy boy looked sporty, a much better deal than her dad.

Wishing Henry had sent his music ahead of him, Leigh focused on sticking, hanging and draping, taking off her heels to climb on dining chairs with tinsel. Might be best to go OTT and make random and bizarre look like some kind of an ironic statement.

At the swish of the door she looked up, expecting the manager, but it was a different kind of boss.

"Just checking on the state of play," he said, with less than a smile.

"Feel free, Mr Hart." she said, as if she couldn't care less what he did, and kept her back to him. So the stroke of her buttocks was a surprise that made her jump, secretly. Her shoulders tightened but she didn't turn.

"You've got flair," he said. "But then I knew that."

Hearing him take a step away, she looked down on his gleaming gelled head and smelt his aftershave. He was looking around the room now, appraising her efforts. Quickly she returned to her task as if he wasn't there, filling the silence with snatches of *Winter Wonderland* as a hum. When he said something about 'an excess of foliage' she ignored it. If he touched her again, she might have to wrap the tinsel round his throat and tie it tight!

"It's time to hold out an olive branch," he said, looking up at her, "if you won't come near the mistletoe."

"Hold what you like," she said quietly, as if her mind was elsewhere. "Mind the holly, though. It's got a nasty prick."

That was one to tell her dad if he had the strength to slap his thigh. But Kyle was grinning as if this was foreplay. She could scream and accuse him of assault, of sexual harassment, and however much she lied he'd still be guilty.

"Come down," he said.

She began to sing as if she hadn't heard him. With a sudden

movement he grabbed a chair leg. Tilted, Leigh screamed.

"I've got your attention now," he said, holding out a hand in mock chivalry.

Leigh pushed at his chest. Then they both heard footsteps bounding up the stairs and a cry of, "It's the cavalry!" Pause. "With crackers!"

Henry was flushed, in a scarlet pom-pom hat with white Santa beard attached. From his gloved hand he swung a large plastic bag that showed the corner of a gold cardboard box. He looked cheerfully from Leigh to Kyle.

"Everything under control, boss?" he asked.

"Very promising," said Kyle, briskly. "I'll leave you both to it and see you later."

As he clipped down the stairs in the shoes Leigh once removed for him, Henry gave her an anxious glance and mouthed, "Are you OK?"

Leigh didn't so much shake her head as rattle it.

"Come here, you," said Henry, and held her.

It must be Christmas. Even without a drink, or any audible verse of *In The Bleak Midwinter* on the air, she felt like crying and that made her swear instead.

Running a finger along Arthur's mantelpiece, Annie collected more dust than she'd imagined. Some of it came from a younger Carole, framed in holiday mode with sunburned shoulders, smiling brightly between an empty vase and a Get Well card. She'd be appalled by such poor housekeeping. But then it wasn't her house anymore.

"Annie!"

So he was awake again. His sleeps were getting shorter. The cry was almost boisterous now and Annie much preferred it to the weak, apologetic version with a hairline crack in it. It was the sound of the Art Capaldi she knew.

She hurried up to the master bedroom and found a reminder that the body hadn't caught up with the voice. With weight lost from his cheeks and chin, his face had the looseness of a baggy jumper. Sometimes she thought even his eyes had aged, and Leigh would probably suggest those brows needed plucking. His hair cried out for a cut, so loudly Leigh might hear it in London, but he wasn't listening.

"I dreamed I was at Mandela's funeral."

Annie didn't ask whether he was remembering the Outspan boycott at university. She replayed the image: Art Capaldi, chair of the Anti-Apartheid Soc., with the juice from a dozen oranges trickling down and matting his hair, pips sticking. Her image, not his, because she only watched. Not her style.

She told him about the Soweto choir paying tribute to the great man in the supermarket, a film she'd watched three times on YouTube now. But he interrupted.

"I can't. I'll blubber. And I miss that dopey dog too," he said. "She really died while I was under the knife? God, that's loyalty for you!"

Annie saw that for Janey he really might cry. But then he looked around the room. "What's the time?"

Always the first question when he woke, but she didn't understand why. His watch had stopped in hospital so she'd bought a new one for Christmas, very much like one she'd chosen for him soon after they met. Perhaps she should present it early. Why wait?

"Eleven twenty-eight," she said. "Thursday. Don't ask me how many shopping days till Christmas. Are you hungry?"

"Not for salad," he said. "Anyone sent me a hamper with Stilton yet?"

"Don't wind me up, Arthur Capaldi. You know that'd clog your arteries. And scare off the housekeeper the first time she opened the fridge."

"Don't call yourself that," he said, softly, reaching out his hand. "You know you're more than that to me."

He'd been out of hospital for four days and she hadn't asked him yet exactly what she was. Could her love-of-his-life status have changed, like everything else, since the rupture and the heart surgery? Buying his food and vacuuming his carpets made her his housekeeper. The careful, fearful business known as *wound care,* along with bringing him water so he could take his painkillers, blood-thinning pills, antibiotics and beta blockers – and plumping his pillows – made her a kind of nurse. And only Leigh had asked about work, leave and financial implications.

"Carer, then," she told him, hand in his.

"Yes, you've always cared, haven't you? Unlike some wives I could mention."

"You do remember Carole flew over from Cyprus when you were out of it?"

"A bit pointless if she was going to clear off again before I came

189

back."

He didn't seem to want a detailed account of those NHS days and that was fine by Annie, who had no desire to relive them, with their shocks and aftershocks and endless stretches of disconnected time. But since Carole was back in Edinburgh and promising to visit, she reminded him that he'd been breathing through a tube at the point in question.

"The weak and silent type," he said. "Yes. But Carole usually has plenty to say for herself."

"She was worried about you, Arthur, of course she was."

"Who needs a wife with an ex like you?"

"If that's supposed to be charming," she smiled, "you can do better. Don't tell me you haven't had lots of practice in hospital."

He protested, and said he'd love a cup of tea. Annie pulled the curtains. The frost still clung hard under a washed-out sky that was all cloud. Looking back at the king-sized bed where, over his longest marriage – not yet technically over – he must have made love to Carole hundreds of times, a thousand or more (was that possible?) she felt for the first time a kind of interloper.

"I'll get that tea," she said. "Don't ask for sugar."

"No, Matron. Wouldn't dream of it."

"I'll wash your hair later," she told him. It looked in need of that red berry and vanilla crush shampoo she'd seen in the en-suite bathroom, which Carole had obviously decided to live without, along with the rom-com DVDs and Michael Bublé's Greatest Hits. And her husband.

"I'm a lucky boy!"

It was the right line but the wrong delivery: smile too thin, the acting unconvincing.

"Do you want to shave after that?" she asked.

Now that he could sit up in bed, he liked to manage that task for himself with a towel to catch the foam, but she wondered what he thought when he saw himself in the mirror she set against his raised knees on the duvet.

"You like me rugged, don't you? You used to."

Leigh would tell him there was a difference between rugged and down-and-out. Annie just smiled and headed downstairs.

From the kitchen she heard him ease himself out of bed with an intake of breath. He was going to the bathroom. The potty was still under the bed but determination must be a good thing.

"You all right?" she called up. "Would you like some help?"

"I'm fine! I can piss for myself!"

Had she forgotten that serrated edge? Was it there all along? In any case, he was allowed to be sharp. Searching the cupboards, she told herself she must stop working through Arthur's biscuit supply. There were enough packets for a midnight feast in an Enid Blyton dorm.

Upstairs she heard him stumble. Running, calling his name, she found him holding the banister, the fly of his pyjama bottoms partially open and spilling hairs. His face was closed-in, his eyes dark. She took his arm.

"I made a bit of a mess," he said. "I hate this! I feel useless."

"It's all right, darling."

Such a word, but he didn't seem to register it as she led him back to bed, only muttering, "It's not, though. It's not all right. I'm too young for this crap."

Annie had felt too young: to be a mum, to head up a hospital school. But she could see this was different, disempowering. She assured him that it was temporary and he had to be patient – which of course, he'd never been in his life. Having settled him down, physically at least, she cleaned up the toilet seat and bathroom floor before returning to the kettle for his tea.

Day Four of being home (his, not hers) and she had no idea how she felt anymore.

Looking out of the kitchen window she saw a familiar body emerge from a taxi, two-tone cowboy boots first. Carole's hair was preposterously blonde for a woman of fifty-three, her tan made her eyes look very blue and her jacket parted to reveal the low neck to her top. Annie reminded herself how much she always liked this woman as she hurried to reach the door before the bell rang. But didn't she used to look fluffier and less tarty?

Carole announced her name and, instead of cheek kisses, gave her an unexpected hug.

"I'd forgotten how bitter Edinburgh is," she said, stepping inside and removing her boots – quite a protracted business which involved holding on to the wall. No suitcase, just a large handbag. "How are you, Annie? Is he running you ragged?"

"He's doing well," she said, "just not as well as he'd like."

191

Carole's look was both sympathetic and knowing. "You must think I'm a heartless cow."

"I think it must have been difficult for you."

"It turns out you're the best wife he had – by a long way. He'd already come to that conclusion himself a while back, and told me so..."

Annie had to interrupt and talk of tea, forgetting until she was reminded that Carole only drank coffee, strong.

"Maybe I should face him," added Carole, hesitating at the foot of the stairs. "Do you think he will have heard me already? Do I need body armour?"

Annie told her he'd probably be watching a film by now, or listening to Queen again.

"Is he behaving like a teenager? No, don't answer that," Carole told her. "I'm sorry, Annie – that you've got landed like this. I didn't take my phone because I hate that availability thing. I didn't want Arthur texting asking which button to press on the washing machine or what day the bin men come. It never crossed my mind..."

Annie said it wouldn't; it hadn't crossed hers either. They'd been through this at the hospital but Carole was unaccustomed to guilt.

"We're used to his bad habits," she continued. "I suppose he has to start eating like a grown-up and stop getting bladdered."

"Booze is banned. But I'm not sure he's really registered that at the moment because he's too beaten-up post-op."

"Good luck!" Carole's smile vanished. "You don't have to do this, you know."

Annie faced the worktop as the kettle bubbled. "I know."

She should do! Her mother had told her so, and her ex-colleagues – and even Leigh, once, although her position wasn't entirely clear, given that she'd also said, "You can't abandon him, Mum, when he's got no one!" Poor Leigh was struggling rather and pretending nothing could dent her at the same time.

"I know," Annie repeated. "It's a choice and it's made, like yours."

She hoped that didn't sound critical, or like a reminder that was also a warning. She put Carole's coffee on the table.

"I'm still his wife, Annie."

The tone was light rather than combative. As if the words were up in the air and she didn't know where they'd land.

"Of course, but..."

"I know, I left him. I needed time out. But everything's changed, hasn't it?" She stood. "I must talk to him, even if he hates me. You understand?" She placed a warm, soft hand on Annie's arm. "Maybe no one really stops loving Arthur."

"I think Lorelei did!"

They both laughed, freely but conspiratorially too. Annie said if Lorelei turned up they'd get an injunction. Carole said they'd plant land mines on the drive.

Then she disappeared upstairs, her coffee untouched on the kitchen table. Annie could have followed her, but there were good reasons to stay and turn on the radio. She bypassed a Chopin Étude: too delicate and poignant, not thick enough to blot out voices if they rose. *I'm Still Standing* thudded in on some nostalgic pop station and made her smile because he was, or would be. He could surprise himself and she'd make sure he did.

She'd never fought Carole over anything and she didn't want to start. The phone rang; it was a friend of Arthur's who called herself *James-and-Lilith*. Annie had a set patter now, like a salesperson in a call centre, answering the doubtful "Carole?" with a brisk explanation: "No, his first wife, Annie," and moving on to a health-made-simple account. Really she should record something…

As she ended the call, Carole rejoined her with a smile that didn't match her filling eyes.

"Told me to fuck off," she said, standing as if she didn't plan to sit down.

"Oh, Carole, I'm sorry. He doesn't mean it. It's the medication, and the shock still..."

Carole looked at the coffee but from a distance. "You're very kind, Annie. He doesn't deserve you. Crises don't bring out the best in him."

"Don't go, Carole."

"Annie!" came from upstairs.

"Wait, Carole. Drink your coffee. I'll be back."

Hurrying upstairs, she imagined his frustration, knowing that below him the women would be focused on him. As she stepped through the bedroom doorway he called, "Get rid of her, Annie. She came to gloat. Don't give her house room."

"She's concerned, Arthur. Come on, take it easy. No stress."

"She's a bitch."

His face twisted as he spat the word. Annie turned away. "You don't mean that. Have some more water. You've hardly touched your glass."

"I'm not thirsty. It has no taste."

He pushed it away. In a reflex she reached to stop its wobble and chink but between them they spilt the water on his bedside unit. Holding back an apology, she hurried to fetch a hand towel. When she returned she found him lying still, facing the wall.

"Are you tired?" she asked.

"Wouldn't you be?" he muttered, without turning.

"I'll be back, Arthur," she told him, her tenderness full of purpose.

She leaned across to stroke her fingers down the length of his stiff, broad back. He didn't move.

As she reached the door he said, his voice muffled with his mouth under the duvet, "I know you will. Just ignore me. I'm full of spleen."

"It's all right."

"Sorry, darling."

She smiled and nodded. He needed to apologise to Carole too but his eyes had lightened now. In them was a trace of the boyish Art she'd first seen in the Students' Union Bar with a pint of Guinness and a hand-knitted stripy scarf that almost reached down to his sandals.

Stopping in the doorway she asked, "What was it you wanted, when you called me?"

"Just you," he murmured.

"I'm here," she said, left the door ajar and stepped downstairs.

In the lounge Carole was wandering, examining the objects on the surfaces. Even Annie knew which holidays they represented. What had he done to make Carole leave this lovely house behind?

"We should talk, Annie," Carole said, turning with a decorated wooden bowl in her hand. She blew off dust that puffed into the air, then rested it on the shelf. "I hope you don't believe everything he's told you."

"I don't," she answered: a slipping-out surprise.

"Sometimes people start decomposing long before they die, or bits of them do. In Arthur's case, empathy. He's all ego again, like a little boy who can be terribly sweet and appealing but only until he's crossed. Empathy's just self-control really – and without it…"

"Carole…" Annie didn't want to hear this now. It seemed unfair and disloyal with him lying in bed upstairs and the two of them perfectly well and on their feet.

"I know. You always loved him and you don't want to stop now. I loved him too but if the person you're with has no interest in your feelings anymore... well, your feelings look elsewhere. I'm not ready to give up on that. I know you tried. Dating would have done you so much good, Annie, trust me. Art Capaldi's not the only man in the world."

Annie remembered the determined enthusiasm for Italian, painting and am-dram that had so obviously bolstered him after he stood down from the board and became a sleeping partner, a consultant rarely needed and not often wanted. Maybe that ego of his had taken more of a knock than it could stand, and chipped away edges that had been smooth.

She started to remind Carole, who interrupted gently.

"Of course, life gives us plenty of excuses. But in the end we owe it to our significant others to give them something better than the worst of us." She sighed lightly. "Don't you think?"

She was peachy still, thought Annie. The toy boy, if that was really what he was, had a good deal whatever her birth certificate said. Carole Capaldi: soft-skinned, uninhibited and curvy, with home-made cake thrown in. Annie had never kidded herself that Arthur had anything to remember with regret or longing from his first marriage that Carole didn't offer in his third, and with easier good humour.

"I'll drop by, Annie. I'll give you breaks if you're determined to devote yourself to nursing and cosseting."

"He'll get better, Carole. I'm sure."

"But you don't have to sacrifice yourself. You really don't."

"I'm not!"

She knew she sounded hurt. Carole reached out a hand, with an "Oh, Annie, please don't be offended."

"I'm not," she said again, voice lower and edges blurred.

But suddenly the connection that had always surprised other people felt more broken than loose. Carole hadn't laid pity on her before and like the kids on the wards, she couldn't bear it.

Arms out, Carole was offering an embrace and she had to accept it. Only the beautiful glass bead necklace Arthur had made for her himself felt cool. They agreed to stay in touch.

"Make no promises, Annie, not yet," said Carole as she hurried onto the drive.

Chapter Two

Coralie was asleep in her roll neck and jeans, face down on top of Ethan's bed. One socked foot stuck out under his jacket, which he'd used to cover her. What time was it now? The hut was lit by candles, and around it the darkness hung heavy across the land and sky, but afternoon had only just faded away. Crystel stood with her coffee mug in both hands, looking out.

"Like a stage curtain," she whispered. "You know, with bright lights behind it."

"Keep it closed," said Ethan, "for now. Another show begins tomorrow. The cast will be rehearsing as we sleep."

They giggled about tap dancing deer and jiving ants. Crystel had noticed that everything seemed funnier now, as well as childlike but much more serious. Ethan squeezed her hand. Crystel lifted up her mouth and he accepted the invitation. With a jumper of his hanging loose down to her knees and over her hands, she'd stopped shivering now – even though it was possible to trace their breath through the candlelight. The kiss was long. Not a bed kiss, but light, playful and tender.

She wondered how it would feel when she was back in London. How would she remember this, and him, when she was on a bus or in the supermarket, or Lou wanted her to find a babysitter and go to some club? Would it seem like a movie or a crazy dream that swerved off in directions she couldn't follow?

A lyric went through her head, one of her mum's old favourites: *I'll give it all up for you.* Nothing she'd miss. Heels and vodka, River Island and celebrity magazines. Nothing as real as the trees. And if she tried to forget him, and the reality that the TV News kept on ducking because it was just too scary… how could she? Coralie wouldn't let her.

Ethan was smiling at her, his fingers stroking hers. "What are you thinking about?"

"Leaving. Going back. And how it won't seem like home anymore."

Home. For Crystel it had a new definition. With no sensible economic plan and no engagement ring, Ethan Garrett was her home all the same, but she dared not say so. Spoken out loud it would be scary, embarrassing too.

Coralie sat up. "Is it Christmas yet?"

"Not long now," said Crystel.

Ethan thought Coralie looked disbelieving. He remembered that excitement.

"How many seconds?"

"You don't need to worry about that," said Ethan, "because one of my friends gave us a pot of casserole and by the time you've forked every kidney bean and butterbean and chewed every slippery crescent of onion and disc of carrot, it'll be January."

Coralie's laugh was a protest and involved a jump, fists in the air.

"That's too long! Christmas will be over!"

"Oh dear," said Ethan. "I'd better boil you that egg."

Coralie began laughing helplessly as Ethan pretended to search under cushions and books, muttering, "I'm sure Ellie the hen sat here."

A joke was what Lou would think of all of it. Madam too. Even on the phone she'd heard Leigh Capaldi's gawp when she explained about a guy who lived in a shepherd's hut with no car, TV or computer. A guy she'd met on a train.

"Like Romeo and Juliet, across a crowded tube?"

Crystel thought there was envy along with the are-you-serious incredulity. "Kind of. Yeah."

An old actor had talked like that on some chat show sofa, about his first sight of his wife of umpteen years, and said it wasn't love as much as recognition. Crystel supposed she must be a romantic deep down to remember something like that. And maybe once she'd heard the word she'd been waiting for it to happen, on some bus or street or tube, until it did. Recognition. The differences were just details to learn.

She'd tried to tell Madam about Ferningstone, choosing her words carefully and trying to dodge the embarrassment: "a sustainable, sharing community." The response was the kind of wordless noise that dropped down like a barrier. Leigh Capaldi wasn't going there.

"My love life's unsustainable," she muttered darkly. "Or at least, it was. It's going to have to be speed dating. Most men don't deserve more than two minutes."

Then she'd apologised and wished Crystel well, said she deserved a break and paused. "Don't be too trusting. Your eco hippie might be more typically male than he seems."

Crystel smiled, remembering that. He had longer hair than her, might weigh a little less and knew more about ancient civilisations than football or cars. He was the guy she'd never expected or imagined. Catching her watching him, he smiled at her, ladle in hand.

"What?" he asked, knowing exactly.

"Oh," she said. "Just."

Had she ever felt so happy? And his casserole smelt good. Crystel looked at her watch, wishing time would stop, right there. It was cold outside and all she knew about labyrinths came from movies with monsters thrashing their tails and roaring in the darkness, but she didn't want to be late.

Arthur had been asleep since two and now he was cross that he'd missed the daylight. Annie sat the laptop on a pillow first, then a cushion, then a tray, but the height wasn't right, or the reach. Arthur shook his head and pushed it away.

"They give you cancer anyway," he said.

"You don't feel like getting up, just for a bit, and sitting at your desk? Or the kitchen table? I can work around you."

"No," he said, and grimaced as if she'd just punched the wound. "It's not that I don't feel like it. I can't. It hurts too much. I couldn't concentrate anyway. Can't you use my password and order it all for me? Choose your own present!"

Annie's ideas about boycotting huge, greedy tax evaders and supporting local businesses were greeted with a throaty sigh and lifted eyes, and, "Of course, but just not now!"

She told him it was his money and she'd follow orders, no problem. "Like a good P.A.," she murmured, hoping the smile would be returned.

"Don't," he said, appealing, one hand towards her.

It reminded her of student days when they'd made love on a Sunday afternoon or evening, and she'd got up afterwards to dress and leave, because she had work to do. "Don't," he'd beg, smiling and drawing her attention to what was on offer if she stayed. And always reaching out a hand to pull her back onto the bed or wrapping his arms around her and challenging her to escape if she could.

"Don't call yourself that. You keep doing it. Nurse, housekeeper, secretary. You're my wife."

Sitting on the bed, she let him thumb the palm of her hand in a circular motion familiar from long ago.

"I'm not, though, Arthur."

"Don't say that! You're here! We've always belonged together. You know that."

Perhaps it wasn't the time to point out that for most of his adult life he'd been unshakably certain that he belonged with someone younger and more exciting. Lorelei had been beautiful, in a waif-like, gamine way, like a cross between a heroin addict and a saint who never fed her body because her fragile spirit needed all her energy. "What can I say, Annie?" he'd asked. "I'm in love with her. She's cast a spell on me."

For a big, capable man he could be helpless. She'd told him so, in a letter he probably didn't open and certainly never kept.

"I wonder," she murmured, the memory spilling over, "where Lorelei is now."

Arthur withdrew his hand. "Why are you being cruel?"

"I don't mean to be."

"It's not like you."

Perhaps because it was hard to know who she was? But no, this wasn't fair. "It's not cruelty, Arthur. The past flashes back. Or perhaps it's always with us, a layer below the present. So she's here, between us still, in her absence..."

"Get an exorcist!" Arthur laughed. "She's out of our lives, Annie – where Carole should stay. I don't want to see her either. She's a reminder."

He was appealing again, and stroked her thigh.

"But she really *is* your wife."

He shook his head.

"And she's my friend," continued Annie, "and I appreciate her support."

"Well I don't! They send nurses, don't they? What do we need her for? Two's company and three is definitely a crowd when Carole's the third."

Looking towards the far wall, Annie focused on the faintly outlined space where she knew a wedding photo of Carole and Arthur used to be. She wanted to ask him for the truth, as he saw it, about what happened to drive Carole into infidelity. Carole, who used to squeeze his arm, laugh at his jokes... and once, when she didn't know Annie was approaching from the Ladies, nestled against him to kiss his neck in a restaurant and run her hand right down from his shoulder, over his chest and under the table. For a moment Annie felt again the electric current across the Bombay Tandoori, stunning something that was better put out of its misery.

"Anyway, you're a better friend than Carole could ever be. I should know. All those years, always there for me." He smiled, straightening. "But it's different now. Annie Capaldi, will you marry me?"

She smiled too, but she didn't answer. It was a gesture, surely, not a question.

"Don't make me sweat," he said. "I'm serious."

"Arthur, you're not divorced from Carole yet. And you're still... well, you're in recovery. Let's just take things slowly."

"When I could be dead by spring? What for? So you can decide whether you still love me now that I'm an invalid who can't satisfy your needs?"

Annie stood. "Firstly, you've been told you could live a long life, a healthy, active life..."

"If I give up drinking and chips!"

"Yes, and you will. Otherwise I'm leaving now. Secondly, if you mean the kind of needs that went unsatisfied in me from the day you walked out, I think I they can go unmet for a couple more weeks."

Annie looked away, reaching for papers to tidy.

"Annie, sweetheart, I'm sorry! Don't keep throwing it in my face. What can I tell you? I never wanted you to live like a nun." He took her hand and she sat again.

"No. You told me so. But I lived like one anyway."

"You could have got yourself a vibrator! Have a look in the drawers in case Carole left one behind."

"Funny, Arthur."

Annie could tell he didn't really want to talk about sex, because now the humiliation was his. And he didn't really want to talk about divorce or remarriage either. The past filled the space between them and spilt out all over the house and the city, even down the railway line to London. But for now this bedroom was all they had and soon he'd be repeating his invitation to her to share it.

"My darling," he said, "tell me we have a future, an incentive to go on walks and eat celery. And then order yourself a sexy dress for Christmas, for when we go out to dinner. And heels. You never wear heels anymore." He grinned. "I need to change the subject. More tea? I think mine got cold."

Thankful for tea's tendency to do that through conversation that had no beginning or end, Annie picked up his mug and agreed.

"It's not the same without sugar."

"You'll get used to it," she told him. He'd made bigger adjustments.

"You're a hard woman," he threw after her as she crossed to the landing.

There Annie stooped to pick bits from the carpet. White bits on colour; brown bits on cream. Where did they come from? And why couldn't she leave them alone, like she did at home, where they mixed with the flecks and did nothing to disturb her equilibrium? Because this house wasn't hers and yet she had responsibility, a duty of care for it as well as for him.

Why are you there, Annie? Gillie had asked in a text. *No choice,* she'd answered. *Careful what you choose,* had been the reply, with excessive kisses. Now she didn't always answer Gillie's texts, because short as they were, they made her feel so exposed.

If she asked him, did he ever sleep with Gillie, would he lie? Would *he* remember?

In the kitchen she looked at the calendar, where Carole's handwriting had scheduled in a couple of plans months ahead. A photograph of frost on a hillside, broken by the jagged darkness of a dead tree, seemed oddly bleak on the butter-yellow walls. She realised that in her morning quietness, afraid to turn on the radio or TV for fear of waking Art, she hadn't recognised the date.

It was their unofficial anniversary, before any wedding. On this day, an age ago, they'd become a couple – which in those days, for her, meant snogging. Not in this instance with the taste of alcohol, under cover of *Nights In White Satin* at the end of a party, but by daylight, outside a West End cinema where they'd met one Saturday afternoon.

"I wasn't sure you'd come," he said, smiling as she approached in boots and a maxi skirt that the December wind wrapped around her legs.

"I said I would," she told him, smiling too. "Do girls generally stand you up, then?"

"Oi! Less cheek," he said. "Never. But other girls aren't you. You're a cool customer. I don't know what you're thinking."

His hair had been ridiculously long, and layered. He reminded her of John Donne in the Portrait Gallery not so far away but she didn't tell him that, not then, because he'd love that idea and he was cocky enough. But insecure too? Had he really doubted that she'd show?

Whether she'd said anything to that, denying being cool or inscrutable, Annie couldn't remember. Maybe it was all ironic, because surely he could detect her delight and relief to be there with him, at the right cinema and on time, and to see his smile. He'd kissed her cheek and said how cold her skin was, and then he'd taken her hand in her old purple gloves and said, "I know what I'm thinking."

"I'd be worried if you didn't," she said.

"So can you read me?" he'd persisted as they queued in the foyer and he unwrapped his scarf. "What am I thinking?"

She knew. But she wasn't going to tell him. Not just in case what was on his mind was the price of tickets or the politics of Vanessa Redgrave, but because she wanted him to say it himself, out loud, in public.

She shrugged, eyes bright and empty.

"About this," he said, and kissed her. And kissed her again and again, until the cashier butted in because they'd reached the front of the queue.

They didn't see much of the film and when they emerged into the Christmas-lit London darkness, her mouth felt wet and swollen and her skin tight and burning.

A year later they celebrated the date as their anniversary, even though, as Arthur pointed out to their friends, she wouldn't sleep with him for what he called *an eternity*. Probably a fortnight. She tried to explain that she'd loved him from the cinema on, but that she couldn't be sure. He'd had a lot of girls and it was in his kiss, the confidence of habit. He was just too good at all of it: words, hands, timing, smiles. Of course she doubted everything but her own feelings. Why her?

"You're like Anne Boleyn," he said once, during that *eternity* of stopping short. "You want me in your power. I'm there. I'm bewitched."

Another time he called it a test, a cruel one, and wanted to know whether he'd passed, with urgent kisses and all-over touches. And when she'd decided to spend the night with him in her student bed, she'd looked in the mirror afterwards to find some new version of herself: rosy, shining, electrified. It made her giggle. But even then she was afraid to let it show, slipping back to him in darkness and hoping that she didn't illuminate it like Blackpool.

Now, making his tea decades later, Annie doubted whether the date would mean anything to him anymore. He probably muddled the three weddings. For years, when Leigh was a child, she'd suspected he wouldn't remember her birthday without Carole to choose a card with the right embossed number, address the envelope and put it in front of him to sign.

She must phone Leigh, and try to talk to her, really talk. Not to force her to come for Christmas, or to offload any kind of burden, but to communicate somehow, to break through. If Leigh would only speak to Carole's girls, it might help like it used to, but she seemed determined to go it alone these days.

In spite of the rain against the window, and even without the aroma of Carole's cooking, this was a kitchen some might call beautiful. Sunny walls, Mediterranean tiles underfoot and soft, well-polished wood all invited family to fill the space and friends to pile on in. Now it felt like a field lying fallow. Annie gave a quick wipe to the Aga she'd kept on admiring from a respectful distance, still not entirely sure how to use it.

It was a welcoming house and, if she looked properly, she was sure she'd find all those tasteful decorations Carole must have chosen and hung with effortless design flair each year. But she wished Christmas was over.

The labyrinth was in the big hall at Ferningstone. The usual seats, microphone and screen had gone, making way for tea lights marking out a path to the centre.

"Not a maze," Ethan had told Coralie. "A maze is like a puzzle. You can choose which way to go and you can get lost. A labyrinth is a path to the centre and out again."

When he'd explained about life being a journey she'd said, "Like on *Strictly,*" and it made her smile when Ethan didn't understand, never having watched celebs in sequins strutting their stuff on a ballroom floor.

Crystel liked the idea of going in to find your true self and then out again into the world. Coralie just liked the candlelight, and kept saying, "So pretty!" and, "Like magic!" But really, Crystel had the feeling they should be silent, like people in church. Crystel could see, from Coralie's bounce and the tug on her hand, that she wanted to twirl and skip her way to the centre. She kept asking if she could go first, until Ethan suggested that she followed him.

"Like a puppy," she said.

Hoping she wouldn't yap as well as frisk, Crystel watched her walk the path between the tiny, flickering flames. Smiling, she saw her begin to focus, head down. Even from outside the circle, Crystel could feel the warmth on her own cheeks in the cold space.

Ahead of Coralie, Ethan heard her fall quiet, the little wordless noises replaced by concentration as her footsteps became lighter and slower. Even a child could feel it: some kind of gentle power taking hold, stilling, connecting with a deep place. They were together but separate too, each alone on a journey to the centre of their own soul.

Ethan had walked a labyrinth before, outside a Welsh village church in sunlight, the pattern marked out with wooden stumps and not so different from a game in a playground. There Coralie would have jumped, bridged the gaps, balanced and hopped. And there the only sound had been the wind and everywhere the green had been lush and free. No distractions. Nothing but Nature alive and untamed, and a path to take into peace. Here, in a wintry room, the darkness was speckled with starry flame. With a five-year-old in tow, he felt stirred by excitement too.

Crystel stood back. She tended to leave it to Lou to jump in with a splash. She was the toes-first dipper, the inch-by-inch wader. Then she'd keep going, always one more length, pushing herself. But this was different. It'd be crazy to rush into something that claimed to be a metaphor for life. If her being had the deep core of a centre that was her soul and she was about to discover it, then shouldn't she feel ready? Didn't it all feel risky enough? Lou would never have come here, to this crazy, intense place. Lou would think she'd had her soul snatched and her brains with it. Even Lucie would direct her to church and the Bible, not dreaminess and mystery.

Crystel felt cut loose. The life she'd lived hadn't been like his. She looked around her at the others. The jumper-and-jeaned teenagers with their mother could have been born in the Seventies. What did the word 'urban' mean to them? Where were their piercings, music feeds, tattoos, hoods? Where was their attitude? The man with a grey beard looked like one of Jesus's disciples, apart from the old coat and baggy cords. The only face that wasn't white belonged to a bright-eyed Asian who talked like the commentator on Royal weddings.

Coralie had forgotten her now. She was walking her way back, eyes low, a smile on her face. Ethan had given himself up to it, whatever it was, to this big symbol. Maybe he knew the path his life had to take but he'd been heading in that direction for years. For her, it was a sudden U turn, a jack knife. All because of a hippie on a tube who could be a head case, his brain rewired by all that cannabis he used to smoke.

Someone was at her shoulder, an old man with a peace sign on his sweatshirt. "It's a choice, to enter or not enter."

Yes, she got that, and she hadn't made it yet. But what else would her choice mean? She'd thought the whole idea was so cool in theory and so pretty at first sight. So why was she standing there, spectating like the outsider she was, dumb and motionless and... kind of afraid?

It was just about a spiritual path and finding yourself and all that deep stuff she'd always liked at a distance. Now she was meant to start walking. Coralie had almost worked her way back. She could see Ethan was aglow, innocent as a choirboy.

Then the quiet was broken by a gasp and a sob. A woman bent at the middle as if she'd been mugged. Crystel had seen that before, but this woman hadn't lost her money even though she might have plenty of it. She just looked like she'd give it all up, everything, like that song again. Because God was calling? What did it mean?

Someone reached out a hand like a lifebelt over the water but Ethan was quickest. He stepped across the flames and put an arm around the woman, who could barely stand. She slumped against him and whimpered. His arms were loose around her.

Coralie skipped out, looking across to the weeping woman with a question mark furrowing her smooth forehead. She took Crystel's hand. Hers was always so warm, and soft as butter. Sometimes it made Crystel want to cry herself. Now it held tight.

"Why is that lady crying?" she whispered. "Did she burn her

finger?"

"I don't know," Crystel told her. "Maybe it's too much." Too much what? Coralie's face asked the question. "Too much emotion."

"What emotion?"

"Maybe people feel different things when they walk the labyrinth."

"It's a happy labyrinth!" said Coralie. "I want to walk it again."

She looked back, hesitating, still holding Crystel's hand. Was that allowed, wondered Crystel? If this path was life and the centre was the core of your being, was it a one-off?

The woman was outside the circle now, blowing her nose. Ethan stood with her. Another woman sat beside her, one arm around her. Crystel supposed she'd made a mess of her life, but didn't everyone? Wasn't that why places like Ferningstone existed, because people screwed up everything, including the earth?

"What did you think, as you were walking?" Crystel asked Coralie.

"I didn't think!" she cried, as if it was a funny question. "I just felt happy with the magic."

"It's not really magic..." Crystel stopped. Who got to define these words? Coralie felt something good but Crystel didn't trust it. What was she afraid of?

"Why don't you come with me this time? I'll show you. You can't get lost!"

It was the kind of question and the kind of face that only allowed one answer.

"Yeah, go on then."

She followed Coralie into the labyrinth.

Ever since Leigh's colleagues had begun to arrive at the party she'd been feeling disconnected, like a visitor who'd only dropped in from another time to observe and would soon be making a getaway in the Tardis. Preferably before the trouble started. Maybe it was the mineral water bubbling up her nose while the rest of them were tipping back the wine and beer, but everyone seemed boring and seriously stupid. In the theatre, faced with conversation like this as dialogue about Christmas itself *(not doing much really, just seeing family)* and the remaining run-up *(being behind with everything, with loads to do and running out of time)* any audience would walk, and demand a refund.

Henry had got stuck down the other end of the table with some husbands who didn't make much effort to pretend they chose to be there. But at least, thanks to a babysitter with a virus, Francoise Hart hadn't materialised.

Admittedly ice cream desserts weren't especially festive but Leigh pretended she didn't hear Kyle's comment, "What, no plum pudding and brandy butter?" She did wonder, by the time the last bowl of kulfi was cleared, whether certain stomachs might be too swollen to be jiggled about to Henry's dance compilation. But soon everyone bar the two reluctant husbands was up and shaking something. Not a pretty sight.

Leigh bought some time and space in the Ladies, but when she returned Kyle was dancing – with Henry. Or rather, his hips were swinging into Henry's and their butts meeting, to the delight of whooping women. Not much point in giving either of them a glare but how drunk could Henry really be, at three minutes to ten? *"Judas,"* she mouthed at him from the table the moment he glanced her way. But if he saw he didn't seem to care. No one came to drag her up to dance. No one cared.

Maybe she'd get through this better with booze after all. Filling her glass, she looked up to find Kyle, no visible traces of sweat on his hair or his purple shirt, his mouth still loose from laughing and his lips moist with the beer she smelt as he leaned towards her.

"Party pooper," he said. "Dance with me."

"I'm nowhere near as good as Henry."

He murmured close to her ear, "I know how good you are."

"Sorry, boss," she told him, "I just need to put my head down the toilet. As tradition demands."

He put his hand on her arm. "You look incredible."

Of course she did. That was insurance, against something she couldn't identify. In a silk camisole top she'd kept in her bag all day with perfume, skin-tight new jeans and long earrings, she was the class act who didn't have to try.

Her look was meant to be cool. "You're the one who's hard to believe."

Kyle only smiled. He didn't even seem to wonder whether the abandoned husbands might lip read. His body language was about as hard to interpret as a Miley Cyrus video.

"It's Christmas, Miss Capaldi," he said, straightening. "I'm allowed to rub up against your tits."

"I must have missed that verse," she told him. "Which carol would that be in?" On the dance floor, Henry was looking at the door. "Oh look," said Leigh, following his gaze and finding a short, delicate woman with a large baby bump. "That must be your wife."

At once he was rushing to embrace her, kissing both cheeks, reaching an arm around her and murmuring something in her ear that came with a smile. Not a trace of guilt or panic, just delight. And the words, "What a lovely surprise!"

Leigh realised she was staring. Why was she watching this? A hand took hers and pulled her up.

"Let's dance," said Henry.

"I feel sick," she bleated.

"No you don't. Come on. Everyone loves Cher."

"Do you believe in life after love?" the diva sang, with the help of a dozen women.

"Not for a moment," said Leigh. "Not after and not before."

She'd dance until her shoes pinched or her legs failed, or the first person called a cab. Then she'd leave.

Chapter Three

How long was it, thought Leigh, since she'd gone to bed stone cold sober after a party? It was true what they said about distance. Towards the end when she sneaked away, she'd felt like some kind of anthropologist watching the chimps. And they weren't as funny as they thought they were, especially one guy who was using his wife as a crutch but whose tongue was even less under control than his legs.

As she cleaned her teeth hard and drew a little pale blood from the gums, she watched her bare face in the mirror. The eyes that looked back were clear, her lashes long and thick, skin good, hair holding its shape. But this woman was not as pretty as Kyle's wife and nowhere near as nice. Leigh spat into the basin and thought of Crystel because the bathroom was missing her. Christmas must be fun with a five-year-old. Was Kyle a fun, careless daddy? The French mummy was neatly pregnant, celebrity fashion: no all-over splurge and sag with boobs dropping like over-ripe mangoes, just a bump that knew its place.

Francoise Hart deserved to know and if Leigh had been drunk she could have talked herself into sharing. Not with an *EastEnders* scene but a note in a Christmas card, in best handwriting, from a well-wisher. A sister on the side of Truth. But it'd be like trashing her house, kicking over the tree and stealing the presents from underneath. Just like Lorelei had done. Leigh would never forgive her for snatching the future away along with her (fun, careless) daddy and rewriting her past.

If Kyle's wife was happy loving him, she was lucky to be stupid.

Like her own mother? Was she happy loving her dad – as he was, future uncertain and present pretty shit? Because he didn't sound happy to be loved.

Christmas in Edinburgh wouldn't be what he'd call *a blast* but she couldn't really duck it. If Henry couldn't find some nice young man to take away in her place, maybe he had an elderly aunt who looked like Maggie Smith who'd escort him.

She took her laptop out of its case and, sitting it on the bed, typed a letter of resignation not much longer than a tweet. People wasted too many words, she thought, as she settled down to try and sleep. And most of them were some kind of manipulation.

Picturing Kyle trying to jive in a long red hat with a white trim, she remembered the Secret Santa lunch to come, and the raspberry wine gum penis that had once seemed a suitable gift to throw in the sack, in the hope that some lucky dipper would squeal. What had happened to Christmas anyway? Adults were sick. Crystel got to wake each day to a shepherd or donkey behind an advent calendar window, and sing *Rudolf the Red-Nosed Reindeer* on the way to school.

Everything was such crap: Kyle deceiving his nice-as-pie wife, her father's lousy heart, the job and the weather, the government, the X-Factor and low-life footballers, and brainless Barbie who never learned any better.

Leigh realised she wanted to cry on someone's shoulder and there was no one out there who wouldn't be either asleep or in no fit state to listen. With the possible exception of Crystel, who'd probably be wearing dungarees when she came back, if she ever came back at all, and smelling of patchouli.

Closing her eyes, she knew she was much too sharp for sleep.

Who said December was a bad time to look for jobs? It worked for Dustin Hoffman in that film her dad used to blub over.

Charities, she tapped in. Why not? There seemed to be one natural disaster after another; she couldn't stand watching the News anymore. Maybe it was time for a change of direction.

Crystel hadn't planned to leave Coralie at Rick and Layla's place. That was where she'd crashed out in her clothes, having taken to three-year-old Benji like a rather scruffy teddy to be cuddled, patted and led around. Ethan told Crystel she'd be happy to wake in the kids' room, where he'd carried her – even if her alarm clock was Benji bouncing on top of her.

But as Ethan led Crystel back to the hut, their arms hanging close in the darkness but separate, he wasn't sure what sleeping arrangements she expected herself.

"Tell me what you thought about the labyrinth," he said. "Or what you felt."

"Which?" she asked.

"Are they different?"

"Yeah! Very!"

"You were glad you went?" he checked, because she'd said so little since and he'd been too busy with the woman who'd broken down – or opened up – to see Crystel on her journey and to read her.

She didn't answer at once. "Yes," she said. "And I'm glad I came too."

"Here?"

"Here. But..."

He heard her sigh. He wished he could see her face. "You won't be coming back?"

"I don't know. I can't say. I don't have any words, Ethan. I'm not like you."

"We don't need words," he said, hearing his own uncertainty and reaching for her hand.

The moon wasn't quite full but when it broke free from clouds above his hut, he wanted to clap. Or bow down and worship. By its light he could see her cheek, then both eyes as she turned.

Crystel kissed him. Her tongue was sweet and spicy in his mouth. He could taste the cloves and the honey.

"My first Christmas kiss," he said.

She was used to the steps now. He opened the door, shocked by the noise because the silence felt thick, full. He felt for the candle and matches on the shelf by the door. All he could see was his sofa, not yet a bed, narrow and creased. He knew from experience that the warmth they'd met, as they swapped outside for in, had a life expectancy of three minutes, two. He'd never made the conversion so quickly.

He dared not assume. Should he unroll his sleeping bag and slip inside? Did she need the space?

Even in the dim light, Crystel could feel Ethan's awkwardness. It made her smile.

"Come here, Ethan," she told him. "I need warming up."

Really, she thought as he pressed himself close, she needed him to take off her clothes. Crystel couldn't tell him now, but he seemed to understand.

Waking, Annie listened. Had Arthur called? Cried out in pain? Eyes adjusting to the darkness, she processed the room again. Not hers and not yet familiar, it felt like a bedroom in a film, the sort where a betrayed Emma Thompson would emote. Curtains: heavy, expensive fabric she would love to wear as a dress, for an occasion too special for her diary. Carpet: deep-pile buttermilk, unstained. Only careful guests had slept here, in the firm spare bed with its crisp white sheets. Once she'd done her first wash and iron, it would never look the same again.

There was nothing to hear. Glancing at the time shining from the square face of a square, silver-framed clock, she felt a silent sigh inside, where the indigestion had a habit of lying at night. Four minutes past twelve, and she was ageing. Wakefulness, digestive problems and skin that felt dry enough to crack were just the start. Oh, poor Annie, she thought, shaking her head at her own ego. On the other side of the wall, Arthur was older still, the age difference expanding as other things shrank.

Once, in a year she couldn't be bothered to pin down but would probably be illustrated with velvet flares (Art's), they had got up at four twelve, or thereabouts, to catch a train and see the sun rise on a Sunday. It was his idea, and he'd called her stodgy when she didn't embrace it with the same wide-eyed excitement. Partly because she remembered his insistence a few weeks earlier on breakfast at Heathrow at a similarly ungodly hour: an experience that in practice had no glamour at all – just space, a plastic wrap round the croissant and a zaniness that cooled even before she took the lid off her coffee. Did anyone use the word *zany* anymore?

The sun simply couldn't rise without them that morning, he'd said, and she'd given in because there was no chance of sleep once he was struck by a spontaneous urge. Annie could picture the train that he'd called as private as the bedroom, and the foreplay she'd had to cut short all the same. They were in one of those old compartments that made murders possible in movies, with doors that opened so the hero could tell the villain the game was up, or the Nazi could check the papers of the Jew or POW with a forged identity.

"We wouldn't be the first couple to do it here," Arthur told her, as if that was an inducement when it only made her wonder about the stains on the grubby upholstery.

"You're insatiable," she told him. "You've had it twice tonight."

"Ah," he said, "but now it's morning."

So she'd said it wasn't quite, and if it had been, the whole thing was pointless. But soon they were watching the sky lighten to a cool, murky grey, through a window that was murky too, and he was shaking a panto fist at the sun that had risen too soon and only to hide. So by the sea at Thorpe-le-Soken, chosen because he liked the name whichever accent he used to pronounce it, dawn was more of a comedy sketch than a romantic escapade. And not always funny, because although they were too late for sunrise over the water, they were much too early for a coffee anywhere at all.

But they'd been wildly, stupidly young. That was really the only point. Because otherwise where was the thrill in the wrestling wind, or the salt spray colder than any shower when he insisted on daring the waves up close? His hand felt different now. The veins were risen and thick, bruised by needles, and his skin was harder. Did her memory really still hold the warmth of the young hand along with the empty town and the milky light?

Memory was what she willed or allowed. There must be airbrushing, even reconstruction built in. *We cannot conquer time.* But Auden's grandiose verb was a joke, because time couldn't even be paused. It was faster than light and more slippery than water, with no container that could keep it still enough for a surface and a volume. Or even a form.

She supposed that was why people, who struggled to hold it back, liked to schedule it, pretended it was a line along a classroom wall for them to label, or needed God behind it. To find some sense of control.

"You're a control freak, Mum." Leigh's words, once, not so long ago. Leigh with her gadgets, online diary and high-voltage London lifestyle.

"You need to loosen up." To quote Arthur, a dozen times over the years, sometimes paraphrased and in varying tones and locations.

Work was Annie's sense. Arthur Capaldi had always been the opposite: the madness? She would have seen all this so long ago, surely, if she'd only stopped to think?

Upstairs he was… what, gasping? Pain? A bad dream? Annie set foot on the stairs, but lightly, in case he was sleeping through it. On the turn she stopped, listening. Not the sound of sex, not exactly – not as she'd heard it outside Leigh's room when she was home from uni one weekend, with a floppy-haired Tory studying Politics and Economics and something to prove with her yelps and moans. This was different but it made her feel much the same.

Had it stopped now? Creeping up to the landing, Annie saw half the bed through the open door, the duvet mounding, and an arm reaching out for the box of tissues in its embroidered case.

Annie felt something catch. A sob that knew it had no chance of escape but took her breath by the throat and shook it. No words. No thinking. And he'd needed neither, only release. Only a kind of living. And it didn't matter, not to her. She didn't have to remember, or make it a scene or a symbol. That was choice. Some wives would smile indulgently, like the mothers of small boys who'd discovered a little body part to explore. Carole wouldn't have cried, for God's sake. Annie waited a moment. It was remarkable really, that after everything, he had the desire, the life force, when some men would lie daunted by the demands of Scrabble. She heard him groan as he straightened again and tried to find a way to lie.

"Fuck," he muttered, and she almost giggled, but the tightness came back.

Time for work. Wanking was healthier for the patient than fags and this patient didn't hate her like Declan.

"Can't you sleep?" she whispered in the doorway.

He didn't move. His eyes were closed. For a moment Annie thought his heart had stopped. Then he turned his head away.

Did he know he'd been caught? She should have stayed away, frozen on the landing like a burglar. Now he was humiliated.

"It's all right," she said. *"I love you,"* she added, but not aloud. "You could have painkillers now, if you need them."

He didn't shake or nod. Annie laid a hand on his shoulder, above the duvet. The fleecy fabric felt warm and soft but he hated pyjamas almost as much as she loved them.

"I'll let you sleep," she murmured, and slipped away. Her bare feet felt cold now. "Call me if you need anything."

He wouldn't call, not for a long time, unless he had no choice. Let him sleep, she thought, on the stairs. Maybe sleep was the only defence and escape, a manipulator of time – but then again, the biggest thief of all. She remembered the days before Leigh could word an argument when she wouldn't go to bed because she hated the idea of waking life carrying on without her. And as for Christmas Eve, or rather, Christmas morning, beginning much too early to catch a rising sun ...

There must be kids out there who knew the number of hours to go before that particular midnight, the minutes even. As the shopper and cook she should at least make some lists. In the kitchen, Carole's decorated block of coloured squares for note-making gathered dust without her. Annie blew the lime green surface and tore the page away.

Schedule, she wrote and underlined.

Chapter Four

Since Kyle was out of the office and no one seemed to know where or why, Leigh left her resignation letter on his desk. There was the inevitable *follow-up* to nights like the Christmas party, with mime-like grimaces about headaches, nausea and noise, and in-joke laughter that shut her out. Henry said everyone went to a club after she left – apart, apparently, from Kyle and Francoise, who had their last-minute babysitter to consider.

"How the hell," muttered Henry as he brought her a coffee, "did a shit like that pull a cute Frenchwoman with real manners?"

It hadn't gone unnoticed that aside from the pregnant Francoise, Leigh was the only one not drinking. "Something you're not telling us?" from one joker had been followed dangerously quickly by a glance at the father of the baby inside the bump. But the music had been too loud for most dancers to hear, and of those who did, Leigh was probably the only one with crystal-clear recall. She'd always found football crowds Neanderthal. Now she thought she'd rather be surrounded by thugs threatening to chop off a referee's goolies than by well-paid professionals who couldn't resist that kind of fishing.

She had no intention of squirming. And in Kyle's absence, with productivity sinking to an all-time low around her and mince pies on the menu for lunch, she scrolled through job vacancies, making no attempt to switch screens when anyone approached. What began as speculative became intent, determined. Having eventually found something worth pursuing, she downloaded an application form.

No one would miss her. And since Henry was back with his ex, she'd done true love a favour by ducking out of the Christmas getaway. Later if not sooner, she'd take a step out and up in her career. In the meantime there'd be slumping to do, with turkey, chocolate and tinsel TV. Although how she could jolly her father along without sherry, Baileys, beer, wine or cider, egg nog – or the winter Pimms he'd called the healthy option last year because of the orange slices – she had no idea.

As a couple of the others came back from a fag break she decided to take time out to call Edinburgh. Not that she'd had a proper conversation with her dad since he came out of hospital. Her mother said it just took time and he'd get his old self back before long.

His mobile rang so long she almost gave up. Then he answered weakly, as if he was speaking a few feet from the phone. It was a very dubious "Leigh?" As if in spite of the name on his screen he was worried someone might have stolen her phone.

"How's it going, Dad?"

"Oh, you know, much the same. Can't sleep, can't drink, can't do jack shit. Daytime TV is eroding my will to live. I've hired a hit-man to eliminate that presenter, you know? That show where fat guys fight over which of them impregnated an even fatter woman who looks like she could wrestle them all to the floor."

Leigh chuckled. But it was just the start of a rant about the hospital, for showing it on the ward – just, he reckoned, so that being out cold on an operating table seemed a better option than remaining conscious with garbage like that on screen. He'd always been opinionated, but this was tiring. She felt like holding the phone at arm's length. A couple of times she tried to butt in and redirect, but he returned to the same topic. It must be the drugs, or shock, or maybe the pain.

"Are you up to reading?" Leigh asked, but apparently that took too much energy. And he claimed he was wasting away.

"Your mother does her best but you know she's not up to..." he lowered his voice... "Carole's standard."

"Dad! Don't let her hear you, for God's sake!"

"It's too cold for salads and she won't let me have pastry or pasta..."

"I should think not!"

"It's a conspiracy! What's the point of being alive if I can't have a hot toddy or some whipped cream on home-made apple pie?"

It was hard to tell whether he was joking, or half-joking at least, and the voice she was trying to read wasn't quite as familiar as it should be. Like his face, last time she saw it. There was a moment's silence when she expected him to ask about her, or work, or her social life, but he didn't. She couldn't hear a thing.

"Dad? You O.K?"

"Fine and dandy," he said, darkly this time.

"I'm coming for Christmas after all, Dad, if you'll have me."

"If you've got nothing better to do."

"Dad..."

"Sneak a bottle or two into your suitcase, will you? We can slip some gin into our tonic and no one will know the difference."

Leigh sighed. "Stop messing about. It's not funny. Look after yourself, Dad. You've got to give that heart of yours a chance."

"Ah, my heart belongs to your mother, darling. Only I'm not sure she wants it."

What was she meant to say to that when she had no idea whether it was some kind of bleak joke or a fantasy? "Dad..."

"It's the truth. *I can see clearly now the rain has gone. I can see all obstacles in my way.*"

"I'll let you rest, Dad. I'm at work. Got to go. See you soon!"

"Great."

The word felt heavy with sadness, as if he only wanted to mean it. She didn't say she loved him, because in her head the word felt out of place, spiked with pity he didn't need. And because she wasn't sure she'd mean it, not just now. But if not now, when he might easily have died and Christmas was coming fast, then when? What was so hard?

Maybe she wouldn't look for jobs in Scotland after all. Too complicated. She'd be at risk of claustrophobia, mediation, dependency. London suited her better. Anyone could be alone there.

At the station Coralie's hug was more of a ride. She was in no hurry to climb down from Ethan's chest. There was almost no one on the platform but then the sign said ten forty-six and this was the country.

"Thanks for having us," Crystel told him.

They were under cover of the station roof now, but his hair was already flat with rain. Her own dripped thinly from the curls around her hat. Only Coralie was waterproof in her hooded coat, but it was getting tight and short in the sleeves.

"She'll be needing a new one soon," she said, "and they cost silly money, the good ones. I'm not paying a fiver so some poor teenagers in India can work for peanuts in a factory that could collapse any minute."

But if no one bought those cheap coats would those women be out of work? Thinking threw up so many questions and Ethan didn't have all the answers.

"I can't give you cash right now," he said, "but maybe…"

"No! That's not what I meant!" Did he think that because he'd been inside her, taking her somewhere she'd never been, he had to dress her daughter? She had no idea anyway where his money came from. Maybe his archaeologist father paid into some account every week. All that talking they'd done, about Gaia and God, and fracking and bees, and walking a candlelit journey into her deepest being, and she still didn't know the things most people began with, and ended with too.

"I know you didn't," he said, hoping he didn't sound hurt.

"I don't want your money, Ethan. You've given me much more than that."

He believed she would have kissed him then, if Coralie hadn't been dangling between them. Ethan mouthed, *"I love you"* but it was bigger than that. The two of them made him feel the future was worth fighting for.

The train approached. He put Coralie down but the first thing she did was reach up, puckering. His hand reached out to Crystel and he didn't want to let go.

"Thanks," she said, and took Coralie towards the carriage door. "For everything, I mean."

Watching, Ethan waited only a moment before he followed, wading through a puddle that left the last few inches of his jeans dark and heavy with rainwater. As they stepped inside, Coralie turned, waving. Crystel didn't.

They were finding a seat. He walked parallel along the platform until he found the place where Crystel reached up with her bag while Coralie sat by the window, waving again and pressing her nose flat onto the glass. At once she was blowing, smearing and using a finger to make a letter or a shape. He grinned back and winked. Then he waved like a Royal and saw her giggle. The doors had closed. He needed to see Crystel, but she was taking off her hat, busy.

As the train began to move, she looked out at last, leaning so her breasts curved out in her green jumper. He saw her face open one last time.

She wasn't coming back.

Ethan walked away, feeling his phone in his pocket. No, he told himself. Not while he felt as if no words would cover it, and the ones he could try might scare her. But if he gave her too much space for time to fill, with her old life or real life, then the distance would stretch and grow until they could never close it up again. Already the world they were heading for would seem like home. That was the way with holidays. They ran their course, even for boarding school boys who didn't belong in term-time.

It was over.

In the carriage, Crystel produced Coralie's colouring book. As a snowman's body filled with dark pink felt tip strokes, Crystel placed her phone on her lap. Ahead of her she had family waiting, real family, qualified and tested. Big decisions couldn't be made in two days. She needed perspective. Maybe Lucie would understand, or come close. Watching her face in the glass, she saw the mouth Ethan had kissed lift in a smile as it remembered.

When Arthur woke from a long after-lunch sleep, Annie reminded him that the nurse was coming soon. She suggested that he combed his hair himself, but his face creased as if every stroke pulled at a stitch.

"Let me," she said, and he handed over the brush. It felt good to be gentle and slow, like she'd been with baby Leigh.

"I've been thinking," Arthur announced, "that we should have a party."

Annie gave his hair a couple more brushstrokes before she stepped away and looked, waiting. Best not voice any of the knee-jerk responses that sprang to mind. Was there an ironic punch line?

"A *Staying Alive* party. You know my disco moves are legendary. A *still here for Christmas so no crossing me off your present list* party." He grinned. "Bring a bottle, of course."

"Arthur… it's a bit sudden – and very late. You know how busy people's diaries are in the last week before Christmas."

"You never liked parties." He sighed loudly through his nose. Then he lowered himself back down from a propped-up position, pulling the duvet up to his pyjama collar.

"I've never had much opportunity," she said, the sentence tailing away as she wondered what it meant. "Or reason, I suppose."

"You've had plenty of birthdays."

"But I've chosen to ignore them for quite some time." Carole was great at parties, of course. "I think you'd find it very tiring just now."

"No shit, Sherlock!"

He'd got that one long ago from teenager Leigh. Looking across the room and out of the window, Annie hoped the nurse might be early.

"If you want to explain what you have in mind... if you think you can get up?"

"I thought I could hold court from my bedroom." He laughed. "I'll get up! It'll give me something to get up *for*. There's an address book somewhere with phone numbers, unless Carole took that too. I'll call people myself. You don't have to lay on a spread like she did. Tesco mince pies and crisps will do as long as you mull some wine."

"Arthur, can we wait a bit?"

"Until I'm dead? I'm all for the rest of you enjoying a good wake but I'd rather get to raise a glass myself."

"Don't. I'm going to keep you alive!"

He put out a hand. "Don't panic. You can drown the wine in orange juice. I'll just have the one. You know it'll do me good to have people round and get away from this body of mine. And this bed, and these walls. It'll be great. How about next Monday? Nobody will be booked on a Monday."

"You're serious."

"I'm always serious these days. It must be catching."

Annie picked up a tissue, tucked half-hidden under the edge of the duvet. It was only as she held it that she realised what gave it stiffness. His semen had dried; the thing was sculpted.

Now she felt him watching her. Should she just slip out to the bathroom without a word and flush it down the loo?

"What the fuck can I do?" he cried as she turned towards the door. "Do you think I don't know you're only here out of duty – or nostalgia? Don't treat me like a grubby old man when all I want is to make love to you and wipe the rest away."

"Please stop." Annie stood near the door, tissue in hand, looking back at him.

"But I can't give you what you deserve. I'm sorry, Annie. I'm sorry for everything except our marriage, which I threw away. I never was good enough for you and now I can't even give you great sex. I should have carried you up to your bed that night at your place, after the restaurant with no booze, and reminded you how it used to be."

Annie looked away, back towards the door. Some part of her wanted to hurl it back at him: the truth. He couldn't handle it. And she'd be left to handle him.

"I remember how it used to be," she said. Better than he did, she supposed. "It's all right, Arthur, really."

"But it's not! How can it be? I'm a useless heap of a half-man, lying here thinking of sex and dancing when I can't even face a bath and *Countdown* leaves me wasted. I want to make you happy."

"I'm glad to be here with you."

"You don't look glad. I haven't seen you smile, not once."

It wasn't true. Annie looked across to the bedroom window, as if something was happening outside too. *"I will if you will,"* she could have said. Now he reached out a hand.

"Ignore me, Annie. I'm a brute. I can't think straight. You're just sympathetic."

Annie wondered what kind of a smile her mouth was managing now. Professional? Determined? Fun wasn't her strong point, not any more. Carole would have chatted, of course, about everyone she'd met in town. Stories were one of Carole's many and obvious strengths and Annie supposed she was one of them now. Perhaps she always had been.

"And I'm grateful, darling. I am. I'll get better, get myself back. By next Monday I'll be on my feet and ready to jive."

The doorbell rang. Annie was still holding the crisp meringue of a tissue when she greeted the nurse. As she made more tea, she imagined the kitchen full of guests in paper hats. He'd love it, and why shouldn't he?

Once, long ago, he'd told her in a different kitchen, "You're too sensible, Annie. You need to let your imagination run wild." She'd been wearing maternity dungarees at the time, and he'd been reading out a list of daytime and evening classes, steering her away from the studious and the practical. So when she signed up for Design, she made her clock crazy, assisted by imagination and limited technique. It had a rainbow as a drunk might see one, asymmetric curves and odd angles, and no shape that anyone could have labelled. By the time she'd finished she'd developed a warm affection for it, as well as pride.

"Let's see, then!" Arthur had cried, when she came back with a brown paper package.

She hid it behind her back and shook her head. "Uh-huh. You'll have to wait. It's going to be an extra birthday present, your best."

He laughed out loud on his birthday, when he peeled away the wrapping paper. And then, before she could be hurt, he told her he loved it, and kissed her, and told her how clever she was.

"I can safely say," he added, grinning, "that you've redefined creativity. Pushed the boundaries." And his arms showed how far.

So the rainbow clock hung on their bedroom wall in the flat and then the maisonette, requiring a lot of dusting, until he didn't see it anymore. When he left he abandoned it, along with more conventional material possessions, for love of Lorelei. And she didn't suppose he'd given it a thought since. But it had been a mistake to give it to Leigh when she moved into a place of her own. Not her style at all. Without an explanation she'd probably thought her mother was having a bizarre kind of mid-life crisis. Well, Annie hoped it had raised a pound or two for Oxfam – rather than decorating a landfill site, where flies jumped from soiled nappies and rotting veg to crawl from one o'clock to two. But she certainly wasn't going to ask.

Taking the tea up to the bedroom she found the nurse recommending good TV and admitting to a crush on 'the archaeologist with a kind smile'.

"Oh," said Annie, "Mark Garrett? I met him in a churchyard. He had a son from another time."

She glanced at Arthur, who showed no signs of remembering that before he left her for Lorelei he kept telling her how much he wanted a boy next.

"That Garrett poser's full of himself," he said. "I bet he's not really a professor."

"A walk in the park would do Arthur good, don't you think?" Annie asked the nurse.

"It's going to bucket down!" objected Arthur. "There are other ways to exercise. Aren't there, Constanza?"

It turned out that on her day off Nurse Constanza danced, in a Zumba class. Annie could imagine her, with that thick black hair loose and her wide hips swaying – another exciting woman, free. She said she'd recommend it to anyone – in Arthur's case, once he felt a little stronger, maybe in the New Year. The conversation jumped to Monday's party, in one step.

"Great idea!" said the nurse. "For lifting the spirits. But with sense too. Good rules."

"Annie will see to those," said Arthur. "Rules are her speciality." He clapped.

Annie wasn't sure which woman that was for.

Chapter Five

December 23rd

In the end Leigh didn't care. Christmas began early when she called in sick, asking to speak to Kyle. She kept the words as few and as predictable as possible, hoping the message was clear: that she knew he knew she was lying, but he'd better not take any kind of action, or say anything but *Get well soon.*

On the train up to Edinburgh she smiled to herself, confident that he'd believe her capable of blackmail – even though she'd rather eat a crispy crème doughnut than tell his poor, sweet wife. It was quite civilised travelling First Class at her dad's expense but why her parents had to hold a Christmas party at five o'clock on 23rd December she couldn't imagine. She was pretty sure it wasn't her mother's idea. So she couldn't let her spend all day in Carole's kitchen without offering to count the glasses and butter some French bread.

Her dad must be missing his golf but not as much as he missed the pub and Carole's cooking. The party was a drinking excuse, an opportunity under cover of a crowd. God! She'd better attach herself to him like a defender to a striker and stop him scoring a single unit.

Her question, "What's the deal, Mum, between you and Dad?" hadn't been answered yet. Her mother was more evasive than ever, blocking with medical reports. But she'd find out on arrival – when she'd either be allocated the second bedroom with its built-in wardrobe and roomy shower, or the third, where she'd last slept... oh, four summers ago now, with Gordon, who in her mother's conversation was always described as 'poor'.

Gordon: now a Facebook friend and married, in spite of swearing when Leigh ended it that he'd love her forever. Those four years had given him a life. They'd only left her with a past that could once have had a future. Gordon thought so.

"Speed dating?" her mother had echoed, as if it was a phrase in some foreign language she'd never learned.

Her dad thought it was an amusing idea, until he met the outcome in Gordon.

Leigh took herself back to the present. A Happy Christmas message to Gordon and wife via Facebook wouldn't hurt. In the photo he looked happy, head to head with his ordinary-looking wife. Happier than she could have made him.

She was scrolling down through hangovers, the price of turkeys and retail panic when she heard a Slade ring tone burst from her own phone. Shaking her head at Henry's idea of a joke, she avoided eye contact with the sixty-plus CEO type opposite, and his business-lunch stomach.

Her mother asked where she was.

"Not sure exactly," she said, "but I'll be there at 15:48."

"Oh, as late as that?"

"You're not stressing, are you? No one will come at five, unless they've got another party to go on to later."

Her mother said she didn't really think that applied, given the average age of the guests.

"So now you tell me I'm the only one under thirty! Was I supposed to bring sherry?"

"In fact Carole's girls might call in."

"They've got names and they're full-grown women, Mum!"

Her volume might have risen. She caught the edge of the exec's disapproval and decided to keep her eyes over his shoulder. Phone calls were probably a downgradable offence in First Class.

"It'd be good to see them though," she said, aiming for a better tone. Her mother had a way of bringing out the bitch in her and she was getting so tired of it.

She asked for a guest list but her mother just said, "Oh, mainly the usual suspects, I suppose." Then she added, "Are you bringing a man?"

Leigh's mouth fell open. "What man? Do you want me to ask around the carriage and see if there are any takers?"

She gave the receding exec a smile. He picked up the tablet he'd discarded earlier.

"Carole's bringing her... partner."

"What! Are you serious?" Leigh found one hand supporting the side

226

of her head.

"At least, he's joining us later. Carole's here now, with some rice salad and a chilli."

"Hello, Leigh! Can't wait to catch up!" called Carole, the smile audible. On a training day recently Leigh had been told to smile on the phone. It was a rule Carole lived by but Leigh reckoned that personally she'd need a longer and more intensive course.

"Hi Carole!" Leigh wasn't sure she was adult enough for this. Didn't her father hate Carole? Was Lorelei on the guest list too? What would those 'girls' of Carole's make of her toy boy? "All right," she told her mother, the words like sighs. "See you later."

Glancing out of the window at the dull, streaky sky and the sea creeping around the shore, she thought it all looked more ghostly than festive. Was her father out of bed? For a moment she pictured him barefoot on the doormat, greeting guests with his pyjama trousers hanging low and a bottle of vodka in one hand.

The trolley rattled up. She bought a coffee and tried to remember Christmases. It was probably another December 23rd when as a pre-school blonde she made Lorelei cry – silently, unable to speak – all because she'd found a present, wrapped and hidden under a bed. So, being about three years old, she'd ripped it open like a lion with a kill – and left a give-away trail of card, cellophane and shiny paper as well as bits of dolly clothing that wouldn't stay on the plastic limbs. She didn't suppose she could retrieve many scenes from her infant life but she could still picture her first step-mum in that one. Lorelei had knelt dumb on the floor, helpless with grief but horror and outrage too. As if the mess was entrails! She was scarier, in her quiet, dark-eyed way, than Miss Trunchbull.

That was the last Christmas with Daddy until Carole came along.

In between, all Leigh could bring back was the sofa, the telly, her grandparents dozing and her mother apologising for food that wouldn't present itself properly or on time. Unless they were visiting her religious Uncle Greg, in a house that was like a den but less fun and where no one could eat without 'grace'. When Leigh was little she didn't mind taking a turn and saying, "Thank you, Jesus, for chipolatas and turkey," but when Uncle Heathen (her dad's idea) asked her once, in her teens, she said, "We thank thee, blessed turkey, for the sacrifice. Now let's gobble". Cue anti-festive silence, followed by apologies from her mother that she refused to echo herself. Even at that age Leigh couldn't see the point of her mother and uncle being brother and sister if they were just going to behave like strangers once a year.

"I want a sister," she told her mother one year, when she was still at primary school. She'd heard so many people say that Christmas was wonderful for children, but it wasn't the same for just one. And it had taken her years to get the idea that her parents wouldn't be making any more babies together, even though whenever they met, her dad always kissed her mum on both cheeks.

A sudden, surprise memory broke through – of catching her mother holding a wedding photo as if it was a picture of dying puppy, with her mouth wobbling.

But had she really? It seemed so unlikely. Sometimes Leigh doubted whether old people actually remembered their youth at all, even when they seemed to live in it. Her own narrative of childhood felt ragged and patched. The images might just be photographs, or illustrations she'd drawn in her head from dialogue overheard when she was meant to be asleep. She didn't trust any of it. So all that counted was now, and looking back was as pointless as trying to guess where she'd be next Christmas.

Or who she'd be? A highly-paid executive, but cooler and sharper than the one facing her, who had her in his sights and thought she couldn't tell. He looked up from his tablet and gave her an unexpected smile.

"Home for Christmas?" he asked.

"Not exactly."

Lou still hadn't found the top she was looking for but Coralie wanted to know when they were having the pizza her auntie had promised.

"Last shop," said Lou.

The windows had giant snowflakes drawn in industrial glitter glue, but Crystel felt hot. It must be all the well-wrapped bodies already swinging plastic bags as they wove between the racks. At the far end she noticed a winding queue at the check-out. Lou picked up a red shoe with a six inch heel and golden stars.

"Insane!" said Crystel.

"Meant to be! I like a challenge!"

But with both feet red and starry she teetered into Crystel, who left her to see sense and moved on with Coralie. In the kids' section, Coralie tried on an alien headband with antennae. The silver from the colliding balls flecked her hair.

Now Lou called from behind, holding up a small pink fleecy top. "Look, Crys," she said.

On one side it read, *I may look like a girlie...* in loopy, sparkly letters with flowers. Grinning, Lou turned it to show her the back: *but I'm a badass baby.*

"Nice," said Crystel.

"Bad what?" asked Coralie.

"I told you she's a good reader," Crystel said.

"Badass," said Coralie. "I'm a badass baby."

"Thanks, Lou."

Lou laughed but Crystel didn't. She guessed Coralie was remembering what that mean girl had said about her daddy. "It's rude, sweetheart."

"You left your sense of humour in that Green place," muttered Lou.

"What green place? The elves were green," said Coralie, who hadn't wanted to go in Santa's grotto enough to wait in line more than three minutes. "It was white inside, you could see, but the snow wasn't real."

Crystel ignored her sister. Coralie seemed to think it would be snowing by Christmas Eve. As they walked back through the Women's racks Lou held a gold stretch top against her jacket. Crystel pulled a face.

"What?" asked Lou.

"It's... cheap."

"Well yeah, else how do I afford it?"

"You know what I mean. You've got nicer things – a whole wardrobe full of tops."

"Yeah, so? *A whole wardrobe full of tops,*" she echoed, prissily. "Go and live in a hut then and leave me here to shop."

"That rhymes!" cried Coralie. "I like it in Ethan's hut. It's so quiet you can hear the stars sing if you really try."

"I got X-Factor for that!" laughed Lou.

But as they walked out of the shop talking pizza, she tapped fingers against the side of her head, and when Coralie turned to watch a baby in a buggy kicking his padded feet and laughing she muttered to Crystel, "You're no fun like this, letting everything get spoiled. People have to live. We can't all be poets and woodcutters."

A year ago Crystel didn't think twice about consuming, always wanting more, wasting and wanting. People had to do better than that but she couldn't make it sound convincing in her head, the way Ethan would say it. Lou probably wouldn't thank her for the spotty cotton shopping bag she'd bought her for Christmas, folded in a little tiny pocket so you could keep it in your handbag and never need a plastic one again. She'd think she was preaching.

But Coralie was talking about trees breathing for the earth and Lou listened to her – until her phone rang, anyway. Ethan said he understood why people couldn't face the truth about the ice melting and carbon addiction, because once you get it, you can't live with that understanding unless you change the way you see the world and how you live in it.

Lou didn't want to change but now Crystel couldn't go back. It wasn't home anymore. And she missed him.

Ethan knew it couldn't be much later than five. Not so many miles away the shops would still be full, but he felt the quiet descend like the darkness. He sat down on a log, letting everything settle. For now he wanted to be alone. He wanted to hear the life in the silence and feel his own pulse as he breathed it in. Tomorrow would be a different kind of day and he wanted to remember this taste and this sound, this smell of wood and earth, growth and fire.

Why her? Just because. Why now? Because it was time.

"I love her," he murmured.

If only he could write a poem about love that added something to the world, something completely new that redefined love like Van Gogh redefined loneliness! But love said everything. It was an enormous word, so big it swallowed a hundred others, perhaps a thousand. There was nothing else.

I love you. On the screen of his phone it looked so small, but he let it stand alone. He pressed Send. Then he focused on his hand, trying to relive hers joined with it, and his mouth, locked onto hers. Sex was just a metaphor. (*"Yeah, right, Ethan!"* That was Daph in his head.) But everything that mattered most was a poem. And they had a deeper connection that was just as wordless.

She must be busy. Of course she was. She had a child, work and a family. The message was there, waiting. She would find it, and it would bring her back, wherever she was, to the truth.

He had a train to catch tomorrow, but he didn't need a map to know the distance between Crystel's world and the Kensington hotel. He had one jumper that might do for dinner and he could wash his hair when he arrived. It'd be the kind of place with expensive little tubes and sachets laid out in the en-suite bathroom, and bright white slippers, maybe a robe. So he could travel light. Mentally he worded and reworded an explanation for the presents he hadn't bought, searching for a variation that didn't sound mean or superior. But he would have liked to find something for Coralie that was just right.

Ethan realised how distracted he must be, because he hadn't meditated all day, not even in his lunch break on the farm. He closed his eyes but the pure blue was hard to find, even when he tried to hear Messiaen's E Major, the one he believed held heaven. So stupid to give up the flute when he could have made birdsong in the dark and played for Coralie, taught her too.

Even in the middle of a field, surrounded by silence, peace on earth was hard to find.

Slowly brushing her hair, Annie breathed deeply, and glanced with a smile at the giant Happy Christmas card from the doctors, nurses, other teachers and kids. Including Emmy: *Miss you come back soon sorry for your trouble x*

Looking at Declan's name, each letter pressed hard into the paper and some way from the last, she wondered how much coaxing, bribery or coercion had been necessary. Sanamir's oddly Victorian script was in turquoise glitter pen, also used to draw little flowers: *Thinking of you with kindness in this festive season.* For an overwhelming moment Annie felt a longing for the party she'd missed, the one she'd organised annually for twenty-four years and called work. All those kids now adults, or in some cases, not. She started to name them all but faltered, distressed. They were something she couldn't forget, mustn't. If there was a heaven, she'd see them all there one day, even Declan, and there wouldn't be a wheelchair or injury in sight.

Ha! The sentiment of Christmas, already.

Seeing Leigh from Arthur's spare room window, she felt an unexpected surge of emotion. Not that she could see her daughter's face under the black umbrella. In her heeled boots Leigh walked stiffly and, in spite of the briskness, Annie didn't imagine she was eager to spend Christmas in the bosom of her family. Even as a child Leigh disliked magic – although she once called Lorelei a wicked witch.

Annie put down the hairbrush. There was nothing to hurry for anyway and nothing more to do now. Carole had seen to that and might as well answer the door as well. Glancing in the mirror, Annie felt sure Leigh would disapprove of her dark blue top in spite of its sequins around the neckline, or the long blue skirt that curved round her stomach and wasn't quite the same shade. In spite of the foundation she'd borrowed from Carole, she looked pale. Some ten or twelve years ago her daughter had remarked, as if she really should be ashamed, "Mum, the bags under your eyes could carry the shopping." Presumably now they could manage Christmas, without a trolley.

From the landing she heard Carole cry, "Leigh's here!" and waited for the embracing to finish. She heard the umbrella being shaken outside and the door close, then, "Where is he?"

Before Annie had descended to the hallway, Leigh was being shown through to the lounge. Her priority, as it should be, was to see her dad: up, dressed and claiming to be 'distinguished' in a smooth red sweater and some new trousers Carole had brought as an early present. Hearing his loud, cheery greeting, Annie imagined him pulling the waistband yet again to prove he'd shrunk two whole sizes, and proudly tightening his belt.

Annie stopped and put her smile in place. She walked towards the lounge, where Leigh turned to her.

"I wondered where you were!"

Holding her, Annie breathed it, felt her thinness and how cold she was, underdressed as always. But she censored the commentary, murmuring, "Lovely to see you. So glad you could come," as if she was practising for the guests she hardly knew. Leigh pulled away.

"I'd love a cup of tea, Mum. It's horrible out there."

Annie took orders. Everyone ignored Arthur's half-hearted 'joke' request for champagne, which he then amended to 'proper' coffee. Annie left the three of them, the voices mingling as she supposed they did in families reunited for Christmas. Feeling surplus to requirements, she told herself not to be so needy and slipped on a CD of King's College carols, not sure anyone would notice.

Reaching for the cafetiere, she thought maybe she'd just 'forget' and make him tea. Otherwise he'd only ask how many spoonfuls she'd used or how long she'd left it before she pushed down. Looking out of the window on the darkness closing in, she realised that they'd passed the shortest day. And had she ever, once, celebrated like she always meant to – that the worst was theoretically over once again, and dark days were starting to shade towards light?

"On the up, then," she muttered wryly, and only noticed her daughter behind her once the words were out there, incriminating her.

"Things must be bad," said Leigh, wondering why her mother had to look like a headmistress even at a party. The steam from the kettle clouded around hair that was already limp. Did caring for the patient leave her no time for a cut? She couldn't look much paler if she dusted herself with face powder like Hilda.

Annie felt wrong-footed. She looked back at her daughter, puzzled. There were so many answers.

"Talking to yourself," explained Leigh. "Shall I take my bags up and unpack? I want to change before people arrive." She was thinking the new wine-red dress, even though she might clash with her father.

"Ah, yes... the forget-me-not room."

"O.K."

Was it her imagination, wondered Leigh, or was that said with firmness and care? So her parents weren't sharing a bed, not even for post-surgery companionship. Probably for the best, if he didn't want to die on the job and leave her mum on a manslaughter charge. No wonder he looked dark in spite of the over-stretched grins.

Leigh remembered when Carole chose the wallpaper just as Cath Kidston exploded and flowery prints were fashionable again, but she'd never considered what the little blue blooms might be until Gordon said, "Forget-me-nots," with a kind of quiet affection. Gordon was the only boyfriend who not only bought her flowers but could name them all.

Now that she stood in the doorway looking at the wallpaper, Leigh also remembered squeezing into that single bed with Gordon. The memories were vivid enough for her to wonder why she lost patience with him so quickly. But there was plenty of forgetting going on this particular Christmas – or had better be. Carole forgetting her marriage vows. Her mother forgetting her father forgetting his. Didn't middle-age teach people anything?

"Good to meet you, Gordon," her dad had said, looking at his double denim (before that was back in fashion) and telling her, the moment he could feasibly be out of earshot, "All in blue!" as if it was some kind of joke.

Apparently for her father, Gordon would always be the Blue Engine, and after a few drinks he found that even more amusing because this Gordon was anything but a show-off or bighead, and could admittedly be slow at times. And knowing nothing about Alex Salmond or any form of politics whatsoever put him on the back foot once her dad expressed his astonishment: "It must be lovely to live in a bubble!"

Sometimes things and people looked different with hindsight and it was hard to think what Gordon had done wrong apart from break his promise to forget-her-not. For such a nice guy he wore a thick skin, and it was only when she dumped him after nine months or so of treating him in a way that her mother called 'careless and disrespectful' that she remembered he'd won the Drama prize at school. The skin turned out to be a costume. Out of role, he exposed the hurt: very few words necessary. It explained the lines he'd learned for the Speed Dating presentation, probably rehearsed with the sister who dragged him along because she needed moral support. The sister who apparently held on to grudges, because she refused Leigh's friendship request.

"Sorry, Gordon," said Leigh to the mirror on the wardrobe door.

She pictured poor Gordon gelling his hair in front of that same pane of glass before he faced her father, when what he needed to brush up on was his current affairs, Art and History. Well, as her dad had observed with undisguised pleasure once it was over, Gordon was 'history now'. "I always preferred Percy," he'd added, and Carole said, "Ignore his smut, Leigh," while he protested, "The Green Engine!" and Leigh countered, "You're looking more and more like The Fat Controller, Dad!"

Leigh expected this Christmas to be banter-free as well as celibate. So much to look forward to! And she could have been Mrs Blue Engine by now, with a kid or two chuffing alongside and kindness every day.

She heard her mother below, clattering.

Annie binned teabags, wondering whether the forget-me-not room was up to Carole's kind of scratch. It occurred to her that Leigh was like that Snow Queen in the story she used to read her, with a shard of glass for a heart. Pulling a face, she wished thoughts could be rewound and deleted. As if she had any right to judge, given her own love life – or life, threaded feebly with beads of love she was too ashamed to wear.

Aware of Leigh moving around, opening wardrobe doors and drawers, Annie felt sure she'd spot some kind of difference and complain. Then through the choirboys and organ she heard something unexpected. It made her venture quietly towards the lounge.

As she looked in, Carole turned towards her, eyes widening. Arthur's head was on her chest, and one ringed and manicured hand was on his hair.

Annie stood, then took a step into the room, two. As if nothing had happened, nothing at all. Just as she had so many years earlier, the first time she'd accepted an invitation to dinner and walked in on them just there, no space between them, the pair of them smiling with the knowing intimacy of dahlias vivid and heady on the same stem. Still that was what they were: bright and showy together.

He lifted his head from Carole's chest. Now all the party shine had gone. Carole picked a hair from her top and held it between red fingernails.

"It's good to see you two are friends again," said Annie.

Carole crossed to the wastepaper basket and dropped the hair before she looked back and said, "I certainly hope so." And smiled.

Leigh was on the stairs now in her heels. Annie realised she still held the tray of teacups. Arriving, Leigh took the last one and sat next to her father, planting a kiss on his forehead and then wiping the lipstick away with a tissue.

"You're cold," Leigh told him.

"Nothing a Scotch wouldn't sort," he said.

"Behave!" cried Leigh. She wanted to ask Carole when her toy boy was arriving but this was Christmas all over, eggshells everywhere she put her feet. And her mother looked scrambled.

In fact, her mother had left the room.

It was called St John's. Crystel and her mum sat on either side of Coralie, with Lucie on the end of the row, waving and beaming at everyone because this was her church and she was at home. It was where Coralie had been christened, with Lucie and her Kenny as godparents, but Crystel hadn't got round to bringing her back more than a couple of times since. She felt awkward, especially when faces she'd forgotten smiled as if they remembered.

Her mum had said Lucie must have pulled a few strings with the minister back then because of her being a single mum but she didn't believe it. It wasn't that kind of church.

It was the crib service this afternoon and the scene was big and chunky, with solid wooden figures that must have been carved by people living a different life.

"They've got mouths like us," Coralie whispered, because the wooden faces were African.

The church was candle-lit and decorated with holly that looked real but Coralie wanted to test the prickles with a fingertip.

"Is that why the berries are red?" she asked, looking at her forefinger as if there was blood on it.

A shabby Somali in a hoodie sat in front of them. Crystel's mother wrinkled her nose.

"What's that smell?" asked Coralie, as the organ rose into a chorus Crystel recognised.

"Shh," said Crystel, her eyes on the choir and lots more mouths like theirs. Then she added, "It's what poverty smells like." Ethan's voice was here with her now, everywhere.

"No one's too poor to wash," said her mother.

"Shh!" Crystel told her. "He'll hear you."

"He won't speak English!"

"He's what church is for – isn't he?!"

"Everyone welcome," whispered Lucie.

That what it said outside. Her mum had wanted 'a proper church', which meant swaying her hips and clapping and shouting out loud, but this one was nearer and Crystel liked the quietness. There wasn't any fuss.

"Is Ethan coming?" asked Coralie.

"No, sweetie. He's at Ferningstone."

The music rang to a stop. A short, middle-aged woman in jeans and a spotty silk top welcomed everyone, and thanked all the children who'd been giving Mary and Joseph a place to stay in the last couple of weeks. She was holding knitted figures with wobbly smiles. Coralie turned to Crystel.

"We didn't have them! Can they stay with us tonight?"

Crystel whispered that they'd see. It was a kids' story, but way better than Santa and his elves or a snowman that always had to melt in the end. The woman placed a big, golden star with sharp geometric angles on the end of a stick above the roof of the stable. Someone must have lit a big candle behind it because the scene glowed brightly now.

"Is it magic?" asked Coralie.

"In a way, I guess it is," Crystel told her. Her mother frowned, but Crystel supposed love was a kind of magic when you thought about it.

"Way better than magic," said Lucie, her face so bright and sure that Crystel wished she'd led a good life too, and easy.

There was a Bible reading and she saw her mother nodding seriously under her new hat but she didn't really believe in a virgin falling pregnant with God's child, did she? She hadn't been so happy when Crystel had found herself in the same condition and claimed she didn't know how.

Wondering how she'd feel if that boy who couldn't control his urges walked in now, with the same swing of a walk, she realised she forgave him long ago. No point blaming a puppy for wagging its tail.

If it was a choice between Finn and Ethan A. Garrett, plenty of people would say she belonged with her own kind. Even her mother might forget the way she used to spit Finn's name and give him her vote. They'd call it facing facts, all of them. As opposed to dreaming.

There was a prayer to say and Crystel wished she could make them work – like a recipe or spell. They were poetry really, another kind of language, beautiful and sleepy but exciting too, once you let them be new. If God was love then God was good and great. But wasn't love the power, and God just a way to make a character out of an idea?

When they came to the reading about the baby being born, Coralie whispered, "I love Baby Jesus."

Of course she did. Lucie agreed with a big smile and who wouldn't? Crystel felt so much love for her own baby that she could have cried, like a sentimental old woman. But what about the nails and the cross, and that bloody beating? Wasn't the message that love always had to die?

Her gran used to sing, "Were you there when they crucified my Lord?" and once, apparently, she answered with, "No, or I would've untied him and set him free, like Robin Hood." She must have just seen the movie with the creepy Sheriff. Granddad George thought it was a funny story when he heard it but he didn't disapprove like her gran. He just thought it made her brave.

But love was in the sadness. That was the point. And Crystel felt it now, through the candlelight, with organ chords roaring up as if an olden-days king had been crowned. If she couldn't be with Ethan, then she'd always love him, and he'd be there every Christmas. Not like Finn, who could be hanging back, chewing gum in the shadows like a ghost come back to haunt her. Ethan was part of her now, like God was part of believers but not really there all the same.

Coralie didn't know the Lord's Prayer, and Crystel found gaps breaking in. But there was something about 'the power and the glory' that lifted inside her when she mumbled it. When it ended, Coralie kept her head bowed as they rose for another carol. They were two lines into the verse before she opened her eyes and stood up.

Her smile was like the one she wore on her birthday when she'd blown out the candles and made a wish.

"Don't ask," she whispered. "It's a secret."

Crystel shook her head as she sang.

Emerging from the bathroom with a washed and touched-up face, Annie was surprised to find Leigh waiting for her.

"What's wrong, Mum?"

"Nothing."

"Right."

"You know I'm not a party person."

"That's what I told Dad. He thinks you're upset. He's been throwing a wobbly about calling round to cancel. But we talked him round. It'll do him good, won't it?"

Annie would say the same about any one of her pupils who tried to duck out of the Christmas party. No one had even told her whether Declan behaved or Emmy refused to join in.

"Yes, I hope so."

"So don't spoil it for him. There's nothing to be jealous of. Carole told me she wouldn't have him back even if he begged on bended knee."

Leigh watched her mother's face for a reaction because she knew she'd said that with some vehemence. But she sighed because there was nothing in that face to see. It made her want to rattle her till the feelings fell out.

Annie followed her daughter to the top of the stairs, their arms close but not touching.

"You'd prefer it if Dad hated Carole like he hates Lorelei?"

Annie stopped and frowned. "Not at all," she said. "Hate's overrated."

Leigh laughed. "Oh, Mum, hate's fuel!"

Annie almost said it would be better in that case if the fire went out. Ashes: the word that filled her head was so fragile, light enough to be scattered on air, streaking, smearing and breaking on a fingertip.

By the time she'd greeted the first couple on the doorstep minutes later, Arthur had some fuel of his own, in a whisky glass. He stood awkwardly as his guests seemed unsure whether he was safe to hug. Annie looked at Carole but she was quite at home, smiling as she waited to kiss French-style. No concern whatever.

"You can't stop him drinking at his own party, Mum," murmured Leigh, picking up a matching glass and taking a sip. "He'd rather be dead."

"I'm going to check the oven," said Annie. For ashes, she thought. She could almost taste them.

"Do you want any help?" Leigh could see her mother was stressed but nobody was going to let him get hammered. Would she never learn to lighten up?

"I'm fine," said Annie and walked away, realising she was still in her slippers. With a wild laugh silent inside, she thought about stuffing them with Carole's mushroom pâté and arranging them in the centre of the display on the dining table.

From the lounge she heard laughter. She opened the oven door, the heat catching her cheeks and spreading through her neck, her ears. The foil crackled under the whirr of the fan. Noticing the food congealed on oven gloves – something Carole would never have allowed – she attempted to scrape off the solids with a knife, and cut her finger just enough to draw a speck of blood that stretched into a bead before she sucked it away.

A rhythm she recognised beat into the room as the volume surged. *All right now. Baby it's all right now.*

Chapter Six

One minute to midnight

Annie realised her mistake around ten fifteen when Arthur began to flag. It hadn't occurred to her to put a time for *Carriages* on the invitations. Cutting off *Wham!* Arthur fell back onto the sofa, removed his jumper with a show of a struggle and asked for something 'soothing and mellifluous', as well as water. Quite a hint, especially when she said, "You must be tired." But the few who seemed to notice the difference were begged to stay by a host who declared he was 'fine'.

Around this time Carole's extra-mature daughters Sarah and Lizzie dropped by in passing, with social skills Annie doubted she'd ever match. It was good to see Leigh catching up with Sarah, her favourite 'big sister' who used to lie on the sofa wrapped in bandages dotted with red felt tip so that Nurse Leigh could make her better. Maybe they'd keep in closer touch now both their mothers had been separated from the same man.

Carole herself was on such typically relaxed and welcoming form that Annie wondered how many of the guests had any idea she didn't live there. Or that she'd abandoned Arthur for a man she admitted wasn't quite forty, especially as the man in question failed to show. It was Leigh who reported to Annie that he'd sent Carole a text claiming a temperature.

"Oh," said Annie on auto-response, "that's a shame."

"Or a lie," said Leigh, and added meaningfully that Sarah and Lizzie had never met him.

"Leigh, no one makes people up!"

"There are shades of lie," Leigh told her. "Come to my office for a day and you'll see most of them."

But Annie could understand the mysterious toy boy staying away from a party at a house his woman still co-owned, hosted by her husband. She'd quite like to be absent herself.

Now one of Arthur's old colleagues was asleep with his mouth open, revealing smoker's teeth, and a friend of Carole's seemed unable to stop giggling whenever she tried to move from the sofa without a wobble. The rest were oddly stable, the men propped up with carbohydrate and the women either driving or sobered by the sight of their host trying to fool his heart.

Somehow proceedings lurched on and Annie tried not to watch the time. Mingling with plates was safe but unrewarding; bathroom breaks helped. Surely, she thought, emerging from one around midnight, it would be over soon?

Returning to the lounge she found Arthur waiting for her, beckoning her. Pointing to the clock like John Travolta on a flashing disco floor, he called for silence. About fifteen guests remained, most of them dancing to *The Locomotion*.

"Shut Kylie up, Leigh!" he repeated, waving an arm towards the CD player.

The giggler, whose name was Gerrie, leaned forward as if to propel herself up but dropped back again as the music stopped.

"It's Christmas!" he cried, pointing to the second hand racing on past midnight. "I want to make an announcement."

"Are you pregnant, Artie?" asked Gerrie, and giggled.

In the quiet Annie thought she sounded like a cartoon with the vocals on the wrong speed.

"I'm alive," said Arthur, and repeated it, with more triumphant force.

Leigh clapped and put a boss-like arm on his back.

"Thank God," muttered Carole beside Annie.

A cheer gathered itself up until he stopped it with both hands.

"And only a very little bit pissed," he said, "so if I sit down now that's not the booze, it's the surgery. Swear to God." Annie knew that phrase, such a give-away. "And I don't know how much longer I've got, but I want to enjoy every minute of it."

More cheers. Was that embarrassment Annie felt now, in the warm room, spiking the air?

"I need my sleep now, but I wanted to see Christmas in with this woman beside me, this woman who's always been my rock." He looked round, towards Carole. Her smile was frozen. Annie looked away. "My

241

Annie," he said, and held out his hand. "Here to save me like an angel should."

Annie felt as if she shrank from the inside. "I'm no angel, Art."

"Ah, but angels say that," he continued. "It's an angel thing to say. God knows who you are and what you've always been to me."

God? It really must be Christmas, thought Annie. She realised Leigh was looking anxiously from one parent to another, thinking perhaps that what she'd been was his ex, his reject.

"This angel says bedtime, Arthur," she said. "Happy Christmas, everyone!"

Through the chorus and the kissing, he broke through again. "She's the one. I know that now. And I'm so glad she's here. Here's to the rest of my life, with my Annie by my side where she belongs!"

Carole was still smiling but Annie had no idea how. Her own face felt stiff as she let him take her hand.

"All right, Dad," Leigh told him. "Let these people go home."

"Yes, do!" cried Annie and suddenly the words were back, jostling, jolly, empty and repetitive, as coats were fetched and scarves claimed.

Carole kissed her cheek and told her she could easily come back at around eleven to help clear up, no problem. Annie told her there was no need, thanked her and said, "Don't catch that flu!" with a cheerful smile as she held the door. It seemed a matter of seconds before she was alone and locking up, in a hall that felt cold enough to make her shiver.

"Dad's in bed," said Leigh as she began to load glasses onto a tray in the lounge. "He wants you." She paused, and for a moment Annie thought she might blush. "To say goodnight. Just leave all this."

Annie nodded. But by the time she'd loaded the dishwasher, Arthur was asleep.

Leigh emerged from the bathroom, with her make-up wiped away and skin so clear Annie felt a sudden tenderness for the child she remained. And anxiety that in that silky robe she must be frozen, even in a post-party house still warm and sweet.

"I hope someone enjoyed that," said Annie, "or bits of it anyway."

Leigh raised her eyebrows, which Annie realised were plucked rather well. People had such odd ways of spending their money and time. Like parties. She wondered whose idea it was, in the first place, for people to dress up, overeat and drink to excess, shout over music or wiggle and shake as if they didn't know how foolish they looked.

"It had its moments," said Leigh, with no trace of a smile.

"I didn't realise you were such a good dancer," Annie told her.

"I guess that's relative." Leigh wasn't in the mood to make small talk with her own mother like this. "Dad didn't need to humiliate Carole like that, in front of everybody. *Her* friends."

"I hope that wasn't the intention."

"Mum, talk to me! You're not at work now. He's a total shambles, a liability."

Annie didn't know how to answer. In retrospect any humiliation had been scattergun: hers, Carole's, but Arthur's too and even Leigh's, in her outrage at... what, exactly? At emotion in those old enough to know better? And emotion held in check, for safety's sake?

"He's not himself," she said, fully aware that he was also more himself than ever. "I'm done in now," she added, and wished she was the kind of mother who could count on a hug to make the difference words couldn't manage.

"O.K.," said Leigh, suddenly much too exhausted herself for any of this. "Yeah."

"Sleep well," said Annie.

"You too."

Ethan didn't know why they had to watch through the credits at the end when his father's name had been at the start, almost as tall on the screen as the series title. It was a repeat anyway, but his dad knew he hadn't seen it and it would have been mean when asked, "Do you fancy taking a look?" to say, "Not really," even though he knew this stuff, could have fronted the programme himself with a bit of last-minute revision. And it was a lot better than the chat show on the TV in the hotel lounge, with Hollywood guests making jet-lagged smiles and trying not to look piqued when the host took the piss.

"What do you think? Camera angles obtrusive in the tomb?"

"Depends whether they're trying to show you as an action hero or a professor."

His father smiled. "Both, surely."

"It's perfect, then."

Daph might have contributed a lot more if she and Martin hadn't crashed out shortly after arrival. The others were due at various points before afternoon tea, which was when Ethan supposed a day called

Christmas Eve would really begin, regardless of the date on the clock he was facing on his dad's hotel room dressing table.

"Is it the flying that bothers you?"

Ethan wasn't sure whether that was about his sister, or the star of the show and the camera crew. "Flying bothers me," he said slowly. "It's the single most damaging thing an individual can do, in terms of carbon. I don't have to tell you that."

"So I should stick to writing books that no one reads."

"Dad, I'm not going to tell you what to do."

His father sipped his brandy. "Why not?"

"Because you know. Of course you know."

His father watched the liquid in his glass, studied it as he tilted it. Ethan was unnerved by his composure. They might have been debating the future of Atlantis.

"Look, Dad, I'm not anyone's judge or jury. We have to live by our own rules. And it isn't personal."

Ethan would have liked to share something else that was. Someone. It might redirect the conversation but his dad would see it as a statement just as ideological, or political, as the one he'd skirted round. As if he'd selected Crystel because she was a black single mum from North London who'd never been to a museum that wasn't Tussaud's.

His father turned off the TV. "Are you sure?"

"I'm going to bed now," he told his father. "Good work – on the show."

As he left for his own room two doors down, his father said, "I'm glad you came."

Ethan nodded. In his room he turned on his phone.

X it said. So little, and enough too. Switching off again, he told himself words weren't always necessary and sometimes they got in the way, clouded, misled. It didn't matter what she said or didn't say. He loved her anyway.

With only one job to do, Crystel took Coralie to her parents and arrived at Leigh Capaldi's apartment, only to find a note. *Happy Christmas, Crystel. I had to head north – parent problems. Just give the place a quick onceover and enjoy the afternoon with Coralie. There's a bit extra so you can treat yourself. Thanks, L. x*

Counting the notes she found four twenties over and above. "Shit," she murmured. "Thanks, L." She tucked them away.

Still, with no one here the place hardly needed cleaning for Christmas. Employers like Mrs Harris knew the morning off, especially on Christmas Eve, was worth more than the money, but she couldn't expect Leigh Capaldi to understand that without a daughter. Even though she'd nearly lost her dad.

The place didn't have one string of tinsel, just the kind of tree that pretended to be modern art so people would pay more and feel good about it. Glassy white in a corner, with spikes like icicles, it looked sad: a Billy No Mates abandoned by the other trees without a single robin to cheer it up. A bit like Madam herself. But a wodge of cash and a crazy clock, an X and a sorry didn't make them best friends forever.

Crystel padded into the softly-carpeted lounge to enjoy the under-floor heating. Dusting the DVDs, she noticed one lying across the top. It was an old movie she'd been trying to name with Ethan, because the Amish community reminded her, in a way, of Ferningstone. *Witness:* a love story about two people who'd always love each other but would live their lives apart.

Her gran believed in signs. Crystel shook the duster out of the window, looking down on streets shining with colour, some of it on the move as the wind stirred a trio of thin city trees veiling the apartment block. She remembered another movie, one she loved as a little girl, where the father heard his son calling him from the top of a mountain, summoning him to the secret garden.

Ethan was out there, thinking of her too.

She took out her phone, held it, entered his name and put it away again. The sooner she finished, the sooner Christmas would start.

22:51. From the spare room Leigh could hear her mother clearing debris. By the time she joined her downstairs, all evidence of the night before had disappeared.

"I'm so glad you managed to sleep in," Annie told her, offering coffee.

Leigh thought there might be jealousy in the mix. Her mother didn't look remotely refreshed and hadn't bothered with clothes or make-up. In her slippers and fleecy dressing gown she looked bag-lady old. Leigh would never allow herself...

"I might hit the shops," she announced, "before they get too mad."

245

"On Christmas Eve? I think oases of calm might be hard to find. I'm going to the supermarket myself but maybe we could stagger it, so as not to leave your dad alone…"

Leigh frowned. In case he strung himself up with tinsel at the idea of a total ban on booze? No, in case he filled up while they were gone!

"He's not a child, Mum. You can't control his every move…"

"Control! As if anyone could! I just want to help him… to help himself."

Leigh turned away and investigated the breadbin. She guessed he'd rather have a year doing what the hell he wanted than thirty years of restrictions. She'd probably be the same, except that no one could ever see around the next corner. And even an inhibited, middle-class mother who never broke any rules could be an enigma, impossible to decode.

Having dropped a couple of wholemeal slices in the toaster, Leigh turned on her phone. Just a few drunken texts from various friends she hadn't actually seen for weeks or months, with festive well-wishes. Nothing from Kyle to delete unread. Maybe he was her Lorelei, the big mistake soon righted by some male equivalent of Carole, capable and understanding. Except…

"Mum," she said, to her back at the sink as the toaster pinged, "honestly… would it be a relief if Carole came back to Dad and you could go back to work, and your life?"

There, thought Leigh. She'd said it now.

Annie didn't move. She ran the tap and listened to the water, shaking her head as if she might not stop.

"Mum?"

Leigh wanted to be gentle; maybe she needed more practice. She only felt impatience now. How could this woman mother her, and let herself be loved, when she needed some kind of help to just be herself?

Annie wiped her hands on the towel, turned and tried to smile. "That's like asking me whether I'd be relieved if he died." She opened the fridge, staring at the contents but for a moment identifying nothing.

"It's not! For God's sake!" Leigh ignored the low-fat spread her mother pushed towards her on the kitchen table. "I thought the job was everything to you …"

Annie looked up, trying to read the question. She wasn't sure whether she heard respect or an accusation.

"It's not that simple," she told her quietly. "Nothing's ever

246

everything."

"What does that mean?"

Annie held one hand in another. The arthritis was becoming bothersome. It was probably the Edinburgh weather. The kitchen clock sounded louder than ever. Wasn't time enough of a problem without the relentless sound of it, taunting? He was upstairs and she'd loved him so long, without the words to label and explain.

"He's asleep. I looked in," continued Leigh. "Look, all I'm saying is, this can't be easy. God knows I love him but *he's* not easy."

"Life isn't." Annie tried the statement with the other L word but it was much too true. "But like he said, he's still with us, and we're together, and we have plenty to eat – or will do, soon. Edinburgh's not a war zone. We're the lucky ones."

"Yeah," said Leigh. Conversation over, then. Someone had better tie her mother to a couch and keep her there until she 'owned up' the way teachers said. "Any marmalade?"

It arrived in front of her as she scrolled through Facebook. "I don't know why I bother with social media when the best anyone can do is sugar-coated Virgin Marys and guinea pigs in Santa hats."

"Bah humbug," muttered Annie and poured the coffee.

Relatives arrived at Mark Garrett's chosen hotel in dribs and drabs, some more bedraggled than others as the weather teased, with sun broken by sheeting downpours. The room temperature everywhere felt balmy to Ethan, who turned off the radiator in his room, pulled off his sweater and supposed his T-shirt would look better ironed.

"You could save energy and turn the heating down," he told the manager at the reception desk, all in black with a bright white collar and handkerchief peaking over his pocket, but a red paper hat angled slightly on his gleaming hair.

"People like to be cosy at Christmas, sir," was the response.

"It'd be cooler on Bondi Beach," said Ethan, but the guy only smiled.

His father appeared to tell him Evelyn had a cold and wouldn't be joining them, passing him the phone.

"I'll be thinking of your mother," she told him, "along with Tom, like I always do, every day. And you too, Ethan. Bless you."

"Thanks," he told her. "Happy Christmas."

Had he considered her once since he'd waved goodbye, talking mermaids? No need for guilt, Ethan told himself. Everyone needed somebody to think of each day, but he had Crystel, Coralie too, and that felt like some kind of limit when he threw in his mother as well as his dad and sister.

Up to twenty of them now gathered in the bar, exchanging family news, repeating the headlines with each new arrival. Name labels would have come in handy. Sitting in an oversized leather armchair, Ethan faced the clock. There were aunts, uncles and cousins, most of them last seen at the funeral. With each new meet-and-greet he felt more like an actor with lines to deliver.

"No, I'm a kind of casual labourer, farm work mainly, some peeling veg at Ferningstone when the numbers are up."

"No, I didn't finish the Masters. It didn't seem to matter much."

"No, in the middle of a field, in a shepherd's hut."

"No, but I might see if I could teach a poetry class."

"Nothing at the moment, nothing much anyway, nothing worth finishing. Life's a poem if you read it… you know, carefully."

"It's a community dedicated to a change of consciousness. To a global awakening, a kind of uprising of people who love the earth and one another."

That was what you might call a conversation-stopper. One cousin suggested loving one another was a Christmas-only thing. One uncle who used to be in the R.A.F. repeated *uprising* and talked about not holding with 'students breaking windows and occupying the City'. Ethan was explaining that he stood by Gandhi's ideals of non-violence when his sister handed him a glass of mulled wine.

"Get off your soapbox, Ethan," she told him. "It's party time."

Mince pies and cream, vegetable crisps and marzipan stars coated in chocolate were soon followed by cocktails, which then made way, before Ethan was remotely ready, for a four course meal in the dining room, where the starched red tablecloths were as thick as the canvas roof on his new home.

"Worth stealing, eh!" laughed Uncle Trevor, admiring the sheen on the cutlery.

Daph was the one who stole lipstick when she was about twelve. Ethan said if she didn't put it back, he'd tell, but she didn't believe him and she was right. "Wuss," she called him, producing it from her pocket outside the shop and applying the dark red sheen so she could pout at him.

The menu was in French too, the font looped, with a silver star at the beginning and end of each dish. Ethan pictured Crystel grinning incredulously, as if it was all a cross between a fairy tale and a joke. He didn't want to know how much this cost per head, but he wished he knew what his mother would say. What she'd look like, ten years on. Whether she'd ask him the same questions, with answers that all began with denials and led to dead ends. Or whether she'd have reconnected with the girl on the beach at last...

The clock said 7:34 and it was his turn to order.

"I'm full already," he said. "Really."

Protests, of course, insistence and a note of irritation or two. They were dancing as the ship went down, all over the world, but must he be the one to shout *Iceberg?* And wouldn't that be a sick kind of joke given the big, green melt?

"He'll have the veggie option," Daph told the waiter, and the ordering resumed.

Glasses were refilled but Ethan shook his head, having already exceeded his alcohol intake for the year in one day. Losing all clarity was tempting, but this would never happen again, and he'd be unavailable if it did. Maybe it could be a poem in its own way.

Soon the starters arrived and Ethan found himself staring at the minimal arrangement on the huge plate: char-grilled vegetable slices vivid with colour, their tips dipping in a speckled pool of creamy sauce. Conversation thickened, most of it across or beyond Ethan. He watched, observing, trying to understand but unwilling to fit.

Until the main course was cleared away, no one mentioned the anniversary. But around nine his father stood and toasted "an absent wife, mother, niece, cousin ..." Her name, mumbled on a loop, sounded like a mantra. Not the official one on the printed envelopes but her middle name, the one that only his father used, and not so often. Not Catherine but "Joy".

It was the name she wore barefoot in rock pools. It was the name he thought she'd lost – and he'd overlooked, like a typo.

Silent with his glass half-raised, Ethan felt as if he had slipped into a corner in shadow. Or was a figure left behind a steamed-up glass, peering through at the colour. He stood and the linen napkin fell from his lap.

"I've just learned to love my mother," he said.

Silence. His father said his name but he couldn't tell the tone. His own voice seemed a thing apart from him and heat rose up to his head. Daph passed him a glass of water, muttering, "Lightweight!", but instead of taking it he put his wine glass down on the cloth, spilling a little.

"It's too late now."

"Ethan, it's not. It's all right." It was his father, looking very sober. Not his camera face.

"It's never all right without love. Then we're just consumers and competitors. We're data." He looked around but he'd never been good at projecting and he wasn't sure all the hearing aids worked in crowds. "We have to learn to love the earth again, like we did as children, but it's almost too late."

A great-uncle was asking a great-aunt what he'd said. The embarrassment of those who knew was swamp-thick.

"We've got to hug more trees," reported Daph, glancing at the immaculate festive one with symmetrical and coordinated decorations, all in purple and gold.

"It's Christmas, Ethan," his father pointed out.

"I'm not trying to spoil anything..."

"Try harder," said Daph.

"We have to stop abusing the earth and endangering the lives of the poorest who suffer first. We have to protect the future for generations who'll live with climate chaos. Or die."

Daphne shook her head. "I have something to say too." Her projection was impressive. "There's a reason I'm drinking mineral water. We're having a baby." She looked quickly at Martin, who smiled awkwardly and placed his hand on hers.

Then Daph looked back at Ethan. Her eyes were wide.

Another toast, no name at all. As the congratulations became kisses and questions followed, Ethan sat down. He tipped the water in his glass, sipped it, listened.

He would be an uncle, she told him, and he could teach their child to love the earth.

Ethan smiled. "Thank you," he said, because she meant it, in her way. But at the same time it meant nothing. It was a peace offering, a gesture, not recognition of unavoidable truth. Not a commitment. And he felt like a father already. Waiting for his turn, he embraced her, shook Martin's hand. People were settling again. The waiters were pouring a different wine for dessert. Wouldn't cholesterol soon be clamping someone's heart?

Ethan stood again.

"In fact," he said, "I love someone else and I should be with her now."

The lifted faces were suddenly open.

"Her name's Crystel and I think… do you mind if I go – now, while there's still transport?"

Why would anyone mind? They'd toast his departure! He dropped his napkin in a firmly angled sculpture on the table. Someone pointed out the time.

"Go," said his father. "We'll all be here till the morning after Boxing Day. Bring her back with you."

"Yes, hire a lecture room," said Daph, "and show us a Powerpoint."

"Get a taxi," said his father, producing his wallet, but Ethan said it was fine. The tubes were on a weekend service. Through the good wishes he didn't mention that he didn't know exactly where to go.

The stairs were steep and something inside him was shaking.

After Scrabble, Leigh and Arthur agreed to watch *Cabaret*. Not Annie's idea of a festive movie, but when she said it was 'dark' Leigh teased her about preferring *White Christmas,* even though she didn't, and Arthur groaned. After making them coffee she went to her bedroom and called Hilda, whose dissatisfaction loomed large through her stage whispers.

"It's all very serious here," she said. "Greg wanted me to go to church at midnight but we have to go at eleven tomorrow anyway."

"I wouldn't mind," said Annie. No kitchen, no booze (well, only a sip from a gold chalice) and no manic TV. And generous candlelight.

Hilda ignored that and asked fondly of Arthur, who had apparently impressed her more than usual by what she called attempting to beat her to the grave. Annie was vague, with phrases like 'getting there' and 'taking it easy now'.

"I'm sorry I missed the do," said Hilda. "I always liked Carole's parties. She doesn't serve mince pies cold from the packet."

"True," said Annie, trying to picture her mother joining in the Locomotion. "But it's all very quiet here, really."

Hilda seemed unconvinced. Annie used Christmas-long-ago as a prompt for familiar rosy childhood memories – from a time when people knew how to have real, honest-to-goodness fun with a piano, a bread board and a blindfold. She heard her mother's pleasure in the retelling, wondering how much variation there might be each time. Barely listening, she was surprised all of a sudden to hear her sniff and guessed at a tear to wipe away. Reminded that she wasn't really old, she told herself it wasn't over yet. Ahead lay more to lose, to regret or romanticise.

"Happy Christmas, Mum," she said, realising how odd it would be if she never got to say that again. If she didn't have much time left to love her mother properly, she should do it. Nothing else would be enough.

She returned to the lounge to find Arthur ready for bed.

"The sooner I go, the sooner I'll be opening my stocking," he said, eyes stretched in an impression of a five-year-old.

Half an hour later Leigh was fully absorbed by her own phone, so Annie went upstairs to discard clothes that felt increasingly restrictive and take comfort from her softly forgiving pyjamas and wraparound dressing gown.

"Annie," she heard, heading back downstairs.

Annie grimaced because she'd been creeping, careful to avoid the creaks. She waited and he called again. The door was just slightly ajar the way he liked it, letting a chink of light through. Annie stepped inside. He turned the dimmer switch by his side of the bed, illuminating himself in a light that was soft and warm. He looked wide-awake.

"Did I wake you? I'm sorry."

"Not exactly. You kept me awake. Your presence downstairs. And how much I owe you."

Annie said nothing but she was where she had to be, that was all – which reminded her of Hilda, so she told him about the phone call, with as much diversionary humour as she could muster.

He patted the bed. "Come closer, darling. I can't see you."

"Not such a bad thing," she muttered and sat on his bed, careful still. "Can I get you anything?"

"I've got what I want," he said, "right here. You know why I love you, don't you?"

He used to know, she remembered that much. There were locations, but they slipped away without captions. Maybe people never remembered what they didn't really believe.

"Because you never stopped loving me, whatever, whoever. Only I didn't see – or maybe I did, all along. That's why you're here and I'll always love you for that."

She knew that smile. It went with touch. Reaching out he stroked hair that had looked and felt so different decades earlier, the last time. In the gentleness of the touch Annie felt heat, and tightness where she breathed.

"It's a double bed, darling. Stay with me tonight. I want to wake up with you on Christmas morning."

Leaning towards her, he kissed her cheek. With a forefinger she wiped the wetness away, but she hadn't moved.

"I won't jump you, much as I'd like to. Your virginity's safe with me."

Annie breathed out, surprised by how much sound she made.

"You must be so tired," she said, "and I'm not sleeping well. I'd disturb you, reading until the early hours." She kissed his forehead and pulled away. "Big day tomorrow!"

"I won't give up," he called as she left the room after checking there was nothing else she could fetch him. "I'm wooing you – as best I can. And this time I won't let you go!"

Leigh was on the landing when Annie stepped out into the light.

"Is he rewriting history?"

Annie smiled. "Selective memory," she whispered. "We're all good at both."

"It's only the present that counts," said Leigh. "And the bigger the better!"

Annie smiled, kissed her goodnight and closed the bedroom door.

23:13 said the digital alarm clock and Crystel was wide awake. Beside her, Coralie slept on her back, the rhythm of her breathing so low and peaceful it was hard to believe that twice in the last four hours she'd whispered, "Mummy, is it time?"

This was the room where Lou had spent her teens, the room she'd given up when Crystel brought Coralie home from the hospital five years ago, and laid her in a cot that only just fitted between the bed and the door. Even now Lou didn't seem to need independence, but then she always did as she chose. Crystel hadn't heard her come in yet. Lou might be the bad girl but she brought in money and her *understanding of family planning,* as their dad had put it once, was *better than some people's.* As if family entered into Lou's mind any more than planning anything but her social life.

"Come on," Finn had said, pressed hard against her, "it's all right, I'm a Catholic boy. I know what to do. Trust me."

He'd never said he loved her and she respected him for that, at least. She was the one who chose to pretend, when only a Sunday School teacher would trust him with a fiver.

Ethan had been shocked underneath, must have been. "So you're twenty?"

Lou had a theory that housework was more ageing than cigarettes but Crystel knew it was being a mother that made her feel thirty sometimes. Not that she told him about the back of Finn's brother's car because with Ethan it was so different there should be another word. And maybe there was, only she'd never said it or even thought it. Lovemaking. Remembering, she stretched, turned, wishing she could find a way to lie still, the way she'd lain with him outlining her, his arms around her waist.

"We don't grow up till we're forty-two or three, at least," Granddad George had told her once. "And I'm a late developer."

But young was no fun anymore with the earth so sick and lashing out. What her granddad meant by growing up was understanding other people and maybe she couldn't really know Ethan inside out, even by some kind of magic. She'd never even *cleaned* a private school.

He'd told her about Samantha, the kind of girl who could take off to find herself with a backpack and a credit card. The kind who liked to tweet quotes from philosophers and revolutionaries. Crystel tried not to despise her, because she'd freed Ethan A. Garrett to fall in love with her on a train – which was beautiful as well as silly.

Maybe if she pretended he was there, holding her now, she could feel the peace again.

Coralie sat up. "Is it Christmas Day?"

"Not yet, little one," Crystel told her.

She flattened herself face-down, and Crystel slowly stroked the back of her neck until she was asleep again. Ethan had gentle hands. There were always places to clean and people with no time to clean them. There were children who needed minding while rich parents worked, and courses she could do so they'd let her. A nursery at Ferningstone, not for plants but little kids... Nothing was impossible. It couldn't be, even saving the planet for Coralie, and their own children, hers with Ethan.

23:37. Crystel eased her way out of the bed and took her phone to the bathroom. Turning it on, she found missed calls, five of them, and two texts, all his. *I'm on the way xxxx* followed by *Where are you? I'm outside the flat. XX* The last one was 11:31, just as she'd been thinking... He couldn't have gone far. His phone was ringing now.

"Ethan, I'm at Mum's. Have you got your notebook?"

"Yes, same one. I've got a pencil somewhere."

She heard his relief, his smile stretching like hers. She gave him the address and directions, repeated, improved. "It's not far," she said. "Is it raining? It's torrential, I can hear it!" Crystel peered out into the darkness through glass steamed by her breath. "There's a bus, should be..."

"I'll walk. How long will that take?"

"Fifteen minutes? Twelve with your legs."

"See you in twelve. If that's all right..."

"It's all right."

"I sent you a message."

"You sent loads."

"Before that, yesterday. Three words."

Crystel realised he couldn't see her grin but perhaps he guessed. "I've got four," she said, "for when you arrive."

A few years ago she would have sent other texts around the moment the exchange was finished, all beginning omg. She'd even sent one when she knew what Finn had in mind.

Now this was a world she hadn't known. In the bathroom mirror Crystel smiled at the shine in her eyes. Better do some explaining before her dad found a skinny white hippie dripping on the doorstep. Downstairs they were still watching TV, or snoozing in front of it.

Under the tree in the lounge was the strange shape of the rainbow clock she'd almost left at home because it stuck out of any bag like a squashed guitar. Ethan could give it to Coralie. It was him all over; he might have made it himself. She'd love it.

Annie turned the alarm clock beside the bed that was beginning to feel

255

familiar, like all the shapes she reached for in the dark. The end of a day and not much left of 2013: the year Mandela died, and made a number people would remember, like those 27 years in prison. After they'd forgotten the Philippines and Syria, like she'd been trying – mostly quite successfully – to do.

"I need a hero!" she sang with Gillie once, at one of her New Year parties, no men allowed. Some year or other, undistinguished now. Annie wanted this one over – just so another could begin?

No hands to move on Carole's clock, just digits to hypnotise. Annie waited.

Gone midnight. Christmas Day, and not a snowflake in sight as she parted the curtains. No chance of Kalashnikovs being sacrificed to love, or the doors of Abu Ghraib opening wide. Just people primed to leak tears over *Silent Night* or clutch a tissue through *It's A Wonderful Life.* Which could be a form of soul therapy but wouldn't peace on earth do a better, more enduring job?

Annie remembered that from the stars she couldn't see for all the light pollution, life on earth had sparked. It was wild and ridiculous that hearts and minds had been born up there in the blackness where there was nothing to grasp or even see. No wonder babies in mangers still made a kind of beautiful sense, until the love and peace got nailed to a cross. All such a muddle, really, with Santa muscling in with Rudolph and the elves. But had she ever looked out into the night sky for a sleigh, or checked the carpet for sooty footsteps like Arthur claimed he'd done for years, until his dad debunked the whole caboodle with a wink? Maybe she was always an unimaginative child, preferring sums to magic. She hadn't lied to Leigh, or pretended – not about Father Christmas, anyway. Only, mostly, about Daddy who left.

Words. The latest were a cue, pressing, waiting and unanswered.

But now was not the time.

About the Author

Sue Hampton is an ex-teacher who has been a full-time writer since 08. She is the author of more than 20 varied novels for children and teenagers, set in the past, present and future and across genres like humour, mystery and fantasy as well as real-world human drama. Her hero Michael Morpurgo has praised three of her titles: "Beautifully written" THE WATERHOUSE GIRL, "terrific" JUST FOR ONE DAY and "enthralling" SPIRIT AND FIRE. She already has one adult novel called ARIA, existing in e-book and audiobook form. Inspired by the work of George Eliot, Virginia Woolf and Carol Shields, she also admires Siobhan Dowd and Susan Fletcher, and writes from character and with passion. She enjoys visiting schools – more than 500 so far - to inspire children of all ages to read and write. Sue lost all her hair to alopecia in 1981 but decided in 09 to walk bareheaded in the world with an important message to share about respect and identity. As an Ambassador for Alopecia UK, she embraces difference and individuality in life and in her work. An eco-activist, she sees herself as a keyboard warrior in more ways than one.

Sue lives in Hertfordshire with her husband, author and poet Leslie Tate. Together, as #authorsinlove, they present to writers' groups and library groups, and run Berkhamsted Live, a mixed-arts show. Sue has appeared at various book festivals (Lincoln, Alton, Flamstead and Lyme Regis, plus the Seed Festival) and like Leslie will be at Banbury Literary Live 2015.

About the Publisher

Magic Oxygen Limited is a sustainable publishing house based in Lyme Regis, Dorset. As well as delivering great content to their readers, it is also the home of the Magic Oxygen Literary Prize.

This is a global writing competition like no other. Not only do they offer a share of an impressive prize fund, they plant a tree for every entry in their tropical Word Forest, situated beside the Kundeni Primary School in Bore, Kenya. The project is coordinated by forestry expert, Ru Hartwell of Community Carbon Link.

Bore is a remote community that has suffered greatly from deforestation. As well as reintroducing biodiversity, creating an income for the village, providing food, medicine and water purifiers, trees planted near the equator are also the most efficient at capturing carbon from the atmosphere. Each tree in the Word Forest will lock up 250kg of CO_2 and keep our planet a little bit cooler too!

Magic Oxygen publish the shortlist and winners in an anthology and plant an additional tree for every copy sold.

Visit MagicOxygen.co.uk to find out about the next MOLP, then spread news of it far and wide on your blogs and social media and be part of a pioneering literary legacy.

Copyright Images

The images on the back cover are used with permission as follows:
Nelson Mandela - courtesy of South Africa The Good News via Wikimedia Commons

London - Courtesy of kloniwotski (Flickr) via Wikimedia Commons

St Dunstan in the East Church Garden courtesy of Free Man http://www.geograph.org.uk/profile/117712

Edinburgh - courtesy of Kim Traynor via Wikimedia Commons

Angel of the North - courtesy of David Wilson Clarke

Stevie Winwood and Free in Amsterdam - courtesy of the Netherlands National Archives

Annie Julia Margaret Cameron - courtesy of the Getty's Open Content Program

9 780957 562134